# Overdue:

## Mystery, Adventure, and the World's Lost Books

Curated by

Jon Black & M.H. Norris

**Overdue: Tales of Mystery and Adventure**
An 18thWall Productions book published by
arrangement with Jon Black & M.H. Norris
*verba mea in minibus*
*desiderium meum*
Cover by Johannes Chazot
Jacket Design and Book Design by Adventure on Earth Productions
Illustration by Fio Trethewey



ISBN-13: 978-1-946033-19-2

# Table of Contents

prologue

# Wicker Man

## M.H. Norris

The autopsy suite itself was filled the typical scents: antiseptic, bleach, and chemicals. Yet the smell of burned flesh overpowered the usual suspects.

Dr. Rosella Tassoni stepped into the autopsy suite and studied the room. Along the far wall lay monitors that held the x-ray images. For Rosella, it helped tell her the story of what happened to the victim—and that much closer to giving this John Doe a voice.

The room itself was spacious, a welcome change to some of the spaces she'd previously had to work with. A desk sat to her left, spartan save for some paperwork.

The victim in question laid on a table in the middle of the room. Laid might be a loose term, Rosella noted. The body was curled up in the fetal position. The face was hard to see, covered by the body, the head facing downward towards the chest. The hands were fused to the legs, making attaining fingerprints virtually impossible. The Médecin Légiste had taken one look at the case and asked for someone more qualified.

But first, she headed to the bins to her right and donned a surgical gown, mask, and booties, and grabbed a pair of gloves. As she turned on the recording, she faced the victim.

"This is Dr. Rosella Tassoni at the Institut de Médecine in Quimper, France. Today is August 13, 2019 and the time is 14:27. On behalf of The Booker Foundation, I am examining the remains of a John Doe found on the archaeological site near the coast."

Rosella felt a chill run up her spine. She still wasn't sure how her name and credentials had crossed the desks of Jake Booker and Dr. Vivian Cuinnsey, but she was grateful for this chance.

Approximately 20 miles away sat the biggest archaeological find in modern history. Through a series of events, Doctor Cuinnsey and Mr. Booker had discovered Merlin's tomb.

Merlin.

THE Merlin.

Of course, every academic in the world was vying for the chance to get to look at the tomb and its contents. Rosella liked to think her own application had helped draw The Booker Foundation's attention her way.

She had a real chance to be the envy of academics across the globe. Which made this autopsy one of the most important she'd ever conducted. At the moment, Rosella was doing her best not to feel the pressure.

Stepping away from the x-ray images, she turned towards the charred body. "Today, I'll be creating a biological profile to see if ascertaining the identity is possible."

The skull was examined, some of the facial features—particularly on the lower half were still attached. The expressions were frozen in agony.

Now came the difficult part. She needed to try and get the body into a supine position on the table. Ideally, while keeping it as intact as possible. Slowly, she worked the body so it was on its back. Her estimate was that the victim weighed around 220 pounds. Checking the preliminary forms, she saw that she was off by a couple of pounds, but close.

First, Rosella began working with one of the legs, trying to fight against both rigor mortis and the tightness of the burns. It was slow work, but eventually she got the right foot to rest on the table.

Looking at the torso, Rosella paused. She could see that the burns covered significantly less of the body there. But that wasn't what gave her pause. It looked like an envelope was against the torso. The edges were lightly singed but Rosella realized there was a good chance that the contents would be salvageable.

Did the victim die to protect whatever was in that envelope?

It took her over an hour to get the envelope free. The need to preserve evidence, along with Rosella's tendency to use meticulous care, made the process draw on. But finally, she got the envelope free.

She sat it to the side and continued her examination.

Taking off her gloves, she walked over to the laptop set up and entered her findings into FORDISC to help her build the profile. It began crunching the numbers and she went to her exterior examination.

"The x-rays of the lungs indicate that the cause of death was asphyxiation."

Normally, she would start at the head and work her way down the body. But having read the notes from the initial autopsy made her change her usual tactics.

As morbid as it sounded, this was one of those cases where she was especially glad she didn't have to deal with the living. Severe burns covered most of the body—the metatarsals were even charred, a process that could take hours. "The x-rays do not show any signs of bruising on the phalanges, metatarsal bones, intermediate cuneiform bone, lateral cuneiform bone, navicular bone, and the calcaneus."

It was hard to even tell a shoe size from the remains of the feet that greeted her. There was no soft tissue left below the knees, revealing the bones.

Sliding on a new pair of gloves, she carefully brought the magnifier over the remains of the right foot. While not specifically part of why she'd been called, she'd be remiss if she didn't do a thorough job and make sure that there wasn't something the ML missed due to the lack of subject expertise.

One thing of note: the victim had several places along both arms that looked like defensive wounds. There, almost completely masked by burns, was bruising. The victim tried to fight back. Burns covered most of the body, ranging from extreme third degree burns on the lower half of the body to slightly less on the upper half. It made it tricky to tell what was what.

Still, it was enough that it was proving hard to identify the body.

A knock at the door broke her out of her thoughts and she turned off the recording and took off her gloves. "Come in?"

An intern entered the room. "The Medical Records finally arrived and are in the system for your review."

"Thank you." She nodded as the intern left and then went over to her laptop, minimizing the previous program and opening the facilities system with her temporary login.

She sent the x-rays of the victim in front of her to one of the screens on the far wall and sent the corresponding x-ray from the file to another. Moving to stand in front of them, she began her examination.

Around the time the victim was discovered, a researcher went missing. The Booker Foundation was concerned that the missing researcher and the body found on their property were one and the same. Rosella's task was to see if the remains in front of her belonged to Dr. Jonathan Sanchez.

It would be a shame if it was. He was a great source of information on the Celtic Civilization. They'd debate mythology for hours. He was one of the ones who pushed her to take the cases she did.

Currently, she had the toros up, looking for a distinct injury she'd seen on the x-ray. It took her a minute to find it, both due to its age and its size, but sure enough, there was a remodeled fracture on the right clavicle from a college football injury.

Going to the computer she switched to the left femur for both files and returned to her examination. This was a hair more obvious, as the childhood fracture had been more complete than the clavicle.

One injury in common could be a coincidence, but two was good enough for a confirmation in anthropological circles.

The body in front of her was Dr. Jonathan Sanchez. It was a shame that so bright a mind ended up with such a painful and dramatic end. Consulting the file, she read over how the body had been found and felt her eyes widen.

There was no way.

Going to a folder on her desk, she opened it to find some crime scene photos. Sure enough, it confirmed what she had read.

Turning to Dr. Sanchez's remains, she saw it in a slightly different light. "What happened that someone burned you alive in a Wicker Man?"

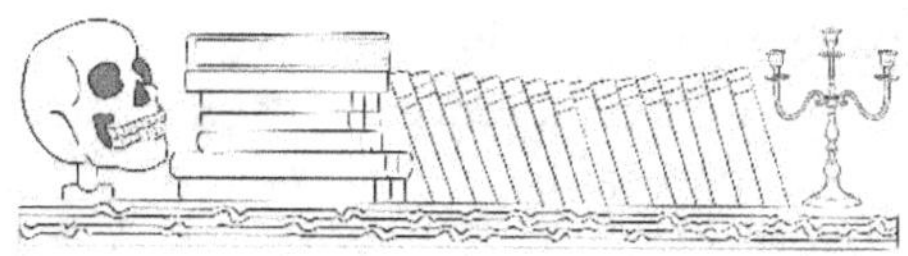

The most noticeable feature was a ziggurat-like tomb. To the casual observer, this building would be nondescript, but standing a couple of stories tall, this was a feat of ancient architecture. As Rosella stared at it, she wondered how they managed to get the clay all the way here to build it. It certainly wasn't indigenous to the area. To get it here, to the edge of France, without what we imagine as the necessary miracles of modern machinery.

That alone could cause Rosella to spend far too long investigating. Even ignoring it was far out of her traditional area.

The shiver went down her spine at the sight of Merlin's tomb. Soon, she too would get the chance to go inside. Unlike the pyramids of Egypt, this looked significantly smaller. To Rosella, it was one of the most beautiful things she'd ever seen.

Sadly, she needed to look away. That was not why she was there today.

The black circle that stood about a dozen yards from where she was standing finally drew her attention. At its base, it had a circumference of about ten feet. Like delicate spider webs, charred grass branched away.

Thankfully none got near the tomb. The wind had been blowing in the right direction that day.

A small guard house sat at the entrance to the valley. The entire area was fenced off to discourage unwanted guests. Inside the enclosure, there were a handful of people scurrying around, most going into the tomb itself.

"This is one of my favorite places to enjoy the view as well."

She turned to see a man approaching her. Standing just a couple of inches taller than Rosella, he looked like he could be a member of the excavation crew. The trio of flannel, levis, and work boots certainly didn't help convince you otherwise.

"Mr. Booker! It's an honor to meet you."

Jake Booker smiled—the soft smile of a southern gentleman—and shook her hand. "Pleasure is all mine. Thank you again for being willing to fly all this way on such short notice. Vivian is disappointed she can't be here, I know she would love to discuss some of your papers on Arthurian Legends."

"Perhaps we can do it another time." Rosella turned back to the tomb. The sea wind blew at them up on the bluff, making Rosella glad she'd pulled her hair back. "Walk me through this, if you can."

"We keep a single guard here at night and the rest is done off site. We focus most of our security on the site itself, not the approach. Unbeknownst to us, there was a blind spot."

"Let me guess, it's a certain circle."

Jake Booker nodded, his face grim. "An oversight we have since corrected."

He pointed to the guard house that was situated about a hundred yards from the tomb at the entrance to the valley. Between it and the circle, several temporary buildings stood. It wasn't hard to see how that would be a blind spot after all.

"It was the billowing smoke and the smell that caught the guard's attention. By that point, nearly the whole thing was in flames." Jake pulled out his phone and held it out, a video ready to play. He pressed play and Rosella couldn't help but stare in morbid fascination at a burning Wicker Man. "Unfortunately, it took the fire department over a half hour to get here and almost another hour to get the fire under control. Locals say that they could see the tops of the flames over the bluff."

He pointed behind them where in the distance, a small town sat.

"I'm sorry to report that your John Doe is in fact your missing researcher. I'm waiting on the official dental records report but based on my Biological Profile, and particularly his previous injuries, the body is a match for Dr. Jonathan Sanchez."

Jake's head bowed slightly. "I was afraid of that."

Rosella turned to face the valley again. "Someone was very angry with him. I've been told that the remains of the Wicker Man are being stored at your facility?"

"They are, I can get you access if you'd like it."

"I would, thank you." On one hand, examining the Wicker Man would be beneficial to the investigation. But Rosella also was far too well aware that she may never get a chance like this to study a Wicker Man built for their "intended" purpose.

And that was an opportunity she was not about to miss out on.

He held out a lanyard carrying an access badge. Rosela took it, taking great care to make sure that she did not seem too eager. Looking at it, it was a badge for access to both the site below and the warehouse in Quimper that was currently serving as a place to study the newly discovered treasures.

In the land of academia, this was the golden ticket.

Jake Booker also handed her a business card. "My number. If you need anything, don't hesitate to ask."

"Thank you, Mr. Booker."

"Jake." He nodded.

"Rosella." She put the card away. "If I can get a list of what Dr. Sanchez was directly working on before his death, I can try and discover what happened. Has the Wicker Man been properly examined?"

"Not by anyone with expertise in the field. Speaking of, what do you make of the Wicker Man?"

"This is a site where a myth became something more. It's weird that another myth occurred mere feet away." She nodded to the taped off area. "You see, there's no actual evidence that the Celts sacrificed people in Wicker Men. The documentary evidence is thin, with severe internal problems."

"But, what about the book, the horror movie? The awful American remake?" Jake gave her an incredulous look.

"Bought into the hype. The Celts are an interesting group. We believe they settled into the area that is now the United Kingdom around 1200 BC. But the first reference we have to them is from the Romans. The Romans referred to them as 'Galli,' which means barbarians. Now keep in mind that this 'barbaric race' held back the Roman assault, through a mix of Roman mismanagement and their own tactics, and did so for decades. So, excuse me if I take what he said about them with a grain of salt."

"What did he say?" Jake asked.

"All the Gauls are keen on religious observances; because of this those who contract more serious illnesses, as well as those involved in hazardous undertakings, either make or promise to make human sacrifices, and use the Druids to perform these on their behalf. The reason for this is that they believe in 'a life for a life'; otherwise, the gods cannot be placated. Their public sacrifices are always of this type. Sometimes they use images of enormous size; they weave them from sticks, fill them with living men, and set fire to them. Once they are fully alight the men die. They think that those caught thieving or robbing or committing other crimes are particularly pleasing as sacrifices to the gods; but if they are short of such people, innocent men will serve equally well."

"So wait, you're saying that the entire myth of a Wicker Man was started because Julius Caesar lost a war? Did you just quote Caesar from memory?" Jake seemed impressed.

"Arguably." Her eyes lit up. "Inarguably."

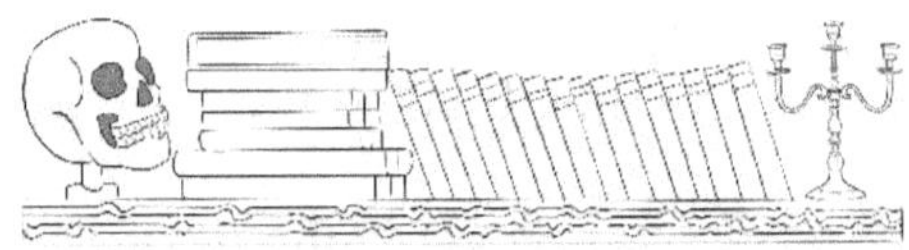

Rosella pulled her rental car past the guard house and into the small parking area. While there were a few people in the small shelter that were working on various artifacts and preparing them for transport, the site was mostly empty. Walking over—solely for the purpose of getting a feel for the crime scene of course—Rosella saw a couple of people leaned over papyrus. The symbols on it, she vaguely recognized from her studies into Egyptian mythology.

Rosella took a deep breath. The air of course smelled of the sea, but also a faint tinge of burned wood. It added a sour element to the crisp sea air she'd been enjoying up on the hillside. Though, it wasn't the usual suspects when it came to wood.

She could faintly hear the waves crash on the shore as she made her way to the burned circle.

The smell of burned wood grew stronger as she approached the circle. Wrinkling her nose, she noted that it didn't smell how she'd imagine the indigenous trees burning. But she couldn't quite place what it was.

It was quite obvious that while the center of the circle was the epicenter, the fire had spread wide. Considering the reports of the Wicker Man, it was no surprise.

Despite the fact the body had been discovered almost 48 hours ago, there was still a slight feeling of heat coming from the circle.

Its sheer mass gave her a hint about the dramatic nature of the crime.

Looking over her shoulder at the tomb, Rosella wondered why someone would choose such a dramatic scene next to such an historic site. What statement were they trying to make? What were the papers that Dr. Sanchez protected in death? And who didn't want them to see the light of day?

While not quite in the shadow of the tomb, Rosella felt its weight as she thought about the investigation ahead.

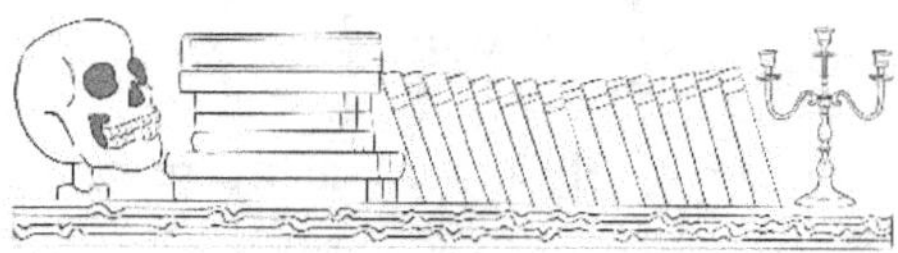

The complex where academics from across the globe were examining artifacts from The Merlin Collection was easily one of the most exciting things Rosella had seen.

For now, she was led to a side room. But 'room' was an understatement, considering this room was the size of a small warehouse. Taking up a portion of the center of the room was the remains of an actual Wicker Man.

Chills went up her arms at the site of the remains.

It was beautiful.

Perhaps Rosella shouldn't use that word to describe something that had helped to kill a human being, her own friend. But she couldn't help it. Several different types of wood—all unfortunately all too common like Oak, Ash, and Birch—came together to form this structure. Even with most of the bottom half burned away, it was still almost as long as she was tall.

Someone took the time to weave a figure of over 10 feet like one would make a chair. It wouldn't have been easy. Nor would it have been easy to hide.

It lay on its back, its eyeless face facing the ceiling—and indirectly her.

Gowned up, wearing gloves and booties, she circled the Wicker Man.

The wood itself was not overly brittle which means that narrowed the timeline of its creation to 6-8 weeks. Was someone plotting this for that long?

Rosella continued her circle, at times running her hand along the Wicker Man and admiring the craftsmanship. Despite its purpose, this truly was a work of art.

On the far side of the room, a handful of people were working on a device. A series of cables had been set up, with a harness, so that people could examine the Wicker Man more thoroughly without touching the object.

"How's it looking, Dr. Tassoni?"

She turned to see Jake Booker walking in. "I told you it's fine if you call me Rosella."

He grinned. "What do you think?"

"It's a work of art." She turned back to it. "Such a shame that someone with this level of craftsmanship resorted to something like this.

"A shame." He turned towards where a couple of technicians were setting up what looked to be a harness. "If you want a closer overhead look, we've got this."

"Am I right in assuming you haven't tested that yet."

Jake shrugged his shoulder. "Not at this site."

For science. She could get in that contraption for science.

"For science."

Carefully she stepped onto the harness and allowed them to lower her to the ground and secure her feet. The last thing Rosella wanted to do was hit the Wicker Man with a stray kick. The technician walked her through some hand signals, indicating what direction she'd want to go. Beside him was another piece of machinery that would raise him to be closer to Rosella's eyeline. The two would have to work together to make sure she saw what she needed to.

Someone handed her the tool belt she'd prepared.

A steady hum filled the room. After a moment of anticipation, she was brought over to the head of the Wicker Man. Goosebumps covered her arms in anticipation of being the first person to examine an actual Wicker Man.

As she rose higher than the Wicker Man was tall, Rosella couldn't help but wonder how someone was able to hide something this big, get it to the site of the tomb, and shove a man inside one of the legs.

Not for the first time, she wondered why someone would go

through all the trouble to do that in the first place.

First order of business: observe the construction. Perhaps she'd find some clues there. She needed something more substantial than excellent workmanship.

Rosella had never been so much in love with a stack of wood as she was now. Whoever had gone to the trouble had at least made it worth their effort.

Moving slowly, she studied it when she noticed something that seemed out of place in the jumble of wood.

Where a person's heart would be, it looked as if there was a box hidden within the branches. Not much larger than a coat-sized gift box, it sat in an opaque container.

Raising herself slightly, she turned. "Jake, I think I have something you'll want to see."

She heard some clanging and after a moment saw Jake standing slightly over the Wicker Man. "What is it?

"Take a look at this." She shone a light on the box. "There's something inside."

He studied where her light shone for a moment, brow furrowed slightly. "Any idea what it is?"

She shook her head. "The container is opaque."

"Are you able to get to it?"

Rosella felt her face slightly scrunch in thought. "In theory, yes. But I don't see a way to it without damaging the torso of the Wicker Man."

"Which might be frowned on by some people."

"That's an understatement. But someone took great pains to hide this inside of there. And I'd wager it has something to do with why Dr. Sanchez was murdered."

"I say we ask forgiveness instead of permission." Jake gave her a knowing grin that Rosella returned.

She carefully excavated Wicker Man's chest. In a process that wasn't unlike her past digs, she removed the wood layer by layer, taking care to disturb as little of the evidence as possible.

Jack Booker stayed where he was, watching her work intentionally.

Taking painstaking effort, Rosella made her way to the box. Ideally, she wanted to disturb it as little as possible. Finally, she was able to remove it from where it had been put. She handed it to Jake.

"Want to come down so we can pop this open?"

Rosella nodded and maneuvered herself back to her landing point and with the help of some of the lab techs, she was able to get out of the harness fairly quickly. Her limbs stung slightly with pins and needles as they woke up after being in that position for so long. She rolled her shoulders a couple of times before she accepted her blazer and put it back on.

They wove their way to the far side and Jake opened a door to an empty lab. "You can use this as a base for your investigation if you'd like. Right now, no one is using it."

It took every ounce of Rosella's self-control not to react to that statement in a dramatic fashion. "Thank you, I certainly appreciate it."

He sat the box down on the table. Rosella took a minute to study the box. It was made of wood but a different type than the Wicker Man. Perhaps this was elder?

"I wonder if this was someone's way of making a coffin."

Jake raised an eyebrow at her statement.

"Whatever is in here, I imagine our killer wanted to make it disappear."

Grabbing a pair of fresh gloves Rosella turned on the recording app on her phone before putting them on. "This is Dr. Rosella Tassoni."

She nodded to Jake. "And this is Jake Booker."

"We are examining a box found in the torso of the Wicker Man in which the body of Dr. Jonathan Sanchez was found." Rosella grabbed a tape measure and began to carefully measure the box, Jake documenting the results on paper while she announced the aloud for the recording.

"Despite being in a place where it was exposed to high heat, the box remains relatively intact." Rosella began feeling along the edges, hoping to find some sort of catch she could use to open it.

Finding one, she took great care to open the box. It was sealed so Rosella had to take great care. Grabbing a small knife, she began to try and pry the wooden top open.

A folio lay inside, the leather faded and worn with age. After taking pictures of the now open box, Rosella lifted the folio out with the utmost of care. Even through the gloves, she could feel how brittle it was.

Sitting it on the table, she unwrapped the bands that held it together. It opened and miraculously stayed together. Inside were papers, hundreds of them.

Rosella recognized the language, but as she delicately handled the pages, she marveled over the script.

"What language is that?" Jake broke the silence.

"I believe it is Celtic." Rosella lifted the paper, she was fairly certain it was parchment and placed it on the table. Grabbing a magnifier, she studied the paper more closely. As she did so, she described in as much detail as she could about what she was seeing.

"What is it?"

Rosella looked at the papers in front of her. "Without being able to read it, I can only speculate."

"Feel free."

"I have a feeling that this is a book, perhaps something lost. We find out what it is and we might unlock the key to Dr. Sanchez's murder."

"You said it is Celtic, right?"

Rosella nodded.

"Perhaps I need to give Vivian a call."

Rosella nodded, but paused. "That's odd."

"What is?"

Separating some of the papers, she took a look at them. "These are modern English. An academic article by the looks of them."

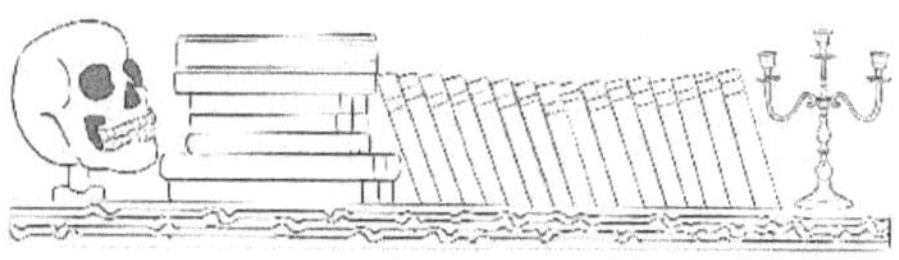

Where Rosella kept her workspace clean to a point where it almost felt cold, Dr. Jonathan Sanchez did not.

His "office" at the facility was tiny. Honestly, it was little more than a glorified cubical. But despite its small size, it was packed with notes, books, and some artifacts.

The wrap-around desk was covered in papers—some manuscripts, some translations, and still more documents that even resisted her ability to parse. There were photographs tacked to every spare bit of the walls. Some were of his family—a wife and two daughters (neither out of elementary school). Others were artifacts. Still, others were maps.

Rosella had yet to find rhyme or reason to it.

"What was an expert in Ancient Rome doing with a Celtic Manuscript?" Rosella looked at papers by his laptop.

Jake looked up from his papers. "Perhaps some overlap? Or was he asked to consult?"

"Maybe." She flipped through a few more pages. "Any estimates on when Dr. Cuinnsey—"

"I'm sure she won't mind you calling her Vivian." Jake smiled at her.

Rosella cleared her throat. "Any idea when Vivian will have at least an initial idea of what the text was about?"

"With the time difference, it may be a few hours before she can take a look."

"We'll have to make do in the meantime." She continued glancing at his notes. "Anything interesting on your side?"

While Rosella had found plenty of interesting things on the desk, notes on some of the Latin texts that had been found in the tomb, outlines for potential scholarly articles, and more, none of them did anything to help Rosella with the problem that was solving this case.

"You mentioned earlier that a lot of the modern lore surrounding Wicker Men was born out of, excuse the less than academic terms, Caesar's spite."

"I did. There are a lot of scholars who would agree with me on the subject as well."

Jake held up a folder. "Well, it seems as if Dr. Sanchez thought it wasn't a hoax."

"What are you talking about?"

Jake handed her the folder and she opened it up to review the contents. "He has an article coming out in a journal next month that says the opposite of what this says."

"Does he?" Jake eyed the folder. "I wonder what changed his mind about the whole thing?"

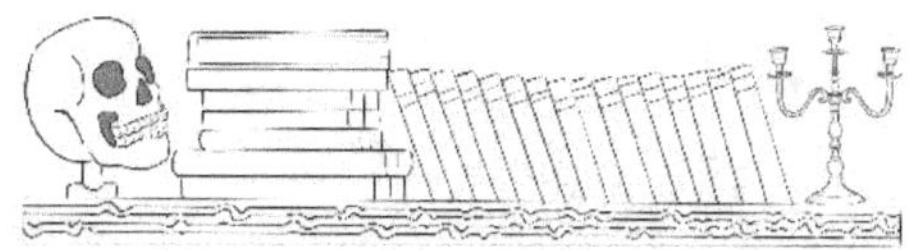

Due to the nature of this particular historical site, there were a dozen Celtic experts working on the project. On top of them, there were at least 10 research assistants hiding in cubicles in a large open room.

They had taken over one corner of the large facility. Professors and archeologists occupied the handful of offices.

It was yet another time that Rosella wished she had time to pause and enjoy. In a temperature-controlled room to one side sat dozens of artifacts. Maps took up walls along with photographs of more and some that included various texts. History lived and breathed around her.

Technically, Rosella was checking the bits of text to make sure none represented her mystery text. If that required her examining each and every one of them…

It was late in the workday, but the academics that bustled around the space showed no indication of going home.

As she walked by, she heard a voice with a thick Welsh accent call out from one of the offices. “Dr. Tassoni?”

Doubling back, she stuck her head into the office to see two gentlemen having a meeting. Both were middle aged and had a pile of papers between them. Unlike Dr. Sanchez’s office which was the textbook definition of organized clutter, this office was very straight and neat.

Of course, it was not the office she’d had to examine with a fine-tooth comb…

The man behind the desk stood up and walked over holding out his hand. “I heard you were paying a visit. Lovely to see you again!”

She smiled, holding out her own hand. “Dr. Sampson.”

“Seamus, come meet Dr. Rosella Tassoni.” Dr. Byron Sampson waved the other man over. Dr. Sampson had more salt than pepper in his hair, but his eyes twinkled with a joy for knowledge. A portly man with a Welsh accent, he managed to seem like both a jovial grandfather and a determined researcher.

“As an undergrad, she attended one of my lectures and then proceeded to bombard me with questions about The Morrigan for an hour.”

Rosella laughed. “If memory serves, I did buy you coffee first.”

“That you did. This is Dr. Seamus Fitzpatrick, he specializes in Celtic Literature. He can write so beautifully in that style, you would think it came from that period. Seamus, this is Dr. Rosella Tassoni.”

Unlike Dr. Sampson, Dr. Fitzpatrick appeared to be about ten years younger and fifty pounds lighter. His red hair was just starting to bleach into white.

“Pleasure to meet you, Lass.” He shook her hand. “What brings you to our little slice of academic paradise?”

“She’s here investigating that nasty business with Jonathan.” Dr. Sampson had a sour look.

“Right. That horrid business. You’re an investigator?”

“Forensic Anthropologist.” Rosella looked around the room, eyeing a statue in a class case and knelt down ot examine it.

“Don’t let her fool you, Seamus. She also has a passion for looking at mythology. She’s wasted on the police of the world.”

“Please, Dr. Sampson—” Rosella bit back a chuckle as she stood again.

“Rosella, please. You aren’t an undergrad student anymore. You can call me Byron.”

“Byron, we are all entirely too busy to sing my praises.” She rejoined the group.

“Nonsense.” He waved her into the office. “Is there anything we can do to help with your investigation?”

He waved at a chair but Rosella shook her head. “I’d hate to interrupt your meeting.”

Dr. Fitzpatrick laughed. “Please, this is nothing more than one academic trying to talk his colleague out of some of the scotch I know is hiding in his desk.”

“Seamus! Don’t give away all my secrets.” Byron was already pulling out three glasses. “Join us, Rosella. Perhaps we can give you some insight. I just got back from the States, went to a conference and teased some of what I discovered”

He poured the drinks, handing them to both people. Rosella

took her glass and took a sip. “What can you tell me about Dr. Sanchez?”

“He preferred to work alone. Then again, must of us do.” Fitzpatrick mused. “No one wants to share any more credit than necessary.”

“Everyone wants their moment in the academic spotlight,” Rosella mused.

“And there is a lot of spotlight to be had in this project,” Byron countered.

“What did both of you think of his work?”

“I thought he was very dedicated to his work.” Byron leaned back in his chair.

“But you have to be, to be selected to work on this project. What about you, Dr. Fitzpatrick?”

“Out of everyone here, Jon wanted the fame the least. He was one of those who were here to learn, not for recognition.”

Rosella leaned back, processing the answers but before she could respond, Byron scoffed. “Please, no researcher here is here for the fun of it. You must publish or perish and I heard that Jonathan was racing to publish a piece.” Byron let out an annoyed huff.

“And you aren’t, Byron?” Fitzpatrick retorted.

The office fell silent, all three lost in their own thoughts.

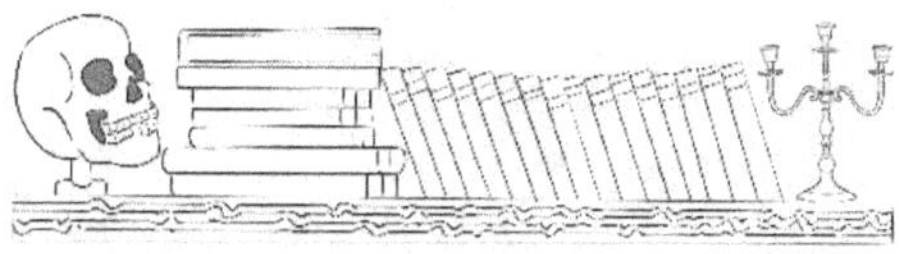

Traditionally, when Rosella got involved in an investigation like this, she left the confirming of alibis to the authorities and instead focused on other aspects of the case.

Of course, this wasn’t a traditional case, not only did she know the victim in question but also there was the whole “not a bad idea to impress the Booker Foundation” principle.

For a large chunk of the researchers, the job was easy. They were all together at the town pub drinking what Americans would consider a large amount but was in fact just another night out for a lot of European countries.

Eying the time stamp on the bottom of the screen, Rosella sat back and watched the scene play out. On a clipboard, she had a picture of everyone who worked in the department and one by one, she marked them off. It took her around four watch-throughs (thankfully at four times the rate) to confirm who had been in the pub.

With over half the department cleared, she had to turn to the rest. A handful of others were at a dinner party—Rosella had statements by numerous witnesses confirming that. Another researcher was out of the country all together.

That left two for Rosella to track and they were the most interesting. Fitzpatrick and Bryon were acting as each other's alibis. Both claimed they drove to Paris where Byron reportedly caught an early flight while Fitzpatrick had brunch with an associate before coming back.

Byron then took the train from Paris to Quimper a few days later where Fitzpatrick picked him up. Already, Rosella had footage of him speaking at a conference—one she'd considered attending.

Luckily, between Jake's contacts here in France and her's in the FBI, there were people looking into confirming where the pair where during the window in question. Sure enough, there was an email in her inbox. Clicking it, she reviewed the information before opening the attached files.

If the pair drove straight to Paris, why were they at the Quimper Regional Airport during the window of opportunity?

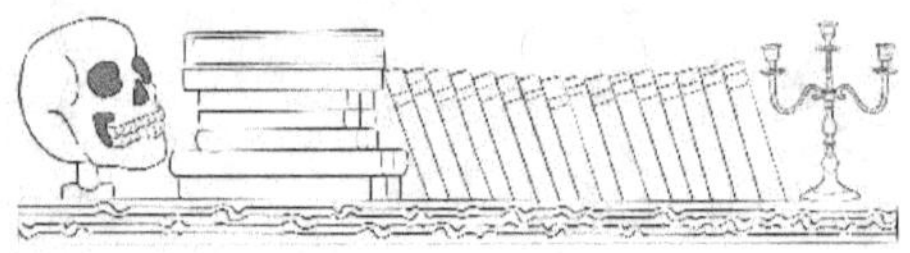

Something that Byron had said. The old publish or perish adage that lived in the world of academia. Would someone murder to stop a publication?

And if so, who?

"Any progress?"

She turned to see Jake Booker standing in the doorway. "I've got a theory."

He walked in, staring at the projection. "Which is?"

"This article is what got Jonathan Sanhez killed."

Jake's hands slip into his pocket as he stares at the productions. "Why?"

"Because that's not the real article. Well, it mostly is." Rosella walked over to her computer and put up a new document. Where the previous document had been 11 pages, this document was 15. "Fun fact, before an article is published, it often makes the rounds in the academic community for people to read over. Because it deals with mythology, I received Jonathan Sanchez's paper to review."

Pulling it up, she turned her laptop so that Jake could see. "The one found in the Wicker Man is close but it's missing pages on a single source."

Rosella went over and grabbed the envelope that Sanchez had been found with. Opening it, she pulled out a small book. "One of the greatest things I have ever been allowed to touch. I suspect—though I cannot read early Celtic languages—this belonged to Merlin himself."

Jake stared at the book. "I understand there's the whole publish or perish saying in academia, but I thought that was more hyperbole than anything."

"Unfortunately, I've seen people kill for less." Rosella shrugged, looking at the book. "Something in this must have been worth killing over."

Jake came closer, looking over her shoulder at the pages. "Perhaps Vivian can give us some insight into what it says."

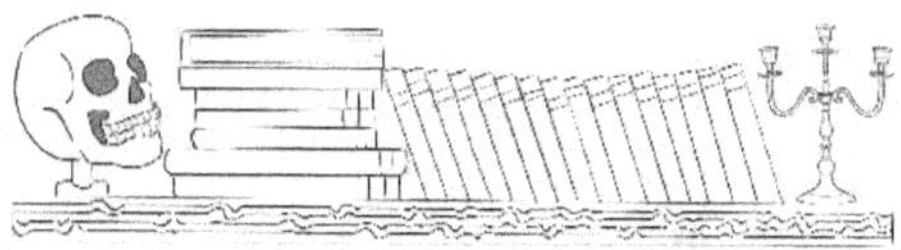

One of the reasons Rosella preferred field-work to staying in a lab was that there was nothing like being outside. Especially on days like today where there was the hint of the approaching autumn in the breeze.

The tomb was in front of her, the spot where Jonathan Sanchez died to her right. While the charred earth remained, the smell of burning wood had dissipated.

"Rosella?"

She turned to see Jake, Byron, and Dr. Fitzpatrick walking

towards her. Outwardly, Jake walked as if he if owned the place—which was not entirely inaccurate. Meanwhile, the two academics strode across the clearly, heads on a swivel looking around as if trying to decipher any clues as to why they were there in the first place.

"Until this tomb was discovered, the majority of the world had dismissed King Arthur and the legends surrounding him as nothing more than fantastical tales. But then…"

Pointing at the tomb, she paused briefly. "Then they found this. The tomb of Merlin himself. And with it we discovered manuscripts and priceless treasures that otherwise would have been lost to history. And you two, you were selected to come and help oversee the project."

"Rosella, I fail to see where this is going." Dr. Fitzpatrick waved his hands at the tomb. "Why are we here?"

"Why is any academic here? To discover knowledge that was previously lost. To prove what many of us believed. Merlin was a real person. Camelot was a real place, and regain the lost knowledge." Taking a deep breath of the sea air, Rosella focused back on the two men. "In a place where a myth became so much more, someone tried to bring life to another, false story."

Even Jake had, at this point, crossed his arm and was giving a questioning look.

Shaking her head she plowed on. "There's so much we don't know. So much that has been guessed at. For example? Did the Celtics use Wicker Man to sacrifice people?"

"Of course they did." Byron was emphatic and took a step forward. "I thought better of you, Rosella. Surely you don't buy the theory that it's purely made up."

"A lot of people have done a lot less out of spite. Surely as an academic you know that." She countered. Honestly, it didn't matter what she believed. It mattered what he believed.

"Once again, I fail to see what that has to do with anything." Dr. Fitzpatrick's body language was between casual and defensive, as if not sure which way this conversation would turn.

"Everything, or perhaps nothing. I do have another question for you however." Reaching into her bag, Rosella pulled out a piece of paper. "The pair of you both told the police that Dr. Fitzpatrick had taken Byron to the airport so he could catch a plane to America for his conference."

Both nodded before Byron spoke up. "Seamus used the opportunity to meet up with an old colleague."

Rosella showed a photograph of Dr. Fitzpatrick with another individual. "Yes, the next morning. You were already on the way to America at that point. Both of you hundreds of kilometers from the recently discovered body."

Pulling out a photograph, Rosella carefully placed her fingers as to hide one important corner before turning it around. "And Byron, that's you in the airport at Paris catching your flight, isn't it?"

"Yes."

Removing her finger, she handed over the piece of paper. "Check the timestamp."

Jake looked and looked up at the pair of academics. "The fire crew responded at 10:30."

"Right, you see, Jake, I was looking over this case and things didn't quite add up. Any way I tossed it, there were pieces that just didn't make sense. But I have a few contacts here in France and a couple at Quantico. They were more than happy to get a copy of footage to confirm your alibi."

"Of course. I made a speech first thing the next morning in front of a room full of people. Clearly, I was in America."

"Dr. Tassoni, what exactly are you getting at?"

"It's a six-hour drive to Paris and their airport from here. Why didn't you choose to go through the regional airport? Why cause Dr. Fitzpatrick to drive all the way to Paris?"

"I'd hardly say I was forced. The drive was quite lovely and we spent the entire time discussing some of the recent discoveries with the project." Dr. Fitzpatrick crossed his arms.

"Rosella, can you please get to the point of this?" Jake was looking at the photo still.

Opening the folder, she pulled out several documents. "You two made a show of leaving the facility shortly after lunch and you were not seen on property the rest of the day."

"Correct."

"Dr. Fitzpatrick, did you know that your neighbor filed a noise complaint the night that Dr. Jonathan Sanchez was killed?"

He took a step back. "I'm not sure what this has to do with

anything."

"You were using the cover of the newly fallen night to get the Wicker Man here. They complained about their neighbor—you—using heavy machinery."

"By that point I would have been in Paris." He shook his head with a grin.

"You never went to Paris. Instead, the pair of you chartered a flight out of the airport at Quimper and did your level best to keep it as off the books as possible. Sanchez is dead. Byron, you have a marvelous alibi of being out of the country—and conveniently close to the back-up—while Dr. Fitzpatrick is left behind to subtly leave clues for the investigators to find."

She took a step towards them. "And then Mr. Booker calls me and I'm sure you thought you'd manage to sneak this past my inexperienced eyes."

Rosella handed the entire folder to Jake. "But you forgot one tiny yet important detail. Jonathan was my friend as well. I made Mr. Booker here call in a favor to get me this information."

"Mr. Booker, with all due respect, you cannot seriously believe her. We've been on this project for months. You hand-selected us."

"I did. But perhaps my judgment was off on this one."

Rosella waved at the security shack and after a minute, she saw a couple of police cars making their way towards them.

"How dare you both. You were both trusted with the research job of a lifetime, one academics the world over, myself included, would have given anything for. And you abused it. You murdered a fellow researcher and tried to edit their paper. And for what?"

After handing over the evidence Rosella had managed to accumulate and both men had been placed in the back of the cars.

Jake turned to Rosella. "Thank you for helping me get to the bottom of this."

"Jon was a friend. It was my honor to help bring him justice."

"Perhaps you'd be open to a future collaboration."

"I would love that."

He turned towards the tomb. "As an extra thank you, would you like to spend a few days here, properly exploring?"

Rosella bit her lip. "Can I take a raincheck? I have a previous engagement in a few days back Stateside. I promised a colleague

I would speak to her class."

"After that then."

She smiled as the pair turned and made their way back to their cars. "I look forward to it."

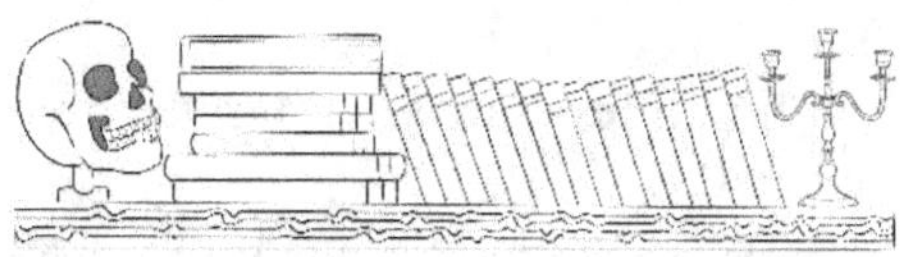

**Two Months Later – Huntington, New York**

If Rosella didn't get out of the hospital soon, she was going to scream. It had been weeks of pain, morphine, and an utter lack of silence. Her arm was in a sling that was positioned so it would not move. It would be another two weeks before she'd move to one that would allow her to start physical therapy.

The worst part was that she didn't even remember how she ended up in this condition. There were flashes, glimpses that made no sense.

In-between visits from doctors, she tried to pass the time with the help of her Kindle. But what she wanted more than anything was to be out of this hospital bed and somewhere, honestly anywhere, else.

As her door opened, Rosella braced herself for another doctor to come and tell her yet another reason she had to stay longer.

"Now, I thought you were supposed to come back to France after your talk, not get run through the meat grinder."

Rosella turned to see Jake Booker standing there with a bouquet of violets in his hands. She laughed. "A case came up and I guess it didn't end well."

"You guess?" He came and took the seat beside her bed after placing the violets and their vase on a table to the side.

"To be honest, I'm missing about four hours there at the end." She turned. "How is everything after the whole mess I left behind?"

"Regrouping. They're resilient. If anything, they're angry at Fitzpatrick and Samson. I'm looking for some people to replace them. Vivian's doing the interviews, since it's more her field of expertise. But this whole mess got us thinking."

"About?"

“According to Viv, you found an old manuscript that provided details into Celtic religious practices. A lot of what was there was previously unknown and would have been lost to history if not for the project and of course your help saving it.”

Rosella stared at Jake. “So, what were you thinking about?”

“Would you like to do it again?”

She blinked at him a few times. “I’m not sure if it's morphine or if I heard you right.”

Jake laughed. “We’re thinking of creating a lost books project. You’d be stationed in Washington DC so that you can continue your work with the FBI while the main headquarters is in Houston.”

He laid a tablet on her lap and it showed a beautiful office space with windows that faced the US Capitol. “In between cases, you could work with us to help find these books and to secure ones that are brought to us.”

“I can’t afford that office.” Rosella looked at the pictures.

“I can. It will be good to have two locations—not have all our eggs in a single basket. So, what do you think?”

Rosella shifted position, wincing as her shoulder gave a twinge of pain. “And what, help you find lost books?”

“You said it yourself, it’s an opportunity most academics would give anything for.” Jake leaned back in his chair.

# Wholly Holy

## Kara Dennison

Everyone at the wake had interesting stories to tell about Faye's father. How he'd shown up to his Shakespearean comedy class on the day of finals dressed as Malvolio, right down to the crossed garters and yellow stockings. How he surprised his 101 and 201 students by randomly taking off for unannounced bass fishing trips and leaving a literal "Gone Fishin'" note on the classroom door. Hell, the fact that past and present students were even showing up to a professor's family's wake—invited, but not pressured—said more about Dr. Chase Lundgren's life than any of their stories ever would.

Faye's favorite story seemed anemic by comparison. It was simple, almost childish, but still the closest to her heart. The most "Dad" thing about her dad.

On nights when she couldn't sleep, she'd open her bedroom door and turn on her nightstand lamp. Her dad was a light sleeper, and the light shining from across the hall through her parents' open bedroom door was enough to wake him. That was their agreed-upon beacon: the Dad-Signal. And no matter how tired he was, he responded.

Eventually there was something of a script between them. Same words, same rhythms. Even the inflection seemed part of the ritual.

"Can't sleep, Faye-Faye?"

"Mm-mm."

"Want to hear about the stars?"

"Mm-hmm."

And he'd lie next to her, on top of her quilt, arms tucked behind his head like they were outdoors looking up at the stars. The story he told was a jumble of images, tales of knights and magic and holy kings. She never stayed awake long enough to hear it through to the end, eventually slipping into comfortably dark dreams of chivalry and magic.

She eventually outgrew the Dad-Signal, and she couldn't remember ever invoking it as a teenager. But her first night away at college left her feeling unexpectedly homesick. She crept out into the dorm's bright-lit halls at 2-something and called her dad's cell phone. She expected no answer, or a bleary reply asking if she was okay.

She didn't even make it through one full ring before her dad picked up.

"Can't sleep, Faye-Faye?"

Instead, she talked a bit about how glad she was that he'd inspired so many students and how amazing it was to see them all—so many ages, so many backgrounds. A sign of just how far his influence had spread over the years. Then she went to a back booth and drowned herself in what her dad's favorite restaurant dubbed "Irish nachos."

The rest of the guests left her alone. Good. She couldn't handle talking to anyone right now. Not that she didn't want to; she just wouldn't sure how long her mask would hold before the tears came spilling out. It felt like one more word would break the dam. And regardless of the events of the week, she couldn't handle being thirty years old and crying like a child in front of mostly strangers.

"Faye Lundgren?"

Shoot.

Faye took a deep breath, swallowed, and looked up at the woman across from her. "Can I help you?"

"We've never met."

"No kidding."

The woman smiled. "I can come back at a less fraught time, if you'd like."

"No… if you're cornering me at my dad's wake, clearly there's something you want very badly. Might as well get it over with."

The smile held—but it seemed to waver a little. *You got me there.* "My name is Dr. Cuinnsey. I come from a group dedicated to… how shall I put this? Securing and storing important books. We were in contact with your father a few years ago concerning an item in his collection, but unfortunately we were never able to complete negotiations."

Faye felt a wave of weariness spread over her. Was that all? Here? Now? "You're welcome to pick through his library before I do. There's nothing in there I was particularly attached to. Not big into academics." She waved a hand, then let it drop on the table. "Have at it."

"I'm afraid what we're looking for is a bit more… *secured* than that."

"Sorry?"

Dr. Cuinnsey looked around; something washed quickly over her face, a realization that perhaps this wasn't the place or time. She reached into her bag and pulled out a business card. "Call me when you're feeling up to it. It looks like you might need your space right now. I'm sorry."

Before Faye could respond, the woman made a quiet exit. She went back to her Irish nachos, turning the card over in her hand.

The Booker Foundation.

"Let me guess. You want… a… *book.*"

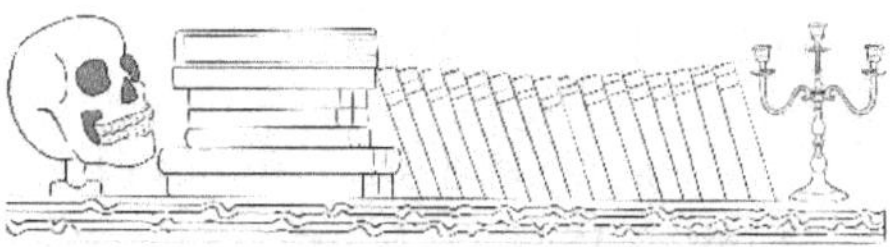

Faye had never taken much of an interest in her father's work. Not out of any particular dislike. It just seemed *wrong* to her to analyze stories so deeply. Stories were for telling and reading and listening to. Reading was her escape from study. It was her fun when her homework was over. It was why, even though she loved to read, she always hated English class. It felt like the teachers were corrupting her hobby by making her be academic about it.

But she wasn't fool enough to think that her disinterest meant there was no merit to it. Her father was smart. She knew that. His students and peers loved and admired him. He'd written book after book, given lecture after lecture, about the importance of discrete lines of text in massive works of fiction. And she'd pointedly ignored it. Not out of disrespect… though the gnawing demons of grief would come around lately to tell her that's *certainly* how he'd seen it. She'd never bypassed anything of personal importance. Not that she could recall, anyway. Just the overly literary. She was more that content to let other people delve into that.

Uncle John was one of those people. Not an actual uncle; one of Dr. Lundgren's associates from the college. He was a good guy, smart, despite being a bit on the conspiracy theorist side. None of that flat Earth, hollow Earth, chemtrail, what have you. Only the purest historical conspiracies, with a bit of MK-ULTRA sprinkled in just to keep his feet on the ground. It kept him firmly in the realm of entertainingly eccentric, provided you kept him on calm topics.

By all accounts, Professor John Prestern was highly regarded by his students, ranging from general appreciation to the occasional crush (though Uncle John was the only source for this claim). To Faye, he'd always been a dinner guest, an occasional visitor, a presenter of perfectly-chosen birthday presents. Clearly liked by the family, but occasionally referred to via a "you know" tilt of the head. And, at the moment, helping Faye clear out some of her father's belongings.

"Anything? Really?" Uncle John's eyes roamed over the living room bookcase as though it were a dessert tray. "You've been through it already?"

"You know me." Faye looked up from her phone. "Not into the academic side. I'd rather they go to someone who'll love them." And, not that she'd say it aloud, but the less she had to dig into the clutter of the family home, the better. Just coming here brought back memories; actually getting to work had been a bigger emotional blow than she'd expected.

Despite the open offer, and despite his excitement of just moments ago, Uncle John was selective. A book here, a book there. Nothing he made a mad dive for. Each pick was thoughtful, almost introspective. Faye suspected every book he chose had a story behind it. *I bought him this one for Christmas,* or *We wrote opposing dissertations on this one.* Whatever it was academics did for fun.

“Thanks for flying all this way,” Faye murmured as Uncle John scoured the shelves. “I know it’s a hike from London.”

“How could I not? It was for Chase.” He smiled over his shoulder at Faye—a sad smile of shared loss. “And for you, of course.”

“Thanks. You’ll be heading back soon, then?”

“Yeah, probably in the next day or so.” His hand rested over the spine of an encyclopedia. “And you’re sure I can take *anything?* Really?”

Faye snorted. “If you can carry it home, you can have it. I promise.” She left him to his devices and went to the kitchen to make a pot of coffee. When she returned, he was stacking a surprisingly small number of volumes on a nearby table. Just odds and ends. Nothing exciting. But they seemed important to him.

“By the way,” he said absentmindedly as he began searching for something to pack them in. “There’s something your father wanted you to have.”

“Something I don’t already know about?” Faye sipped on her own coffee, sliding the second mug next to the short pile of books.

“Mm. Well, I’m fairly sure you don’t, at any rate.”

Faye raised her eyebrows, but the inquiring expression got her nothing. “So, um… am I going to find out what it is, or…”

“Here.” Uncle John took out his wallet and unzipped a hidden pocket, producing a small key with a worn paper tag on it. “Fox Point Credit Union, box 504. Let me know when you get it.”

“Thanks.” Faye took the key, turning it over in her hand. “So, uh, no hints?”

Uncle John smiled. He had an easy, disarming smile, one that calmed you as soon as you saw it. He only used it when there was nothing to worry about. “I’ll just say it’s a bit more than your usual light reading.” He knocked back the rest of his coffee, then swept up his plastic bag of books in one hand. “I’ll be at the hotel another few days. Ring me when you’re caught up.”

And he was gone with a slam of the screen door.

The house was suddenly empty again. Faye had thought for the longest time that quiet was what she wanted more than anything right now. But the conversation (and the helping hand clearing out some books) had been more welcome than she had expected.

There was a void now. One she couldn't handle. She wanted someone there. Anyone.

The lady of the other day sprang to mind. Dr. Quincy? Quinn? Whatever her name was, she'd wanted to talk. And, well, Faye was willing to listen to anyone right now. She dug up the card she'd been left with ("Cuinnsey," that was it) and shot a quick text to the number printed on it.

"Now's a good a time as any," followed by her address.

She expected a sudden knock at the door, or a phone call with vague instructions. Instead, she got a text back only moments later: *Running errands. Meet you at yours in half an hour?*

The unexpectedly human response put Faye a bit at ease. In half an hour was, in fact, fine. It gave her time to lie down for a few minutes, get into a headspace that wasn't quite so post-mortem. And, more importantly, it gave her brain a few minutes to realize that the name wasn't *quite* as unfamiliar as she'd first thought.

Half an hour passed unexpectedly quickly, and Faye found herself bolting upright from the sofa at the sound of the doorbell. She greeted Dr. Cuinnsey, smart and put together, feeling a bit like she'd just rolled out of bed after an earthquake.

"I *do* know you," Faye said on opening the door. "You and Dad worked together on a paper once. Something about Celtic bear-gods."

Dr. Cuinnsey smiled. "I hardly expected to be remembered for that, but I'm flattered. May I?"

Faye stepped aside, watching the tidy woman pick her way through the disaster of a house.

"Sit, um, anywhere you can find. I'm sorry."

"You've been through a lot lately. I understand." Dr. Cuinnsey chose a spot on the living room sofa just opposite the bookshelf. She stared at it thoughtfully, seeming to take it in, like a photo or a piece of scenery. "I apologize for how I confronted you before."

"Eh." It was all Faye had. "Coffee?" She didn't wait for a response, rushing off to the kitchen to freshen hers up and make a second mug for her guest. When Faye came back, Dr. Cuinnsey had walked to the bookshelf and begun running her fingers along the spines.

"Uh, you can take anything there you like. Seriously. I want it to go to people who will care."

"Again, thank you. And…" Dr. Cuinnsey paused over a tattered volume devoted to *Piers Ploughman.* "I may. But that's not what I'm here for."

"Right." Faye took a spot on the floor, her back against the wall. "You're here for something super-secret."

"You could say that."

"Hate to tell you, but Dad didn't really keep any secrets." She paused, her eyes caught by the lock box key on the coffee table. "Well. Okay. One secret. In a safety deposit box. But that's fairly new news to me."

The woman raised her eyebrows, her gray eyes lighting up. "That's likely what I'm looking for, then."

"You don't even know what it is. How can you be so sure?"

Dr. Cuinnsey pursed her lips. It was like watching someone riffle through a mental Rolodex: there were a dozen ways she could say what she was going to say next, but she needed to kick off with the right one. Just that pause made Faye a little edgy.

"Look, if you're implying my dad was into some weird sort of business…"

"Oh, I know Dr. Lundgren was what he seemed. No more, no less. I admired him greatly, and I was told the feeling was mutual. There was one sticking point between us, though." She steeped her fingers and pressed them to her lips. "There was an item in his possession that he considered safest with him. And I consider it safest with us."

"This Booker Foundation."

A nod.

Faye snorted, raising her coffee mug to her lips in preparation for a sip. "Is this where I find out Dad's been hiding some sort of Biblical face-melting artifact from us for all these years?"

"Well, minus the face-melting bit."

Faye lowered the mug slowly.

"I know you're not a fan of, erm, 'academics.'" Dr. Cuinnsey managed to say this without sounding condescending. "So, suffice to say that your father was believed to be in possession of a very rare piece of writing whose mere existence has been the subject of debate for centuries."

"But it *does* exist."

Dr. Cuinnsey nodded. "Unless your father was an exceptional liar, the proofs he gave that he was in possession of such a text were beyond adequate. Frankly, the only reason for doubt we have is his unwillingness to produce it when we requested it."

Faye rolled her half-empty coffee mug between her hands. "So, my father had something you wanted. Which is top-tier important. And he wouldn't give it to you. And now it's mine… and I don't know what it is. In fact, all I know of it is that you want it." And that she was meant to go over it soon with a family friend. But she left that part out.

She fixed Dr. Cuinnsey with a curious look. The woman seemed intelligent and aboveboard. She'd never heard her father mention Dr. Cuinnsey as an untrustworthy entity. Even so.

"So, when do you start proving to me that I should give it to you?"

Faye was not expecting the satisfied smile she got in return. She wasn't sure if she'd passed a test or proved a point, but she far preferred the smile to a fight or a shouting match.

"I'll make you a deal, Ms. Lundgren. Go and get the book from your father's belongings, and decide for yourself where it belongs. I promise, I will honor whatever choice you make." Dr. Cuinnsey finished her coffee in one long tip of the mug, then set it down and got to her feet. "Should you choose to hand it over to the Foundation, you will be compensated."

"How much?"

An eyebrow raise. "I wouldn't want to sway your decision in advance. Suffice to say, you will receive what it's worth. Once you understand what we're dealing with here, I'm sure you'll be able to make a decent estimate."

"And if I decide not to give it to you?"

"Your choice. But I highly recommend that if you do not sell it to the Foundation, you destroy it at once. It would be a tragic loss, but better than the alternative. I'm sure there are many other people in the world who wouldn't be quite so scrupulous with it."

Faye felt the back of her neck go cold. "You're making it sound awfully dire."

Dr. Cuinnsey's face was placid.

“What *is* this book, anyway? Dad’s library is enormous, and that’s even giving things away left and right.”

“The author is Kyot. The book is *Parzifal.* Assuming Dr. Lundgren was telling the truth, the rest should be easy.”

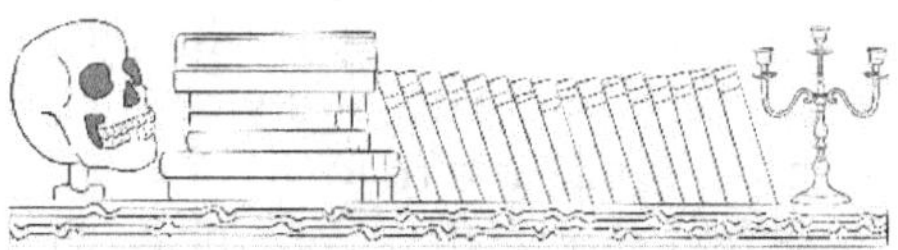

As far as Faye could gather, it went a bit like this:

Hundreds of years ago, there was a writer named Chrétien. He wrote a story that a lot of people liked, but he never actually got around to finishing it.

Not long after, another writer named Wolfram came along and wrote his own, longer, more detailed story based on Chrétien’s. Except he claimed not to *like* Chrétien’s. Not only that, he claimed his source wasn’t that original story, but rather another book entirely, by someone named Kyot. And Kyot’s book was based on *another* book, by someone named Flegetanis.

(It was at this point in Faye’s reading that she remembered why she preferred to just let stories happen to her instead of getting too deeply involved. She was four writers deep before she’d even completely figured out what she was supposed to be looking for.)

Upon finding the writings of Flegetanis, Kyot traveled across Europe to write his own book, which then inspired Wolfram’s. And… oh, boy, here was the kicker, here was the great big nasty go-home-and-take-a-nap kicker… this book was about the Holy Freaking Grail. Specifically, about how it’s very real, and about who it belongs to and what it enables them to do.

Most historians believed that Kyot was an invention of Wolfram’s, either as metafiction or because he hated criticism and thought that saying his story was Totally True would protect him from haters. Then there was Dr. Lundgren, who not only believed there was a Kyot and a Flegetanis, but also claimed to *have* the book in question.

That was what Dr. Cuinnsey wanted: an ancient book that proved that a literal Biblical relic existed. That told where it was, what it did, and who it belonged to. A book that, apparently, had now been willed to Faye. A book that, *also* apparently, she was meant to chat about with someone who would *absolutely* believe whatever this alleged book put forward, to God knows what end.

She could understand now why the relative stranger was so adamant about it being either turned in or destroyed. At best, it was a forgery. But even a forgery could lead to some pretty messed-up stuff. People started cults and harmed other people in the name of much, *much* less. There only needed to be something reasonably genuine-looking to turn to.

At worst, it was real. And if that were the case… Faye couldn't even imagine what would happen if it became common knowledge. The seat of pretty much every major world religion would want to get their hands on it. Conspiracy theorists, zealots, all of them would have their own uses for it. And God forbid anyone ever traced just who was named as the keepers of the Grail. They'd be worshipped. Killed. Both in no particular order.

If *Parzival* were to leave Faye's sight, if it were to get out of her hands, there was no telling what disasters would happen, or how quickly. It had to be secured, quickly and without incident.

All of these thoughts were swimming around in Faye's mind, bumping into each other like confused guppies, as she stared into her father's safety deposit box at the bank, emptied out save for a small, bright green sticky note bearing four words.

*Come and get it.*

It was in Uncle John's handwriting.

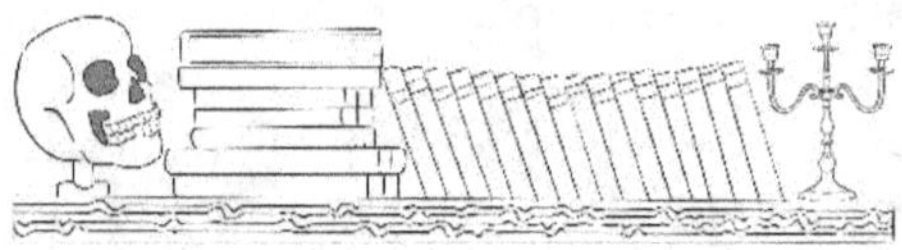

The lady at Customs wanted to be there even less than Faye did; it radiated. "And where will you be staying while you're here?"

Faye stifled a yawn. "With my Uncle John."

"Where's he, then?"

"Golders Green." As in London. As in England. Not in the hotel like he'd said. No, he'd checked out *several* days early, as it happened. And this was where Faye had ended up: on the trail of a book that might not exist. Though given the effort being put in by all parties, she was leaning more toward the Does Exist camp.

"Maternal or paternal uncle?"

"Does it matter?"

The Customs lady gave her a pointed look over her bifocals. Faye suddenly felt like she was smuggling in seven handbags of drugs and a few farm animals.

"Paternal," she said quickly. Somehow, she felt that explaining that "uncle" was only a nickname would make things far worse.

"How long are you staying?"

*Until I've managed to wrest the secrets of one of mankind's greatest mysteries from the hands of my dad's nutjob college buddy.* "About six or seven days."

The cross-examination ended, and Faye took her passport and hand luggage and moved on. She was only slightly relieved to hear the person behind her get just as much push-back. It was clearly just the way of things at Heathrow first thing in the morning.

Uncle John had a bedsit in an old three-story house. Faye's father had been to visit before. Apparently, it was cozy, mostly book-filled, and *didn't* have a board covered with thumbtacks and red string. It was also a relatively short walk from the tube station and easy to find with GPS.

She hadn't called ahead. She hadn't felt like it. Between knowing he was expecting her and really, really hating being taunted all the way to England, she couldn't find any desire to do him any favors.

It had also crossed her mind to let the Booker Foundation deal with him one on one, especially considering the whole trip was going to happen on their dime one way or the other. But the last thing he needed was knowledge that there were *more* things out there he didn't know about.

Besides, she'd rehearsed one hell of a speech for him.

Her opening gamut ran over and over in her head as she knocked on the door of the house. An older woman, stout and pleasant-faced, greeted Faye. The landlady, clearly. Not the person to let loose on.

"Hi, um. Is Professor Prestern in? I'm his niece. He's expecting me."

The landlady looked oddly embarrassed. "Oh, no, love. I'm so sorry, but he's gone out." Her tone made it sound as though she took the blame entirely. "I don't know when he'll be back. Come in, set your bags down, I'll make you some tea and we'll sort you out."

Good. Lovely. Figures. Of course. Faye took the invitation with a quiet bob of the head. "Did he say where he was going? And, er, did he mention having any company coming in?"

"He didn't mention guests, no. But he's gone to his house in Cornwall."

"Since when does Uncle John have a house in Cornwall?"

The landlady led Faye into a small, tidy kitchen. What little she'd seen of the boarding house was oddly tiny and vertical compared to what she was used to. Standing there felt like putting her eye up to the window of an intricately furnished dollhouse and imagining herself inside.

"Since as long as I've known him, really." The landlady went about the tea ritual: bags, an electric kettle Faye found herself wanting for her apartment, a foil-topped glass bottle of milk out of a skinny little refrigerator. "He goes out there for research, he says. Researching what, I don't know. It's all a bit beyond me."

"I know how you feel." The tea was in her hands soon after. She wasn't sure what to do with it, so she just let it steep, water wicking up the string and slowly wetting the tag. "So, he didn't say anything about when he'd be coming back? Just up and left?"

The landlady chuckled, doctoring her tea with milk and sugar with a sort of blind familiarity. "He does that, the professor. He'll pack a bag and take off. Just shouts he'll be back and runs out the door. Could be a day, a week." She mused over her mug. "Once he was gone three months. Wasn't half cross when he came home and saw I'd rented the room out again."

Faye briefly considered just dropping it all. Just getting a hotel room, seeing London, enjoying herself, and going home. Forget Uncle John, forget Kyot, just let it all handle itself. If the Foundation wanted the book that badly, *they* could chase it all the way to Cornwall. They could deal with whatever it was or wasn't, and she could take a nap.

If that same Foundation wasn't footing the entire bill, she'd likely have gone with the idea. But the thought of looking Dr. Cuinnsey in the eye and explaining she'd frittered away the group's money with nothing to show for it was six different types of unappealing.

Inhale. Exhale. "You think I could have his address?"

Whether it was thanks to a desire to bring family together or spite at her tenant's unpredictable ways, the landlady had no trouble presenting Faye with an address, directions to Paddington Station, and a spare room where she could have a lie-in and set off the next day. Fortunately, she slept hard: one nice dream (the one she had occasionally about the neverending plate of shrimp quesadillas) and nothing else she could remember.

One mitigating factor of the entire mess was the newness of it all. As Faye settled in on the train's quiet car, she had to admit that there as something a bit romantic about it all. A five-hour train ride near home would have been a slog, but she had a whole new nation of countryside to watch. (And, as immature as it sounded, a whole new variety of cheap train food to acclimate to.)

An hour or so in, she popped open her laptop and searched out Wolfram's *Parzival.* If nothing else, she could familiarize herself with the whole mess before she got there.

"Right," she muttered quietly to herself. "Book One."

*How Gamuret of Anjou at the death of his father, King Gandein, refused to become his brother's vassal, and went forth to seek fame and love-guerdon for himself...*

Faye shut the laptop again.

Just a glance at the page had been eye-crossingly full of odd names and terms. Fair play to people who liked it, but she much preferred her father's stories. They flowed like molten stardust from one scene to the next, free of lengthy family trees and full audits of armor and weaponry. She rode the stories like enchanted horses into sleep, galloping alongside nameless knights who needed no description save for the valor they demonstrated.

The words of the stories came to mind in the same meter, like an often-watched movie: "The cascade over the northern summit pointed the knights to their king," it began, careening off into adventure after adventure.

She realized she would never hear those stories again, not outside her own thoughts, and suddenly the train ride felt just a longer.

Alighting from the train in Bodmin left her in a little stone station, oddly exactly as she'd imagined it might look. It was another 14 miles by bus before she even stepped into Camelford, where Uncle John's home-away-from-home apparently was. The novelty of the situation was beginning to disappear.

It came back when she hit Camelford. She'd always assumed the little English villages on television must be highly stylized and almost completely fictional, but this looked like it had spilled straight from a movie. The thought occurred to her yet again: leave the book, leave Uncle John, enjoy your time here.

No. Not when she was practically on his doorstep. Just another block or two going by his landlady's directions, and she could get in and take care of this nonsense. And *then* she'd relax on someone else's dime.

The scribbled directions led Faye to a house that gave off the impression of deserving its own name. It looked like a Lilac Copse or a Chestnut Corner—not an 18 Hunters' Way.

There was no car out front, no lights visible in the front windows. She rang the bell nonetheless. From somewhere inside, a grand chime sounded. She waited a minute, two minutes, then rang again. This time she waited five minutes. Still nothing.

Expecting nothing, she gave the front door a little push; it creaked inward. Fine, then. She walked into the front hall, peering through the quiet house lit only by the afternoon sun peeking through the curtained windows. It was tidy, hardly what she'd expect of Uncle John, decorated sparsely but pleasantly with photos and personal belongings. The air smelled of potpourri and the universal smell of Someone Else's Home, with an edge of dust.

A floorboard creaked somewhere toward the back of the house. She followed the sound, finding another door, also ajar. Pushing this one revealed a cozy but decently-sized study, lined with bookshelves and display cases at capacity. The centerpiece was a worn desk littered with books and papers and a few neglected mugs of tea. And sitting at the desk, of course, was Uncle John.

He didn't look up at her, but she knew he knew she was there. He was making her wait.

She'd always seen him in three-piece suits or dressed all the way down to jeans and a faded T-shirt. Now, behind his desk, he looked far more like a respected professor than a tolerable conspiracy theorist: buttoned-down shirt with collar and sleeves unbuttoned, a cardigan thrown hastily over, and reading glasses perched dangerously low on his nose. In his hand, a bit of light reading: a small, ancient-looking book, leather-bound with metal corners. In this brief moment, he was everyone's favorite professor. And it seemed almost wrong to break that illusion.

"I'm here."

"So, you are." He didn't look up from the little book, but his tone was calm, almost jovial. "And in excellent time. You must have set off the day after I did."

"Why did you lie to me?"

Uncle John raised his head, pulling his glasses off his face with a quick, punctuating motion. "I don't recall lying to you."

"You said we'd meet and discuss this thing Dad left for us."

"Yes, and here we are." He closed the book and raised it, giving it a little shake. "As promised. Have a seat. You're probably exhausted. I'll put the kettle on."

As Uncle John rose from his desk chair, Faye leaned backward, shutting the office door. "No, thank you. I'm fine. They refilled my tea on the train a *lot.*"

He sat down again slowly, his cheerful expression straining slightly. "At least pull up a chair, then."

"Is that the *Parzival?*"

"It's been quiet without your father to chat with."

"Uncle John, is that the book?"

He sighed, his expression world-weary. "We don't have to talk shop right away, do we? You're finally over here! There are so many places I've wanted to take you!"

"Is it—"

*"Yes,* it's the bloody book! Christ!" Uncle John's fist came down on the desk with an unexpectedly loud *slam,* jostling the discarded mugs. Faye reared back slightly, eyes still fixed on him.

"That's really all you're here for, isn't it?" He put a hand over the small volume. "To take it and go. To sell it off to… who was it? Professor Hailey? Collins and Muhafaz? I didn't actually catch that bit."

Faye felt the back of her neck prickle. She wasn't sure whether it was with fear or… guilt? Why did she feel guilty?

Uncle John was more than willing to help make that clear. "I told you, didn't I? It was your father's. It was for *us.* To go through *together.*" He laughed. "And at the first opportunity you want to get rid of it, just because you don't fancy a bit of reading."

The guilt joined forces with insult and stung.

"If you knew. Faye, if you *knew* how important this book was to *you.* To *me.* You wouldn't sell it. You wouldn't even let it out of your sight."

"Why, though?" Faye did finally take a seat. She felt the exhaustion hit her brain, then her legs. "I know what it is. I know it's yet another thing about the really real truth of the Holy Grail, for serious this time, you guys."

Uncle John gave what Faye thought at first was a short sigh, but realized when he started muttering under his breath had been a scoffing laugh. "'For serious this time.' Honestly, how many holy vessels has someone important bled into?"

"Still. What does any of this have to do with either of us beyond the fact that it's here in this room?"

Uncle John looked at Faye with what she could only parse as pity. "Faye Lundgren, this book is our everything. And you are the key to it all."

"Just so you know, that last bit sounded really apocalyptic and kind of insane."

If he registered her comment, or even heard it, he didn't show any sign of having done so. He was leafing through the book, scribbling things down on a piece of paper as he did.

"There are pages missing," he muttered. "That must be why Chase wanted us together. You have what's missing. It's the only possible explanation."

"How? Until a couple of days ago, I didn't even know that thing existed. He never talked about it with me at all."

Uncle John looked at Faye pointedly over the rims of his glasses. "Now, I'm not entirely sure I believe that."

She laughed, spreading her hands out helplessly. "Okay? You don't *have* to. But that's the truth. We never talked about Grails or anything like that. He had his thing, I had mine."

"No… no. There's something. Something you know, something you're supposed to do." He stared at the book. Faye could see a little clump of long, skinny stubs of vellum sticking out between the pages.

"There's some missing."

"Yes, well spotted." Uncle John's tone was tetchy. But it was a nice change from the impassioned fervor of earlier. This was much closer to what she was used to: the thoughtful, professorial tone he and he father shared when approaching an issue. “It’s not uncommon for a book this old to be incomplete. Vellum is durable, but that doesn’t mean bits won’t go missing.”

Faye leaned closer over the desk. “No, those look like they were taken out on purpose.”

Uncle John looked up at Faye, then down at the book. “How do you figure?”

“The cuts are really straight, see? And fairly even across that whole little set. Whatever was in this bit was taken out deliberately.” She peered more closely at the book. “And it must be recent, because the edges don’t have the same soft wear to them as the rest of the page edges. This was *really* recent.”

“And also *really* important.” Uncle John tapped a finger on the leftmost page, then the right. “There should be coordinates between here and here. On the missing pages.”

Faye shook her head. “I don’t know. I really don’t. I’m sorry. Look.” She paused, collecting her thoughts. “Tell you what. Okay? I’ll help you to the end of this. To, you know, figure out whatever it is you’re looking to do. And then when that’s done, we can decide together what we do with the book. Okay?”

She flashed him a hopeful smile. In all honesty, his behavior here in his home office convinced her more than ever that she needed to get this little chunk of heavy reading material out of her life. If it was making him preach this sort of oddness, who knew what someone else might do with it.

“Mm.” He gave a noncommittal grunt. It was clear he still wasn’t sure he could trust her. Then, slowly, he eased up, looking her in the eye calmly. The defensiveness had begun to melt away.

“With the missing pages, there’s only so much I can do. But between local legend and good hunches, I do have a ‘first pick’ for places to visit. Care to come with?”

She didn’t. But she said she did.

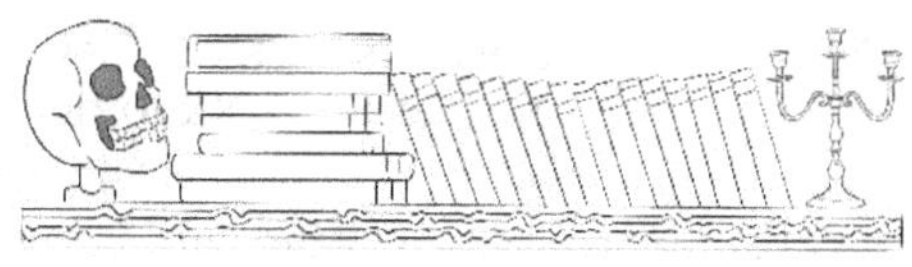

A calm sleep in a small-town guest room made the anxiety of previous days seem to vanish. Faye awoke in the well-appointed little room Uncle John had pointed her to. Barely big enough for a bed, a steamer trunk, and a wardrobe, but it felt like enough.

She was sitting by the room's one tall, narrow window, just enjoying the fact that she was looking out at an autumnal English town in her pajamas. For the briefest of moments there was no book, no Grail, no money on the line.

Then her phone buzzed.

*Any luck?*

Dr. Cuinnsey, of course. Faye realized she'd been out of touch for longer than she'd promised.

*I have seen it,* she said. *Things got a little complicated. Have to play along to get it back.*

Faye watched the little bouncy ellipses idle as a response came. One, two, three minutes. It must have been a hell of a message. Then:

*Stay safe.*

The filter snapped off her vision again, and she remembered where she was.

Uncle John had rented a car for the day, a boxy little Citröen that smelled like a smoker had recently tried to hide the fact that they'd had a smoke in it. The route wasn't long, Uncle John said, and they'd be walking more than driving.

"Do you know the story of Parzival?" he asked casually as they set off.

"I… started it. I didn't get past love-guerdons."

The professor chuckled. "Can't blame you. They aren't enticing reads in their original format." He stared at the road ahead. "Parzifal was a no one. A nothing. A backwoods boy whose mother deliberately kept him from learning of chivalry. He'd lost a father and brothers in battle, you see, and she didn't want to lose a son, too.

"But chivalric blood flows strong. It always wins out eventually. He saw some knights washing their armor in a stream near his house, and he ran home to tell his mother he'd just seen angels. He described them, and she asked him why he thought they were angels? Because, of course, she had told him that angels are the most beautiful thing you will ever see.

“She knew there was no keeping him away. So, she sent him to Camelot to follow his destiny.” He laughed quietly. “Family trait, I suppose.”

Faye stared out the window at the landscape rolling past them. “And then he went off and became a great knight, I suppose.”

“Oh, no. He was terrible. His lack of manners and education caused more harm than even he could ever know. He ended up spending years having to earn his way back into the grace of God. He finally did, of course. And he found the Grail. For the second time.”

“The second?”

“I’ll let you read the rest for yourself.” Uncle John grinned. And, to be fair, he had hooked her. At least a bit. “Suffice to say, he became the new Grail King, the new steward of the holy vessel. And his descendants would follow in his footsteps: one family in the east, one in the west. Of course, this was back when the world was much larger. No Internet or air travel. So, the job could theoretically be held down by one person in this day and age, don’t you think?”

“Er…” Faye tossed him a wobbly smile. “Sure.”

The rest of the drive went on in silence, Faye occasionally glancing at the little leather-bound book between them, wrapped in a soft towel. *You had better be worth this, I swear.*

There was a place to park, and then, seemingly, a lot of nothing.

“It’s about a two-hour walk,” Uncle John said brightly, taking the book and a shoulder bag from the car. “Hope you’re ready.”

She very much wasn’t.

The hike was sprinkled with small talk: work, memories of her father, future plans. They eventually crested a hill—“Showery Tor,” based on the map Faye had brought up on her phone—and could see another in the distance.

“That’s where we’re going. Brown Willy.”

Faye choked.

“It’s a long shot, but there are good odds we’ll get what we’re looking for there.”

“I’m not climbing your Brown Willy.”

Uncle John trudged ahead, ignoring the jab. Faye rushed behind.

"So, you're saying you think there's… what, the literal Grail there? Don't you think someone would have found it by now if so?"

"Faye. There are so many things in this world still unfound in plain sight. There are things that took thousands, *millions* of years for humans to find. A few hundred is still fairly recent in the grand scheme of things."

That was actually a fair point. "And what's got you thinking that… God. That *Brown Willy* is what you're looking for?"

"Location, for one. If nothing else, Cornwall is a fairly agreed-upon hub for the activities of these stories. For another, the hill has legends of its own. Some say a great king is buried underneath it. What if it's not a king, but something *belonging* to a king, eh?" Uncle John grinned. "And there are those who believe that the hill is charged with great universal energy. Again, there could be more than one explanation."

"Who believes this again?"

"Ah…" He hesitated. "UFO cult."

"Oh, well, if *they* believe it, jackpot."

Uncle John's expression settled into one of eternal patience. "Right for the wrong reasons. It can happen."

When they reached the top of the hill, Faye collapsed gratefully onto one of the many rocks scattered here. Her legs were sore and burning. She was used to running around on her feet doing temp work, but no office ever made her hike uphill for an hour.

Uncle John, on the other hand, was looking around at the various rocks, tapping his chin with one finger. "I'm not entirely sure where to begin. There's a cave under here, but it's never been excavated. If we need to dig our way down, there's an issue. But I can't believe there's not *some* way to get in without actually pulling the whole thing apart."

"I feel like that wouldn't go over well with the locals," Faye mused. "Don't expect they want people's hands all over their Brow—"

"Faye."

She smiled. Frankly, this was the only way she was going to keep her sanity. If she let her sense of humor slip, she might remember what she was actually in the middle of doing.

"Right. The northern summit is our best bet, but what then?"

“The cascade over the northern summit,” Faye blurted out.

Uncle John snapped his head around. “What?”

“It’s… I don’t know. It’s just stories Dad told me. But they were about stars, not *rocks*. They wouldn’t be helpful here.”

“No, no.” He stepped back, casting an eye over the field of stones. “What if that’s actually what was on the missing pages? Not navigation by the stars, but navigation into the caves via the stones?”

Faye shrugged helplessly. *“Maybe?”*

“No one’s entirely sure what the rock formations are for, or why things are spread out this way. Only that it’s a man-made arrangement. There are theories that it’s something to do with the equinox and all that, because it’s always to do with the equinox. But what *if.”* He rounded the tall cairn that stood at the very peak of the hill. On the opposite side was a small semicircle of stones, shaped almost like a comet. “The cascade over the northern summit!”

“Anyone could have done that. Tourists could have been playing with them.”

“Maybe. We’ll find out, I suppose. Tell me more.”

Faye closed her eyes, racking her brain for whatever of her father’s stories she could remember. Uncle John stood still whenever she rattled through any actual battles or plot points. But when the stars came into play, their movement guiding the heroes of her tale to their next destination, he’d move among the stones on the hill, like a giant game of connect-the-dots.

The oddest part was that it seemed to be working. Each time he moved, he found a new landmark. Though, to Faye’s eyes, he seemed to be walking in circles.

“Couldn’t they just say which one it is?”

“And make it easy for just anyone who found it? Don’t be silly. What’s next?”

“Um… well, the last thing I remember—”

“Just the stars, Faye.”

“The last thing I remember about the stars is Orion’s Belt.”

Uncle John looked around. “So, we’re looking for three stones in a row near where I am now. Aha!” He spotted it and stepped over about three feet. “Anything else?”

“Nothing about the stars.”

Uncle John got to his knees and began tapping his hands over the rocks, the soil, anything near the three stones. "There must be something here if that's the end."

"To be fair, I always fell asleep before he finished."

"Shouldn't matter. If he told it the same way every time, he'd remember."

Faye shook her head. "I don't know. I don't think the stories are part of it."

"It's fallen in line with the stones so far."

"Sure, but… if the pages are missing, how could Dad have known the stories to tell them to me?"

Uncle John's hand stilled for a moment, the fingers curling in on themselves into a loose fist. "Ah. Well. Who knows, eh? What came next?"

"Nothing about the stars. But let's see." Faye rubbed her forehead, as though that would bring the memories forward. "Something something…Orion's belt led the way to the castle of the maiden, and the moon-light glinted off the tip of his sword as—"

"Ah!" Uncle John's surprised exclamation cut her off. "Of course. Orion's belt, Orion's sword." He glanced to the side. Sure enough, there was a line of three slightly smaller stones. "That last one should be what we're looking for."

Faye glanced down at the row of stones. The last one was circular, almost artificially so, and seemed to be set deep into the ground, almost like the reset button on a piece of electronics. It was visible, but difficult to interact with unless you knew it was there. She tapped it with her sneaker. Nothing happened.

"Try pressing it."

"I just did."

"With your finger."

Faye shrugged and reached down, poking the stone firmly with her thumb.

The hill rumbled gently at first, then increasing power. The cairn at the northern summit started to collapse and fall away, the rocks sliding toward the opposite face of the hill. Uncle John ran to it as Faye squatted motionless, staring at her hand.

"Over here! Faye! It worked!"

"What? No way." She ran to Uncle John's side. Sure enough, the cairn had fallen away to reveal a pit sinking deep into the hill, with hand and footholds carved into the stone wall lining it. "Oh, my God."

"Come on, then." The professor popped a small flashlight from his jacket pocket and clicked it on, grabbing it between his teeth. He wasted no time in making his way down the makeshift ladder. Faye watched the white light recede farther and farther.

She patted her back pocket in vain hopes that maybe, *just* maybe, she'd somehow worked the *Parzival* into her back pocket without remember and could just take off. No such luck. She sighed and followed, picking her way down the ancient handholds.

When her sneakers hit the ground, Uncle John was already a few feet ahead. He was shining the flashlight around the chamber below the hill in awe. There was nothing there, though: no carvings or paintings on the walls, nothing left behind by other errant travelers, and certainly no Grail. But there was a tunnel leading off into the distance.

"Shall we?" Uncle John was beaming like a kid at Christmas.

There was really no other choice at this point.

There were no handy torches to light as they walked down the tunnel—something Faye had always assumed was standard issue in ancient structures. Uncle John didn't seem to mind, though. He was flicking the flashlight back and forth across the path, practically vibrating with excitement even though there was nothing to see but dirt and stone, and nothing to smell but wet earth and faint smoke.

"Aren't you glad I didn't leave the book for you, Faye? If I had, you'd never see *this.*"

"Yeah." She swallowed. "Yeah, about that. Um… the stuff you were saying earlier about this being a thing for you and Dad and me."

"Oh, yes, of course. You never read the stories, did you?" He pulled the *Parzifal* from his back pocket and tossed it idly to Faye. She opened it, peering at what little she could make out in the dim light of the flashlight. There wasn't much to see, considering it was all in smudged Old French.

"Did your father ever mention how we met?"

"Something about working together on a project."

He nodded. "This. This was it. The two of us, Chase and me, dissecting this book. Bit by bit. It was only ever a page at a time. He'd photocopy or transcribe a piece, say it was all he had, but I knew, I *knew.* And then one day I saw it. Just *there* on his desk, right in front of me, like bait on a hook. He didn't let me look at the whole thing. Said all things considered he'd rather I not get to into it. Whatever the hell he meant by that. But we talked about it.

"He told me something he'd never told anyone else. He had dreams. Dreams like the ones in that book. The visions the Grail Kings would see. Visions of a vessel, a Grail, that provided neverending blessing and sustenance. Dreams of stars, dreams of heroes. It was a calling, to come and find his destiny. And Faye?" He paused.

"I had those dreams, too."

She stared down at the book in silence.

"We traced our family trees, and what do you think we found? A common ancestor. It was us, Faye, *us.* We were the eastern and western kings! *Us!* Centuries of travel moved things around, of course, but it was us. And we had a destiny. One he never pursued."

Faye exhaled slowly. "Dad took those pages out himself, didn't he?"

No answer.

"He did. And I know why."

Uncle John continued walking, but Faye stopped in her tracks, holding the book tightly in her hands.

"He knew you'd get like this, didn't he?"

"Your father never wanted to see his duties through. *Our* duties. Now we have a chance. Now that he's gone, we can reclaim our places."

Faye shook her head, taking a step backwards. "No. Look. We're not doing this, okay? It's been an experience, I can tell my kids about it someday, but we're going home now. Okay?"

"We're not done yet."

"Maybe you're not, but I'm done as hell." Faye took another two steps backwards, then tried to turn and run. But Uncle John grabbed the collar of her shirt before she could get away. The book flew out of her hands, bouncing off the wall of the tunnel and hitting the floor.

"No. I can't do this without you." He pulled her back toward him, gripping her left wrist tightly in his hand and dragging her with him. "It has to be both of us. I have to know."

Faye struggled to no avail. Uncle John wasn't a large man by any means, but he was tenacious enough that she knew she would only hurt herself trying to make another break for it. The tunnel ahead opened into a wider room. From within shone a light, dim but visible. It wasn't an opening to the outside; it shone from something in the room itself.

"The stone responded to you," he muttered. "But it would have responded to both of us, right? Right. Of course. Two families, two people. Why wouldn't it?" He was talking to himself now, breathless, frantic. "That's not what chooses, anyway."

"What are you—"

"The Grail, Faye. The Grail chooses. God, why couldn't you just read a damn *book?"*

On the last word, he slung her ahead of him into the room. It was round, about the size of a respectable dining room, with a long table in the center. Grand chairs were positioned all around it. Most were covered in piles of dust, but a few had stray bones in them. One, the one closest to the entrance, held a skeleton, the head lolled forward as though it had fallen asleep and simply forgotten to wake up.

The table itself was almost entirely bare, a thick layer of dust blanketing it more like a sheet of padding than a tablecloth. Faye couldn't even begin to estimate how many years it had been since anything had disturbed it. An intrusive though flickered by—*Leave a handprint in it!*—then let her be.

In the middle of the table, and the only thing on it, was a large golden dish. Somehow it had survived the years of dust-layering, marred with only a few dark specks of something she couldn't discern. In the bottom of the dish was about an inch or so of clear water.

"What is that?"

Uncle John shot Faye a disgusted look. *"What* is that. Have you been asleep this whole time?"

"But… the Grail is a cup, isn't it? That's, like, for a casserole or something."

If he heard her, he'd tuned her out, stepping up to the table until he was between two of the chairs. The professor was staring at the golden dish, the excitement gone from his face. He looked almost placid now, but she could see that every muscle in his body was tensed. He held his hands out, as though preparing to lean forward and pick up the dish, but otherwise didn't move.

"Maybe we should leave it alone." Faye looked at the skeletal visitors, the piles of bones and dust. "I feel like things don't go well for people who try to take it."

"People it doesn't belong to, maybe." Uncle John laughed calmly. "Come here." His voice was encouraging, almost pleasant.

Faye stepped forward until she was alongside him, a chair between them. She stared down at the dish. A tingle went down her spine; whether it was from a sense of divine right or abject terror, she couldn't be sure. She'd never really experienced either before.

No, she knew what it was now. It was the dark spots. That was blood, all right.

"The Grail chooses its guardian," Uncle John said quietly, almost reverently, pointing to the rim of the vessel. The scrollwork etched along it was beginning to warp, as though pondering those in its presence. "It names its own king, gives its own command."

"Oh."

*Click.*

Faye glanced over at Uncle John. Blocking her view of him was the business end of a small handgun.

"However." His voice was still calm. "If its chosen owner suddenly becomes unavailable, I'm sure it will happily take a replacement."

"What the *hell?"*

He cast her a sad glance. "Personally, I think it will make the right choice. You have shown it no interest, given it no thought." A smirk twitched the corner of his lip up. "You might even sell it off if it came to you."

"Look, if it wants me, you—" She stopped. Did she really want to hand over a holy artifact to this guy? She didn't even want him to have the book when she thought it might be fake. But there was also the fact that she really, *really* did not want to die. And at the moment, she wasn't sure which took priority.

"It doesn't work that way. It *will* have its owner. But it wouldn't." His hand faltered for just a moment. "Just because Chase favored you doesn't mean it will. Just because he said he didn't want to see me get involved doesn't mean I shouldn't. No. No, this is…"

The scrollwork began to resolve slowly. They both stared, breathless for entirely different reasons.

*IOHN PRESTERN*

Faye closed her eyes, letting out an exhausted sigh of relief as she heard Uncle John drop the gun on the floor of the cave. She wasn't even ready to process what this could mean overall; she just knew she wasn't dead.

Meanwhile, he had snatched up the Grail in both hands and drunk the clear water in it, like a dying man in a desert. He stopped, coughing and spluttering, holding the dish out in front of him as he tried to catch his breath. Faye felt the floor rumble underneath her and grabbed the edge of the table to steady herself. But when she looked around, she didn't see any signs of the room shaking.

"Hah… Chase… what do you think of that, eh?" Uncle John had regained his composure and was laughing under his words. He tucked the Grail against his hip like a laundry basket. "Always so proud of your academics. Always so happy with keeping your nose out of the 'theoretical' fields. But look where it's gotten you, eh?"

He and Faye locked eyes. And he smiled.

"You were never fit for this."

In that moment, Faye knew she wasn't the one being spoken to.

The rumbling grew louder, and Faye realized it wasn't coming from the floor. It was coming from something moving across it: a chair. A moment after she realized it, Uncle John's legs were swept out from under him by a new chair that had slid in from somewhere along the shadowy edges of the wall, forcing him to sit down at the table. The dish flew out of his hands, resuming its original spot.

"What in the…" He tried to push himself back, but the chair remained firmly in place. He tried to climb up over it, but he couldn't get his legs out. He struggled in every possible direction. Then he looked back at the dish on the table. His name was warping into a new one:

*DINDRANE.*

"Wait… No. No, it's wrong! It's all wrong!"

Now the cave really was starting to rumble. Faye backed away as Uncle John grabbed for her arm, looking at her with terror in his eyes.

"Faye!"

She shook her head, but words wouldn't come out.

"No, don't leave me! This isn't what I wanted!" He laughed. "He was right, you know! He was always right, your father! Come on, let's get out of here together, eh? It'll be like none of this—"

The rumbling, she realized, was coming from above. The cairn was re-forming. She dashed for the tunnel, the professor yelling after her helplessly.

Faye ran hell-for-leather for the exit, stopping only to snatch up the *Parzival* as she went. She clenched the book between her teeth as she climbed, dust and leather on her tongue. The stones were flying around above her like leaves in a whirlwind. When she was close enough to manage, she pushed herself out with what little strength she had left.

She rolled a few feet down the hill, the stones of the cairn clacking back into place behind her. And then, everything was silent.

For a moment, Faye lay on the ground, her hand on the book, the dry grass tickling her cheek.

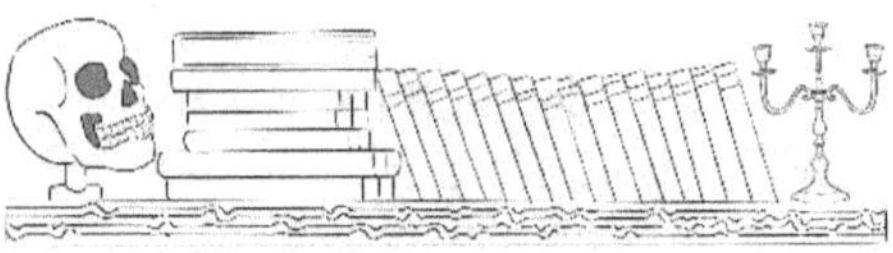

Dr. Cuinnsey stared at the little book on the coffee table between them. "That's it? That's the *Parzival?"*

Faye nodded. "The real thing. Though… as much as I appreciate your offer, I won't be selling it to you."

“Ms. Lundgren.” The woman’s tone went slightly sharp; not angry, but scolding. *Do you know what you’re saying?* “I’m sure you’re a very trustworthy person, but having this out in the world could cause untold amounts of chaos.”

“I agree. Having a book out there that tells you how to find the real Holy Grail would be a terrible thing.” Faye rested a hand on the book. “And again, I will not be selling this to you.”

Dr. Cuinnsey opened her mouth to protest again, but stopped herself. “I’m not sure I quite understand.”

Faye laughed. “Actually, you probably do. I didn’t, though. I had to do some research.” She took her phone out of her pocket and tapped over to a screenshot she’d saved. “Do you know who ‘Dindrane’ is?”

“Yes. She was Parzival’s long-lost sister. A nun.”

“Do you know how she died?”

“Remind me.”

Faye put the phone down; she remembered this bit by now. “She and her brother came to a castle where a princess lay dying from an evil enchantment. Only the blood of a virgin could cure it, so all virgins who came to the castle were forced to bleed into a large dish. Dindrane cured the princess, but bled to death in the process.”

*How many holy vessels has someone important bled into?* Two, Uncle John. That was just it.

“You believe… this is a map to a decoy Grail?” Dr. Cuinnsey tapped the book, her expression dubious.

“Uncle John believed Dad was guarding this book for a reason. Because of a calling. I don’t necessarily think he was wrong; just off about what that calling was.” It would explain their strange friendship, too: “baiting” Uncle John with talk of the Grail, but never giving him enough to go on. It wasn’t to protect the Grail. It was to protect his friend.

“It’s a shame, really.” Dr. Cuinnsey cracked a smile. “It’s a bit romantic to think your family could have been protecting the Grail.”

“Who says we’re not?” Faye picked up the book. “The most I can ask for is your silence. Decoys are no good if everyone knows they’re a decoy.”

“You said ‘we.’”

Faye sighed, turning the book over in her hands. "Yeah. Well. This is a lot bigger than me not being into academia at this point. I don't like the idea of letting someone else down. Or, you know. Contributing to the onset of the apocalypse."

The conversation was over without much difficulty. Dr. Cuinnsey obligingly picked up her bag and gave Faye a quick nod. "I can't really push you for a sale under these circumstances, I suppose. Though, is there anything I can do for you?"

"Maybe." Faye flipped through the book, her lip curling into a smile. "If you find any really aggressive treasure hunters—"

"I'll give them your number."

"Read my mind."

# Perpetual Happiness

## Heidi J. Hewett

### Chapter 1

**Houston, 2018**

Carl Rosenstein, a heavy-set, soft-spoken man in his late forties, with a sensitive mouth and wire-rimmed glasses, believed in being early. Especially for any event of importance. Which was the only reason this particular blind date didn't end in his death.

Carl naturally had no idea he was in such jeopardy, or he never would have flown three and a half hours to meet "Evelyn" at two o'clock on a Sunday afternoon at the River Oaks Barnes & Noble in Houston. His heart thumped in his chest rather more rapidly than he was used to experiencing, but that was entirely due to the fact that after a life of mostly academic celibacy he was going on a date. He pulled open the door to the entrance for two middle-aged women who had just stepped up onto the curb, remembering to smile at the last minute—not too much, just a little—in case one of them was the person he had come to meet.

Neither noticed him. They passed through the entryway displaying self-help books on one side and books on bonsai, crochet, and papermaking on the other, and Carl reached hastily for the second door.

"Allow me," he murmured. This time they looked at him and paused in their conversation to thank him, but a quick glimpse of their faces had convinced him neither was Evelyn. He was wise enough to know that people put up their best profile pictures. He was quite prepared for Evelyn in person to be shorter, taller, fatter, and several (even many) years older. But he was fairly confident he would be able to recognize her from the photo he had been staring at on his computer for the last three weeks as if willing her image to suddenly come to life and speak. It was too soon to use words like *love,* but however she appeared in person, Carl was sure he would be able to accept her, and grow, with a respectable elapse of time, to love her, because he was a sensible man and it was her mind he valued.

Inside the double doors he stopped short, his daydreams instantly derailed by a gaudy display of history books, much of it pseudo-history in his opinion. To his immense annoyance, prominently displayed in the place of honor, elevated above the rest, was a book with a title in one-inch capitals, *THE RENYIN PLOT: BLOOD, SEX, AND THE SECRETS OF ETERNAL LIFE.* Below its title was a woman dressed like a Ming dynasty courtesan, simpering behind a fan while drawing a stiletto from her hair, which was rubbish if one cared anything about historical accuracy. It took another few seconds for his angry, indignant mind to process the author's name underneath: *HYACINTH BUTTON.*

*Hyacinth!* he steamed. *Of course!* He thought. *Of course,* this was exactly the sort of popular tripe she would have produced. He wished her joy of it, he thought sourly, all the way to her bank.

In vain, he tried to reclaim his earlier, anticipatory mood of a man looking forward to meeting the woman to whom, if all went well, he might one day propose. Thinking of Hyacinth had ruined everything. Even the jitters he had previously been experiencing seemed placid compared to the bitter, roiling state into which he had been plunged. Drat, the woman! She had turned out exactly as he would have predicted: a sell-out. A *provocateur.* He wondered how she had changed. In his imagination, she was still a young associate professor of thirty. His fingers itched as he thought about picking up the book and turning it over, opening its cover, to see if there was a picture of her. But he would not touch it.

Glancing at his watch, he confirmed what he already knew, that he was early. That gave him a reassuring, satisfying feeling. Plenty of time to get coffee and settle himself. So that Evelyn would come to him and not the other way around. She would recognize him by the blue-and-gold striped tie and University of Toronto lapel pin he was wearing, as they had agreed.

As he took his place in line for the cafe, a new and ghastly thought struck him that perhaps Evelyn was Hyacinth herself, posing online to torment him for some twisted reason of her own. Perhaps no one would show up at two o'clock! Or, worse, maybe it would be Hyacinth herself, come to laugh at him for falling for her demented joke at his expense.

*No,* he told himself firmly. He was too sensible to allow imagination to run away on him. He could trust the impression he had of her, formed through their enthusiastic discussions of the Yongle Emperor, Zhu Du, and early 15th century China. Evelyn had resisted his initial questions about herself, but he judged her circumspection-wise, given the online nature of their relationship. And he had adapted, respecting her reluctance to share personal details over the Internet. From then on, the substance of their conversations had been almost entirely scholarly. She certainly knew her early Ming dynasty.

He glanced at his watch and chose a seat at a table for two—private, but not too far away from the main part of the cafe—choosing a chair against the wall so Evelyn's first sight of him when she arrived wouldn't be the small, balding spot that had begun to form at the back of his head.

Drinking his coffee, he scanned the women he could see in the store. A woman sitting with her friend at another table laughed. He hoped for a minute it might be her because she looked friendly, but he didn't think it was. Anyway, it was unlikely, wasn't it, that Evelyn would have come with a friend? Unless that was what women who went on blind dates did. The more he thought about it, the more reasonable that seemed. Evelyn had no more guarantees about him than he had about her.

The idea that she might, at this very moment, be feeling as much trepidation and uncertainty as he was made him feel more confident. Perhaps she was wandering the stacks, killing time. He wished, suddenly, that he'd thought to pick up a book first himself. It would have given him something to do and felt less odd than sitting by himself, nursing ~~along~~ a cup of coffee, surreptitiously observing other customers. He hoped he looked like a businessman with a layover and not what he actually was: a slightly desperate, increasingly nervous, middle-aged man waiting for a blind date who might not show up.

He had just looked down at his wristwatch again when he heard the chair scrape across from him.

"Is this seat taken?" the woman asked, sitting down before he could reply.

He stared. "Excuse me," he interrupted her because she had begun some conversation about the unseasonably hot weather Houston was having. "Are you Evelyn?" he asked. But he already knew the answer and felt a corresponding sickness in the pit of his stomach. The woman sitting across from him was in her early 30s, possibly of Italian ancestry, with large brown eyes and shoulder-length brown hair, done up in a twist. Even with the heat outside, she was wearing a long-sleeved blouse.

*Not Evelyn,* his brain told him. *Not remotely, even possibly Evelyn.*

"Are you Professor Carl Rosenstein?" she countered.

"Yes," he reluctantly admitted.

"Then you're in luck," she said briskly, putting her left hand in her purse—she seemed to favor her right arm he noticed. "Because I'm not Evelyn. Or rather, the person you have been corresponding with who calls herself 'Evelyn.'"

Carl experienced a brief sensation as if the walls were buckling inward.

"My name's Dr. Rosella Tassoni." She produced a card and set it on the tabletop between them. "Forensic Mythologist."

"Forensic what?"

"Mythologist." She waved her hand dismissively. "It's a thing. We understand you're an expert on Emperor Yongle's Encyclopedia."

"Well, early Ming dynasty history. That's my area of study, yes," Carl said cautiously.

The card wasn't a business card exactly. At least, it didn't have Dr. Tassoni's information the way one would expect. There was only a stylized image of an open book and a street address. No city.

He fixed her with a stern expression. "Did Professor Button put you up to this?" he demanded, in exactly the same *don't lie to me now* tone he would have used on a student he suspected of plagiarism.

Dr. Tassoni sat back. Her mouth pressed into a firm line, and she studied him for a moment through narrowed eyes. “She said you were the best.”

Carl struggled to find words. He wanted to storm out of there. He wanted to shake his finger under this young woman’s nose and say “I knew it!” He wanted to send a message to Hyacinth warning her to leave him alone. But he was also, in some tiny, locked away part of his heart, secretly elated: *the best!* Hyacinth, with whom he had violently disagreed about nearly every subject in Chinese political and intellectual history, had told someone he was the best in his field!

“Now, Ms. Tassoni,” he began.

“Doctor.”

“This won’t do—,” he said, but she cut him short.

She tapped the card on the table with one finger. “Don’t look around. Can you see the Chinese woman with the sunglasses standing by the door?”

His heart had started thumping rapidly again. He gave a small, curt nod.

“Good. Consider her your guardian angel. At least for the time being. Spill coffee on yourself and get up.”

“What?” Carl said, appalled. He had never in his life intentionally made a mess.

“We are being watched. Wait for me to walk away and then make it look as if you’ve accidentally ruined your suit and need to leave. Go to this address as soon as you make your exit. Guan-yin will run intercept and deal with anyone who follows you.”

“This is insane,” Carl said.

She smiled and stood up, putting her purse over her shoulder. *“Ciao,* Professor. If we’re lucky and you make it out of here alive, I’ll see you at the Foundation.”

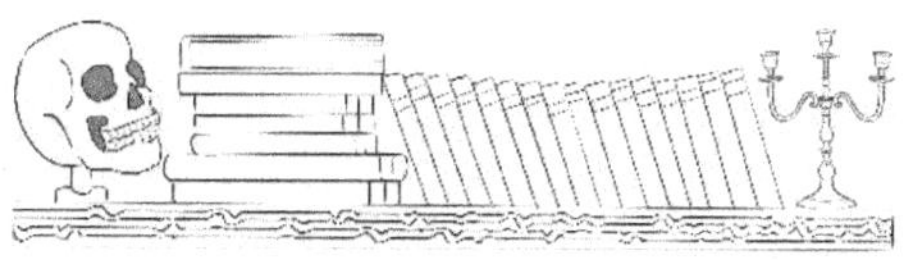

Pale, sweating from the exertion of his walk through Market Square Park where the taxi had let him out, Carl found his way to the two-story building at the end of a row of commercial brick storefronts. He double-checked the card clutched in his hand. The glass door in front of him was unmarked, but it was the only building left. At worst, they would send him away. Perhaps they might give him directions. He risked a quick, anxious glance over his shoulder and pulled open the door.

Instantly the smell of old furniture and even older books hit him. Carl felt safe for the first time since leaving home, and his entire soul quivered in gratitude. A young man sat behind the executive desk in the lobby. He looked up and took in Carl's coffee-stained suit and rumpled appearance without a hint of curiosity. "Yes?" he asked.

"Is this—well, I don't know what. Someone—a Dr. Rosella Tassoni—gave me this," Carl stammered, presenting the card.

The young man didn't glance at it. He nodded vigorously and started tapping at the laptop computer in front of him.

"She said something about a foundation?" Carl continued.

The young man cradled the desk phone in the crook of his neck, announcing "He's here," into the receiver. "You want me to send him back?" He hung up and addressed Carl without looking at him. "She'll be right out."

"Oh," Carl said. "I'll…wait here, then, shall I?"

"Yep."

Carl glanced around curiously at the wooden bookcases, leather chairs, paintings, and antiques tastefully displayed by recessed spot lighting. He felt relieved. Surely these people would protect him. Anyone who valued old books and art *had* to be on the side of Good. Focusing on an antique bronze tripod censer displayed under glass, he drifted closer to inspect its lotus-pattern design. Mid-fourteen hundreds, he guessed. Probably created during the time of the Ming Emperor Xuande. Quite striking. He wondered how it had come to be there. It had to be worth several thousand, at least. Was this some kind of private museum?

The polished floorboards creaked and Carl turned around. A dark-haired woman, professionally yet comfortably dressed in a crisply pressed pantsuit and heels, advanced toward him with her hand outstretched.

"Professor Rosenstein?" she asked. "I'm so glad you were able to make it."

"So am I," Carl said feelingly. He shook hands. Her hand was cool in his, and he was embarrassed again by his overheated, disheveled state.

If she noticed, she didn't give any indication. "Why don't we talk in Mr. Booker's office?" she suggested, gesturing with her head.

Carl fell into step behind her.

"Were you followed?" she asked with polite interest as if she was asking him how his flight to Houston had been.

"I really have no idea," Carl said. He had started to sweat again. "I'm a history professor. I have no experience of this sort of thing."

"Oh, history is a much more dangerous profession than one might imagine," she said. Smiling at him, she gestured toward the open door to a comfortably furnished, wood-paneled office. "Please take a seat," she said. "I'm afraid we have a lot to discuss and not much time."

"Who *are* you people?" Carl blurted out.

"Please," she said again, and Carl sank into one of the padded leather chairs in front of the desk.

"Bourbon?" she asked.

Carl hesitated and then nodded dumbly.

She crossed the room to a bar, built into the wall and surrounded by bookshelves, and took down one of the half-empty bottles. Carl studied the painting above the desk and the pictures on the wall, many of which featured a handsome, buff man with thick, silvered hair doing adventurous things wholly beyond Carl's imagination, like piloting helicopters, or boats, or leaning against a safari jeep somewhere in the wilds of Africa. The clink as the lip of the bottle touched the cut glass tumbler made him look back over to the bar.

"I am Vivian Cuinnsey, professor of Celtic Linguistics. And this," she half-turned and waved her free hand around her, "is the Booker Foundation." She set the bottle down, screwed on the cap, picked up the tumbler with three fingertips, and handed it to him.

"Thank you."

"You'll need it." She watched him, waiting, arms folded across her chest. On the first sip, the liquor scorched a path down his throat, and he grimaced involuntarily.

"If I may say so, you have the look of a man who thinks he is dreaming and expects to wake up," she said. Her mouth twisted into a wry smile. "I have news for you: You won't." She drew out her chair and sat down behind the desk. "But you're the one who has to decide if that's good news or bad."

Shuddering, Carl took a second, bigger sip, knowing the sensation would be just as unpleasant and welcoming it anyway.

"Have you heard the rumors? On the dark web? Someone calling himself Dao Yan. You recognize the name, of course."

Carl's eyes widened behind his glasses. *"Dao Yan?* The monk?"

"That's the name he's using. I say 'he' for convenience only. But you can see why, when someone claims to have obtained a priceless artifact and uses as a pseudonym the name of a 15th-century monk, we immediately thought of the *Yongle Encyclopedia.*"

*"Leishu,"* Carl said automatically. "It's not really an encyclopedia, at least in the Western sense. More like a compendium, categorized writings. More commonly called the *Yongle dadian.* 'The Great Canon of Yongle' might be the best translation."

The bourbon had started to work its magic, kindling a pleasant glow in his belly that made learning that some person or persons unknown wanted to kill him feel not quite, perhaps, as bad as he had first thought. Put in perspective, it was only the *second*-worst thing that had happened to him. The first being Hyacinth.

Dr. Cuinnsey was smiling. "Your knowledge of the subject proves my point. You are fortunate we've been monitoring your discussions with 'Evelyn,'" she said.

Carl went bright red to the roots of his thinning hair.

"You have nothing to be ashamed of, Professor," Dr. Cuinnsey said dryly. "All quite chaste and above board, wasn't it? Apart from some rather gratuitous intellectual flattery."

The red faded to pink but stayed. Inside his breast, shame was quickly becoming indignation, mixed with a good deal of fear. "Those were private conversations. I was under the impression all communication through the dating service was confidential," he said, shifting in his chair. He considered getting up and walking out on principle.

Dr. Cuinnsey stopped him. "We were intrigued by the extent of your knowledge of the *Yongle dadian,* which is why we think you are exactly the man we need for this recovery assignment."

"What assignment?" Carl said, bewildered. Then, recovering his gravity, he continued "Is this a joke? Did Professor Button—"

He was cut short by the door to the office opening. Dr. Rosella Tassoni stuck her head in, carrying a carafe with tea in it. She smiled when she saw Carl.

"Oh, good!" she said, sounding relieved. "You made it!" She started to say something to Dr. Cuinnsey, but her words were lost under the sound of another woman outside in the hall—a voice that made Carl's blood run cold.

"Is he in here?" it said, and a lithe, middle-aged Chinese-American woman with short, bobbed hair squeezed eagerly past Dr. Tassoni.

"Carl!" she exclaimed with obvious delight. She threw herself sideways into the chair next to him. "I *knew* you'd come!"

Carl ignored her greeting and turned to face Dr. Cuinnsey across the desk. "No," he said. "Absolutely not."

## Chapter 2

**Yale University, 2007**

It had been a rather dull panel, with the usual parading of erudition, until Hyacinth Button, who had arrived late, set a cat among the pigeons by suggesting the four-year reign of Emperor Jianwen was a historical interpolation promulgated by late 16th-century neo-Confucian scholars.

The room exploded. Professor Ryland stood up and said it was a preposterous misreading of Zhu Lu's *Annals*. Professor Cho asked contemptuously why Emperor Yongle had carried out the purge of 1402. Professor Li demanded Professor Button cite her sources and asked where she stood on another controversial 16th-century idea, that Jiawen had, in fact, survived the coup and lived out his days in a Buddhist monastery outside of Suzhou. Then Professor Kirchoff turned on Professor Li for dignifying such nonsense with his line of questioning.

Hyacinth sat back with a saucy smile on her face.

Carl watched her through the fracas. In fact, his eyes had rarely left her since she first entered the lecture hall. She was a striking young woman: a trim figure in a red silk blouse and short black pencil skirt, with silky black hair that hung like a curtain around her oval face. She moved with restless energy—there was a lively spark in her that seemed capable of setting all the dignified deadwood in the room alight.

Her head shifted a fraction at that very moment and her gaze locked onto his as if she had caught him staring. She winked and Carl's head dropped. He studied the knot in his left shoelace and pretended to be engrossed by the pattern of the oriental carpet under his chair.

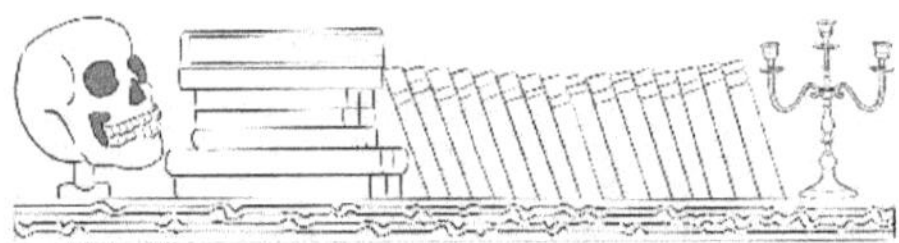

After the final lecture of the day, during the dinner break, Carl sought out the East Asian Reading Room on the second floor of the Sterling Library, a mini-library of its own containing the university's Chinese, Japanese, and Korean language reference materials, as well as bound volumes of journals. He found the long, rectangular room inviting, with buttery-yellow wood and study tables with *shoji* rice paper dividers. To his left were the stacks: a lower level and an upper level, with a narrow balcony running the length of the room. Although he had never visited Yale before, Carl felt immediately at home. He was even happier to see the study room was empty.

He climbed the small stair to the upper level and went in search of Liao Pin's *Yongle Palace Murals* among the Oversize. Almost immediately, he became sidetracked, brushing his finger along the tops of the spines as he read the titles, stopping now and then to gently ease a book out and study it briefly. He lost track of time. He might have been there fifteen minutes, maybe even half an hour, browsing, but when he pulled out Zhang Sheng's book on the *Yongle dadian,* he let out a surprised yelp. A pair of sparkling, obsidian eyes were inspecting him through the gap in the bookshelf. He had been sure he was alone in the reading room.

"Hello," she said. "What do you have there?"

He held up the title. *"Yongle dadian yanjiu ziliao jikan."*

Her eyes twinkled. "I see we gravitate to the same things. You're not going to the cocktail reception before the keynote?"

"Not really my thing," Carl mumbled. "Thought I'd…."

She nodded. "Seek the company of old friends? I understand completely. I like you," she said.

"You do?" he stammered.

"Hyacinth Button. Associate Professor of History and East Asian Languages and Civilizations, U of C. What's your name?"

"Professor Rosenstein, History, Asia-Pacific Studies, Acting Chair, University of Toronto."

She smiled slyly. "And does Professor Rosenstein, Acting Chair, have a name?"

His throat had closed up. "Carl," he finally managed.

"Hello, Carl," she said, and first the fingers and then a long, shapely arm extended through the bookshelf.

He gave the fingertips a very wary shake and the hand was withdrawn.

"You were at the Mencius panel?" she said, making it sound like a question. Except that he knew she had seen him there, so she must already know the answer. "You didn't join the crying hordes thirsting for my blood," she observed.

"No."

"Why not?" she asked. "Do you think Jianwen's reign was a late 16th-century invention?"

Carl couldn't suppress a derisive snort. "Certainly not! Zhu Di wouldn't have spent years waging a civil war against his nephew if Emperor Hongwu had died in 1402 instead of 1398."

He peered at her curiously, shyly. "You don't *really* believe T'u Shu-fang and Zhu Lu just *made up* four years of history?" he challenged.

She tossed her long, silky black hair. "If anyone had bothered to ask, I might have explained that I meant Emperor Hongwu intended Zhu Di to inherit and that the Jianwen emperor's claim was therefore illegitimate."

Carl smiled contemptuously. He knew now she must be pulling his leg. "You don't mean to tell me you take the *Veritable Records* at face value?" he said. "Or are you arguing Yongle's usurpation was justified by the ancestral injunctions, as he claimed because Jiawen had forfeited the mandate of heaven through misrule?"

"Maybe. Maybe Jiawen was only the second son of a lesser concubine," she responded coolly.

"When he ascended the throne, Yongle had Dao Yan rewrite the *Veritable Records of Hongwu's Reign*—three times—and destroy the originals!" he said, feeling his face flush against his will. He returned the reference book to its place on the shelf with a firm push.

Her head appeared around the corner at the end of the row.

"You don't know that," she said. She looked him up and down: the sandy hair, not yet thinning, parted neatly on the side, wire-rimmed glasses, a slight chubbiness to the face, the suggestion of a cupid's bow in the line of the upper lip.

She took a step toward him and he instinctively retreated, wishing he still had Zhang Sheng's book between them. He bumped up against the back wall, trapped between the stacks.

"Look," he said, with all the professorial stuffiness he could muster, "even Zhu Di had to defend himself from the accusation he wasn't Empress Ma's son. It's obvious it was nothing more than a transparent fiction to discredit his nephew."

She said nothing. Her mouth curved into a faint, mocking smile, and her eyes glittered with intent he couldn't read. She reached forward as if she were going to take his face in her hands. Carl drew back, but she had unhooked his glasses from behind his ears and lifted them off his face. Instantly everything in the room, including Hyacinth two inches in front of him, went soft and fuzzy.

Her smile became more natural. She set his glasses down on top of a row of books at shoulder height.

"What are—?"

She leaned forward, her dark eyelashes fluttering closed, and her lips melted into his mouth. The softness went to his head. And to his groin. Sparkling, tingling fireworks seemed to flare to life all over. Without meaning to, he found himself pressing his lips into hers, prolonging the sweetness of the kiss, giving it an edge of urgency.

She separated and stood, looking at him, as if waiting for him to say something.

"What was—why?" he managed.

She looked searchingly at him, her head on one side. "I wanted to see what you would do."

He was stunned, tongue-tied.

The smile disappeared into a frown. "Did you like it?"

"Did I—?" He cleared his throat. "Yes."

The smile came back, like sunshine breaking through—no, blazing through… before he completed his thought, to his wonder, she kissed him again! This time he closed his eyes and let the fluttering sensation flood through him. His hands came up, grazing her upper arms, wanting but not daring, to hold her. He had expected—he didn't know what he had expected—something floral, perhaps, because of her name. But she smelled like pear. A scented shampoo, perhaps. It was utterly delicious.

He felt her shoulders shifting, her torso twisting. Carl pulled away.

"What are you doing?" he asked, his breath short. But he could see what she was doing. She was tugging the hem of her silk shirt from her waistband. Mesmerized, he watched her hands move up to undo the buttons below her collar.

"Have you ever done it in a library before?" she asked.

Scandalized, frozen like a small, desert mammal about to be devoured by a snake, Carl wasn't even able to shake his head.

"It's even better, surrounded by books. Everything's better with books. I just love books, don't you?"

Desire, something so strong it felt more like nausea, turned his stomach.

She twisted the front clasp of her bra, releasing it. She set her hands on her hips.

"Well," she asked. "What are you going do?"

## Chapter 3

**Houston, 2018**

She was thinner than he remembered, Carl thought when Hyacinth dropped into the chair next to him across from Dr. Cuinnsey. She had always been slim—the kind of woman genetically incapable of holding onto weight—but there was a gaunt quality to her now. He could see the faint outlines of her ribs just below her throat under the relaxed scoop-necked top she was wearing. Crows' feet stamped the corners of her eyes, but she appeared to have just as much energy as ever.

"Nonsense," she said, addressing Dr. Cuinnsey. *"Of course,*

Carl will go with me."

"I will not," he said, still not looking at her.

"Oh, come on!" She laid one hand on his sleeve and he moved his arm away. "You don't mean to tell me you'd give up a chance at finding a lost *juan,"* she said.

"Wait, what? Someone's found a lost *juan* of the *Yongle dadian?"*

Hyacinth frowned at him. "Haven't you been following the chat boards? Everyone's buzzing about this find 'Dao Yan' is hinting at. You really are behind the times."

Carl turned to Dr. Cuinnsey. *"This* is the recovery assignment? You want me—"

"You and me, actually," Hyacinth interjected. "Us."

*"Us,"* Carl amended bitterly, "to what? Steal a *juan* some fellow calling himself Dao Yan has discovered?"

"Not *steal,* Carl," Hyacinth said. "Dao Yan doesn't have it yet. He only says he has access to it and is going to get it soon. Finish your drink, Carl."

"No. And we're supposed to swoop in and snatch it first?" He looked from one woman to the other in disbelief.

"Something like that," Dr. Cuinnsey said enigmatically.

"Think about it, Carl!" Hyacinth urged. "We're talking about a volume from the *Yongle dadian* no one has seen in five hundred years! And who knows what it contains? Maybe texts hundreds of years older than that!

Inside his soul, Carl struggled mightily.

"Aren't you at least curious?" she demanded. "You're telling me you wouldn't give your eyeteeth to be the one who finds it?"

Carl refused to be baited.

Dr. Cuinnsey leaned forward, elbows propped on the desk blotter, steepling her fingers. "Are you familiar with the term *catfishing?* You would likely be dead now if Guan-yin hadn't intercepted the man waiting outside with a syringe of metoprolol. Do you take a beta-blocker, Professor Rosenstein?"

"I do," Carl mumbled. "Heart problems."

She nodded.

A fresh wave of mortification flooded through him, turning his stomach sour. *Did Hyacinth know about his 'date'? Had these Booker people made her privy to his online conversations too?*

He hadn't written anything *especially* embarrassing, he thought, wracking his brains, saved only by 'Evelyn's' clear preference to engage at a cerebral level. But certain expressions in which he had been too free in his praise now came back to haunt him. He had admired her and had wanted desperately to be liked by her.

*Her!* He still thought of 'Evelyn' as a real woman. He was going to have to rethink everything he had thought and felt in the last three months! Dizziness clouded his head and his eyes lost focus.

"No," he gulped. He shook his head more firmly. "Not until Professor Button admits Jiawen was the legitimate successor of Emperor Hongwu."

Hyacinth twisted in her chair and drew back, stung. "What? Really?"

"Not unless she admits the Yongle emperor had his father's records rewritten to expunge Jiawen as Zhu Lu described. Admit Jiawen was Hongwu's legitimate heir, or I won't." Carl said stubbornly before turning to the other two. "And you—whoever you are—can find yourself some other sinologist."

"Oh my God! I can't believe you'd be this petty!" Hyacinth said.

"Admit it," Carl said. "You never thought Jiawen's reign was a late Ming dynasty hoax. You just said it for the fun of it, because you wanted to watch the old fogies' heads explode."

Hyacinth threw up her hands. "Fine! Okay. It was a bit of a joke."

"So, you don't believe the account in the *Veritable Records* in which Emperor Hongwu names Zhu Di as his successor on his death bed?" he demanded.

"No! That's a patently apocryphal story. Only slightly less ridiculous than the one in which he watches the palace burn and publicly mourns his nephew's death as an unnecessary tragedy."

"Do you still claim to believe the rumor that Jiawen escaped through a secret tunnel and disguised himself as a Buddhist monk?"

"Of course not!" she said hotly. "Only a lunatic would think Jiawen didn't die in that fire. And if he had, you can be sure Zhu Di would have made sure he *got* killed."

"Yet at the time you insisted, willfully insisted—"

"Oh, for goodness' sake, Carl! I was only trying to shake things up in that horrible, dry conference."

"So, now you're saying that you *never* believed—"

Dr. Tassoni had turned her head to talk to someone out in the hall and now turned back. "We'd better get going. Guan-yin says the front is being watched. Go out the back," she said, and then disappeared.

Carl goggled at the open doorway where she had been standing.

"You have your passport?" Dr. Cuinnsey asked.

Carl's hand moved to the inside breast pocket of his suit coat automatically, but Dr. Cuinnsey didn't need to see it. She was removing two envelopes from a drawer behind the desk. "These are for you," she said, pushing them forward.

Hyacinth had hers open at once while Carl was still reaching for his. He caught a flash of pale pink paper.

Dr. Cuinnsey and Hyacinth were already on their feet, shaking hands. Carl looked down into his own envelope to see a similar, staggering amount of Chinese yuan, along with an Amex Gold card and an Air China plane ticket.

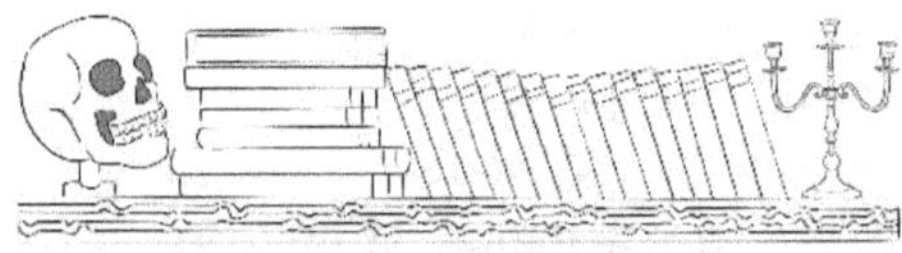

"I don't even have my luggage," Carl objected as they exited the taxi.

"Buy what you need when we get there," Hyacinth said blithely. She herself carried only a light, over-the-shoulder traveling bag. "I'm sure you can find a travel kit of some kind at the airport."

Carl thought about his overnight bag with his clothes and his pills and the library book he had left in his hotel room and fervently hoped he'd be able somehow to reclaim them when he got back. Whenever that was.

"I'll meet you at the gate," Hyacinth said and vanished into the crowd, leaving him to navigate the George Bush Intercontinental Airport on his own. And that, he thought with grim resignation, was just like the Hyacinth he remembered.

He waited through the security line, where they inspected his boarding pass and he felt compelled to explain to a disinterested official that he had lost his luggage and that even though he was Canadian, flying internationally out of an American airport on a recently purchased plane ticket with no bags, there was nothing in the least suspicious about his trip.

Once in Terminal D, he was able to find a small convenience store selling travel supplies where he picked up a small kit with a mini-toothbrush, toothpaste, soap, and shampoo in a tiny less-than-one-ounce bottle. The toiletries did not extend as far as including shaving cream and a razor. He'd have to purchase those in Beijing.

At the cash register, recalling he had not had anything to eat since lunchtime apart from half a cup of coffee and a tumbler of bourbon, he added a bag of smoked almonds to his little pile of necessities. While the clerk was ringing up his purchases, he drifted over to the book display with a half-formed thought of buying something to read on the plane, and there, among the Tom Clancys and Stephan Kings and James Pattersons and Nora Roberts, *THE RENYIN PLOT: BLOOD, SEX, AND THE SECRETS OF ETERNAL LIFE* smacked him in the face.

Grunting with surprise, he picked up the paperback and turned it over in his hands without thinking. He noticed she was at Rice University now. His eyes darted down the book description, and the lines of his mouth deepened. It promised to be as lurid and spicy as the title made it sound.

"This too," he said, holding the book out along with his TD Bank debit card. The clerk nodded.

A yeasty, warm, salty smell drifted into his unconscious, and Carl's stomach stirred with longing. Hyacinth reappeared as abruptly as she had disappeared, gnawing at a soft pretzel sticking out of a white paper bag.

"My book!" she said delightedly through a mouthful, seeing the bookstand next to the register. "Have you read it?"

"Certainly not." Carl said, watching the clerk bag items out of the corner of his eye.

She made a face. "There's no need to be rude."

The cashier handed him his receipt and bag, and Carl hurriedly thanked him.

Hyacinth had already started to walk away, trusting he would follow. Carl took several quick steps to catch up.

"I wasn't being rude," he said, jogging every third step to keep up. "It's sensationalized pseudo-history, and you know it. *'The secrets of eternal life,'* for goodness' sake." He did not add what he wished he could say, that she was better than this.

She tossed her head. "You've gotten old and boring, Carl," she said.

"I have *always* been boring," he replied, unfazed.

"Academics writing for other academics? Fighting over how many angels can stand on the head of a pin? Someone's got to write history for ordinary people. You're no better than the Yongle emperor, collecting all the knowledge he could find and locking it away."

She had finally got under his skin. "It's not 'locking it away,'" Carl said stiffly. "It's being a *steward.* Preserving. Passing the burning torch to the next generation."

Hyacinth scoffed. "The emperor claimed he had consolidated all knowledge—*'a book that can satisfy all possible inquiries'*—but you can't tell me the project wasn't primarily a power play to solidify his claim to dynastic succession among the scholarly court faction who had backed his nephew. With the added bonus of keeping them busy for the next five years." She craned her neck, reading the gate numbers as they moved through the crowd. A plane at International Arrivals must have unloaded because they suddenly seemed to be swimming upstream. "The entire project was blighted from conception. He didn't care about preserving or sharing knowledge, just *capturing* it."

She stopped so abruptly that Carl almost stepped on her heel. Hyacinth plunged right, forcing the crowd to part, and he panted along behind.

They emerged from the river of people into the gate area. She headed for a tall, bearded man with a full head of wavy brown hair who was standing in front of one of the TV screens with a rolling carry-on bag and a satchel slung over one shoulder of his tweed jacket.

He looked around. "Oh, ah!" he said.

"The emperor didn't care about the Encyclopedia. It was

finished in 1408, the *sixth* year of his twenty-two-year-long reign, and there's no record that he ever consulted it," Hyacinth said. "And this is Andrew," she added, with a smile so wide it looked like her face might crack.

"Hullo," said the man affably. He turned and stretched out his hand to Carl.

"Professor Rosenstein," Hyacinth supplied.

Carl shook the proffered hand. "And you are—?" he ventured, wondering how this unexpected third person fit into their assignment.

"Didn't I tell you?" Hyacinth interrupted as Andrew opened his mouth. She slipped her arm through his and patted him. "Andrew is my husband."

Carl shot Hyacinth a look that meant *you couldn't have mentioned that before?* which she missed entirely because she was staring up adoringly into Andrew's face.

"Didn't bring a bag?" Andrew asked. His eyes flicked up and down.

Carl gritted his teeth and smoothed his stained shirtfront and tie. "Left in a bit of a hurry."

"Well, no worries. Anything can be replaced."

"Yes, yes it can," Carl said and directed another look in Hyacinth's direction. She wasn't looking at him, but her smile had a fixed quality that suggested she heard everything and knew exactly what he meant.

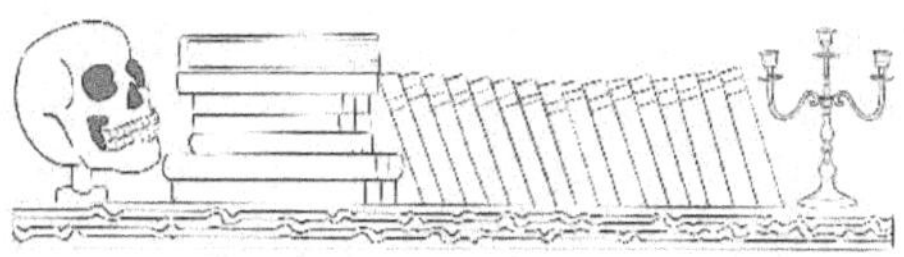

They had seats D, E, and F, and ended up sitting with Hyacinth on one side, Carl on the other, and Andrew in the middle.

"Economy, Christ!" Andrew complained. "You think the Foundation might have sprung for first class." He smiled apologetically. "Sorry. Comes from being married to a fabulously successful woman. I've gotten spoiled. I'm going soft, aren't I, darling?" He nudged Hyacinth's elbow, but she had her head buried in a sheaf of papers and ignored him.

"Are you—do you come from the U.K.?" Carl asked

tentatively. “Bit of an accent.”

“Yes, well. Leeds.”

“Mmm. My mother’s side, if you go back far enough, hails from Scotland,” Carl said.

“Really? Where? My grandfather was from Aberdeen.”

“Drumnadrochit.”

Andrew nodded and smiled. “Ah! Been there once on a visit. Small world, isn’t it?”

“I suppose so,” Carl agreed, thinking darkly that both he and this virtual stranger had slept with the same woman. How much, if anything, had Hyacinth told Andrew about her past? “Have you, er, been in the States long?”

Andrew frowned, recalling. “’98? ’97? Thereabouts at any rate. Met Hyacinth at a show in Chicago in 2012—one of my shows,” he added, seeing Carl’s blank expression. “Photographer.”

“Oh?” said Carl politely. “What kinds of things do you take pictures of?”

Andrew gave him a pitying look. “It’s—I—Art. Really can’t explain.” He retrieved an mp3 player and a tiny case containing a set of wireless earbuds from his satchel. “Look here,” he said to Carl. “You don’t mind, do you? Always use ’em. Long flights.”

“Please,” said Carl, frankly relieved not to have to make conversation and trying not to show it.

He folded his hands on his lap and watched the flight attendants moving through the cabin. He was desperately missing his library book and had started to wonder if he could get away with taking out Hyacinth’s book to read without her noticing, which he doubted. Hyacinth surprised him by leaning over Andrew’s armrest to say, “So, how did this ‘Evelyn’ find you?”

Carl flushed. “Really isn’t worth going into,” he mumbled.

“Oh, I think it might be very important. For our assignment,” she insisted. Hyacinth set her elbow on the armrest and propped her chin on her hand expectantly.

“Well, the department secretary—administrator—Peggy, has been after me for a while to, ‘get out there.’ Try one of these dating sites people use nowadays. I don’t know—I guess I thought, why not. And that’s how I met…Evelyn. I saw her picture and I asked her if she would like to chat,” Carl said, mortified.

"Go on," Hyacinth said.

"I didn't expect it would amount to much, but after a couple of pleasantries she asked about my work at the university, if I had published any books, and things sort of took off from there."

"What did you think of her? Did you like her?" Hyacinth asked.

He hesitated, but honesty won out. "I did. I had no idea."

"You think Dao Yan was behind it?" she asked eagerly. "Not the real Dao Yan. Not the 15th century monk, obviously. But whoever is using that name to make claims online about a mysterious artifact? I mean, who else could it be? It stands to reason."

"Chicken or pork?" the flight attendant asked him.

Carl turned to his right. "Uh, chicken, please."

The attendant handed him a covered plastic tray.

"Andrew!" Hyacinth said, nudging his arm.

"What? Oh," Andrew said, removing his earbuds.

"Chicken or pork?"

"Pork."

"Ma'am?"

Carl sat back against his seat to allow the attendant to reach past, handing Andrew his dinner tray. Internally he kept dredging up bits of his conversations online. Had the whole thing been simply a ploy to get information from him? *What had he said?* He had been so focused on getting to know Evelyn that he had almost no recollection of what he himself had written.

He popped off the lid to his dinner tray and surveyed the compartmentalized contents.

They had discussed the *Yongle dadian,* he remembered, and the possible fate of the bulk of the manuscript of which so few volumes had survived. Had he brought that up or had she? Or *he?* He shuddered. It was still hard to think of 'Evelyn' as nothing more than a front. Only in hindsight could he realize how much her conversations had meant to him and that he was really a man in love. In love with a mirage. Worse. With someone who'd manipulated him and actively wished him harm. He'd swallowed the bait with desperate eagerness. Hook, line, and sinker.

Hyacinth was saying something, alternating between cutting up her food into tiny bites and waving her knife and fork to add emphasis to her conversation. "But in *theory* it's possible, isn't it?" she was saying. "Ginseng, turmeric, *Rhodiola rosea,* green tea—people take all kinds of herbal supplements for longevity. I mean, it's not *eternal* life—that's preposterous—but extending life…."

"I'm sorry," Carl said because she was looking at him expectantly. "Are we talking about Zhu Houcong's elixirs?"

"Yes!"

"Who?" Andrew asked.

"The Jiajing Emperor," Carl explained, now wondering if Andrew had read any of his wife's books. "1521 to 1567, twelfth emperor of the Ming dynasty."

"Isn't it at least possible, in all his experimenting, he might have stumbled on something scientifically useful? Maybe not in the right quantities, or mixed with a lot of other stuff, but still," Hyacinth argued.

"Quackery. People have been poisoning themselves for thousands of years in the pursuit of eternal life," Carl said. His lips pressed into a thin, disapproving line. "The fifteenth-century Italian Marsilio Ficino's belief in the *elixir vitae,* drinking blood, cooked with sugar, if necessary, to make it palatable, for example. Not to mention the more garden-variety ingestion of jade, gold, arsenic, sulfur. Sun Simiao's *Danjing yaojue* is full of alchemical formulas for so-called 'elixirs of immortality.' And why? Who wants to live forever? Zhu Houcong almost certainly poisoned himself with all the mercury he was ingesting."

Hyacinth waved Carl's objections away. "Trial and error. Clearly, he made a lot of mistakes, but Dao Yan thinks—"

"Who?" Andrew asked.

"Carl and I are just talking, honey. Eat your cookie so you can get back to sounds of the rainforest."

"Oh, right then," Andrew said cheerfully.

Carl was left musing how much Hyacinth actually loved her husband, or whether her show of puppy-like adoration at the gate had been for his benefit.

## Chapter 4

**University of Chicago, 2008**

"Hello!" Carl said, beaming.

Hyacinth launched herself outward through the door of her office. "Carl!" She covered him with kisses and his hands slipped around her waist.

"Get in here," she said playfully, taking hold of his tie.

"Wait—my luggage."

She stopped and peered out into the hall. "That's…a lot of bags, Carl."

"I came straight from the airport. Sorry. Haven't been to my hotel yet. I took book leave. So we can be together. Not just weekends here and there. I'll find an apartment."

"Are you crazy? Of course, you're staying with me." She insisted.

Spring blossomed in Carl's chest. "You're sure? I—didn't want to presume. It's no problem. I can find my own place."

"Are you kidding? Now, get in here." She pulled him into the small office stuffed with books and papers and kicked the door closed with one foot.

"Now, where were we?"

"Mmm," Carl managed between kisses. "What about Professor Wharton?"

"Teaches fifth. History, society, and politics of Maoist China. She won't be back for another hour."

"All right then," Carl said, grinning as she ran her hands over his shirtfront.

"What's your book on?" she asked as she began undoing buttons.

"The role of the magistrates and local administration of the provinces in early Ming China."

Hyacinth groaned. "Who's going to buy that?"

"It's an important but underrated topic to understanding changes in the organization of what was at the time the largest polity in existence. Besides, it's not about making money."

As she took the clip out of her hair, it fell around her face and spilled over her shoulders.

"I forgot," she teased. "It's about making tenure. Publish or perish."

"No," Carl said patiently. "Tracing the evolution of the bureaucratic administration in Imperial China. Adding in my small way to the body of knowledge."

She made a face. "Yes, but provincial officials? Do you have to make history so boring? You should build it around an execution, or sexual indiscretion. Throw in a gory murder or two if you can. Liven things up."

"History is *not* boring," Carl said patiently. "It is the most fascinating subject in the world because it is about real people and real consequences. But you have to open that up, help people see that for themselves, and when you add a lot of stuff on to make it 'interesting,' you are really telling them that history is not interesting in itself." His voice was even and slow, but he had spoken with great feeling. She had stopped and was examining him, her face half smile, half frown.

"You are an extraordinary man, Professor Carl Rosenstein, Acting Chair."

"Not acting. On sabbatical," he corrected. "And not very extraordinary at all, but supremely happy."

Her eyes radiated light.

He ran his fingers through her pear-scented hair, and it felt slick and glossy. He sighed deeply with contentment.

"You can call me the Yongle professor," he said, kissing her bare shoulder as she pulled her blouse away.

She looked up, quizzical.

"*Yongle,* 'perpetual happiness,'" he explained. "Never mind. Attempt at a joke."

"Ah! 'Perpetual happiness,'" she said. Her lips moved by inches up the underside of his jaw. "Of course. I like that."

"Well…perpetual until next January."

"Then we'll have to make the most of our time, won't we?" she breathed in his ear.

## Chapter 5

**Beijing, 2018**

"Over there!" Once through Customs, Hyacinth spotted their guide first, a pretty Asian girl of twenty or so, smiling and waving a sign that read *BOOKER.*

"Not exactly low-profile," Carl muttered.

"Hmm?" Andrew inquired, half-hearing. Hyacinth was already

plowing ahead, pushing through the crowd. Carl anxiously tracked her short, dark bob, afraid of losing her. Hyacinth gave the younger woman a loose hug. When Carl and Andrew caught up, half-bows and enthusiastic greetings were exchanged.

*"Nǐ hǎo!"* the girl waiting for them said, tucking her hair behind one ear. "Meiying," she said. She gave Carl's hand a firm shake. "I'm Professor Button's research assistant."

"Have you spoken with *her*?" Hyacinth asked Meiying.

"She said she'll see you this afternoon. I'll text you when I confirm times."

"Great. Meiying can take you to the hotel," Hyacinth told Andrew without looking at him as she reset her watch. "Carl and I want to visit the library first. Come on, Carl!" she said. She took hold of his elbow and dragged him along. "We'll meet up with you at the hotel when we're done."

"The library?" Carl asked, lengthening his stride to match her pace. "Which library?"

*"The* library," Hyacinth said. "The NLC. I want you to see it."

"We're going to see the *Yongle dadian* that's on display? I thought we were here to see something that's been lost." They pushed through the doors into the open air.

A driver in the taxi line leapt forward to hustle them into his cab.

"Any luggage?" he asked them in Mandarin.

"No. Number 33 Zhongguancun Nandajie, Haidian District," Hyacinth said. She slid across the seat to make room for Carl. She put her bag on her lap and smiled at him. "See? So much easier, traveling without suitcases," she said.

Carl grimaced.

"Don't worry. We won't be here long," she said. She jostled his arm. "Lighten up, Carl. Roll with it."

Carl assumed his most dignified expression. He folded his arms and legs away, out of reach, squeezed against the side of the cab as the taxi driver pulled out from the curb. "Are you working on behalf of the National Library?" he asked. "Surely they have someone who can authenticate the find better than I."

"What? No. The volume doesn't belong to the library."

"Where is it?"

Hyacinth squirmed. "Somewhere safe. I don't have it. I'm

thinking of purchasing it."

Carl's eyes bugged out behind his wire-rimmed glasses. He opened his mouth to say something, but no sound came out.

"I know, I know," Hyacinth said, her voice tight as the taxi weaved in and out of traffic. "Millions. Almost everything I have, in fact. But if it's what I think it is, it'll be worth it. But only if it's the real deal." She leaned toward him, urgent, pleading. "You understand, don't you? It's not just the money. If I publish, and it turns out this thing is a fake, my reputation is shot. I have to be sure. I tried to think of someone. You're the only one I trust."

Carl bit his lip. He didn't want to say yes, but hearing her say that, knowing that he was the only one she felt she could turn to, had set off a small sunburst in his chest lasting all the way to the gray, stone building with the teal, pagoda-style roof that housed the National Museum of Classic Books.

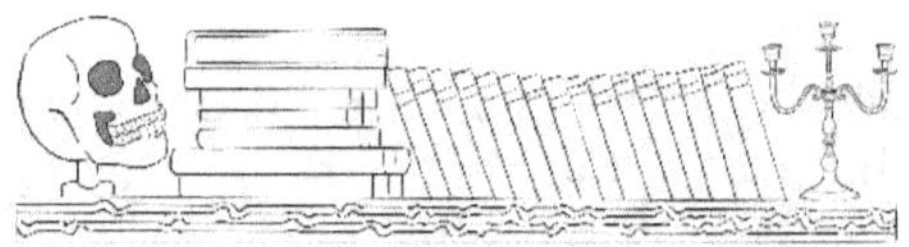

"Marvelous, isn't it?" Carl said in almost a whisper. Under the dark, wood ceiling and muted light of the exhibit hall, even Hyacinth's ebullient personality had become more reserved. They stood, hands unconsciously clasped behind their backs, over one of the glass display tables, lit from within like a jeweler's case, on which a volume of the *Yongle dadian* lay open, displaying two large, white pages with borders of red silk containing orderly columns of Chinese calligraphy.

"The Yongle emperor thought he had collected all the knowledge in the world," Carl murmured, half to himself. "At least as much of the world as was known to them at the time. Philosophy, astronomy, geology, history, medicine, agriculture, art, natural science. They made copies of all the books in the imperial library, *Wenyuan Ge*—what marvelous names the Imperial Chinese had for things! The 'Pavilion of Literary Profundity'—supplemented by any other texts they could lay their hands on, and disaggregated them by chapter, rearranging them to fit seventy-six rhyming categories of the last character of the chapter title.

“The scholars came back to him a year and a half after he commissioned the work, and he sent them out again all over China with orders to gather more books. And when the Hanlin Academy returned to him again in 1408—the index itself took up something like 24,000 pages—the emperor judged his great *leishu* to be complete. And now—of the original eleven thousand volumes? Less than four percent of it remains. It makes one aware of how easily knowledge is lost,” he went on quietly after a momentary, almost religious pause.

He had seen the encyclopedia years ago, housed at the time in the Ancient Books Library, when he had been in Beijing working on his dissertation, but the *Yongle dadian* was just as much a marvel to him now as it had been then: the original was estimated to have contained 370 million Chinese characters, all of them hand-lettered, although woodblock printing had existed at the time, making it a work of art in addition to a record of lost texts.

“It really was a labor of love, wasn’t it?” he said. “And yet in 1861, Weng Tonghe described having seen it in the Pavilion of Respect for the One covered by an inch of dust and scattered in disorder. Thank heavens the scholars who labored so painstakingly on it never knew what would become of their beautiful work.”

“What do you think happened to it?” Hyacinth asked.

Carl shifted as if coming out of a trance. “Oh. The original was almost certainly lost after the sixteenth century. Anything we have now comes from the copy Emperor Jiajing ordered in 1562.”

Hyacinth looked at him with a sly smile. “Do you think he had the original buried with him?”

Carl shrugged regretfully. “Hard to know until someone undertakes an excavation of the Yong Ling Tomb. Although, personally, I think the story in Zhang Chensi’s *Anecdotes* is almost certainly apocryphal. Far more likely it perished—isn’t that strange? One speaks of the fate of books the way one would of people—by fire at the end of the Ming dynasty when Li Zicheng set fire to the Qianqing Palace. This *juan* Dao Yan has been hinting at…it’s not from the original, is it? Because that would be….” He trailed off.

“Beyond priceless. No,” Hyacinth said. “The claim is it’s a lost volume from the 1562 copy. But even so,” she said.

“Indeed,” Carl agreed somberly. “The *Yongle dadian* is not only a treasure itself, but it’s our only link to the other texts it preserved, some as far back as 221 BCE and the Pre-Qin period. Can you imagine what we might find?”

He looked up at Hyacinth. Her eyes danced with excitement, but she was also gnawing nervously at her lower lip.

“What?”

“How would you like to hold one of these in your own hands?” she asked.

Carl stared at her.

“Not one of *these* exactly, but one just like it.

He dropped his voice, even though there was no one in the exhibit hall. “The volume you say is for sale? You know where it is? The person who has it? How did they get it? Have you seen it yet?”

Hyacinth became evasive. “I want her to tell you herself, so you can judge.” She drifted sideways to examine another display. Carl followed her, bursting with curiosity.

“But it’s possible it’s real, isn’t it?” she asked with suppressed eagerness. “I mean, lost *juan* do exist. The Huntington Library just discovered a volume several years back that had been in private ownership.”

“Maybe ninety percent of the copy survived into the Qing dynasty,” Carl said cautiously. “I’m afraid between the Second Opium War and Boxer Rebellion, most of it was lost to fire and looting, but looting,” he went on, “means that some of it ended up as souvenirs.”

Hyacinth was all but bouncing up and down on the balls of her feet.

“You look like the cat that swallowed the canary,” Carl said enviously. “Can you—can I see this *juan?”*

“Not yet,” she said with a quick, forced smile. “Soon. We should get back to the hotel.”

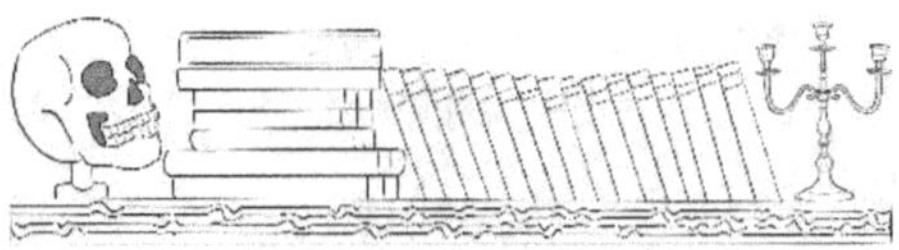

“It’s funny,” Carl said later after Hyacinth had paid the taxi driver.

They stood in an alleyway in front of the door guarded by stone lions that led to the courtyard in which the small hotel was located.

"Funny how?"

Carl made a face. "Not funny, really. Sad, more like. The Yongle emperor. He thought he was keeping all that knowledge safe by collecting it and holding onto it in one place, but the only way to protect knowledge is to share it with as many people as possible." He let Hyacinth proceed him through the entryway. "If he had ordered his scholars to create ten, twenty copies and distribute them throughout China, we might have more of it today."

"You mean, it might actually be a good thing if someone took knowledge out of the Ivory Tower and spread it around to ordinary people?" Hyacinth teased him as they entered the unassuming lobby and approached the reception desk.

"As faithfully as one can," Carl said with a touch of rebuke. Her smile faded. Hyacinth flushed. "Otherwise it isn't really knowledge at all," he finished.

She tossed her head and held out her hand. "Room 3," she said to the concierge in a tailored, plum-colored silk tunic. *"Xiè xiè,"* she thanked him carelessly and turned on her heel.

Carl sighed. His heart sank.

*"Xiānshēng?"* the concierge asked, addressing him.

"Room 5," Carl said. *"Xiè xiè.* Do you know if there's somewhere I can purchase a shaving kit and a clean shirt?"

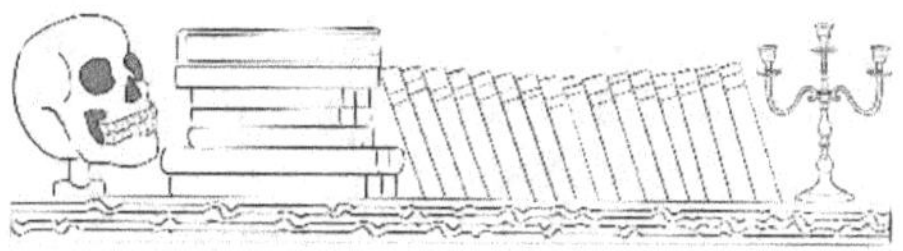

His room was tranquilly spare, with stone wainscoting, white plaster walls, and a dark wood ceiling with the beams exposed like the rungs of a ladder overhead. There was a hanging lantern in one corner with painted glass panels and red tassels, and a decorative scroll wall hanging with Chinese calligraphy, but otherwise, the room contained nothing but the barest essentials: one wooden desk and chair, unpadded, and an uncomfortably firm-looking single bed. The communal bathroom was down the hall, the concierge had informed him.

Carl placed his sack from the airport on the desk and lowered himself onto the bed with his feet hanging over the edge because he had no energy left to remove his shoes. He sat up a moment later and reached into the plastic sack for Hyacinth's book. He dropped back onto the bed with it and unknotted his tie. He had only slept in fits and starts on the overnight flight and weariness seemed to take hold of his limbs. He got as far as removing his glasses and opening *The Renyin Plot,* propping the book on his chest.

When he awoke, it was to a series of thumps and moans. In his sleep-confused state, at first, he couldn't make sense of them, until he realized they were emanating from the adjoining Room 3. He scrambled up out of his bed, fumbling for his glasses, instinctively moving to put as much distance as he could between himself and the connecting wall. Male groans, overlaid by increasingly exuberant female cries. Carl's stomach turned over and his knees felt weak. More pounding and thumping and rattling.

In desperation, Carl snatched his book and fled, locking his door behind him. Even in the hall, he couldn't escape. Shuddering, he plunged forward, down the hall, through the lobby, and out into the street, with Hyacinth's book tucked under his arm. He had no idea how long he had been asleep, but it was still light out, and when he looked at his watch, he saw that it was 2:30 a.m. Houston time. Adjusting for the time change, 3:30 p.m., then. A light, warm drizzle was falling.

He walked, threading his way along the sidewalk, wondering if he should go back to the hotel and ask the concierge to call him a cab, but he had no sense of where to go. He only wanted somewhere quiet, like a bookshop, where he could hide away.

He did not find a bookshop, but, looking to his left, he did see the window of a tea house, and he went in. He brushed at the top of his head to shake off the raindrops and polished his glasses with the end of his tie.

He had dreaded being pounced upon, but the woman behind the front counter only greeted him and asked, in reasonably good English, whether he needed help selecting a tea. The shop was spacious, contemporary, with wall-to-wall glass and white chairs set out around blond wood tables where assorted customers, solitary and couples, sat, working on laptops, reading, drinking their tea, and chatting.

"Oolong," Carl said, fumbling to count out the yuan in his wallet. His attention was distracted by the hunched figure of a woman reading at a table in the corner. Her back was to him, but he couldn't possibly be mistaken because he knew he would recognize her anywhere: Hyacinth.

## Chapter 6

**University of Chicago, 2008**

Carl was a man who wanted very little, who fell easily into new routines and was deeply domestic at heart. Within a week he had cleaned Hyacinth's tiny off-campus faculty housing apartment from top to bottom. The inside of the refrigerator gleamed. It was stocked with individually-sized Tupperware containers he purchased, filled with cut vegetables and fruit for Hyacinth when she left for work. He bought one of the fancy new Keurig machines from a high-end department store so that Hyacinth wouldn't have to stop for coffee in the mornings. He bought bookcases from IKEA and methodically shelved all of Hyacinth's books. Hyacinth herself remarked how everything ran more smoothly since he had moved in, and Carl was more pleased than he thought possible.

His book was not coming along as quickly as he had planned, but the sex was wonderful. For the first time in his life, Carl was suffused with love. It colored everything, enlivening both his research and the little things he did to take care of Hyacinth. Love poured out of him and surrounded him, and he felt it coming back to him in waves, in the way she looked at him, and how she held him, and the kisses she showered on him like rain on thirsty soil.

After about six months, signs of strain began to show. Hyacinth began to be late for dinner. Or she would skip dinner and not come home until eleven o'clock at night. She left the soap on the counter instead of in the dish and habitually forgot to close cabinets. At first, Carl thought she was busy preparing for her classes and researching her new book and he quietly cleaned up after her, but the more he cleaned, the more mess she seemed to leave until he was forced to conclude that she was doing it deliberately.

There was still just as much sex, more in fact, but it had a wild, reckless quality, and she would bounce up immediately, unable to stay still, claiming she had work to do and would disappear into the tiny office with her cup of green tea and stay up past midnight, writing furiously at a breakneck pace. At the end of eight months, she had churned out the first draft to her manuscript, *Death by a Thousand Cuts: An examination of the practice of lingchi, 900-1905.*

Carl, on the other hand, had only managed the first four chapters on provincial administrative practices under the Yongle emperor, taking him up to the year 1408.

January, which at one point had seemed an eternity away, was drawing closer. The faster Hyacinth produced, the slower he seemed to work. To his dismay, he found more often than not he would sink into long periods of staring. Words dried up. He had trouble focusing unless it was on taking care of Hyacinth or the apartment. His research material, which had once seemed so full of life, had turned to dust.

The final straw, Carl realized far too late, might have been when he suggested he rearrange her books alphabetically, by topic, because, as he pointed out, how else could you find what you were looking for? She had agreed enthusiastically, but he couldn't help feeling when he mulled it over years later that he had crossed some invisible line neither of them fully recognized at the time.

## Chapter 7

**Beijing, 2018**

Standing in the tea house, Carl had a passing, insane thought that Hyacinth had somehow managed to dematerialize from her hotel room and fly ahead of him to the tea house, which was impossible. *But if Hyacinth was here, reading....* It was as if his brain had developed a stutter.

"We seem to have an affinity for the same things," Carl said shakily, addressing her. Hyacinth turned around and looked up in surprise. He set his cup and saucer down on the table. "May I join you?" he asked.

A smile lit up her face. "Of course!" she said, although he noticed she had laid both arms over the open book in front of her.

He sat down in the seat across from her, self-consciously trying to hide her book under his arm. *So who was the woman in the room at the hotel?* he asked himself.

Her eyes crinkled with pleasure. "Is that my book?" she asked.

"Yes," he admitted reluctantly, his face turning pink. He set it down on the table.

"You bought it! I *knew* you would read it," she said happily.

"Been here long?" Carl inquired as casually as he could. He took a sip of the scalding hot tea and watched her over the rim of his cup.

"Andrew's bushed," she said. "You know. Transcontinental flights. Couldn't sleep myself. Just didn't feel like it. You?"

"Just shut my eyes for a bit," Carl said, thinking, *she doesn't know,* and then, *should I tell her?*

Hyacinth was still leaning on her book.

"May I ask, in return, what you're reading?" he asked.

Now Hyacinth looked embarrassed. "It's nothing. Just a library book." She tried to close it and slide it off the table into her bag, but she wasn't fast enough.

*"Developments of Provincial Administration in Early Imperial China!"* Carl exclaimed in surprise.

"Yes, well, maybe. I always meant to get around to it," Hyacinth mumbled.

Carl couldn't help it; he was grinning.

"You said no one would ever want to read it," he teased her.

"No one in the *general public,"* Hyacinth said testily. "But I'm not exactly your ordinary woman on the street, am I?"

"No," said Carl with feeling. "You most certainly are not."

She colored. "I meant—"

"I know."

She hid behind her tea cup, even though it had probably gone cold.

*No,* Carl thought. *I should definitely not tell her.* He couldn't be sure it had been Andrew in the room—although it seemed unlikely two strangers would be having sex in Hyacinth's hotel room—but even if Andrew was having an affair, what business was that of Carl's?

"Have you been shopping yet?" Hyacinth asked, bending down

and rummaging in her handbag.

"No, but the concierge did tell me where I might buy shaving supplies."

"I stopped in a drug store," she said, straightening. "While I was out walking."

He took the paper sack from her and looked inside. "Ah! Excellent. Much appreciated."

She rubbed the crook of her neck self-consciously. "I checked. They do carry Lopressor, if you can get your doctor to send your prescription. I'm sorry we couldn't stop for your luggage before we left."

"It was very kind," Carl said. "Thank you." His smile became shy, and his eyes slid away. He reached for his tea cup again. Out of the corner of his eye, he watched Hyacinth running her finger around the rim of her cup.

He couldn't possibly tell Hyacinth of his suspicions, he realized, because, whether it was the right thing to do or not, he wasn't an objective third party. He couldn't cast aspersion upon Andrew because it would look like he wanted Hyacinth for himself, which, he suddenly understood, he did. His heart contracted.

Hyacinth turned her wrist to look at her watch and reached for her handbag. "Did you see Meiying at the hotel?"

Carl was dragged forcibly back into the present.

"Ah!" said Hyacinth, thumbs flying over her phone. "Finally! She was supposed to text me forty-five minutes ago. Meiying says she talked to her and she'll see us now. Ready to see the *juan?"* Hyacinth asked, springing up and starting to clear the table.

"I—yes," he agreed, and hastily gulped down his tea.

"We'll go back to the hotel first," Hyacinth said when they exited the tea house.

"What? No. No need, surely. Is there?" Carl asked, hastening after her. She had started walking purposefully back in the direction they had come.

"You don't want to walk around carrying all that, do you?" she asked. "Come on. It's only a couple of blocks. And it's hardly raining at all. More of a light mist, really."

He caught hold of her elbow and she swung around, off-balance, in surprise.

"Hyacinth," he said. Doing his best to look pleasant and relaxed, he made himself smile. "It's no problem. You said it yourself, Andrew's beat. I don't want to bother him. Let's just go. I really want to see this find of yours. If it is authentic, it could be huge."

"Oh, it will be!" Hyacinth said. "*Life*-changing, in fact." She hesitated. "You're right," she declared, more firmly. "Let's go now. We'll tell Andrew about it at dinner."

She pulled a subway map out of her purse and examined it. "Yellow line," she said. She pointed across the street. "There's an entrance over there."

She folded the map and tucked it into her purse, taking two quick steps toward the curb. Carl gently caught her wrist to stop her from walking out into the street as a car whizzed by.

"Careful," he said.

He looked over his shoulder, judging the cars. Hyacinth turned to look as well, one hand on the strap of her purse. More pedestrians gathered, waiting for a break in the traffic.

Suddenly Carl felt himself viciously shoved from behind, and he toppled forward into the oncoming traffic.

## Chapter 8

**University of Chicago, 2008**

"Since when do you smoke?" Carl asked, looking up at her from the bed.

Hyacinth fumbled inexpertly with the cigarette and a cheap Bic lighter he had never seen before. She folded her naked body back into bed, one arm clasped around her bent knees.

"It helps me think," she said. "And before you ask, yes, I bought a damn ashtray."

"Oh," Carl said. He was still sweating from their mutual exertions and his head felt dizzy. The smoke quickly seemed to pervade the tiny bedroom.

Carl coughed as quietly as he could. "Do you suppose it would be all right—may I open a window?"

She shrugged.

He heaved himself upwards and went to unlatch the window, opening it a half-inch. Chill air swept in.

“There’s something I should tell you,” she said, flicking ash into a plastic ashtray she pulled out of the bedside table drawer. He hadn’t known it was there.

Carl felt as if she were waiting for him to say something, but he didn’t want her to go on. She was avoiding looking at him. Worn out, he collapsed onto the bed and fixed his gaze on the ceiling, as if willing it not to cave in on him, which he was convinced it would if Hyacinth continued.

“I’m seeing someone else,” she said.

He blew his breath out in one short huff and considered this. He wasn’t sure if she was telling the truth or this was just another move in her escalating attempts to provoke him.

“Well?” she demanded sharply.

“Well, I—I suppose that’s…. If you feel that’s what’s right for you,” he began without knowing exactly how he would finish.

“My God!” she exploded bitterly. “What does it take? I just want something! Some reaction from you! Some emotion that shows you’re human. Yell! Cry! Tell me I’m a lying, treacherous bitch! Why can’t you get angry? Don’t you care if I’m cheating on you?”

“That’s not what I’m like. You know that. Have I ever pretended to be anything else?” he asked, genuinely puzzled. His blood was pounding in his ears, but his voice came out preternaturally calm.

“It doesn’t matter,” she said, smoking furiously. “I don’t love you anymore. I’m seeing someone else.”

He watched her stub out her cigarette and reach for another.

*Was it true?* Carl decided it didn’t matter. Plainly she was unhappy with him, and, he decided in a moment of clarity, he was done playing her games. He got up out of the bed.

“Where are you going?” she demanded.

“Home. I’ll have my things packed by the morning.”

“Fine,” she said, the word flying like a bullet through his back to lodge just under his ribcage.

“Goodbye, Hyacinth,” he said quietly.

“You know why they left the *Yongle dadian* to rot?” she shouted after him because she always had to have the last word. “All those texts and extracts of text. Commentaries on commentaries. It had no heart!”

## Chapter 9

**Beijing, 2018**

Car horns blared as Carl twisted and threw himself toward the sidewalk. Hyacinth grabbed hold of his arm with both hands and pulled so that he slid the three inches he needed. He narrowly avoided having his leg crushed, or mangled, or worse. He was shaking and panting and his heart was pounding. The crowd surged forward and around them, people pushing in every direction. His vision spun and he thought he caught a glimpse of a dark-haired woman in sunglasses, but, of course, China was full of dark-haired women.

"Guan-yin!" he wheezed.

"Oh my God!" Hyacinth was saying. "Are you all right?"

"Guan-yin. She was there."

"I thought you told me to be careful!" Hyacinth said. "What on earth were you thinking?"

"Pushed me. Guan-yin. I saw her."

Hyacinth's head turned back and forth. She helped him up. "Where? I didn't see her. Of course, she didn't push you! If she's here, it's because the Booker Foundation sent her to protect you."

"Are you sure about that?" Carl gasped, sucking in great lungfuls of air. "Because I'm not."

"Nonsense. Why would they go to the trouble of sending you all expenses paid to help me recover the *juan* only to try to kill you once you got here?"

"No idea."

"Slow down and breathe, Carl," she said sternly. "You're going to hyperventilate." Her head went over her left shoulder and then she was hauling him along with her, half-running, to cross the street.

"Jesus," he muttered. He fumbled in the breast pocket of his suit coat and pulled out a handkerchief. He was perspiring everywhere and still shaking like a leaf as he stumbled down the stairs of the concrete bunker-like entrance to the subway.

"She had to have been protecting you," Hyacinth said. They bottomed out into the underground station filled with people where she purchased tickets for them. "Someone else knows you're here. Someone who doesn't want you to see Luzheng's *juan.*"

"Wait, who? What?" Carl asked.

"It must be Liu Jichi," she said with conviction.

Carl stopped short in the passageway, provoking voluble complaints as the people behind him were forced to go around.

"Carl!" Hyacinth said sharply.

"Liu Jichi?" he demanded. "The Yongle Emperor's deputy minister of punishment who helped edit the encyclopedia? What the hell is going on?"

Hyacinth took him by the hand and yanked him forward. "Of course, it's not *the* Liu Jichi," she said impatiently. "Whoever it is who's calling himself Liu Jichi. On the Internet. He's been posting to the same chat rooms, attacking Dao Yan."

"How do you know all this?" Carl demanded.

"Because I'm Dao Yan!"

"Wait, *you're* Dao Yan?"

"Yes, keep up, Carl. Don't you see? He doesn't want you to authenticate the find, because that would discredit Dao Yan! He wants to publicly humiliate me!"

"But I thought—," he said. "I thought it was Dao Yan who was posing as Evelyn to…." He ran out of words. The train arrived and the doors slid open.

"Yes. Right."

"But you're Dao Yan," he said. The perspiring crowd of people swept them up and carried them forward.

"Yes!"

"But why?" Carl asked, bewildered. "Why would you do that to me? Pretend to be someone else? My God!" he reeled, realizing he had to rethink the past three months, every conversation, once again!

"Why? I missed you," she said simply as the train picked up speed.

"And you couldn't send me an email? Pick up the phone?" A primal howl had caught in his chest. He stifled it just in time and the words came out sounding strangled.

She gave him a funny look. "After ten years? Out of the blue? And what would you have said?"

Carl didn't know. Nothing made sense since he had left his cozy home in Toronto and boarded a plane, like a fool, wearing his heart on his sleeve.

Hyacinth couldn't meet his eyes. She looked over his shoulder, past his left ear. "Things were…falling apart with Andrew. I signed up on a couple of dating sites—not to do anything!" she added quickly. "I was just…looking at my options. In case I needed to jump. And then—" she paused dramatically. "There you were! I saw your picture. I couldn't believe it. Carl Rosenstein, on an Internet dating site. I wasn't going to do anything. I promised myself I'd leave you alone, but then you sent me that winky emoji *want to chat?* thing and I couldn't resist. Just saying hello, I told myself. I didn't mean to keep going, but, oh, Carl! It was so much fun to talk to you again. And then when you suggested we meet…"

"And what were you going to do then? Show up at two o'clock and say, 'Surprise!'?" he demanded.

"No! I—I don't know—but then Vivian contacted me and said you were in danger. So of course I dropped everything."

"But—who is Evelyn?"

"I don't know. I found a random Shutterstock picture of a middle-aged woman. I thought she looked friendly. I didn't want Andrew to know I was looking. In case he was also looking."

"I can't believe you would do that to me," Carl said with disgust. "I can't believe you would pretend to be someone you're not."

"I'm always pretending to be someone I'm not," Hyacinth said hotly. "We're all masks and personas. Like you and the…the stuffy professor thing."

"But that's what I *am,"* Carl started to say, except that Hyacinth cut him off.

"Can we focus on what's important here? Liu Jichi, or his henchmen, are here in Beijing and they're after you! Oh, hey! Pinganli. This is our stop." She led him out. "We've got to get to Luzheng right away."

Carl hastened after her, afraid of being left behind as she zigzagged down a maze of alleyways off Huguosi Street.

She stopped before a gray, brick wall with a peaked stone roof. An old Chinese woman, frail as a bird, wizened as a prune, bent over a twig broom while sweeping the entryway of a recessed wooden door painted a dull red.

To Carl's amazement, Hyacinth put one fist in front of her

chest, covering it with her other open hand, and bowed with enormous respect. *"Dazhang,"* she said, addressing the old woman, who looked up with flat, black eyes. "This is my friend I was telling you about," she said in Mandarin.

*Dazhang?* The honorific ricocheted wildly around in Carl's head.

"Carl," Hyacinth said, switching back to English, "this is Princess Ning'an."

## Chapter 10

Everything around him seemed to slide diagonally, and for a moment, Carl thought he might faint, but he didn't.

"I'm pleased to make your acquaintance," he said in rusty Mandarin. He read fluently in the language but hadn't spoken it conversationally in years.

The old woman paused in her sweeping and turned her blank gaze upon him.

"I'd like you to tell him what you told me, *Dazhang,"* Hyacinth said.

The old woman studied him and then nodded. She pulled open the door and went inside. Carl followed, with Hyacinth behind him, fairly buzzing with energy. The old woman shuffled ahead on tiny, mincing steps, all her movements slow, and Carl had to fight an impatient urge to offer her his arm and hurry her through the tiled courtyard.

Inside, the house was small and traditional, from the wooden floorboards to the whitewashed walls, the swooping peaked roof, and carved window panels letting natural light in from outside. There were pillar candles set out on a low table. As far as Carl could tell, the house seemed not wired for electricity. An intricately carved, dusty wooden cabinet stood in one corner, and a sliding screen separated the main room from another room beyond it.

The elderly woman gestured for Carl to be seated in one of the two chairs and slowly lowered herself into the other. Hyacinth perched on the edge of the box bed built into the wall.

Slowly the woman leaned her head to one side as if considering Carl, and he waited, feeling his heart beating. When she spoke, it was in a lilting, sing-song voice:

"My name," she said in Mandarin, "is Luzheng. My mother was the Consort Duan. My father was Zhu Houcong."

"Zhu—the Jiajing Emperor?" Carl blurted.

"Shh!" Hyacinth looked sternly at him.

"I'm sorry," Carl told her in English. "This can't be real."

"Shh!"

"But that would mean—"

"I know!" Hyacinth said. "Please continue, *Dazhang.*"

The princess looked down at her wrinkled hands lying placidly in her lap. "My father was a monster. A tyrant with absolute power, obsessed with divination and alchemy. He turned his back on the affairs of state, relying on the Taoist priests and eunuchs to communicate with his ministers while he gave himself over wholly to his search for an elixir of eternal life. He tried everything, including drinking red lead."

"Menstrual blood of virgins," Hyacinth whispered.

"I know what red lead is," Carl whispered back, annoyed.

Hyacinth shushed him again.

"He kept girls, as palace maids, for this purpose, allowing them to consume only mulberry leaves and fresh rainwater, for purity. If a girl became ill, she was thrown out. They could be beaten, or executed, at his whim. Many slowly starved. Finally, in the *renyin* year of the sexagenary cycle, the Imperial Concubine Ning banded together with some of the other consorts and maids in a plot to kill him."

"The Palace Women's Uprising," Carl said under his breath.

The old woman inclined her head briefly. "One night, when he was in my mother's quarters, a group of them pretended to wait upon his pleasure. Then Consort Ning climbed on top of him and tried to strangle him with her hair ribbon while the other women held down his arms and legs, but, in her haste and ignorance, Consort Ning tied a knot which would not tighten around the emperor's neck. The others began to panic, and the one named Zhang Jinlian ran to the empress, throwing herself upon her mercy and confessing the whole plot."

"And the palace eunuchs revived the emperor," Carl finished quietly because the old woman had slumped, seemingly lost in reverie. A prickle ran down the back of his neck.

The woman who called herself Luzheng stirred and met his gaze. "Empress Fang sentenced them all to death by slow slicing, even Zhang Jinlian who had informed on them. My mother hadn't been in the room, but the empress accused her of being part of the conspirators' plot and she was executed with the others and their families.

"When my father recovered, he was furious with the empress, because my mother had been his favorite. He took his revenge upon her when the palace caught fire five years later, he let the empress burn with it, rather than give orders for her rescue."

She stopped, having come to the end of her story.

Carl felt a rising sense of panic, torn between wanting to avoid and being caught by her flat, expressionless gaze.

"And you—?" Carl said.

"I was fortunate. Because Consort Duan had been his favorite, my father gave me to Imperial Noble Consort Shen to be brought up. I was given in marriage to Li He of Ningjin, and bore him a son, Li Cheng'en."

"Might I—" Carl began, clearing his throat. "Perhaps I could trouble you for a glass of water?"

She bowed her head. Hyacinth leaped forward to help her from the chair, but the princess waved her away. Moving with agonizing slowness, she straightened from her chair and went shuffling toward the screened opening.

"Well?" Hyacinth said to him in English, fairly bursting.

"What are you up to? Is this some kind of joke?" he hissed.

"Joke?" she repeated, outraged. "No! Why would I do that—set all this up?"

"I have no idea," he retorted. "Who is she, really?"

"You heard her!"

Carl frowned. "Come on. You mean you believe that…that story? Anyone who'd read your book could tell you what happened the night of the Renyin Plot."

*"Of course,* it sounds like something she heard from someone else. You wouldn't expect her to remember the events on her own! She was only three at the time."

"If she was three…," Carl said, "that would mean she's…." He looked up. The screen slid back and the woman approached, holding out a chipped green cup.

"Four hundred seventy-nine," Hyacinth finished triumphantly.

*"Xiè xiè,"* Carl murmured, taking the fragile porcelain cup from the withered hands. The old woman smiled at him for the first time. He watched her turn and inch back toward her chair.

"That's impossible," Carl said slowly. He brought the cup to his lips and realized his hands were shaking.

"What if," Hyacinth began, her eyes blazing with excitement as they bored into him. "What if, Carl? You said it yourself, the *Yongle dadian* includes medical treatises."

"Yes, but—"

"What if the Jiajing emperor didn't have them all copied, or set some of them aside? What if, buried within all that alchemy and garbage, there was actually something that *worked?* Maybe it doesn't make you live forever but slows the rate of aging? What if she really is Luzheng?"

Carl studied the ancient woman before him, watching her ease herself back down into her chair. "If the emperor had found the formula for some elixir, why didn't he use it on himself?"

Hyacinth was exasperated. "Who knows, Carl? Maybe he did, but then he overdosed on mercury later. Maybe he didn't know what he'd found. Maybe Consort Duan found it and stole the book. Maybe she gave it to her daughter before she was killed."

"What about Luzheng?" Carl asked, feeling self-conscious discussing her under the old woman's bland, watchful glaze. "Isn't there some death date for Princess Ning'an in the imperial records?"

"Of course there would be! No one would believe the truth. You'd have to at least fake your death and change your name, wouldn't you?"

Carl shook his head. "I'm sorry. I just can't."

"Fine!" Hyacinth said. "Whatever. You can believe her story or not. It's the encyclopedia that matters. That's why I brought you here."

"What are you talking about?" Carl asked.

*"Dazhang?"* Hyacinth addressed the old woman. "Can I show him the book?"

The old woman got up again and moved laboriously toward the cabinet. With effort, she bent down. The bottom drawer squeaked as she tugged it open. When she straightened, she held a lacquered box, roughly two feet by one foot in shape.

Carl's blood was rushing in his ears. Hyacinth hovered over his chair, gripping the back.

"Open it!"

"May I?" Carl asked the old woman. He held his hands out and gently took the box from her, setting it on his lap. A loop stretched around an ornamental knot secured the lid. He carefully undid it and pulled back the two flaps. Imperial yellow silk lined the inside of the box, cushioning the book within.

Holding his breath, Carl lifted the heavy volume from its wrappings. Hyacinth took the box and Carl opened the book carefully on his lap. The yellow damask silk covers appeared to be in good condition, although the cardboard was no longer stiff. At a glance, it was easy to see the volume had suffered from damp and decay. There were signs of water damage at the head and tail edges. The covers, when he inspected them closely, had, in fact, been removed at some point and re-attached upside down.

That fit with the damage he noted to the first and last several pages. Quite possibly the cover had been damaged at some point in the past, exposing the first and last short section of text, approximately three to five folio pages he judged, which had likely been removed when the volume had been rebound.

The volume contained two *juan,* each of about twenty folio pages, approximately 16-inches by 10-inches wide, bordered with red silk, on which columns in red and black ink stood out against the white Xuan paper. He grazed with his thumb the punctuation markings that had been impressed on the paper with a round seal and lifted the volume to breathe in the antiquity of the paper and the ink.

"Can you tell?" Hyacinth asked anxiously. "Is it authentic?"

The three sizes of fonts, the marginal lines, 'elephant trunks' and 'fish-tail' markings that guided the assembly of the folio pages—they were all there. There was no doubt in Carl's mind, that despite a somewhat clumsy attempt at repair, the volume he held in his hands was genuine.

Carl turned the stiff, delicate pages, barely touching the edges with the tips of his fingers, and became lost in the book as his eyes skimmed down the columns of Chinese characters, some of which were so old that they were no longer even used.

"My God," he said. "My God."

## Chapter 11

"Is it from the *Yongle dadian?"* Hyacinth asked. She gripped his shoulders.

"I—I'm not a linguist," Carl said slowly. "I'm really not the best person…."

"Carl! I trust you," she said. "Please! That's why I took you to look at the original in the museum. I have to know if this is the real thing. Is it worth $3.5 million?"

He barely heard her, engrossed in what he beheld.

"Carl!" she snapped.

"What? Oh. I have no idea what its market value is, but from what I can tell…yes, this is authentic."

"Dear God," Hyacinth said.

"Where did you get this?" Carl asked the old woman in Mandarin.

Hyacinth was digging into her handbag. "Is it okay, can I write you a check?" She brought out a checkbook. "Or a money order? Would a money order be better?"

"Hyacinth," Carl said, stopping her. "You should really have this authenticated by an expert, and then appraised."

The old woman shifted slightly in her chair. A wary, canny look had come into her eyes.

"Nonsense!" Hyacinth said. She fumbled with the cap of her tortoise shell fountain pen. "I can have that done later. I can't just show this to *anyone,* Carl! We're talking about…about the greatest scientific breakthrough of the—well, ever! Can you imagine? Extending human life two hundred, three hundred, who knows—maybe five hundred years!"

"Hyacinth!" Carl said sharply. "This is an authentic volume of the sixteenth century edition—at least as far as I can tell—but it certainly doesn't belong to this woman. I recognize this. It's the Hynd volume. One of the medical treatises lost, well, it was presumed to be lost in a grammar school library fire in 1986. In Aberdeen." He turned back to the old woman. "How did you come to have it?"

"Oh, boohoo," Andrew's voice cut through the room.Carl

froze, feeling the hard, round, hollow nose of a pistol pressed into the back of his head.

"And here I thought it was going to be so easy," Andrew continued.

"Andrew!" Hyacinth exclaimed. "What the hell are you—?"

"Sit down, darling."

"Certainly not!"

A loud, horrible bang nearly made Carl jump out of his skin. Hyacinth uttered a cry, and when he looked, she had collapsed on the floor as blood spilled from her shattered foot.

"I said *sit down*," Andrew repeated through gritted teeth. "I've put up with five years of you swanning around, having your way in everything, so I know this may be difficult, but now, for once in your selfish life, you're going to have to listen to me. Do you still have the checkbook, darling?"

"You must be out of your mind," Hyacinth spat.

"Hyacinth," Carl said as calmly as he could. "I think perhaps you'd better do what he says."

She tossed her head. "Never!"

"Hyacinth!" Carl said. "Please. Just do it. No amount of money is worth your life."

"Very sensible advice," Andrew said approvingly. "Just make it out for 3.5—no, let's make it an even four, shall we? Four million."

"Over my dead body," she said contemptuously.

Andrew clucked his tongue and shook his head. "What about his?" he suggested. His hand clamped on Carl's shoulder. Andrew turned to the old woman. "Take the book would you?" he said in English. She got up and moved toward Carl with more balance and confidence than she had previously displayed.

"You want it with you in the truck?" the old woman asked. Her English had a faint trace of an accent.

"Yes."

Hyacinth's mouth was hanging open.

"Ready to write that check, dearest? Or do I have to put a bullet through the professor's brain to convince you?"

Hyacinth blinked several times. Her mouth snapped shut and she shook her head. "No," she whispered. "I'll write it. You can have anything. Everything."

Andrew smiled. “That’s the spirit. Four million, I believe, we said?”

The screen slid open again and Meiying entered. “How’re we doing?” she asked.

Hyacinth ripped out the check from her checkbook.

“Be a dear and take that from her,” Andrew said. “Mind! The ink’s drying. Wouldn’t want to smudge that, would we?”

Meiying twitched the check out of Hyacinth’s hand. Hyacinth gave her a nasty, bitter look.

“Splendid,” Andrew said. “Up we go, Carl. You too, Hyacinth, best as you’re able.”

#

Meiying bound their wrists with plastic zip ties while Andrew looked on.

“You’re my research assistant! I can’t believe you’d do this to me,” Hyacinth said to Meiying, who shrugged.

“He pays me a lot better,” she said.

“Let’s get a move on, shall we?” Andrew said. “And no heroics, if you please. Less mess.”

Carl hung his head and allowed himself to be herded along with Hyacinth, limping on her bloody foot, out the back of the house and into the rear of an olive-green army truck.

“She can’t get up there,” Carl observed.

Andrew made a face. “If he tries anything, shoot to kill, darling,” he said as he handed the gun to Meiying. “Up we go then,” he said and hoisted Hyacinth into the back of the truck, letting her drop with a hard thump. “I presume you can manage on your own,” he said to Carl.

Carl crawled in, his movements clumsy with his hands tied behind his back. He scooted on his knees toward Hyacinth.

“Right then,” Andrew said, pleased, and slammed the back hatch shut. He and Meiying disappeared from view. A moment later, Carl heard the engine grumble to life.

“Hyacinth,” Carl whispered. “Hyacinth, are you all right?”

She groaned, which he took as a positive sign.

“Hang on, Hyacinth.” He tried to drag himself closer. The truck lurched forward and Carl fell. His glasses were bent and skewed on his nose.

“Son of a bitch,” Hyacinth muttered thickly.

Carl rolled over until he faced her. The bed of the truck was extremely uncomfortable, jolting and squeaking with every rock and bump.

"Hyacinth."

"Mmm?" she opened her eyes.

"Are you all right?" he asked.

She laughed until it turned into a cough. "Oh, Carl," she said sadly when she had recovered. "What have I dragged you into, you poor man?"

"Nothing I wouldn't go through again, for you," he said stoutly.

"Well," she said, cracking a hollow grin. "Let's not get carried away, shall we? Ow!" she yelled as the truck bounced over a particularly rough patch.

"I find it helps if you can sort of hold your head up," Carl suggested. "Although it does make one's neck rather tired."

Her eyes crinkled.

"This may not be the time to mention it," Carl said, "but I suspect your husband has been cheating on you. Quite possibly with your research assistant."

"Of course, I know he's been cheating!" Hyacinth exclaimed. "With multiple women. For years. That's why we're getting a divorce! I just didn't know she was one of them."

"To be fair," Carl said, "I don't have absolute proof. It may not be Meiying at all."

"Who cares? She's helping him rob me and kidnap—possibly kill—us! I think I'm allowed to suspect her!"

"I'm sorry," he said. "Did you say you were getting a divorce?"

"Yes! Ugh!" Hyacinth declared. She let her head drop.

"It'll hurt more that way," Carl reminded her.

"My neck hurts too much. Yes, I told Andrew a year ago I was done and wanted out."

"I take it he wasn't happy with the proposed terms of the settlement," Carl observed.

"He convinced me I was being hasty and that we should give things more time. But then, a couple months ago, after I became 'Evelyn,' I told him it was no good, that it was you I loved." She stared up at the canvas roof of the truck. "Bastard. I remember catching him later at my computer. I changed my password, but he must have been looking at my account and figured out who you were. He would have realized you could expose his fraud. And then he tried to have you killed!"

"That's okay," said Carl. "It doesn't matter now."

"Of course it matters! Why are you being disgustingly noble about this?"

Carl considered her question. "Because I'm here, with you, and I'm so happy I couldn't possibly hate anyone."

"I can. Complete and utter bastard." She raised her voice. "Can you hear me, Andrew? I said you're a bastard!"

"Not listening, darling!" came the cheerful, muffled reply.

Hyacinth squeezed her eyes shut. "God! He came up with this whole hoax.... And I fell for it," she groaned. "I flew out to Beijing. I met with—her, whoever she really is. I quit my job. I was already working on my next book. I called my agent and rushed it to print, just for the money. I started posting as Dao Yan, hinting at being about to release a find...."

"If it's what I think, it's still a treasure," Carl consoled her. "No one's seen the volume in over thirty years. It was certainly never digitized or properly studied."

"It was in a *grammar school* library?"

"In Scotland. It was donated in 1905 by a fellow named R.S. Hynd who worked for the Hong Kong and Shanghai Banking Corporation," Carl explained. "He'd attended the Aberdeen Grammar School as a boy, along with James Russell Brazier. Both had been at the Siege of Peking in June 1900 when the Hanlin Academy was burned and looted. I expect he picked it up as a Chinese curiosity. Unless, perhaps, he was genuinely trying to rescue it from destruction. Brazier donated one volume to the university in Aberdeen and Brazier's son sold two more to Chester Beatty that ended up in Dublin. The Grammar School probably can't afford it, but I expect Aberdeen University would pay you well to have the volume back, although, perhaps, it really should be donated to the government of China."

She chuckled. "I'll be sure to do that."

"I thought—," Carl began, and then started again. "I thought when I heard—a colleague mentioned having run into you at a conference—that you were married—perhaps, you'd finally found someone who made you happy."

"Happy?" Hyacinth said, twisting to look at Carl as if he'd grown a third head. "Andrew?" she snorted. "The man would rather eat with his hands than wash a fork." The truck pitched forward, coming to a sudden stop. The engine cut out.

"This huge house and between us it was all going to hell," Hyacinth continued bitterly. "I hired a housekeeper *and* a cook, and I can still never find anything when I need it. You have no idea how exhausting it is."

"Really?" Andrew said, appearing at the opening in the back. Beyond him, Carl could see daylight and the outlines of an enormous rubbish heap. Andrew, he saw, was carrying the lacquered box.

"You hurt my feelings," Andrew said. "I didn't think we were *quite* as unhappy as all that."

"Speak for yourself," Hyacinth shot back.

"I'm afraid that's all I will have left to speak for. End of the line for you."

Hyacinth struggled but was unable to sit up. "Agh!" she cried. "Shit, that hurts."

"Where are you taking us?" Carl asked, his mouth dry.

"Did I not make that part clear? No, no. *We're* going. You two stay."

"You can't just leave us here," Hyacinth said angrily.

"Oh, I'm not going to," Andrew said. His right hand came up, and Carl saw the flicker of a lighter.

"What are you doing?!" he shouted as if that would stop him, but there was a smoky smell. One small corner of the canvas had already caught.

"Goodbye, darling," Andrew said. "I'm sorry things didn't work out."

## Chapter 12

"Andrew. Andrew!" Carl shouted, but there was only the empty half-moon of gray sky. He heaved himself toward the back of the truck and blew desperately at the canvas. The smoke was thicker, flame creeping upward. Carl threw his shoulder into the hatch with a bang. The bolts didn't give. He saw to his horror that Hyacinth's eyes had closed and she was lying still.

"Hyacinth! Wake up!" he shouted, clambering toward her, panic choking his throat.

Her eyelids fluttered.

"Stay with me. Stay with me," he muttered. "Look, keep your head down. Put your face against my shirt. If the canvas burns, maybe we can climb through the frame and over the side, as long as the smoke doesn't get us first." He pressed closer to her. "We're going to make it," he said, and he brushed his chin against the top of her head, smoothing her hair.

He heard a faint sound. She was laughing against his shirtfront.

"How do you know?" she said, her voice muffled.

"I know because I love you," he said.

"No, you don't," she said.

"I do," he said with offended dignity.

"Oh, please," she said, her voice gathering strength. "I'm *interesting.* I'm colorful. I say outrageous things. That's why I made C.V. Starr Transnational China Fellow and Associate Director for the Chao Center for Asian Studies. That's why you loved me. If I didn't cause shocking scenes, I'd just be this plain, dull Chinese-American girl no one notices or cares about."

*"I* would care," he said. "I think you are the most wonderful woman in the world. You are clever, and beautiful, and brave in ways I can only dream of being."

"Exactly my point! Because I'm brazen. Because I flout convention."

"No," Carl said with a small, firm shake of his head. "I see the hopes and the fears and the sorrows in your heart, and they shine so *brightly."*

Hyacinth made a convulsive, hiccupy noise, and Carl realized she was crying into his shirt. He snuggled closer to her.

"And this amazing woman, who is so full of life, saw me. Me!" he went on, speaking softly next to her ear. "And thought there was something special, worth loving."

She pressed her forehead into him. The hiccupping subsided. Overhead, there was a tremendous *whoof* as the main part of the canvas caught fire.

"You underestimate yourself," she said. "You are a good, solid, stubborn man who refused to get angry, even when I was doing my best to hurt you."

"I was angry. For many years." He winced. Sparks and shreds of fabric and ash drifted down on them. He turned his face away from them and tried to cover her.

"But you didn't act on it," she said. "You never spoke a harsh word to me. You let me go my own way." Her eyelids fluttered.

"Hyacinth!" Carl said sharply. "Stay with me!"

"Why did you let me go?" she murmured.

"I thought you didn't love me anymore," he said simply. "Hyacinth! Please open your eyes."

Her mouth curved upward. "I have loved you from the moment I saw you at that silly panel." Her eyes opened and crinkled with her smile. Her gaze moved over him, exploring his face like a caress. She laughed faintly. "So gentle, and shy. I winked at you, and you were…so embarrassed. Wouldn't look up for the rest of the hour."

A thunderous boom sounded and the whole truck shook. More sparks and ash rained down. There was a hiss and white smoke billowed everywhere. Carl shut his eyes and coughed violently.

"Well?" a woman's voice said in English heavily accented by Cantonese. "What are you waiting for?"

He craned his neck and looked up. The back hatch was open and a woman in a black leather jacket with sunglasses propped on top of her head stood with her hands on her hips.

"Guan-yin?" Carl managed to croak out.

As the smoke cleared, a man looking like an older version of Indiana Jones with shaggy, silver hair and chiseled physique appeared at her elbow. It took a moment for Carl to mentally place him from the photographs he had seen in Dr. Cuinnsey's office, but this, he assumed must be the founder himself. "Jake Booker?"

The man nodded. "As far as anyone but you knows, I'm gambling in Macau right now." Booker's eyes dropped to the lacquered box he held against his chest. "Professor Rosenstein, well done."

"You have the *juan?"* Carl asked, still dazed, squinting.

Half of Booker's mouth twitched into a smile. "We'll take good care of it."

"But it's—," Carl began, and stopped, because the sound of an ambulance was growing in strength.

"Time to go," Guan-yin said.

"Wait! Hyacinth!" Carl said. "She's not breathing!"

## Chapter 13

**University of Toronto, 2018**

"Hello," Hyacinth said.

"Here! Let me help," Carl offered, leaping to assist her in through the door when it looked for a moment as if she might teeter and collapse on her crutches. "There's a chair over there for you," he said.

"Thanks," she sighed, sinking down. She let him take the crutches and lean them against the bookshelf behind her.

"Wait," Carl said. "I've got a footstool. And a cushion. It helps to elevate it, doesn't it?"

Hyacinth shifted her leg gingerly as Carl helped make her comfortable. She slipped her head through the strap of her handbag, worn crosswise over her chest, and let it drop to the floor next to her.

"This is nice," Hyacinth said, looking around.

"Do you like it?" he asked eagerly.

"I do."

"Your things were delivered yesterday. I had them put everything in the second bedroom. I figured that could be your office. And it can be as messy as you like." He smiled encouragingly at her.

"I prefer to call it 'creative chaos,'" she said with a wry smirk.

"Absolutely. The room is yours."

"And I can leave my books in piles? Papers on my desk?" she teased.

"Whatever works for you. Can I get you something?"

Hyacinth grimaced and looked up at the ceiling. "I'd give anything for a vodka tonic, but I don't think my doctor wants me to mix alcohol with hydrocodone. Do you have hot tea?"

"Darjeeling, Earl Grey, oolong, green?"

"Oolong."

"Be right back," he said.

When he came back from the kitchen, he found Hyacinth leaning on one crutch, on one foot, examining the titles on his bookshelf.

“Here we go,” he said. He moved a potted plant and pulled over the small side table from the couch to stand next to the armchair. “Tea and shortbread.”

“Marvelous man,” she said and hobbled back.

Carl disappeared into the kitchen again and returned with his own Earl Grey. He was appalled to discover she was crying.

“Are you in pain? What’s the matter?” he asked urgently.

She hid her face behind her teacup. “I’m so ashamed,” she said, looking away. “I *completely* fell for the whole, elaborate charade. Can you imagine? Thinking someone could actually be five hundred years old! I’ve been such an idiot.”

“Anyone could have been taken in,” Carl said gallantly.

She shook her head. “No. Not you.” She leaned forward and clasped his hand. “It was my own pride. I wanted to be the one who discovered something sensational. Something big! So big it changed history and science and human life forever.” She shifted to lean on her elbow so she could continue holding his hand across the gap between the armchair and the sofa.

“That library school fire happened in ’86. I can’t believe this entire time someone in Andrew’s family was sitting on the Hynd volume and never told anyone!”

“Maybe they didn’t realize what it was,” Carl suggested.

She rolled her eyes. “I’m a Chinese scholar, who specializes in Chinese history, and no one thinks to ask, ‘Gee, Hyacinth, you’re married to Andrew. Could you take a look at this thing and tell us if it’s important?’”

“You *are* still getting divorced from him, aren’t you?” Carl asked worriedly.

“He tried to kill me, Carl! He *hired* someone to kill *you,* and that’s something I’ll never forgive, unlike you. *Yes,* we’re getting divorced. He can sign the paperwork in his jail cell.”

Carl hid his smile behind his teacup.

Hyacinth let her head sink back and her eyes closed. She gave Carl’s hand a small shake. “I’m so sorry. I’m not myself yet,” she apologized.

“What I don’t understand,” he said delicately, “is why Andrew didn’t just, er, have *you* killed? Why the elderly lady and the elaborate ruse?”

Hyacinth smiled. She opened her eyes and he saw a spark of

her old self dancing in them. “Ironclad prenup. Wouldn’t have been able to touch a penny of my royalties. It all goes to charities. He had to get that check. I wasn’t entirely a fool.”

“Have you talked to the Booker Foundation people? Do you know what happened to the *juan?”*

Hyacinth raised her eyebrows. “They claim they don’t have it.”

“That’s impossible! I saw that fellow—Jake Booker—himself. He was holding the book!”

“I don’t know. Vivian told me the box was empty.”

“Or they have it and they don’t want anyone else to know they do,” Carl said darkly. His brow furrowed in anger.

“So Andrew wanting you dead you’re okay with, but these people make you mad. You are an odd one, Professor Rosenstein, Acting Chair.”

“It’s not right,” Carl insisted. “It may not have been the secret of eternal life, but it’s still a cultural treasure. The book ought to be on display and be available for study.”

“I agree, but the Foundation claims they don’t have it.” She rubbed her thumb across his knuckles, watching him, and his expression gradually softened.

He grinned and gave her a sidelong look. “It was pretty amazing, getting to hold a volume in my hands. Just once.” After a minute, he asked, “Do you really think there could be—I don’t know—an elixir of life?”

Her nose wrinkled. “Doesn’t matter. Who wants to live forever—all your friends, family dying off—if you can’t be with the person you love? The more I think about it, perpetual anything—life, happiness, love—is a fool’s quest. Maybe their fragility makes them more precious, you know?”

Carl squeezed her hand gently and she kissed his hand. Hyacinth set her teacup down on the end table.

“Is there room over there on that sofa with you?” she asked with a slightly wicked grin.

“Certainly! Is your tea hot enough?” he asked as they were resettling her. “Can I get you anything else?”

“No. This is perfect,” she said with a grateful smile. She wrapped her arms around his neck and leaned forward, brushing her nose against his, finding his lips with her lips.

“Oh!” Carl said.

"Is this okay?" she asked.

"Yes! Definitely yes." She still smelled of pear, and he breathed her in, his heart overflowing with love and gratitude. He missed her long hair, although he would never tell her that.

She kissed him again. She murmured in his ear, "I may have lost my chance at the encyclopedia, but I found the real treasure I thought was lost."

# Loredana's Challenge

Liam Hogan

The road snaked up the Italian mountainside in a series of tight switchbacks that had my hire car protesting the low gear. From the valley floor it wasn't obvious there was anything up this way. But I knew there were alpine villages hidden behind the trees and beyond the rocky outcrops. Summer meadows for sturdy cows with clanking brass bells around their thick necks.

That there was also a one-time *Michelin*-starred restaurant was the real surprise and the reason for my autumnal visit.

I let the car proceed at its own relaxed pace. In no particular hurry, I was wary of the treacherous road and glad for the lack of traffic. That too had once been different, as the upgraded but still fragile looking barriers and road markings attested; investment that now seemed unnecessary.

The snake continued winding upwards but a signpost pointed me down a thinner, single-track gravel road, dipping for a while before levelling off and curving through the woods. Narrow passing places had been scooped out of the steep hillside.

There were no cars to pass.

After the gloom of the tree-shrouded canopy, the dazzle of the bright, early afternoon sunshine hit me just as the villa was exposed in all its glory. Maybe there had been method behind the madness after all. Maybe the journey to this out of the way, acclaimed restaurant was part appetiser, part throttle to prevent it from being overrun by eager gourmands.

Once, anyway. Today the small car park was half empty. I slid the Fiat next to a German-registered Mercedes with an open-top, luggage-filled rear, and stood taking it all in.

I'd been wrong about the villa. High up on the walls of the two-storey building, a few feet beneath the moss-covered, tiled roof, I could just about pick out faded letters that spelled "Scuole." An old local school then, converted as the area's younger inhabitants drifted into easier lives in the valleys or even further afield.

A conversion that had saved it from inevitable neglect and decay. Or, more accurately, postponed. Already there were signs that entropy was not to be denied; leaves left to gather along the low walls of the car park, rampant weeds topping the crown of that dry stone wall, and something bulky shrouded in flapping green tarpaulin fouling the view to the side of the repurposed building.

Over the door, the restaurant's name was discretely written in etched glass, the effect rather spoiled by one of the pair of rear lights being on the blink. A staccato editing that intermittently abbreviated "Loredana" to just "dana".

"Do you 'ave a reservation?" the maître d' lurking inside the door asked, with a healthy dose of suspicion. What was it that allowed him so expertly to identify my nationality? Did the fact the owner-cum-head chef (and currently *only* chef) was English sway his assumption?

I peered around him into the sun-lit dining room, heard the soft, sad clatter of cutlery. It was well into what should have been a busy lunch service. I *should* have needed to book a month in advance, at least.

"No," I smiled apologetically. "Perhaps I should come back another time?"

He tutted, frowned, shrugged. "I'll see what I can do."

I stood waiting for a couple of minutes before allowing myself to be led to a square two-seater table. There were a half-dozen such tables much closer to the panoramic windows overlooking the sweep down to the concrete constrained gorge below. Presumably reserved for those who didn't turn up mid-service, unannounced. Whoever they might be for, they'd evidently chosen to stay away.

I counted seven diners, myself not included. A couple of sprightly, silver-haired retirees were picking through their main courses. A snippet of German drifted over the empty tables. The Mercedes owners, I guessed. Tourists indulging in a tour of the region's gastronomic delights, following a guide book a couple of years out of date. Or perhaps there were no other places of note that didn't require more significant detours.

They did not look, I thought, entirely enchanted with their meals.

Two Italian businessmen were more vocal, though their wine glasses took up more room than their plates. And, dwarfed by their table for six, a modern family—a youngish couple with a single, sullen child—sat dressed in their Sunday best, possibly celebrating a birthday. Though again, the celebration appeared muted, the echo in the dining room or perhaps the disappointment lying heavy on their spirits.

After a while the waiter condescended to take my order. I regarded him with professional interest. As far as I could tell, his criminal record should have barred him from working here, or indeed, possibly anywhere. So either he'd neglected to mention it when he'd applied or no-one else could be found to take the role.

At least he looked the part. Tall, thin, black hair in a widow's peak. His English was accented by Italian, unlike the maitre d', who'd affected a French twang despite being born and raised in Milan.

"The fish," the waiter observed, "is off."

I assumed he meant off the menu, but who could tell? I chose belly of lamb as an alternative.

When my food came, it was...ok. A little stodgy. Fatty, thanks to the change of main, and as, perhaps, befits a 500 year-old Renaissance recipe. Though in reality the menu was about as similar to fare that you might have found at a Papal banquet as an English curry is to street food in Bangalore. The period dishes had been lightened by the use of local cheeses and regional specialities like buckwheat flecked pizzoccheri, as well as by the salads and seasonal vegetables demanded by modern sensibilities.

As I ate, I reread the old reviews on my iPad, trying to reconcile the two. The glowing reports, the discussion of a culinary revolution, not just in Italian cuisine but a relaxation in the way high-end restaurants served gallery-worthy food. Hand wrangling at the three-month advance bookings required, obstacles for those who simply *must* return. Above all the surprise; the disconnect between appearance and taste.

The appearances, at least, hadn't changed. This was inelegant food by modern standards. Almost rural. The spicing was a little peculiar; a lot of cinnamon, overly heavy on the cloves. At least that was likely to be authentic; 16th century Italian fare lacking all but a smattering of the recent discoveries from the New World. Two and a half years ago the ecstatic ratings had tailed off. Fast. The first disgruntled reports appearing on Trip Advisor, questions about whether the chef had been changed, a sudden *lack* of reviews from the more renowned food critics, as if having visited, they could not bring themselves to write about the disappointing, unfortunate reality.

When the Michelin star was stripped nobody was surprised.

Pushing the plate away, I looked up to find I was alone in the dining room, the other guests having solemnly drifted out, even the pair of soused businessmen having gone quietly. The embezzling waiter stood by the maître d's deserted station, giving me hurry-up eyes.

I waved him over, asked for a coffee and the bill.

The coffee, at least, was good, even if its delivery verged on the surly.

"My compliments," I said, lowering two fifty-euro notes over my credit card as an extravagant tip, but keeping my fingers resting lightly on them. "As it appears service is at an end, perhaps you could ask Dr. Lancroft to join me?"

The way his gaze flickered over and around the tip I guessed he was not used to such largesse. And the way his eyes darted back to meet mine I guessed the use of the honorific was equally as rare and startling. His attention was drawn irresistibly to circle the pair of tawny notes, waiting for my fingers to be withdrawn. I waited as well, until his eyes reluctantly met mine once more and he sighed, compact made. "I'll ask if he can spare you any of his time," he begrudged.

I smiled at his retreating back, but felt tense. If Lancroft did not rise to my bait, if the waiter was incurious enough not to run a check on the name on my card...

It wouldn't show *too* much. A well-established line of credit. Links to the Houston-based Booker Foundation. That *might* pique the good Doctor of Medieval History's interest. And hopefully make sure I hadn't come a long way merely for an overpriced meal

I wouldn't be writing home about.

A snatch of a surprising baritone escaped the kitchens, accompanied by the clatter of empty wine bottles. Something from the Marriage of Figaro? The maître d' had talents my web search had not revealed. Any moment now he and the waiter would return and begin stacking chairs onto tables. Or maybe they didn't bother to sweep between services, the customers too few to make that much of a mess, the oft-delayed promise of future salary too distant.

I'd finished the potent coffee by the time the owner-chef arrived. The man looked frazzled, worried, nervous. His long face drawn, sleeves spattered with sauce and meat juices. He was the least chef-looking chef I'd ever seen. No surprise there, I guess, though I also struggled to imagine him in the tweed and casual wear of academia.

"Mr...?" he half asked, a hand marred by frequent pot-burns resting on the back of the unused chair across from me.

"Withy," I replied, echoing the name on the credit card. "Samuel Withy. And you, of course, are Dr. Jacob Lancroft."

He squinted at that. "Should I know you, Mr. Withy?"

"No, indeed not! But I have a small proposition for you." I placed an envelope on the table before us. He sat, delicately lifting the unsealed flap with a finger laced by the thin lines of a sharp knife, peaked in at the sheaf of crisp euros.

"And this is for?"

The narrative was in the details, even if they don't pick up on them directly. The lowly hire car parked outside—and the fact I turned down the Milan rental's generous offer of an upgrade—should speak volumes, if anyone was listening. The money on the table was not mine. I was merely an employee, a messenger, an intermediary. There was, therefore, most likely no more money within the lining of my jacket. But my employer might have much deeper pockets.

Deep enough to drag this restaurant out of the hole it had fallen into, these last two years?

That would be Dr. Lancroft's hope, anyway.

Of course, this being Italy, wads of cash from strange men might be viewed with a high degree of unease. Even if the bearer had shown no signs that they understood the local dialect, or indeed, the Italian language at all. Even if the money *was* desperately needed.

"For your time. Your patience. And your story."

"A reporter?"

"Hardly," I smiled, "I investigate, yes; but not for the newspapers."

"Tax, then?"

I almost laughed, but tapped the unmarked envelope instead. "No." *Obviously*.

He fidgeted in his chair. "I do not think my story interesting enough to warrant such an amount."

"Still, I would like to hear it."

"I hardly know where to begin."

"As I mentioned, I am an investigator, of sorts. Assume then, perhaps, that I already know your story. The broad details anyway. I've read your doctorial thesis," I said and his eyebrows raised. "*Loredana vs Bartolomeo: The First Celebrity Chef Feud*." A paper which on its own might have snagged my curiosity, though it was the tale of the rise and dramatic fall from culinary grace that had coerced me into turning up in person. "But I want what cannot be gathered from reading such academic papers, or online reviews, or even tax returns. And I want to hear it from your perspective, the things you have kept secret. Perhaps we can start with your rather unusual viva?"

He scowled. A raw nerve hit. Two of them perhaps; the comment about his financial situation, and the facing a panel of professors tasked with deciding whether he deserved his history PhD. "A disaster," he admitted.

"You cooked dishes from the recipe book you discovered? Written by Loredana Marcello?"

"Yes. Damned fool that I am."

"You're not, I think, a trained chef?"

He laughed. "A passionate amateur. Perhaps it was that passion that got me into this pickle. Still, I thought I was onto something. I thought the food was amazing."

"Your examiners disagreed?"

"They were...polite. But unimpressed. I got my PhD anyway, the discovery of a previously unknown medieval book pretty much guaranteed that. However I was furious. I thought they were wrong about my food, how could they *not* be wowed by it? I was sure that there was some jealous reason for their reticence." He shrugged. "Thankfully, I let my anger simmer after the viva and not during."

"Tell me more about the book."

"So that's your interest?" his eyes narrowed, fingers edged towards the envelope as if wishing to claim the prize before I took it back. He resisted. Still English at heart, then. "Ah. I'm afraid your journey has been a wasted one."

I eased back in my chair as two fresh coffees arrived. Waited until the waiter skulked out of earshot before I continued. "You misunderstand. I realise full well that the book is not for sale."

"Well..."

"—Because it has been destroyed."

His face hardened. Reddened as well. He'd lost the blush of the kitchens since he'd sat down, but it was back with a vengeance. "I don't know what you think you know, but—"

I waved his protest away. "As I keep mentioning, Dr. Lancroft, I am an investigator. A very good one. That does not mean I simply discover difficult to find facts, I also play join the dots." Dots that had lead me down the rabbit hole and eventually to here, a fool's errand perhaps, but it was such an unusual case that it demanded to be seen through to the end. I scanned the room once more, noticing fingerprints on the windows. A stray thread beneath one of the cushioned chairs. Cracked glass in a display cabinet of medieval cooking utensils. A whiff of melancholy. "If the book—any part of it—was still around, then your restaurant wouldn't be facing imminent closure. If you had any pages of Loredana's book left, then my employer would pay considerably more than the amount in that envelope."

He mused on that. "You work perhaps for a pharmaceutical company? I thought..."

"An antiquarian. A bibliophile. A man prepared to pay for a story about a rare book, even if that book is almost certainly lost."

"Jake Booker? I'd say the man's more of a treasure hunter."

"See," I smiled good-naturedly. "It is not so very difficult to investigate, is it? We lay out our lives online, and even though some of the areas are not publicly available, I am rather adept at prising them open. Mostly legally, as it happens, though on occasion other means are necessary. But please, we have been sidetracked. Your story. Your thesis?"

He took a sip of his coffee. Some bridge had been crossed. Perhaps because he had already played his one card, the one the waiter had handed him with my request, and my credit card. My link to the Booker Foundation. Like a conjuror's trick, it was ultimately *my* choice of card, not his. And, like the best conjuror's tricks, it worked all the better for not having been spotted.

"I started my research on Bartolomeo Scappi," the academic turned owner-chef explained. "His *Opera dell'arte del cucinare* is well known. It was translated into English as recently as 2008, with the title *The Opera of Bartolomeo Scappi*. Which is the version I read, even before I'd finished my history degree. It took a bit of work on my Italian to allow me to read the original, though that proved worthwhile, in the end." He waved his hand and I noticed the solid gold wedding band. The ring sat loosely, as if Dr. Lancroft was once a somewhat plumper man. Or perhaps the need to remove it before each service meant it was always a size larger than custom dictated.

"But Scappi is a path well trod by other scholars. He is a little too well known for *novel* research, which is the requirement for a successful PhD."

I nodded. "Go on."

"In an antique shop just outside of Sondrio, I discovered Loredana's *Sfida*—challenge—to Bartolomeo. Quite by chance. I had an hour to kill before catching a train to the airport. God alone knows how the manuscript ended up in such a backwater, how it hadn't been snapped up by some other collector. Maybe because it was so evidently a one-off, a print run of one. I paid my own money for it, an amount equal to my student loan that year. But I was flush and perhaps overly carefree with the money—inheritance from my mother's recent death." Dr. Lancroft shrugged, thin shoulders arching towards ears. He had definitely lost weight. "It seemed a good price. Fifth edition copies of Bartolomeo's *Opera*, if you can find them, sell for around 6,000 euros, and this was far rarer, almost certainly unique.

"Loredana was a botanist. More interested in medicine than cuisine. The reasons for her enmity to Bartolomeo are unknown. There's no direct evidence they ever met, though her husband was a diplomat for a while at the Vatican. For a different Pope than either of the two Bartolomeo cooked for. Perhaps it was no more than the traditional feud between different Italian states, between Venetians and Lombards.

"Two years after Bartolomeo published his massive tome on cooking, comprising more than a thousand Renaissance recipes, Loredana issued her challenge, and along with it, her own rather slimmer book, *Una Sfida*. She claimed his *Opera* wasn't all that. Claimed, in a taste test, her recipes would come out on top. That even if Bartolomeo himself cooked her recipes, he would *still* have to judge them superior to his."

Dr. Lancroft smiled. I wondered how often he had told his tale, and to whom. "It was a bold move. Completely out of character with the rest of her writings, with the role of a venerated Dogaressa, even one well known as a scholar. A taunt worded to maximise the impact, the embarrassment. So bold that it would have been hard for Bartolomeo to ignore such a challenge, a public attempt to deflate the bubble of the Pope's favourite chef."

"So, who won?" I asked.

He frowned. "You've read my dissertation. You already know. No one did."

"In your own words, then. Why was Loredana's challenge never resolved?"

"Because things moved slowly in Sixteenth century Italy, especially when a renowned Papal chef drags his feet. And because Loredana died in the December of that year. After that, the contest didn't really matter.

"And then time forgot her, and her story. Her papers, her research, were all lost."

I replaced the empty cup in the little saucer. "Burnt perhaps, or buried on her death?"

He shook his head. "Loredana wrote extensively on cures and treatments for the plague. Three years after her death—while her husband, the Doge, was still alive—Venice had need of her work and reports from that time suggest her remedies were used and judged effective, though surely they could have been little more than a palliative.

"Presumably, her papers and belongings were scattered among other Venetian scholars and doctors as a result of that outbreak, as a result of their need for her knowledge. And so her recipe book—her challenge—might have ended up mixed into another's library. A curio, its true worth not spotted. At least, not until I rediscovered it."

"Let's fast forward. You tried a number of the recipes?"

Lancroft nodded. "And each of them blew me away, even if I wasn't sure I'd got them right."

"At which point," I gently asked, "Did you realise the pages were impregnated with a powerful appetising agent?"

"Hah," he shook his head, whether at my deductions or at how long it had taken him to piece together the unlikely facts. "A process of elimination. Only following the recipes from the book itself seemed to work. Working from a photocopy produced mediocre results. I sent some of the recipes to a chef I knew, he was as unimpressed as my examiners. Then he cooked one in my kitchen, using the original text, and we were both stunned."

"Did he know? Did he realise?"

"No. A one-off, he thought. A fluke. He took a copy of the recipe away but could never quite nail it again. A variant did later appear on one of his menus, I believe, but for its originality, rather than its knockout taste."

He laughed without any real warmth. "Odd that, 'originality', for a 500 year-old recipe."

"And the restaurant?"

His face darkened still further. Though the picture window looked out over the sunlit slopes on the other side of the valley, the temperature seemed to have dropped, the smaller windows at my back had slipped into shade.

"A gamble with the rest of my mother's inheritance. Gone, now, though we had our moment. The trace of whatever it was that rubbed off onto the chef's fingers from Loredana's recipes, as he found his page, or pored over the difficult to read calligraphy, was enough to make almost anything taste divine, to that chef, anyway. That was why my viva didn't get the response I expected. That was why Loredana's challenge was set up the way it was, the recipe book a Trojan horse in Bartolomeo's kitchen, just waiting for him to lick his fingers. But for it to work on an entire service, we needed to introduce more of the appetising agent, as you call it. We started to rip up the book, soaking the pages to make our sauces."

I nodded. All pretty much as I had surmised. "Did the end sneak up on you? The final pages? Or did you reduce the amount, selectively choosing only to use the last precious fragments for food critics and celebrity guests?"

He shook his head. "I wish... Damned fool of a head chef I hired. We were doing well—very well. But I am, as you rightly observed, not a trained chef. I struggled to cope with our workload, with our popularity. So I hired someone to cook the recipes I'd researched.

"At first, I still doctored the sauces, the broths, myself. But even that proved troublesome, now that I wasn't in the kitchen all the time. And," he shrugged and gave his first genuine smile of our conversation, "I was enjoying the spotlight from the front of house, the famous people who were more than happy to have the proprietor sit and dine with them.

"So I took the chef into my confidence. I didn't explain it in any detail, passed it off as a tradition, a silly superstition. But I think he understood more than he let on. He'd come to me, mid-service, when I was flushed by the attention and the wine, and say that'd he'd already used up that day's allocation of pages, beg me to retrieve more. We burnt through the last of them so damned fast."

I made a mental note to investigate the ex-head chef in more detail. It wouldn't be easy. He was serving time for a serious assault on a sous-chef in Turin.

"Do you think the additive was addictive?"

A pair of gimlet eyes bored into mine. "You heard about the French critic?"

I nodded my head, slowly. One of those glowing early reviews had been his. A sharp contrast to the jaded reports he'd been turning in at around that time. I also had on file his account of a return visit. The despair of tasting food that no longer thrilled. A review that went unpublished, because he never made it back down the mountain. A leaden foot on the accelerator, instead of the brake those hair pins demanded. Verdict: Death by misadventure. But the notes he made eloquently capture his anguish at something life-affirming lost.

Even if it wasn't chemically addictive, its absence might have been powerful enough to drive a food-weary man to his death.

"Well. Thank you for your time, Dr. Lancroft. I think I have everything I need."

"I still have a copy of the recipes," he blustered. "I took pictures of each page, before..."

I shook my head. "Do they have the same effect the original had? No, of course not. In any case, I've already seen them. You store them in the cloud. And there are, alas, no clues there. Not according to some experts I had look them over. No hints as to the mysterious appetising agent's formula. And why would there be? When the *Sfida* was intended for another chef."

There was a long awkward silence. "What happens next?"

I picked up my iPad. Pushed my chair back and stood. "Who knows? Perhaps some future historian will find Loredana's lost papers on botany and medicine, shedding light on whatever powerful appetite stimulant she discovered and used to treat the pages of her recipe book. If so, medicine will be all the richer for it. It would be useful for cancer sufferers, and perhaps as a contra-indicator for a new line in appetite suppressants.

"But these are hardly my concern.

"As for your story?" I shrugged on my jacket. "It becomes an electronic reference card in the Booker Foundation's files." A title, and a status: lost to history. And a secondary status, one I was certain would be unique in the Foundation's files: cooked, presumed eaten.

"As for your failing restaurant...well. I suggest you use this," I tapped the still unclaimed envelope, "to pay off what remains of your staff. And then I'd recommend closing the doors. Possibly permanently, certainly in this current incarnation. I'm afraid, Dr. Lancroft, that hearty Renaissance-inspired food will never be quite enough to sustain a restaurant this tucked away. Loredana might work as a less exclusive summer guest house, but..." I shrugged.

Really. There wasn't much more I could say. That Jacob did not already know.

A woman came over as I left. Signora Lancroft. I recognised her from her profile pictures. She looked curious. Concerned. And heavily pregnant.

I hoped, for her sake as much as his, that Dr. Lancroft switched tracks to another career. Perhaps back to academia, where the fact his Renaissance-inspired restaurant had ever been a success would count for more than its ultimate failure.

As I slipped the Fiat into gear, I glanced back. It was only four in the afternoon, but the old school house had been swallowed by the shadow of the mountain and was already lost to sight. A fitting end for an establishment that had cooked its books.

# The Book of Ways

## R. C. Mulhare

*"Yog-Sothoth knows the gate. Yog-Sothoth is the gate. Yog-Sothoth is the key and guardian of the gate. Past, present, future, all are one in Yog-Sothoth."* - "The Dunwich Horror," H.P. Lovecraft

The body lay spread-eagled, face up, on the floor of the back office in Waite's Books and Fine Art, in the midst of a square interlaced with a triangle, traced in chalk on the tiles.

"What is this, some kind of devil stuff?" asked Palmer, one of the older police officers from Gardner, Massachusetts.

Franklin Perry, the sheriff of the city, shook his head. "It's nothing he'd be involved in. I've known him too well and too long."

The deceased, James Reginald Waite, lay stripped completely naked. Throat slashed from ear to ear, no blood stained the tile floor under him. On the victim's bare skin someone had scrawled other sigils, like many-armed spirals ending with eye-shaped knobs and strange lettering, in what looked like blood.

"Could someone have drunk the blood? Are we dealing with vampires?" asked Ashton Fletcher, Perry's red-headed deputy.

"It's probably something a lot more natural," Perry replied. "Is anything missing from any shelves?" In Perry's mind, this could be a robbery gone wrong, but who would go to the trouble of setting up this weird display? Unless they wanted it to look like an occult-related crime. Granted, Waite had auctioned some strange titles in his time. That had raised the ire of some of the more pious locals, but no one had so much as raised a hand against him before this. The worst anyone had done was hang a sign reading *"This store sells obscene books and devil books and should not be patronized!"* on the door.

"Jane, might know," Palmer said. Jane Waite had assisted her father as a business partner after her mother's passing.

"And where is she?" Perry asked.

"According to the folks at the coffee shop next door, she's been away on a book buying trip up north in Maine," DeJasu, one of the detectives coming from the front, explained. "They called it in when one of the clerks came here to get some change. They found the door unlocked and this."

"Liver temp puts the time of death at around 11 p.m., though," Irene Wechsler, the dark-haired girl from the ME's office said, rising from beside the body. "Looks like duct tape residue on his wrists and ankles. Whoever did this bound him, probably killed him, then posed the body post-mortem. Or even while he was dying."

"So where's the blood?" Perry asked, trying to keep an "I can't believe I'm asking this" air out of his voice.

"I'm guessing they collected it in a basin and took it with them," Wechsler replied.

"So why take the clothes?" Fletcher wondered, looking up at Perry then up at Palmer.

"They possibly had DNA evidence on them, if not blood spatter," Wechsler suggested. "Also, stripping the victim established some dominance over him, by humiliating him." Perry stared at her. She smiled at him in a way clearly meant to reassure, but her lack of eye contact canceled it out. "I've read the FBI profiling manuals. I wanted to go into the Bureau, but I couldn't meet the physical requirements."

"But what about the devil markings?" Palmer asked.

"My guess is someone heard the weird stories about some books Waite sold, and they played with that," the tech said.

"So what are we looking for, some kind of wannabe cult kids?" Fletcher frowned.

"I wouldn't go there first," Wechsler looked thoughtful. "The scene is too tidy, too organized."

"Let's locate Jane and see what she can tell us," Perry said.

## Chapter 2

"It's not like he shorted people on the fees he owed them. He was fair about the prices he charged," Jane told Perry the next day, as he sat with her at a table in Brewed for the Best, the coffee shop next door to her and her father's bookstore. She held her cup of coffee in both hands, warming herself on this chilly November day. "I don't know who could do this to him, or why."

"That's what we're trying to figure out," Perry said. From a datebook and some paperwork, they found where she had gone in Maine, assessing a lot from an estate sale. She'd returned a few hours after they contacted her. "I know this is a bad question to ask at a time like this, but could you tell if anything was missing from the store?"

"You think this could be a robbery?"

"That's one of the working theories."

She wagged her head. "I haven't had enough time to go through the whole store, but he kept most of the valuable books in the vault. I checked there and nothing looked out of place."

"Is it possible he'd have opened the vault to pacify a robber?"

"He'd have given them the cash from the drawer or the safe first. Money can be replaced, but books are harder to find."

Perry weighed the next question carefully. "Your father sold some strange books that bothered some folk just for existing. Could someone involved in occult activities or something like that have come here?"

She looked up, her tear-streaked face gathering in confusion. "I don't think so. Most people interested in the esoteric are scholars, academics, people studying folklore and subjects of that nature." She paused, as if something had occurred to her. "There was one, though."

"One what?"

"About two months ago, we acquired a lot of esoteric books from a collector in Cranston, Rhode Island. There's an especially rare text among them. Someone broke a back window and went through the office a week later, but they didn't take anything. He wondered if someone who knew about the book had something to do with it. But he also worried it might just be kids and didn't want to get them in trouble, so he didn't report it."

"Is that book still on the premises?"

"Yes, it's in the back of the vault, in a lot we'd set aside for an auction this weekend."

"If I might ask, what's the book?"

"It's a 19th century edition of a 16th century translation of *The Book of the Ways*, or *Ketab al-Tack* of Rh'as-awl-Aliq."

The words sent a chill down his spine, though he couldn't say why. "Never heard of it, but it's not within my usual range of expertise."

"It's a text from a cult that started in what's now Saudi Arabia," she said. "It flourished, if that's the right word for it, from the 8th century till it was suppressed by the Caliphate."

"So you think someone who knew about the book could have killed your father to get their hands on it. "

"But if it was the same people…how could they go from something as harmless as breaking windows to something as big as killing my father"

"It could be two different groups involved. As cliché as it sounds, I'm going to find out who they are."

"It won't bring my father back."

"No, it won't, but it'll stop them from doing something like this to another family." He paused, wondering if he dared pose the next question. "I have to ask, are you still doing that auction you mentioned?"

"I'd rather withdraw, but we've already had early bids on several titles, including *The Book of the Ways*," she said. "And I could use the money from the sale to help pay for the funeral."

"Is there anyone you can stay with till the sale goes through?"

"I'm staying at the Double Tree Hotel near Route 2, since the auction takes place there."

"I'll make sure management puts extra security on your room. Are you certain there's no way you could get someone else to cover for you?"

"I'm afraid there isn't. There's no one else I trust with our stock and I have too many patrons waiting on this auction."

"I hate putting it this way, but where I'm sitting, I'd think a few rich people with enough ready cash to buy rare books would understand if you withdrew and took the time you need to regroup."

She regarded him patiently, but the tiny frown on her brow said more. "It isn't merely rich people attending the auction. Acquisitions directors from a few major libraries will be there, too."

"Right. I shouldn't have jumped to conclusions."

"There's no harm done, Sheriff Perry," she offered soothingly. "But for now, I need to get back to the shop and put things in order. How soon may I reopen?"

"Once the crime scene people are done with it. And, considering our budget, it won't take long."

## Chapter 3

"You don't think she's in on it, do you? She sounds a little too eager to get back to work," Fletcher suggested, back at the main precinct.

Perry dialed the phone on his desk. "She has a business to run and she made this engagement last year. Given the nature of her business, she has some high profile customers. Also, the store just barely runs in the black. This auction will bring in a lot of revenue."

The line rang several times. "Bear with me," Fletcher said. "She could have got tired of working with her father or how the old man ran the shop. So she hires someone to bump the old man off and make it look like a bunch of Satanists did it."

Perry held up his hand for quiet as the line picked up. "*St. John's Seminary, Dean's office*." a voice on the other end announced.

"Yes, this is Sheriff Franklin Perry of Gardner speaking. I'd like to speak to Father Martin Crowley, if he's available?"

*"One moment please..."* The line clicked. Gregorian chants played as he went on hold. After a few minutes, the line clicked again.

*"Hello, Father Crowley speaking."*

"Martin? It's Frank Perry. Hope I haven't caught you at a bad time?"

*"I'm actually packing to head your way for the weekend. What seems to be the trouble that you aren't calling me 'Marty'?"*

"I have a strange crime scene on my hands. You mind if I email you some photos from it?"

*"Not at all."*

Perry pulled up the email program and sent the photographs to Crowley. For a moment, he heard nothing from the priest's end of the line aside from laptop keys clicking.

Crowley inhaled sharply. *"Franklin, it's a containment circle, and the sigils on the body are things I'd rather never see."*

"Containment for what?"

*"It's used in very dark forms of magick, the sort of thing that makes* the Goetia *look like Glinda the Good Witch."*

"So someone was trying to summon something worse than the Devil? For what reason?"

*"They probably intended the victim as a sacrifice."*

"Stuff just got real."

*"That's James Waite, isn't it?"*

"Yes, it was."

Crowley sighed and went silent for a moment. Then, with a sad warble in the back of his voice, continued *"Waite was a good man and a good businessman. I'd bought a few titles from him over the years."*

"For your classes?"

*"Partly, but mostly on official business."*

"Don't tell me the Church is suppressing books! I thought that went during the Second Vatican Council."

*"The only ones we really pay attention to are the more esoteric and outright questionable works. Modern types like Silver Ravenwolf can rest assured,"* he said with a dryly humorous lilt. *"But one text on Waite's auction list came to our attention,* The Book of the Ways *or* Kitab-al-Tack."

Perry felt his heart skip a beat in his chest. "I heard about that one from Waite's daughter."

Crowley paused. *"What did she tell you?"*

"Not a whole lot, why?"

The line rustled as Crowley drew in a long breath. *"Because that book is something that people involved in certain at-best questionable activities would pay good money to acquire, if not obtain it by any means necessary. It's part of the reason why my colleagues at the Vatican want me to purchase the volume, if at all possible."*

"So how does this tie into Waite's murder."

*"This is definitely cult activity."*

"Cult activity? I thought that was just part of the Satanic Panic that wasn't as big as they say it was."

*"It's a grim possibility that I'd entertain if I were in your place. Those markings aren't the sort of things that teenagers who've listened to too much death metal scribble for fun. This is the work of someone who knows exactly what they're doing."*

"Do you mind if I go with you to this auction? I have a feeling the killer, or killers, may show up."

*"And you worry that I may be next?"*

"If you buy the book, there's reason to be concerned for your safety, Father."

*"I'd deeply appreciate it if you did come with me,"* Crowley said. "*My faith in God protects my soul, but I need to trust in a physical protector for my body.*"

## Chapter 4

The morning of the auction, Perry, with Fletcher as back up, arrived at the Double Tree Hotel. Wearing plain clothes, Perry's sidearm was hidden under his jacket. Lexuses and other high-end cars filled the lot. His older model Honda looked shabby next to them, till a green Ford Taurus with dented fenders pulled up beside it. A tall, slim man in a black suit under a black topcoat emerged into the September gloom, setting a black fedora onto his prematurely silvery head.

"Marty's here," Perry said, getting out of the driver's seat and approaching the newcomer.

"Peace be with you, Frank," the black-clad man offered, extending his hand to Perry.

"And also with you," Perry replied, shaking his hand.

"So you're the priest from the Vatican?" Fletcher asked.

"I've worked under an exorcist there, and I still have contact with him, but I wouldn't say I'm *from* the Vatican," Crowley said, raising one eyebrow in amusement.

"You helping us figure out why someone would kill a man over a book?" Fletcher asked.

"Slow down, Fletch," Perry cautioned.

"Do you know some assassin who could hunt down whoever killed Mr. Waite?" Fletcher asked.

Crowley chuckled. "You've read too many Dan Brown novels. The most I can do is buy the book at the center of all this, but my funds are limited."

"Just one more question? Are you related to *him*?" Fletcher asked, weighting that last word.

"Who?" Perry asked.

"If you mean Aleister Crowley?" Father Martin Crowley replied pointedly. "I get that a lot. He's a collateral relative, not a direct ancestor, as my sister found out when she traced our family tree."

The father glanced toward the hotel entrance, clearly redirecting the conversation. "Shall we go in?"

They walked up the main drive toward the brick carport covering the entrance as a silver Cadillac with Texas plates pulled up, a valet hurrying to open the door. The three men entered through the sliding doors that opened into the lobby. A video screen by the front desk displayed a list of events at the hotel, including "Central Massachusetts HorrorCon" on the third floor and the "North East Fine Books Auction" set in the Windsor Ballroom on the mezzanine level. They took the curved main staircase, following a group of well-dressed people up the steps to the ballroom's open doors.

Across the mezzanine, figures in hooded black robes loped along, hoods raised to hide their faces. Likely people attending the horror convention.

Jane, in a black skirt suit, met them just inside the door. "I was hoping you'd join us."

Perry introduced Jane to Father Crowley. "We've met online. He placed one of the early bids," she said.

"And mine was the other bid," an oily voice affecting a Boston Brahmin accent interrupted them. Behind Jane stood Frazer Jaquith, one of Gardner's "polite society", or what remained of it after the furniture factories had gone elsewhere. The gray suit he wore looked expensive from a distance, but up close showed signs of wear on the cuffs of his trousers.

Though Jane's shoulders set firmly, she kept her face relaxed and neutral. "Yours was one of three early bids on that particular volume," she replied, her voice even.

"Ah, I have some worthy competition in that case?" Jaquith said, before turning his eyes to Father Crowley's Roman collar. "And we have a mackerel snapper as well. Dare I ask what his type is doing here, bidding on such a rare text? Did he sell some church vessels to make the bid?"

Fletcher started reaching under his jacket for whatever weapon he had stowed there. Gesturing to his deputy to back off, Perry looked with concern at the priest, wondering how he'd react both to Jaquith's implications of impropriety and his rather archaic slur of 'mackerel snapper.' Crowley kept his face calm as he replied, "A benefactor has given my colleagues and me the funds to purchase it."

"Then let's hope your benefactors are generous with their funds," Jaquith said, clearly devoid of any sportsmanship, before he stepped into the crowd.

"What's that guy on?" Fletcher grumbled.

"Pay no attention to him. He's always talking big to make himself look big," Jane explained. "Frazer Jaquith's been a thorn in our side for a long time."

"He's been a thorn in the sides of a lot of people in town. He's always calling the precinct on noise complaints that turn out to be nothing," said Perry. "Don't let us keep you from your customers. But if you need anything, Fletch and I are here for you."

"I hope I don't have to ask you for any more help than you've given," she answered, managing a small smile, before moving on to speak with another patron.

They entered the ballroom proper. Rows of gilded chairs filled one side of the room, with a podium and a presentation table in front of them. Behind that stood rows of banquet-style tables draped with maroon table covers on which stood glass and metal or glass and wood cases containing one or a few books.

Once they had checked in with the registration clerk, Perry picked up a copy of the auction catalog from her table. He flipped it open, scanning the pages and the items listed on them. "*Quarto bound in morocco, banded spine with tooled title in gilding.*"

"This is above my grade. What does any of this mean?" he asked.

Crowley looked over his shoulder. "A quarto describes the size of the book, and morocco is the kind of leather used for its covers."

Perry looked further down the list till he came to the entry for The Book. *"The Book of the Ways—awl-Aliq, Rh'as. 700 CE. Translated from the original Arabic by John Dee, 1549. Rendered into modern English, Leslie Armitage 1890. Translated about the same time as Dee's version of the more notorious work by Abdul al-Hazred, awl-Aliq's master. An extremely rare text not seen outside the more thorough occult libraries. First edition, 180 pp. Considered the most detailed treatise on the cult of Yog-Sothoth, "the Guardian of the Gate Who is the Gate". Black leather covers, title tooled on the cover and spine in silver lettering. Light edgewear on covers, slight foxing on edges of pages. Tight binding and internal text clear and clean."*

"Weird stuff. So what or who is this Yog So How do you say this?" Perry asked.

"Allegedly, Yog-Sothoth is one of the so-called Elder Gods whose cultus predated and developed alongside of pre-Christian Judaism," Crowley said.

"Like those Greek and Egyptian gods?"

"More or less, though there's speculation on whether or not these entities exist. If they do, they might dwell in a parallel universe or a pocket on the edge of known space."

"So some kind of aliens pretending to be gods? I think I saw that episode of *Stargate SG-1*," Fletcher joked.

Crowley chuckled, the lines at the corners of his eyes crinkling. "That's a good analogy."

"So who's this Rass-Al-I'm not gonna try to pronounce that name?" Perry said.

"We know only fragments about his life, but his father was a scribe to a much more well-known occult writer, best known for copying down some of Al-Hazred's sayings," Crowley explained. "The younger Rh'as grew up in the service of Yog-Sothoth, and in this book, recorded more of the cult's practices and lore."

"So almost like he grew up in a more erudite version of the Manson Family and wrote about them?" Perry asked.

"The Manson Family in what's now Saudi Arabia, with far fewer distorted flower child culture aspects and far more eldritch creatures from beyond," Crowley said, wryly.

"You mean Manson wasn't an avatar of some weird god?"

Fletcher asked.

"Too soon," Perry warned. "So can we take a look at this book?"

"By all means." Crowley led them through the crowd to the display tables. Auction workers wearing white cotton gloves stood behind some of the tables, talking with patrons. Occasionally, the workers opened a case to remove a book for their inspection. Crowley glanced at the listing in the catalog, then walked along the rows, clearly scanning the numbers on each case. At the very center of the tables, he paused before a case numbered *35*. Within lay a hardcover book, slightly smaller than a typical hardcover and about as thick as a New Testament, covered in slightly worn black leather.

Some part of Perry had expected a weird aura surrounding it, or a small animal skull, even a strange colored jewel embedded in the front cover…something that made its difference obvious. Instead, it was just a book.

"It's small," Fletcher observed.

"Many grimoires don't look like the ominous tomes that Hollywood portrays," Crowley said. "A lot of bookbinders put modest covers on books of this type, to avoid drawing too much attention to them, though it depended on the period." With a dry laugh in his throat, he added, "The jeweled and intricately molded tomes you see in a horror movie might be a dark mirror of the ornate family Bible. The profane will sometimes mimic the trappings of the sacred. But at other times, a more modest approach may be the cleverer, possibly more dangerous guise, since it's less expected."

"You might be on to something there, Padre," a man's voice with a light Texan drawl spoke from behind them. A tall man in a black chambray shirt over neatly pressed blue jeans approached, a black Stetson pushed back on his bushy silver hair.

At that same moment, Jaquith rounded on their table, glaring up at the newcomer from the other side of the Mississippi River. "You again, what brings you this far into the north east?" Jaquith snapped.

"A mix of business and pleasure," the Texan proclaimed. "My company's been exploring a potential natural gas site on the coast, though the geologists are hedging their bets. I'm occupying my time in parts inland."

"And you thought to spend it hobnobbing in the local antiquities market?" Jaquith said, his gaze lowered as if to minimize the fact that he had to look up at the Texan.

Jane approached, putting herself between the two men. At that moment, a small gong by the auctioneer's podium rang and the voice of the auctioneer, Merton Donnell, came over the loudspeaker. "Ladies and gentlemen, if I could have your attention? Thank you for joining us today. The North East Fine Books Auction should commence shortly. If you could take your seats, we'll start the bidding momentarily."

"I take it that's our cue," Perry announced, looking from Jaquith to the Texan to Crowley.

The Texan touched two of his fingers to the brim of his hat. "And may the best man win."

"May the man with the best finances win," Jaquith snapped at the Texan as he walked away toward the seating.

"Thanks. I appreciate you being a good sport about that," the man in the Stetson called back with a wink.

Fletcher looked at Jaquith's back. "I take back every wisecrack I made about you, Father." The deputy bowed his head slightly, but clenched his fists by his sides.

Crowley chuckled lightly as he headed for the seating, Perry and Fletcher trailing him. "There's no harm done. I've dealt with far worse things than the sharp edge of one man's tongue."

Perry and Fletcher sat down on either side of Crowley. Perry scanned the crowd, spotting the Texan to their right, at the end of the same row, while Jaquith had taken a seat in the middle of the front row.

"I don't know if I like that Texan," Fletcher said. "He seems too friendly."

"Jaquith didn't seem to care much for him either, but he doesn't care much for anyone, even from the same town," Perry grimaced.

Once the patrons had seated, Donnell spoke again. "Most of you have probably heard of the tragic passing of James Reginald Waite, a long time seller, just days before today's sale," he said. "I'd like to start with a moment of silence, in his memory." He bowed his head. Crowley crossed himself discreetly and bent his head. Perry glanced down the row, spotting the Texan, hat now in his lap.

A moment passed and Donnell commenced the auction, the assistants bringing up the lots of books, one at a time, in quick succession, including: a set of bound volumes of *The Atlantic Monthly*, in cloth covers very unlike the three-ring binders of *National Wildlife Federation* magazines which Perry's grandfather had on shelves in his den; very large coffee table size art books; a set of Dickens; a leather-bound set of Thackeray; a first edition of William Shirer's *Rise and Fall of the Third Reich*; a first edition of *From Ritual to Romance* by Jessie L. Weston; several letters from famous politicians and authors. Bidding turned fierce over a Christmas card from someone named Luffcroft or something like that.

In time, Jane approached carrying *The Book of the Ways* in her white-gloved hands. "Next, we have Lot 35, an 1890 edition of *Kitab-al-Tack,* written by Rh'as-awl-Aliq, a second-generation student of the infamous Abdul al-Hazrad, author of the *Al-Azif.* This version was rendered into modern-for-its-time English by Leslie Armitage, based on the translation by John Dee, occultist to the stars, or at least one star in particular, Queen Elizabeth the First of England. Bidding will start at five hundred dollars."

Crowley raised his card. "Do I have five hundred twenty-five?"

The Texan raised his hand, two fingers extended. "Five hundred twenty-five. Do I have five hundred fifty?"

Jaquith shot his card up as high as he could reach. "Six thousand!"

The patrons murmured. Donnell gave Jaquith the kind of tired look that anyone in sales management reserved for difficult customers, a dangerous smile quirking the corners of his mouth. "That's not exactly cricket, Jaquith. One thousand, do I hear one thousand?"

The Texan raised his hand. "One thousand. Do I have one thousand four hundred?" Another patron raised her hand. "One thousand four hundred. Do I have one thousand five hundred?" Crowley raised his hand. "One thousand five hundred. One thousand five hundred? Do I have one thousand six hundred?" Jaquith shot up his hand. "One thousand six hundred. Do I have one thousand seven hundred?" Crowley raised his hand, calmly.

The price rose to two thousand, then three, the bids passing among Crowley, Jaquith and the Texan. At three thousand, Crowley frowned slightly, in concern. "I'm reaching my limit," he said softly. "I have only four thousand in my expense account."

"I could spot you a couple thousand," Perry offered.

The bids rose through six thousand to seven thousand. Crowley dropped out with a small shrug and sat back to watch the bidding continue. Most of the bids passed between Jaquith and the Texan, and the patrons watched the progress with the attention of spectators at an intense tennis match. The number passed to the ten thousands, with little sign of abating.

"35,000? Do I hear 35,000?" Donnell called. "35,000 going once, 35,000 going twice. Sold! To Jake Booker of Texas."

The patrons applauded. The Texan, Booker, smiled, nodding in Jaquith's direction, but Jaquith sat with his hands in his lap.

A flash of light exploded in the room and a loud bang shook the tables. Perry grabbed Fletcher and Crowley by an arm, hauling them to the carpeted floor as he hit the deck. *Stun grenade*, he hoped. Patrons screamed and ducked as another flash and another bang shook the room.

Perry poked his head above the backs of the chairs. A cloud of smoke billowed in through an open door to the hallway, shadows moving within it. Donnell bulled toward another door, yanking it open and yelling for the patrons to exit the room in an orderly manner. A fire alarm shrilled, adding to the commotion.

Perry rose, grabbing Crowley by the arm, Fletcher jumping to his feet on the other side. "Stay down, that's probably tear gas," Perry cried. They kept low as the three of them stumbled after the crowd, out into the hallway.

Firefighters armed with chemical fire extinguishers met them in the hallway. "Keep moving!" one of them shouted before stepping into the smoke. They staggered out onto the mezzanine and down the stairs, into the fresh air.

Crowley coughed, staggering toward a wall that ringed a planter, pulling Perry down next to him.

"What was all that?" Fletcher demanded, turning as if to run back inside.

"Someone didn't want the Texan to win that book," Perry said.

Fire trucks and ambulances from several neighboring towns

now filled the parking lot. Crews of EMTs emerged with the wounded, some limping from injuries caused by the crush, some of them coughing and with eyes streaming from the smoke. An EMT approached, checking the three men out, giving them a passing bill of health, but recommended that they check into a hospital for a second opinion.

Crowley reached into his breast pocket, taking out the small black clay pipe there, before putting it back.

"You all right there, Professor Tolkien?" Perry asked, using a high school nickname, given by one of their classmates who'd compared Crowley to the classic fantasy writer for his smoking habits.

"I'm telling myself I don't need any tobacco right now," Crowley replied.

The Texan, Booker, joined them, eyes reddened but otherwise no worse for the wear. "I take it I won't be picking up the book I won, till they let us all back in," he said, his voice gruffer, but keeping his good spirit.

Once the fire chief cleared the ballroom and the smoke had cleared from the air, Perry and Fletcher returned to the scene. No signs of fire damage, aside from some slight scorching on the rug, where the stun grenades had landed. But a few cases on the tables stood empty. Going over the auction catalog, Perry matched up the lost items. A copy of M.R. James's *Collected Ghost Stories* had vanished, but more importantly, *The Book of the Ways* had disappeared from its case.

Leaving the ballroom and going downstairs to the lobby, he approached Jane, who was talking with Booker. "I got some bad news. Jane, you had the M.R. James book?" Perry asked.

She frowned, gravely, clearly divining his thoughts. "Yes, I did. Why?"

"I'm afraid it's been stolen, along with *The Book of the Ways*."

"I guess I won't be collecting my winnings, until we get it back," the Texan's tone was stoic.

"'We'?" Fletcher asked.

"I got a stake in this, least I could do is offer what assistance I can," Booker said.

"I appreciate the offer, but I'd rather you took a step back from the investigation, at least for the time being," Perry politely rebuffed him. "The fact is, there's been a man murdered over this book."

Booker frowned. "If you don't mind my asking, who was murdered?"

"My father, James Waite," Jane explained. "He'd submitted the book for the auction, along with a few other paranormal-related titles."

Booker's eyes softened with compassion, but his jaw set with righteous indignation. "That's horrible."

"I have to ask, were you one of the early bidders?" Perry asked.

Booker relaxed his face. "Yessir, I saw the listing online a day or two before I came up here. That make me a suspect?" he asked with a dry as dust lilt.

"Everyone's a suspect," Fletcher said. Perry darted a glare at his deputy. The younger man had every reason to inform Booker, but not in that manner.

"Rest assured I won't be leaving town for a while yet. Matter of fact, I'm staying at the Colonial Inn across the way," Booker replied. "I know a couple of guys in the Bureau I could call on, if it comes to that."

"Let's hope it doesn't, though I appreciate the offer," Perry said.

"I suppose I should stay in town while you investigate this," Crowley acknowledged. "I'll have to make some phone calls and let my superior know what happened."

"You can call from the station, and you're welcome to crash on my couch, same as in the old days," Perry offered.

## Chapter 5

Back at the station, Perry wrote up what they knew about the case on a whiteboard in his office. Crowley, having made his phone call, seated himself on the couch, reading silently from a book with covers about the same dimensions as *The Book of the Ways*, but with double the number of pages, the red ink on the edges worn from use.

"What's that you got there?" Fletcher asked.

Crowley looked up. "This? It's the *Liturgy of the Hours*. It's a series of Psalms and other Bible readings, a set of them for each day of the year, divided into seven portions known as Hours, to be prayed over the course of a day. It's usually prayed by priests or monks or nuns, but some lay Catholics pray it as well."

"Bible readings, eh? I thought the Vatican used to keep the Bible locked up."

Crowley laughed. "Prior to the invention of movable type, the Church Fathers had to physically chain Bibles to lecterns in churches and libraries, to keep people from stealing them to have their own copy. But they never discouraged people from reading it."

At that moment, an officer stuck her head in through the open doorway. "Chief? There's something you need to see."

Perry turned from the whiteboard as several officers passed by the open door, escorting a group of older teens, clad in black robes with the hoods pushed back from their faces. "What's going on?"

"Started as a routine traffic stop about a couple of miles down the road from the Double Tree," one of the officers, Marcella Duhane, said. "Then it turned not so routine. The kids had flashbang grenades and industrial-grade dust masks in the floorboards of their van."

"Those weren't ours!" one of the teens called. The tallest and oldest glared at him, and a female officer shushed him.

"And yet you're dressed like some persons of interest we spotted in the Double Tree," Perry retorted. "Put the chatty guy in Interview Room One, once they've been booked."

Ten minutes later, Perry let himself into Interview One to question "the chatty guy", Derek Hamilton.

"It's not a crime to have flashbang grenades," Derek snapped, not looking at Perry.

"It's not a crime to own them when you have the proper permits. But you were caught speeding, two miles down Route 68 from the Double Tree Hotel, where someone caused a criminal disturbance using flashbangs."

"That wasn't us," Derek replied, too quickly, looking around the interview room as if hunting for a crevice to crawl into.

"Whoa, calm down, kid. You're going to burst a blood vessel, if your eyes don't spin right around in their sockets."

"Why should you care? You got me locked up and the key thrown away already," Derek replied, trying to sound brash, but the fear making his voice crack.

"I care because people got hurt in that hotel ballroom, and if you were involved in that mess, I don't think you intended for that to happen. All I want to know is who put you and your friends up to this?"

The kid caught Perry's gaze for a microsecond. "How do you know we didn't think it up ourselves?"

"For one thing, you look like someone's after you or holding something over your head."

"If I tell you, it could get my family hurt."

"Who wants to hurt your family?"

"I can't give you that. I've said too much already. He paid my friends and me to dress up like cult goons and look weird. He paid us extra when we agreed to lob the grenades and the smoke bombs, to create a diversion for something else. He didn't say what. But he told us he'd text if we were needed again, and if we didn't hear from him, to just move on."

"You keep saying 'he'. What did 'he' do to scare you so bad?"

"I can't tell you that." Fear had crept back into the kid's demeanor.

"All right. I'm going to need your phone to trace that text."

"You got my phone when your goons made me turn out my pockets," Derek retorted. "Now can I go?"

"I'll put in a word with Judge Hargreaves on your behalf. We're still holding you for causing that commotion in the hotel. That mess you made allowed someone to steal several very rare books."

"Figures. With the money he promised my family, he couldn't afford to pay for his dumb book. If you have to know, I agreed to this to pay for my little sister's asthma meds." Derek snapped his mouth shut, making it definite that he had nothing more to say.

Perry left the interview room to examine the suspects' belongings. He fished out Derek's phone, praying under his breath it wasn't password locked.

To the relief of Aguilar, their tech expert, the phone lacked a password. She found numerous calls and texts from a single number lacking a name, which the phone company traced to a disposable cellphone, now deactivated.

"Someone's been taking notes from *Criminal Minds*," Fletcher muttered.

"Can the phone company track the location of the phone when that last text went out?" Perry asked.

Aguilar rolled her chair back from her console. "They could give us a general idea but not the precise location. Burner phones don't have GPS."

"One of the many things I don't like about *CSI*," Fletcher said. "They make it look so easy to track down the precise location of the creepy caller."

"And reality foiling your chance to be Gil Grissom," Perry added. As the sheriff stepped out of his office, Booker stood up from the chair by the door.

"You again," Fletcher commented suspiciously.

"Been here to give my statement and I thought I'd buy you gents dinner, for all the trouble you're going to," Booker said, hands turned up, open and friendly.

"We'd appreciate that," Perry replied, beckoning Crowley to accompany them.

They followed Booker's Cadillac to the Colonial Inn, a large Federal-period farmhouse now known for its hospitality and its porterhouse steak. Booker treated the officers to the porterhouse. Crowley, on the other hand, chose the scrod haddock.

"It ain't a Friday in Lent," Perry said, teasing gently.

"I stopped eating red meat during an especially tricky infestation case, and I lost the taste for it," Crowley admitted.

"Infestation case? You make it sound like you suss out cockroaches," Fletcher responded.

"When you think about it, evil and malignant spirits are the supernatural equivalent of cockroaches," Crowley said.

"So how does a lawman come to be friends with one of the Lord's men?" Booker asked.

"We were in the same grade at school, starting in junior high," Perry explained. "Afterwards, I went into the military and Marty went into the seminary."

"I was the bookish kid whom some of the larger, more aggressive kids would pick on mercilessly, till Frank came to my defense," Crowley said.

"Not to change the subject, but what's the word on the case so far?" Booker asked. "I suppose it's too soon to ask if you know the whereabouts of the book or who kicked over that anthill in the hotel."

"We know those kids in the robes weren't working alone," Perry shared. "Someone hired them to do the deed, but they're not saying. Something has them spooked."

"It's a start," Booker acknowledged.

"I hate to pry, but what brought you up here besides business?" Crowley asked.

"As in, what's a Texas buckaroo doing in Stephen King country, buying old books?" Booker asked with a hint of whimsy.

"In so many words, yes," Perry said.

"What got you into occult texts? Much less things that usually interest people in the more scholarly, or for that matter esoteric, end of the Lovecraft fan community?" Crowley asked.

"I came across him by way of his grandfather Whipple Philips, who worked with a great-uncle of some degree on my father's side of the family," Booker replied. "Old Whipple was ahead of his times in some ways and a bit of a risk-taker, with the hydroelectric projects he banked on. That got him into geology and the odd things that turn up when you start poking into the earth and what lies within it. Too bad his projects fell apart in a recession in the early 1900s, which lead to the old man's death from a stroke. They say that's what put his grandson Howard Philips Lovecraft into a depressive state, affecting the kid's outlook on the whole cosmos. I've read some of his fiction. Strange stuff, and creepy to think there might be something to the strange beasts from beyond he wrote about."

"That's quite profound and thoughtful," Crowley said.

"I share a passion with that quiet gent from Providence. We both have an interest in archaeology, though I'd be the first to say that's about all we have in common. I'm a lot more outgoing and better-traveled," Booker chuckled. "Dude barely ventured beyond the borders of Rhode Island or New England, at least till later in life, but the world of the past and the world beyond fascinated him."

"And yet you feel a kinship with him?" Crowley asked.

"You got it, Padre. I have time on my hands while the geologists hash out things with the local planning boards. So, for a change of pace, I looked into the antiquities market up here.

That's when I found *The Book of the Ways* in a listing online."

"It's one of the lesser-known texts that Lovecraft is believed to have drawn upon—indirectly, of course, since he was a skeptic and a mechanistic materialist," Crowley explained.

"Hold on," Perry began. "This author wrote horror stories about things that go bump in the night and there's real books of weird magic he referenced, but he didn't believe in it?"

"I get the feeling, reading about him, that he wanted to believe," Booker said. "There's one letter he wrote to a pen-friend when he was younger and still figuring out where he stood in the world. He rants on religion for restricting mankind's progress but couldn't deny how much good people of faith had done to improve the world. It gave me a sense the gent did protest too much."

"And a healthy amount of skepticism does help when you're dealing with the supernatural," Crowley said. With a smirk, he added "I'd be exorcising every other house in Massachusetts if we ascribed preternatural causes to every creaking beam and rustle in the walls. We had one incident where a woman contacted us, claiming her son had a stash of magick books in his room, which turned out to be a stack of roleplaying game manuals. Even if you start dabbling with the real thing, you aren't going to summon a shoggoth just by rolling dice."

Booker laughed outright. Perry snorted under his breath, shaking his head. "You're serious?" Fletcher questioned.

"Things like that you can't make up," Crowley said.

"So all this magic stuff is real, at least in theory?" Perry asked.

"Frazer's *Golden Bough*, a book that details some magical systems and fertility cults, was one of Lovecraft's primary sources of inspiration, along with the work of Margret Murray, and he drew his artistic style from a number of gothic fiction writers who'd gone before him. He also seems to have obtained copies of some early papers by Dr. Margret McConnelly. Tragically, these disappeared when burglars ransacked the apartment in Brooklyn he shared with his wife, Sonia Haft Green, during their short marriage," Booker continued. "An associate of mine's done a fair amount of research on his work and how it related to Dr. McConnell's writings."

"And this book that was stolen today?" Perry asked.

"Of itself, it's harmless, but the information within it could be dangerous in the wrong hands," Crowley said, taking his pipe from his pocket to hold in his fingers. "The rituals it contains are… unsavory at best."

"Animal sacrifice?" Perry asked.

"That's one of the milder practices." Crowley paused, turning the pipe over in his fingers. "Others I hesitate to describe."

"...Human sacrifice?" Perry asked, his mind flashing to the Satanic Panic of the 1980s, when anything fantastic or strange fell under suspicion by panicked parents, religious leaders and even some law enforcement officials.

"Again, that's one of the milder practices. There are others involving cannibalism, involuntary ritual mutilation, and things I don't even want to name," Crowley replied. He paused, breathing easier, then continued. "One copy was found in the possession of a man in Scotland, when a girl he had kidnapped and tried to use as 'a vessel' for Yog-Sothoth, escaped and went to the village police."

"And what's the purpose in this?" Perry asked.

"The same things that many people grasp at: enlightenment and the power they think they obtain from it. Though real enlightenment only brings power over one's self and the ability to improve that self and improve the world around them," Crowley said. "Some would even seek power by trying to bring the apocalypse, if that's possible, if these entities even exist."

"So these Elder Gods might not even be real?"

"As far as we know, there are any number of malignant entities on the spiritual plane that could play along with the person invoking these spells. Pretending to be an Elder God, they would use that person to wreak as much pain and suffering as possible on the people around the one performing the ritual," said Crowley. "At another range of possibility, the rituals might, at the right time and in the right circumstances, pave the way for apocalyptic changes."

"What are we talking about? End of the world? Fire and brimstone? Cities and farms leveled?" Perry asked.

"Dogs and cats living together? Mass hysteria?" Fletcher asked, with a nervous chuckle. Crowley and Booker looked at him, laughing as well.

"Not familiar with that reference," Perry admitted.

Crowley grew more serious. "If the dogs and cats and every other creature on this planet can survive in recognizable forms, once the Elder Gods start reshaping the world."

"So, at the other end of the range of possibility is people using these rituals as an excuse to do horrible things to their fellow human beings," Perry said. "Nothing I haven't dealt with before, except creepy cult activity is involved this time."

"I'm starting to think I bid on a pig in a poke," Booker commented, shaking his head.

"Why anyone would want to end the world, if that's even possible, is beyond me," the sheriff observed.

"For the same reason that doomsday cults like what The People's Temple devolved into, and that groups like Aum Shinrikyo or The Order of the Solar Temple commit the horrors they're known for," Crowley said. "Control. Spreading fear. Making themselves feel greater and stronger than they are. And some, especially in these days, do so to wreak havoc on this planet, because humanity hasn't treated God's good creation or our own civilization very well. They ignore the fact that in doing so, they're no better than the people they rail against."

Perry's phone rang at that moment. "That might be important," Fletcher pointed out.

"One moment," Perry excused himself, getting up, taking his phone from his pocket, and stepping away from the table before accepting the call.

"*Perry?*" Aguilar's voice greeted him. "*I've narrowed down the geographic range of that text.*"

"That's a relief. Where did it come from?"

"*I'm sending you an image with the nearest cell towers marked, but to give you a heads up, it looks like they were in Gardner, close to Route 68.*"

"And close to the hotel," Perry said. "Which means they were near there about the time of the auction, but they could have been anywhere. At least we know we're dealing with a local. Thanks, Aguilar." He switched the phone off, pocketing it.

"Had yet another thought. You think Jaquith could be behind all this?" Fletcher suggested in a low voice.

"It's not impossible. His resources are limited, but I've known someone to take risks like these precisely because their resources are limited," the sheriff reasoned, turning back to their table. "I'm getting a subpoena on Jaquith's financials. Someone paid those kids, and he's starting to look likely."

Crowley reached into the side pocket of his jacket, taking out the tobacco pouch and the pipe tucked there, before sliding them back. "Not exactly friendly to smokers here."

"There's a smoking lounge at the end of the hotel garden. Could show you the way, if you like," Booker offered.

"Temptation is getting the better of me," Crowley admitted, rising and following Booker out of the dining room. Perry kept them in sight, waiting a few moments before following them out into the night.

"You getting the same creepy feeling about this Texan as I am? He's a little too interested in this investigation," Fletcher said, trailing after Perry.

"There is that. And while you're spinning theories, you got one on Crowley?"

"Nothing that doesn't sound like I cribbed it from a novel, though what's to say those novels don't have a toe in reality once in a great while?"

"I don't see Crowley hiring those goons to cause the commotion. I've known him long enough to know it's unlikely. He's assisted in some exorcisms and a friend of mine in the Bridgewater PD consulted him on some cult activity in the woods."

"Well, that's where you go wrong. You're too close to him and he could be using that to his advantage," Fletcher suggested.

"I'll take that on advisement."

They stepped onto the terrace behind the hotel, looking down the slope to a pool area, closed up for the season. The patio also remained otherwise unoccupied on this chilly evening. Crowley lit up his pipe, chuckling at something Booker said, then took a pull on it. The two had clearly struck up a companionable friendship, even in the short amount of time.

Perry nodded toward the pair. "Friendship forged in fire, or smoke anyway." He turned away, intending to go back in from the cold.

A yawp rose from the terrace. Perry turned back as a group of tall, husky figures in violet hooded robes emerged from the hedges surrounding the patio, not so much as a rustle giving away their presence. Crowley dropped his pipe as he stumbled back from the intruders. Booker grabbed a chair from a stack nearby, holding it in front of him like a Clive Beatty-style lion tamer as he tried to step between them and Crowley. Some of the robed persons backed away from him but others lunged at Crowley, tackling him to the pavement. Crowley kneed at one of them, aiming for his attacker's groin, only for them to grab his ankle. Booker managed to ram first one, and then a second, with the chair, till one grabbed the legs of the chair, turning it into a tugging match. Crowley butted his head backward into the chin of the figure holding his arms. A third figure came forward, grabbing Crowley by the hair.

"Let them go!" Perry yelled, rushing for the patio, reaching for his sidearm.

The third figure holding Crowley slapped something soft-looking over the captive's face. "Drop that sponge! Let him go!" Perry yelled. "Hands in the air where I can see them!" The robed figure holding the sponge over Crowley's face turned its hood toward Perry but did not let the priest go. Crowley went limp in his attacker's grasp. Perry fired, but the abductors rose as one, carrying Crowley into the brush.

Booker wrenched the chair free and tossed it after the cluster of figures. One of them stumbled, falling behind the pack. The chair hit them between the shoulders, causing them to measure their length on the lawn.

Perry ran up to the robed figure, pinning them with his foot. Fletcher came up beside them, keeping his sidearm trained on them.

"Fletch, call the house. We need a bus and a crew to search that forest." The hooded figure tried to rise, but Perry pressed his knee harder. "I'd advise you to stay still before my friend here uses you for chair bowling practice." To Booker, he added, "Nice aim."

"I was aiming for the biggest one," Booker replied.

Ten minutes later, a squad roamed through the woods behind the hotel, the beams of their flashlights piercing the shadows. Perry and Fletcher stood over the captured cultist, who sat handcuffed on the same patio chair that had felled him.

"We got some of your friends on criminal disturbance charges," Perry said. "What were a bunch of you doing kidnapping a man armed with nothing but a lighter?"

"I say not a word, I must protect the Way." When the cultist spoke, Perry could hear the capital letter in his voice. They'd found no ID on him and he didn't look like a local.

"What is he on?" Fletcher wondered.

"Doesn't sound like he's on anything," said Detective DeJasu. "He sounds like he's reciting a mantra."

"Or like a captured soldier reciting his name, rank, and serial number to tick off his interrogator," Perry observed. "Sir, this could go worse for you. I can't make the charges go away, but I can keep my guys from hassling you too hard for taking a friend of ours. You don't have to give us your friends' names, just the name of whoever put you up to kidnapping my friend."

"I say not a word, I must protect the Way," the cultist replied.

"This isn't getting us anywhere," Fletcher snarled. He tried pushing past Perry to grab the cultist, but his sheriff pushed him back.

Booker approached. "Hey, what's this 'Way' you keep talking about?"

"Some kind of ooga-booga stuff he's into," Fletcher grumbled. "They must have fed him some line to spout if he got caught."

"Kid, I don't know what yer involved in, but yer likely a better man than whoever put you up to kidnapping a guy, and a priest no less. And if you can't talk to these lawmen just tryin' to save their friend, you can talk to me."

The kid looked at Perry. "I'll talk only to him," he said, indicating the Texan.

Perry nodded, then signaled to Fletcher and the other officers nearby to step back. They did so, but with misgiving squints. The two spoke in low voices for a moment, then Booker turned from the kid and approached Perry.

"Jaquith was behind this, all right," Booker confirmed grimly. "It gets interesting. Our 'friend' says they were gunning for either Crowley or me, whoever they got their hands on first. Seems they're part of a group that calls themselves The Company of the Way."

"And I bet this has everything to do with the book," Perry said. To Fletcher and the other officers, he added, "We have the kid. Call off the search in the woods. They're probably long gone."

## Chapter 6

Once back at the station, Perry called in a favor with the Registrar of Deeds, asking them to look into Jaquith's properties. As expected, he still owned the family mansion on the edge of town. A call to Jaquith's lawyer, Eileen Durless, might prove more revealing.

*"I'm not at liberty to tell you the other properties that my client owns,"* she replied sleepily, clearly at the end of a long day.

"Ms. Durless, I don't ask this lightly. Your client is linked to a theft of property that sold for 35,000 dollars at auction, more importantly, in the panic he intentionally created at the Double Tree Hotel and, most importantly, in the kidnapping of Father Martin Crowley," Perry said, keeping his voice calm despite the anger seething in his heart.

The lawyer did not reply for a moment. *"He still owns a summer house in Holderness, New Hampshire. I can't tell you if he's there or not, but I can send you the address."*

"Much appreciated," Perry thanked her and hung up the phone. The fax machine chirped a moment later. Perry rose and tore off the sheet that emerged, reading it.

"Fletch, have a car go round to Jaquith's house here in Gardner. I doubt he and his little gang are there, but we have to cover all bases," he said.

"You really think he'd stash Crowley there?" Fletcher asked, hesitant.

"He's probably getting cocky now that he has what he wants, so he could be daring enough to go back home." Perry reasoned.

"I dunno, these cult types like to get their prey away from the rest of society. If he's got Crowley, he might not want to get caught dragging him into the family home," Fletcher said. "But, then again, these weirdos are hard to predict." With that, he donned his campaign hat and went out.

True to Fletcher's hypothesis, they found no one there other than a houseboy keeping an eye on the residence in the master's absence.

"I'm calling my contacts in the Bureau, and the chief in Holderness," Perry reached for the phone.

The Worcester field office agreed to send a group of their agents over, but it wasn't until after dawn when Egon Boeteker, the police chief in Holderness returned Perry's call. "*Jaquith's a quiet type. His parties might get a little rowdy, but so don't a number of out of towners staying in their country places.*"

"We're talking about a bit more than weekend deer hunters having a beer blast in their grandfather's summer house," Perry said, shorter than he should have, thanks to the adrenaline and caffeine in his system.

"*Then what are we talking about?*"

"We have reasons to believe he and some...associates of his have taken a kidnapped priest there, along with some stolen property," Perry explained.

Chief Boeteker paused, then spoke. *"That's hard to believe. He hasn't been any trouble before this."*

"There's a first time for everything," Perry said.

The Bureau sent over a group of five agents, including a tall, dark one who looked like he'd started out breaking kneecaps for the Mob, and a short, blond one with rimless glasses, who looked like an unhinged professor. Perry briefed them as well as his unit on the nature of the operation. His men listened with looks of dogged interest, the agents more reflectively, at least until Agent Crazy Professor put up his hand.

"This Jaquith is suspected of being involved with a cult? Of what kind, if you don't mind my asking?"

"He's implicated in the theft of an antique book dealing with the rituals to some alleged god known as Yog-Sothoth—" Perry started to answer.

Agent Crazy Professor sighed, annoyed yet pained. "Not those types. With all due respect, Sheriff Perry, unless we're dealing with dabblers, your man may already be dead—"

Agent Ex-Mobster spoke over the smaller agent. "Don't mind my partner. He's had some experience infiltrating cults, so he might be a bit biased."

"I hope he's wrong and we're dealing with dabblers," Perry said.

At full daylight, Perry led the combined units north to Holderness. Booker traveled in the company of the Feds, on his promise that he'd stay back in the relative safety of their van.

However, the local judge had gone hiking in Heminway Forest and didn't come back to his chambers till nearly nightfall. Complicating Perry's efforts to quickly obtain a warrant, it also inspired Fletcher to theorize the judge had joined the cult.

They approached with no sirens, no beacons, nothing to alert Jaquith and his people, in case they spooked the cult as the law followed the drive to the house. The windows of the old Victorian blazed with light, as if the inhabitants were hosting a dinner party. A row of cars, some luxury and some utility vehicles, stood parked before the building.

"Yea, though I walk through the valley of death, I shall fear no evil," Perry said and killed the motor of his squad car. To Fletcher, in the shotgun seat, he added, "Remember, no heroics. You got the back-up team. I'm leading the forward team."

Fletcher looked up from double checking the clip in his sidearm. "Frank, if this is because I've been uppity the last few days, I was doing my darnedest to help."

"I could tell, and I appreciate it, but I'd rather you kept back in case things go sideways for me," said Perry. With that, he got out, the other officers emerging from the van that had followed them. The squad, along with a few agents, approached the front door as Perry banged on it. No one answered at first.

The door rattled before opening. An older man, clearly a servant or at the least a lookout, emerged. "Mr. Jaquith is engaged, but I can inform him that—"

Perry held up the warrant. "We're authorized to search the property on the suspicion that your boss is holding a kidnapped man, and less importantly that he has stolen property."

The old retainer did not budge, giving Perry a look of shocked surprise that didn't convince him. "Kidnapped man? Stolen property? If anything, Mr. Jaquith is a victim of you and your goon squad harassing him."

"We have the testimony of a kid he hired to help kidnap this man," Perry said, taking a photograph of Crowley from his shirt pocket.

The man blocking their way eyed the photo. "I haven't seen a man who looks like that, not around here." But he quailed back from the door.

"If you've got nothing to hide, why not let us have a look-see anyway?" Agent Ex-Mobster questioned. "The sooner we look, the sooner we're out of your hair."

"Very well, but the master won't like it," the servant said.

They passed into a foyer that opened onto a parlor on the left and a dining room on the right. The parlor betrayed signs of guests of the upper-crust variety: half empty wine glasses and brandy snifters on glass coasters on the furniture. The remains of a light repast lay on the table in the dining room.

From the top of the staircase dominating the foyer, chanting filtered down from at least two floors above.

"I thought these types had their shindigs in the basement, if not out in the woods?" Agent Ex-Mobster asked.

"In the movies, they do. But these sorts will use any space that will fit their cohorts and purposes," Agent Crazy Professor replied.

"If there's anything this case has taught me, it's that fiction's more predictable than life," Perry reflected, mounting the staircase and beckoning the others to follow.

"Mr. Jaquith and his circle can't be disturbed!" the old retainer cried from the foot of the staircase.

"Not after he had a hand in disturbing an auction and kidnapping an unarmed man," Perry said, without a backward glance.

They reached the top floor, its long hallway lined with doors. A single step at one end led to a door standing ajar, the chanting emerging from behind it. Now more distinct, with its words audible but in some language Perry didn't understand.

"Police! We have a warrant!" Perry called, pushing the door open and mounting the stairs behind it, stun gun in hand.

The chanting faltered but did not stop. Perry emerged through an opening in the floor into the attic space. A voice that sounded like Jaquith's intoned a litany of sorts over the chanting:

*"We have no hands but your many limbs,*
*We have no eyes but your many eyes.*
*Efface our past and give the light of What Was.*
*Envelop our present and make of it yours.*
*Enlighten our future that we might know the Way."*

Candles in brackets hanging from the rafters lit the chamber, the air heavy with incense and a scent like dry leaves mixed with burning tobacco, only stronger. Figures in hooded robes stood in a circle around something in the middle of the floor. Tapestries woven with strange geometric designs similar to the ones traced on Waite's body hung tacked to the underside of the roof.

Jaquith, standing in the midst of the circle, peered past the chanting minions. "Perry? How dare you intrude my sacred space! You have no right or need to be here!"

"A warrant based on one of your little friends' testimony and the kidnapping I witnessed says we do," Perry said, coming closer, trying not to breathe too deeply.

The minion closest to Perry shuffled aside, opening the circle, hood falling back to reveal the face of a once respected professor who had fallen on hard times after her colleagues had mocked her research. An altar draped in a plasticized black sheet stood in the middle of the cultists' circle. On top of it lay Crowley, naked, with his ankles bound and wrists tied to his thighs. Three long-healed parallel scars on his chest showed livid in the candlelight, and he lay as still as a carving of a medieval knight on an old tomb. The book at the center of all this lay open beside his head.

Jaquith raised a dagger with a serrated blade above Crowley's head. The priest, the offering, twitched, but made no attempt to rise or break free. "You've come too late," Jaquith gloated. "We're inviting the Key to open the Way."

"I think I came just on time. Now drop the knife, give me the book, and let that man go." Perry ordered.

"Or you'll do what? Your guns don't frighten me when I have the aegis of something far more powerful," Jaquith proclaimed, reaching to caress the pages of the book with his fingertips.

"It's a book. It words contain only as much power as you have," Perry said. The candlelight seemed to grow brighter, halos of strange colors appearing around the flames.

"It's not the words, but that which the words summon," Jaquith retorted, lowering the blade toward Crowley's chest. The knife moved more slowly than Perry expected. *That leafy scent,* he realized. *Salvia,* he thought, recognizing it from a synthetic sample the DEA had presented in a training. Despite his trembling hands, despite the lensing of his sight lines, Perry pulled the trigger on the taser. The dart flew, weird light glinting on the wires connecting it to the cartridge inside, then hit Jaquith in the chest. The man staggered, dropping the dagger before he fell to his knees, shaking.

"Yog will chastise you!" - "The Guardian shall reach through the gate to strike you!" - "Yog shall not be shamed!" the minions cried. But they scattered nonetheless, some retreating to the edges of the room, some trying to rush for the stairs, only for the less affected of Perry's team to catch them.

Perry reached for the radio mic on his shoulder, keying it on by touch. "They're in the attic!" Overhead, where he should have seen the inside of the roof peak, the substance of the world unfolded like the petals of some dark flower. Beyond, reached infinite blackness picked out with pinpricks of light, from the midst of which emerged a glowing whorl-shaped mass in green and violet and other colors he could not name. Long tendrils reached from the whorl toward the world, toward the roof, toward the devotees in the attic, reaching into the heads of some among the cultists. In the midst of the mass, eyes the size of planets gazed out, the three-lobed pupils within pulsating. Chills ran through Perry's nerves, twining into his brain, making it scream and try to crawl into his brain stem.

The room echoed with footsteps booming on the stairs as the second team rushed up. Perry hobbled to the window in the gable and struck it with the butt of his stun gun, cracking the glass. He struck harder with his forearm, shattering the panes, letting the drug-heavy air out and the fresh air in.

"Careful, something nasty's in the incense," he shouted.

The minions surged toward the officers but could not match their strength or number. Perry dropped his Taser, nervelessly. Fletcher knelt behind Jaquith to cuff him. Perry pulled together the shreds of his awareness to untie Crowley. The priest did not move, but he felt warm to the touch. *Still alive,* Perry thought, lifting Crowley to his shoulder in a fireman's sling, limping down the stairs. He felt Crowley's heart beat against the angle of his neck, fast, even a bit shallow, but assuring him that his friend would live. He could swear the scars on the priest's chest had glowed in the candlelight.

Perry staggered out into the night, the world shifting around him, the stars overhead wheeling and casting streaks echoed by the flashing lights of the emergency vehicles. Some of the cult minions struggled against the officers escorting them. Others fled into the woods, a K-9 officer and their human partner rushing after them. Armed with a ritual knife, one cultist tried sneaking up on Agent Crazy Professor, in the act of escorting another cultist. Instead, Agent Ex-Mobster tackled the blade-wielding cultist. Two EMTs approached Perry, reaching for Crowley. A third figure followed them, surrounded by a violet glow, taking something from his shoulders.

Booker came closer, removing his duster and draping it over Crowley's form. "Yer safe now," he told the sheriff. "But I'd let these guys check you out."

"No contest," Perry said, letting the EMTs take Crowley, then relaxing as their colleagues examine him.

## Chapter 7

The visual hallucinations abated by the following morning, allowing Perry to appear at Jaquith's hearing that afternoon. Jaquith's lawyer must have advised him to plead guilty to his involvement in Waite's murder as well as Crowley's kidnapping and the theft of *The Book of the Ways*. That didn't stop the prisoner from glaring daggers in the general direction of Perry and of Jane Waite, who sat together in the spectators' gallery, until the bailiff led him out of the courtroom.

"I should have suspected Jaquith all along," Jane told Perry as they walked down the courthouse steps.

"It would have made sense. He was one of the early bidders," the sheriff said.

"He also tried raising the bid to absurd levels. I doubt he could have amassed that kind of money without liquidating a lot of property," she informed him.

He resisted the urge to ask, *"Why didn't you tell me sooner?"* and instead said, "Must've been a heck of a red flag."

"It was, but we'd dealt with obsessive collectors before. I didn't think much of it at the time. Hindsight is 20-20 and all that, right?"

"Don't be too harsh on yourself, Jane, not at a time like this, not after what you went through this weekend."

At around the same time, according to a call he received later, the hospital released Crowley. Shaken but showing no other sign of physical injury aside from the scrapes and bruises he'd received during the abduction, the priest had orders to consult a psychologist.

Crowley, now clad in a shirt and dress slacks borrowed from Fletcher, sat in Perry's office. The book, in an evidence bag, sat on the desktop. "Why would they try to sacrifice you? Outside of getting back at me for starting the whole investigation," the sheriff asked.

Going through his valise, collected from his green Taurus now in the impound lot behind the precinct, Crowley glanced up. "I'm a person of some authority, and that makes me a more potent sacrifice."

"Are you serious?"

"It was a custom in some magickal systems that involved sacrifice. A child, a virgin, a person of importance, all offer more potent propitiation. At least according to Frazer's descriptions of some alleged practices in Northeastern Europe."

"Please don't tell me you were willing to die back there," Perry said.

Crowley wagged his head. "I was willing to offer my life to protect others, to keep them from suffering at the hands of these people. Even if it meant being sacrificed to a non-existent god by people who chose me for being in the wrong place at the wrong time."

"'Greater love hath no man, if he lay down his life', but to let cultists kill you?"

"I wasn't thrilled by the prospect, but I accepted it as my fate.

"So what happens to the book?" Crowley asked.

"Right now, we're holding it until Booker arrives with proof of sale."

That evening the Texan arrived at the precinct, bringing the bill of sale on Donnell's letterhead. "I gather the book's state's evidence right now. But I paid up to Jane Waite, so beyond that, it belongs to me."

"We dodged a major number of bullets. Jaquith plead guilty and waived his right to a trial. So for legal intents and purposes, it's yours," Perry said. "And to be perfectly frank, I can't get this book out of my precinct soon enough."

Booker nodded, then looked to Crowley. "For what it's worth, for the trouble this book has caused you, Padre, you can consider it yours." He held out the small tome. "It's better if you can put it some place where no one will disturb it."

The priest took a pair of black leatherette driving gloves from his valise, slipping them on before accepting the book. "I appreciate this. My colleagues in Rome will put this away where it won't likely be touched again."

"You're sure it won't get torched?"

Crowley tucked the book into his valise, covering it with a black silk cloth and laying a crucifix on top of it. "I can promise you that won't happen." He closed the valise and locked it. "If *anything*, burning is the last thing that should be done with this. People have burned potentially cursed or occult objects, and their situation grew worse afterwards."

The door opened. Fletcher stepped into the office, his face grave. "Chief? There's a call parked on your line. The warden at North Central Correctional needs to speak to you."

Perry reached for the receiver, picking it up and keying the outside line. "If you gents can excuse me, I'd better take this." Booker and Crowley looked at each other and stepped into the hallway.

*"Sherriff Perry? I'm calling to inform you that Frazer Jaquith has passed away."*

Perry hesitated before asking. "What was the cause of death?" An image popped into his head, of that thing from beyond reaching down to strangle Jaquith in his cell. If he hadn't picked a fight with the wrong prisoner and lost.

*"He garroted himself in his cell this morning with his pants."*

"I'm sorry to hear that."

*"There's more. He chalked some kind of symbols on the walls of his cell,"* the warden added.

"Don't tell me: they look like some kind of weird geometric designs."

*"I'm afraid so."*

"Thanks for informing me." Perry hung up the phone.

"Bad news?" Crowley asked, stepping back into the room.

"You might want to offer a requiem Mass for Jaquith, even if he's anything but one of your flock."

"If there's anyone who needs my prayers, it's him."

"Even after he kidnapped you? Padre, you're a stronger man than Perry and me put together," Booker said, raising an eyebrow in surprise as he looked at Crowley.

"Especially the guy who kidnapped me. I serve a God Who forgave the people who crucified Him. If I'm to serve Him properly, I need to do likewise."

With that, Crowley set his fedora onto his head and walked out of Perry's office, taking the valise with him. He wouldn't swear to it, but to Perry's senses, the air in the room cleared of something heavy and the lights on the ceiling shone brighter. Probably a trick of his mind.

*For Robert Hayes, librarian; Martin J. Donnelly, auctioneer; and Thomas Broadbent, Lovecraft aesthete*

*Written July 11 – August 20th, 2018. Tewksbury, Massachusetts and Providence, Rhode Island.*

Bibliography

Joshi, S.T.. *I Am Providence: The Life And Times of H.P. Lovecraft,* Hippocampus Press, 2011

Lovecraft, H.P.. "The Dunwich Horror", in *H.P. Lovecraft: The Complete Fiction (Barnes and Noble Collectible Edition)*, Barnes and Noble, 2011

—, August Derleth, Donald Wandrei, editors, *Selected Letters I: 1911-1924*, Arkham House Publishing, 1965

Peterson, Nate, editor, *The Starry Wisdom Library: The Catalogue of the Greatest Occult Book Auction of All Time,* P.S. Publishing, 2011

*Necronomicon: The Book of Hell,* Dir. Marcelo Shapces, Barakacine, 2018

# Bring The Fire

## Michael O'Brien

"It looks like an extremely overdone clock," Naomi observed. "Planning to keep time on other planets?"

"It's simply a curiosity, a hobby," answered her uncle Richard. "You spend all day playing World of Elves or whatever. This is what I do with my free time."

She inclined her head over to the table of old books he was failing to subtly block from her view. "Are those diagrams part of your project? They look old. I mean, really old."

"They're simply reference material, Naomi. I'm enjoying giving this project a classic look. Now, that's as much as I'm going to indulge you tonight. You wouldn't understand half of this anyway. Go back to the house and log on to your orcs, and eat something if you want. I will probably be here in the workshop until late."

Reluctantly Naomi stopped slouching against the rough-paneled wall of the workshop. "I don't understand why you aren't working on something more interesting than a reproduction of an antique clock. With a dozen patented gadgets in your portfolio…"

"Which not a single person in the world has heard of, besides the engineers who use them in boring corporate consumer products. One day, young lady, you'll learn that you've got to spend some of your life doing things to please yourself. Otherwise, you become maladjusted. Now I won't tell you again: back to the house."

Naomi sulked her way out the door and heard the deadbolt slide home behind her. Oddly, her mood improved the moment she reached the house and she practically bounded up to her room.

She had a date with her desktop computer. It had nothing to do with elves or orcs, but quite a bit to do with the tiny wireless camera she'd wedged into a knothole in Uncle Richard's workshop. She shoved aside a few Overwatch game character figurines decorating her desk and plugged the receiver into a port on a powered USB hub.

Soon she was grabbing images from the device's video stream, trying to improve their clarity in Photoshop. "Enhance. Zoom seventeen to twenty-three. Enhance," she muttered wryly to herself. Uncle Richard continued to fuss and fiddle with the device, making frequent reference to the books and charts piled on the side table. A man of medium height with sandy hair and a bit more weight than was fashionable, he peered at his work through eyeglass frames in the latest European style.

As near as she could tell, the books he examined had a great deal of Greek and Latin text next to diagrams of the clock-like device her uncle had been fiddling with for the last month and a half. Naomi could recognize the text, but spoke neither language, and the image resolution was barely good enough to guess at the lettering. However, she did recognize large astrological symbols that had been reused in one of her favorite anime series.

The symbol for the Moon appeared above a lengthy passage next to what might be an ornately engraved disk or lens. And one for Mars, yep… Mercury… Jupiter… Maybe Uncle Richard really was planning to tell time on other planets. The intricately geared box he'd begrudgingly showed her did resemble the orrery she'd seen in a science museum once. You could spin its dial and the complicated model of the solar system would spin and revolve, showing you the positions of the planets on any given day in history. Uncle's "clock" had a lot more dials than the orrery, though. The top of the clock sprouted a dizzying array of rods, levers, mirrors, and prisms of inscrutable function.

Someone knocked on the workshop door, and Richard looked startled and expectant simultaneously. He peeked through the curtain, pulled the deadbolt, and opened the door. The man on the other side was tall, with a heavy dark beard and an aspect of rough business about him. His clothes were clean but weather-beaten. He looked furtive and carried a parcel under one arm. Fascinated,

Naomi thought that her little remote camera subterfuge couldn't have been better timed.

Richard ushered the other man in quickly. "You have it, then? I didn't expect you to get it so quickly, Mister…"

"It's still John Doe to you. It's just easier that way. And yes, once I'd tracked down Kemidov, negotiations went quickly." 'Doe' cocked his chin at the parcel. "The book was little more than a curious relic to him."

"Well, that's wonderful. Let me get you your money."

"About that…"

Richard stopped short and raised an eyebrow at his visitor. "Yes…"

"It'll be an extra five thousand, I'm afraid. Kemidov bargained well. The book wasn't precious to him, but he could tell I wanted it pretty bad."

A short silence followed, then Richard barked out a short laugh. "I'll tell you what, John. You've done such a good job, you'll have your extra five. I don't even care what your reasons are." He pulled a lockbox from the shadows under a table and extracted several wads of cash, which he handed to his visitor.

'Doe' eyed the cashbox. "Well, if your budget is that flexible…"

Richard reached casually into his jacket pocket, pointing whatever was inside at the visitor. "Someone once said, 'Large in the purse is not soft in the head.' Take your money and behave yourself. There may be other lucrative work… later."

'Doe' hesitated, then he smirked. "Fine." He set the book on another table, waving his free hand at all the tools, gears, and frames scattered about. "Have fun with your clock-making." He walked out. Richard slid home the deadbolt on the door.

Naomi's uncle carried the parcel over to the best light in the workshop, which by no accident was close to the camera she'd concealed. He unwrapped the parcel slowly. "The last book of the *Codex Astromechanisums*…" he breathed. "It's real." Naomi could see clearly as he turned several pages. "And soon… the world will know."

Naomi decided she didn't like the expression on his face. She couldn't completely identify it… but the image kept her up that night.

“Hey, Booker, I think you’re going to want to look at this.”

Jake Booker looked up irritably from his tablet. While his heart was committed to the Booker Foundation’s cause, recovering the world’s lost literary treasures, his mind sometimes had to spend time managing the fortune he’d made in oil and gas. People he trusted to do their jobs weren’t doing them well enough and he resented having to deal with that, even through a stack of intermediaries. Wasn’t that what they were supposed to be for?

“I’m busy, Chris.”

Chris Blaine waved a tablet at him. “I guarantee this is more interesting. They aren’t very good pictures, but they’re good enough.”

Booker flipped through the images on the tablet. Recognition slowly dawned on him. Booker was an educated man, and knew much more of the world than fossil fuels. “Tell me this isn’t what it looks like.”

The young blond man took a seat without asking. “Well, we think it looks like intact, clearly-labeled diagrams and procedures for an Antikythera Device.” Booker had seen the original in a museum in Athens, resting there after its recovery in 1901 from two thousand years underwater. That environment hadn’t been kind, and much of the mechanism was corroded or missing. Experts had since reconstructed much of the device using advanced imaging techniques, and created various working models according to different hypotheses, but the undeniable fact was that the Greeks had constructed a clockwork computer before the birth of Christ.

“But it isn’t,” Chris continued. “The dials are different, and the mechanism isn’t quite the same as the one from the shipwreck. Plus, it seems to have attachments for peripherals… here, look at the lens-like objects on these levers. We think the instructions describe ways of producing different alignments of the lenses.”

“What for?”

“You got me, boss. A lot of the books’ content isn’t readable from these pictures, and what we can see of the text seems to assume you know what you plan to do with the thing.”

Booker leaned back in his chair. “All right, then. And the point of all this?”

"We got these pictures from a young lady named Naomi Brandt. Her email said she was familiar with our work, and that her uncle had recently come into possession of a book that seems to be the last volume of instructions. The complete set must have valuable information on methods for constructing devices like this. And the books might indirectly unlock some of the mysteries of the actual Antikythera Mechanism. Basically, she thinks the Booker Foundation would want these."

"Do you think so?"

"Without a doubt."

"So do I. My schedule is full until the Second Coming, but you can head on out there. You've got the kind of boy-band face a young lady's likely to appreciate, and maybe that'll help with the negotiations. Get my assistant to set up your travel and accommodations and whatever else." Booker started to get back to his laptop world of PDF files and digital surveys.

"There's one more thing, boss."

Booker looked up as though he'd half-expected there to be. "Yeah?"

"Miss Brandt was very concerned about something she didn't want to put in the email. She said she thinks we should have the books… whether her uncle agrees or not."

Booker closed his eyes and put his hand to his forehead. "Oh. It's one of those."

"Yeah."

"All right. This is your notice that, if you or Miss Brandt are caught doing things you shouldn't, the Booker Foundation will disavow any knowledge of your actions. Now get out of here before I self-destruct in five seconds via paperwork overload."

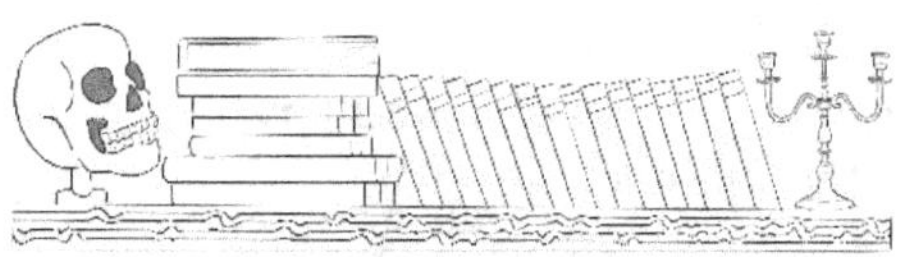

"Thanks for meeting me, Miss Brandt." They sat in a secluded corner of a Starbucks, taking each other's measure over strong coffees and iced pound cake. Naomi was a slight fourteen-year-old with black hair cut in a bob, wearing a t-shirt displaying a Japanese anime character seemingly named *Madoka Magica.*

Chris' knowledge of that particular art form didn't go farther than fragments of his nieces' encyclopedic knowledge. Naomi looked cute and precocious, and Chris suspected that it would be a hard day for her when she learned real life didn't work out like a kids' action romance.

Chris had on a nice suit making him look respectable and bland. Naomi decided that while he was somewhat attractive, he also looked like he was planning to sell her a car. While she wondered what kind of impression he thought he was making on her, it didn't matter that much. She had plenty of other things weighing a lot heavier on her mind.

"Naomi's fine," she replied to his greeting. "And you're Chris?"

"Correct. I have to say I wasn't expecting to be so furtive about this. I'd prefer to be meeting with your uncle. He may not think of selling those texts now, but I hope to change his mind. The Foundation has formidable resources, if not infinite ones. We're usually able to work out an open, mutually satisfactory deal with rare book owners." He felt just a little dirty saying that. Sometimes the previous possessors were reasonably satisfied. Sometimes not so much. But they didn't get their books back, either way. Jake Booker could play hardball, and Chris hated to get a kid like Naomi involved.

She stared into her coffee for a moment. "First of all… I'm not entirely sure he has the legal right to some of the books. Someone came by the other night and I don't think this guy was a reference librarian… you get what I'm saying?" He gave her a cautious nod, and she barely restrained a smirk. Based on the rumors about the Booker Foundation, she'd been expecting someone half-jungle adventurer and half-British superspy. Instead she got… well… a book-seller. Uncle Richard would eat him alive, given the chance.

Naomi continued her spiel. "And anyway, look at these disks. They attach to the main section with rods and levers. From what little I can decipher out of my images, the disks are made from rare metals. I mean, nothing too exotic for an experienced engineer to find. Like, nothing government-restricted, for example, but Wikipedia says they'd still be pretty expensive. Luckily the device doesn't require too much of those materials, because the disks' inside circles are almost as thin as foil."

Chris was feeling a bit bored, though it didn't do to show it. He hadn't even been much for LEGO sets as a kid. "Okay. And?"

"Well… the engraving on them… it's incredibly detailed. I didn't even know you could do that kind of fine, precise work two thousand years ago. That would have been the really expensive part… at least before modern tools and methods."

"So it's pretty."

Naomi began feeling impatient, and it showed. Did Chris not get it? Her uncle had come into possession of several impossible books and this guy acted like it happened to him every day before breakfast. "I'm serious about this, buddy. I didn't have time for much, but I managed to get into his workshop a couple times for a few minutes and get pictures of the disk diagrams. They show a bunch of possible configurations, though I'm unsure for what."

Chris interrupted. "You said in your messages that the workshop was locked. How did you get in?"

Her look grew more impatient. "Let's just say I got in, okay? I'm not stupid or helpless. Now, here's some color printouts of my pics. You can see these six disks are marked with astrological signs, but these two are marked with signs I haven't been able to identify by searching online."

Chris took a deep breath and looked at her notations. She was right, something was interesting about these, but what exactly? "Well… I've seen enough arcane texts to remember these signs are used in alchemy as well as astrology. But while your labeling system seems familiar, I can't place it. What the heck's an Usagi? Or an Ami? And this one's marked Rei, and Makoto here, and then Minako, and Hotaru…?"

She rolled her eyes. "Oh, god. Those signs are the classic astrological symbols for the Moon, Mercury, Mars, Jupiter, Venus, and Saturn. When I see those symbols, I think of characters from a Japanese TV show, okay? The characters from *Sailor Moon* represent the planets of the solar system and get their secret abilities from their planet. Sailor Mercury had water powers, Sailor Mars had fire spells, Venus had charisma and charm, et cetera."

"Ah. Wait—yes, that's why they're familiar! My nieces loved to argue over the subbed and dubbed versions of that show. Maybe they still do. I ended up having to watch at least a dozen episodes in both versions, while they each made their case."

He'd had to listen to hours of their argument. Was every girl under sixteen obsessed with this stuff? With Naomi's smug, superior look getting under his skin, he dredged his memory for additional trivia. "So, obviously, the symbols Haruka and Michiru are Uranus and Neptune—at least in the original Japanese version. Weren't those two cousins or something?"

Naomi snorted. "Yep, something like that. You know more than I'd have thought. You sure your nieces were *making* you watch the show? Anyway, all this is exactly what has me worried."

Chris shook his head. "Cartoon superheroes are making you worried?"

"No, no, about the list of planets in these books! Great Cthulhu, did you not learn anything in school? These copies may be a few centuries old, but like I said, the original *Codex Astromechanisums* was compiled two thousand years ago. And we have no records that suggest anyone knew about Uranus and Neptune back then. Modern science didn't know about them until the eighteenth and nineteenth centuries. You need advanced telescopes to find them and Newton didn't even publish his treatise on optics until 1704."

"Lots of information's been lost over the centuries," Chris sounded less than fully convinced of his own argument. "That's rather the point of Mr. Booker's organization. Hell, until a few decades ago when they scooped some brass gears from the bottom of the Mediterranean, science was sure no one had clockwork computers two thousand years ago…"

"So you see my concern."

Chris nodded slowly. Despite his skepticism, Naomi's story was piquing his curiosity and he found himself taking her more seriously than he had at first glance. "All right. Clearly this device has layers of mysterious science behind it. I still don't see why we can't just try to buy the books from your uncle when he's done making his toy."

Naomi sat back, crossing her arms. "Ever watch *Mythbusters*? The show where they try to replicate urban legends?"

"Yes, I've heard of it. But some of us have things to do besides watch television all the time." Now it was Chris' turn to feel impatient again. This girl's brain didn't seem to contain much more than pop culture and Internet factoids.

"In 2004 and 2006, the Mythbusters tried to replicate the legendary heat ray of the Greek scientist Archimedes. Supposedly he used this invention to set fire to an invading navy, defeating them effortlessly. But despite sunny weather and an impressive array of mirrors, the Mythbusters were unable to make a test boat hot enough to do any real damage."

Impatience drained away as the hair on Chris' neck stood up. Suddenly everything was falling together. "Go on…"

"This was one of the blurrier pictures, but the heading at the top of the page is big enough to work out, and to put through Google Translate." Naomi pulled another color printout from her stack. It was clearly zoomed-in and filtered, but Chris had no trouble using his clues to figure out what the name written with Greek characters starting with 'A' had to be.

"I didn't dare put this in the email. You'd have laughed. I can only do so much with Photoshop filters, but it's pretty clear this page also has the Greek words for 'fire' and 'distance.' My uncle's held rather muffled conversations with shady visitors before this. I don't know if this thing really will work… or even if it's possible… but I don't think Uncle Richard is building a cigarette lighter. I don't like the look in his eyes when he works on it and I want those books in someone else's hands before he finishes."

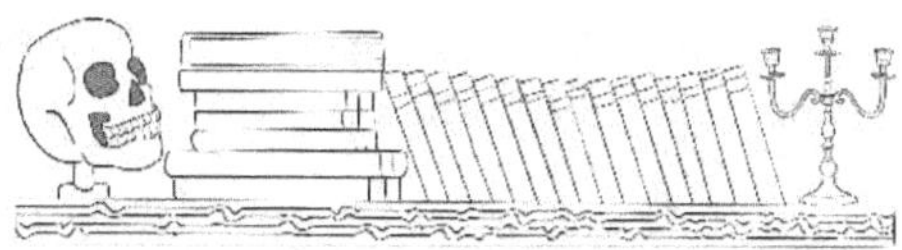

Darkness was falling as Chris stood next to the workshop and Naomi knelt before the lock. Chris kept glancing nervously from the main house to Naomi's work. "How does a fourteen-year-old know how to pick a top-quality deadbolt lock?"

"YouTube. I have an enquiring mind. Once, I found a whole series of videos on getting through locked doors. I don't know if I got my curiosity from my parents, since they've been gone for years, but Uncle Richard has plenty of it. So it's probably—ah ha!—somewhere in my genetic code." She twisted the knob and pushed the door open. "That was easy. That lock's usually a little stickier when it's been sitting for a while. Oh, don't worry about the lights, Uncle Richard often leaves them on. But it probably means he'll be back later tonight, so we shouldn't dawdle."

Chris followed her in, feeling a bit swept-along. He tried to remember if he'd been this self-assured at her age. Naomi's mind jumped from concept to concept like a chain of checker captures, while he tended to think slowly and carefully—with an occasional spark of insight. Still, it wasn't easy to concentrate in here. This workshop resembled a mad inventor's cave of wonders. Intricate, partially finished miniature mechanisms filled rows of shelves. A table on one side groaned under the weight of a stack of old tomes gone crumbly with age. The very nature of his job made Chris want to rush over and examine those books to see which were the ones he'd come for, and to see what else might be worth a negotiation. But enticing as the books were, they could not keep his attention from the enigmatic device in the center of the workshop, sitting under the clearest light. The thing did look like a large brass mechanical clock at first glance, maybe three inches by four by five, with that array of articulated mirrors and supports. He noted that all eight of the disks were in place. Semi-precious gemstones decorated one side of the box, a single stone each on an inscribed arc. Their colors made it clear the gem at the bottom was the golden topaz Sun, while brown Mercury was succeeded by pearlescent Venus, cool blue aquamarine Earth and Moon in moonstone, gleaming red garnet Mars, agate Jupiter and Saturn, and Uranus and Neptune in turquoise. Inscribed rings surrounded Saturn, though there were no signs of them around the other outer planets.

"Your uncle's an artist," Chris said in awe. "I doubt it was necessary to make it so pretty."

Naomi was less favorably impressed. She pointed across the room at a wood-and-cloth dummy standing before a steel partition. The dummy was blackened with fire and parts had burned away, while even the steel behind it was scorched. "I didn't think he'd made it this far on the project. If he's not finished, he must be damn close."

Chris wasn't naïve enough to feel surprise about that kind of language from a teenager. Even had he been, the morbid display held his attention until he consciously forced his gaze away. "I can't deny your uncle's device is mesmerizing, but I'm not here to look at gizmos."

Naomi looked nervous. "Don't you think you'll want the device too? For research?"

"We aren't engineers, the Booker Foundation deals in the written word. I mean, it wouldn't surprise me if the Boss knew someone who knew someone… still. Your uncle may have picked up these books under dubious circumstances, but the device he built is clearly his property." Chris pulled a pair of cotton gloves from a pocket and donned them before gently turning pages with a pair of short forceps, marveling at the contents. It didn't take long to see he hadn't wasted his trip out here. Booker would absolutely want these. Even Dr. Cuinnsey would probably want a look, despite her focus on Celtic writings.

He looked up for a moment. Naomi clearly wanted to pick up the device, but was also clearly afraid to. "Hey, how are you going to explain this to your uncle?" he asked.

"I figure we make it look like someone broke in. Maybe we can even somehow leave clues to suggest the culprit was the John Doe who brought him the last sections of the *Codex*. He'll find out soon enough that your Foundation has them, won't he?"

"Yeah, but we have all sorts of lawyers for those situations. I doubt he can prove prior ownership. Maybe he'd even be willing to drop the matter if we spread hints in the right ears about a few well-compensated lecture tours and a TED Talk or two. He could have crowds of scientists hanging on his every word, maybe even an award or three. Anything's possible!

"But none of that's going to happen while we stand around here. Let's, ah, borrow these books now and sort out the details later." Chris bent down to peer at an intricate chart that included the planetary symbols at the top and cryptic squiggled writing below.

Right then, a key rattled in the deadbolt and the door opened before either Naomi or Chris could move. Richard Brandt walked in, shut and locked the door behind him, then looked up and registered their presence. His face flushed and his jaw clenched. "What—in the hell—is this? Naomi, who is this man? What are you two doing in here? You—you are in more trouble than you can imagine."

Naomi tried an ingratiating young voice on her uncle. "Oh, Uncle Richard! This is my librarian friend, Chris. I talk to him all the time when I'm checking out real books instead of electronic ones, and he got really excited when I told him about your super old books. We were hoping to find you here, but when we knocked, the door was not bolted! So we came in. It's okay, he just wanted to take a look!"

Uncle Richard wasn't buying it. "The door to my workshop was locked, young lady. I can see by his gloves that your friend knows how to handle a precious book, but you shouldn't be in here, and you shouldn't bring your… friend." He clearly didn't believe Chris was a librarian, which was a bit ironic under the circumstances.

Chris tried a gambit from his end. "You have my apologies, Mr. Brandt. Miss Naomi assured me there would be no trouble." Her eyes flashed *thanks for throwing me under the bus* at him, but he tried sounding placatory to them both. "I'm sure she didn't understand how upset you'd be. We'll certainly leave, but I must say, your collection is incredible. I can think of a dozen libraries, mine included, that would pay remarkable sums to acquire these books. I've never even heard of this, this *Codex Astromechanisums* before. And I'm bewildered by that beautiful object over there."

The flattery had at least a little effect. "Young man, I'll make history with that device."

"I know what that is, Uncle," shouted Naomi. "I can see your target over there. That's some kind of heat ray. You're going to blow up tanks and planes with it?"

Richard looked shocked. "Naomi—why in heaven would I want to do that?"

"I heard you. You said that soon, the world would know what you'd created."

"Why—why, yes, of course. Look—look here." He laid the device flat on the table so the array pointed down the room at the dummy. Now the gemstones were on top, and he depressed the topaz gem briefly. Bright light came from the other end of the device, bouncing among mirrors and prisms and gleaming from metal lenses. Pieces swung along arcs, spun in place, and angled themselves as if alive. The effect was dazzling.

"Sunlight was the original source, of course," Richard boasted. "I've substituted a small arc lamp so one need not worry about clouds or darkness." He hid the device's top behind the curve of his free hand while tapping another gem. "I don't think either of you needs to know all the operating details. But look!"

The metal lenses aligned, the engraved tracery upon them glowing incandescent with the light reflected and amplified by the mirrors and prisms. Naomi and Chris felt a wave of heat and watched in fascination as an untouched spot on the dummy brightened and burst into flame. In moments, the burning section had disintegrated and burned away. The metal plate behind the remains of the dummy started glowing with heat before Richard tapped a gem concealed by his hand again. The dazzling light remained, but the steel started cooling as the effect of heat vanished.

"See!" Naomi crowed. "I knew it! It's a heat ray."

"Maybe for Archimedes," Richard replied with just a bit of smugness. "But with some adjustments it could be many more things. A heat source to drive steam turbines or to produce superheated jet engine air via solar power! Perhaps one could even design a thruster for long-distance space probes, the efficiency of its energy conversion is astonishing!" His face fell. "Of course, in production it won't be as pretty as my prototype. We can replace the original gearing with components the ancient Greeks could barely have dreamed of. I'm sure it will end up computer-controlled and stuck in a boring casing of brushed titanium. But it will change the world."

Chris broke the silence first. "Mr. Brandt, I'll get to the point. I'm here because I had to see the books you used to make this. I represent an organization interested in the world's rarest books. They don't usually deal in exotic artifacts, but when the books and the other treasures show up together, sometimes they have to work out special arrangements. We've got connections, and those connections have connections. Let us work together. We want your books, to be sure, but we can also help you reap the rewards you deserve for this… brilliance, if I may say it."

"I'm so sorry, Uncle Brandt," said Naomi. "You were really scaring me. I only figured out bits of what you were doing, I wish you would have told me more. Or maybe I wish I'd figured out nothing at all, considering the awful things I've thought about you lately. I was so wrong about you," she finished miserably.

"These tools can destroy nations," Richard said thoughtfully. "I shouldn't be surprised when they destroy trust. Perhaps it would be better to turn it over to people with more wisdom, or more caution. I suppose I would not mind a little fame and fortune in return."

The three of them gazed at the device, each deep in their own thoughts.

"Well, I'm sure that toy will make someone a very rich man," John Doe said. Chris, Naomi, and Richard stepped back, startled. Doe exited from behind the partition with a small machine pistol trained in their direction. "I'm sorry, but I couldn't stay back there much longer. It got a bit warm behind that plate."

"How—how long have you been back there?" Chris stuttered as he tried to assimilate the surprise and figure out how to react.

"Only a few minutes before you and the young lady broke in," Doe said smugly. "Got inside pretty much the same way, too, considering the sounds you were making with the lock. I was figuring out how to transport all this but barely had time to hide before you worked the door open. At least I moved faster than the two of you did when Richard came in."

"What do you want?" Naomi's Uncle asked with resignation.

"Just what Mister Chris here wants, the books, and your prototype. I was just going to sell it as a weapon, but I don't doubt the Chinese or North Koreans would be fascinated by the other applications you mentioned as well. I'm going to be wealthy enough that being on the run from a government or two will be completely worth it."

Suddenly, Richard lunged for the device. "Not if I can stop…" but before his hands touched the gemstone controls, a controlled burst of three machine pistol rounds smacked into his chest, and he dropped.

"Uncle!" Naomi shrieked. Putting her ear to his chest and lips, she then stood and aimed an incendiary glance of her own at Doe. "You goddam asshole, you didn't have to kill him!"

"Are you sure he's…" Chris started.

"Yes. No pulse, no breathing. Just like on all that television I watch," she snapped at him. He blushed and looked away.

"Now, did I understand correctly that neither of you knows how to operate this device?" Doe asked. Chris looked at Naomi questioningly, and she shook her head silently. "I see. That's probably just as well. I'm sure I can find someone to figure it out. You—you start collecting those books you were looking at. And, little girl, you will pick up the device and bring it to me while I decide if you'd be worth the trouble as a hostage."

"Fuck you!" she yelled. "Come over here and get it yourself and we'll see if you can keep your little gun aimed at us while you do it." The muzzle of the machine pistol swung to point at her.

Chris had begun to gingerly flip the pages of the *Codex* back over before he closed the cover, and stopped suddenly. He was looking at the planetary chart he and Naomi had bickered over. An idea tried to poke though the panic flooding his brain. *Silly space sailors. This is no time for me to be thinking of kids arguing dubs versus subs—wait.* "Naomi. Don't be a fool. Give him the ray gun."

"There. Is. No. Way. I. Will—"

Wishing for telepathy at this moment, Chris tried his best to get through to her. "Naomi, this isn't one of your Japanese television shows. Magic spells aren't going to help us now. You can imagine yourself a cartoon superhero in a cute red skirt all you want, but you are still going to have to give Mister Doe the ray. Don't you understand?" *Please understand.*

Her eyes suddenly widened. "Oh. You're right of course. I'm sorry, Mister, I'll give you the ray." She approached the device slowly, ever aware of the machine pistol. Very carefully, she lifted the device from the table, turned toward Doe… and with a lightning motion pressed the red gem in its engraved orbit. The wave of heat filled the room and Doe's gun glowed cherry red. As his charring and blistering hand dropped the ruined weapon, he instinctively lurched forward to catch it.

Doe's head moved into the burning shaft of light's path.

Neither Naomi nor Chris ever liked to think much about what happened immediately afterwards.

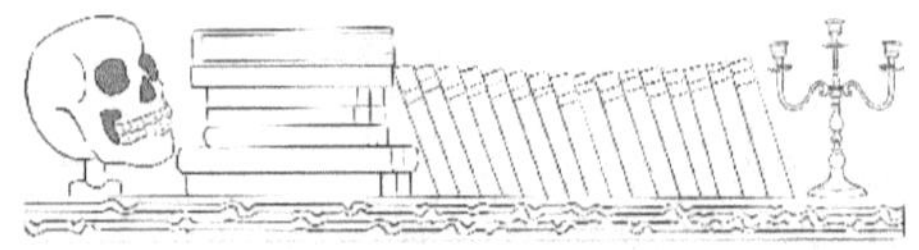

“So, we’ve got the book and the trinket?” Booker asked, feet in cowboy boots up on his desk as he questioned his operative.

“Yes, boss. Miss Brandt, as his closest heir, negotiated a very fair price.”

“Well, the books will go to the conservator and then the stacks, of course, but what are we going to do with a heat ray?”

“I couldn’t tell you, boss. Have it studied by Top Men?”

“Very funny.”

“Well, if it belonged to anyone after her uncle’s death, it would have belonged to Naomi. And she’d just as soon never lay eyes on it again. We certainly couldn’t leave it lying around. Besides, I have unshakeable faith in your ability to turn an adequately-ethical profit on the thing.”

“I refuse to comment. So how’s Miss Brandt doing?”

“Surprisingly well, considering the trauma of her uncle’s death and her guilt for believing such evil things about him. I believe she spent the next week divided between therapy and Netflix.”

“Poor girl. Where she’s going to go from here?”

“Well… we are always looking for Information Technology staff that will fit nicely with our sometimes… unorthodox procedures.”

“Mr. Blaine, she’s fourteen!”

“Call it an internship, maybe? I think she’d like it here. And we’d be lucky to have her.”

Booker examined his operative carefully. Awful concerned with the girl’s welfare. Platonically? It had damn well better be.

“Fine, Blaine. I’ll think about it. Now get out of—hey, no. You know, it was damn lucky she pressed the right button before John Doe ventilated her.”

“Oh, it wasn’t luck at all. Unless it’s lucky she was so quick on the uptake. I was looking at an astronomical diagram and I realized from the notations which planet had to be the trigger. So I told her to give the guy the ray in a way so Doe wouldn’t realize what I was saying.”

"Okay, so you figured it out. But how did she?"

"That's just it, boss, I did tell her which planet. Rei Hino is one of her anime heroines. When I mentioned her television habits, magic spells, and a red skirt, Naomi figured out I was telling her to 'give him the *Rei.*' One of my nieces prefers her foreign cartoons subtitled, and would be glad to explain that Rei Hino is the Japanese secret identity of the super-powered and red-skirted Sailor *Mars*."

# Under Cover

## Sean Michael O'Dea

**The Booker Foundation/Houston/Texas/10 AUG/1827hrs**
When a location looks this innocuous, I know things are going to go south. The narrow, two-story building sits a few blocks off Houston's historic Market Square, capping the end of a quiet commercial row. The red brick and pale mortar looks as though it has weathered hurricanes and sweltering heat for over a century. From the elm tree-shaded street outside, it could easily be an art gallery or trendy wine bar. But as I walk through the unmarked glass door, the smell of old parchment, worn leather, and oiled wood greets me. An array of Old World sofas, inviting leather chairs, and wooden bookcases fill the lobby. Each mahogany sentinels' shelves are decorated with old books of varying discoloration and wear that complement the antiques situated around the room. These have been meticulously placed under recessed lighting or above wall-mounted sconces so their accompanying placards can be easily read. The entire space is clean and, despite its cozy feel, is big enough to host a stuffy charity party.

"*Fancy place. Looks like you should have brought a pipe and a monocle,*" the female voice in my ear says. I feign a scratch so I can tuck my flesh-colored earbud snuggly into place and slightly adjust my fake glasses with an embedded hi-def camera and two wireless transmitters.

"Hi there. Welcome to the Booker Foundation. You must be Mr. Conway?" a young man greets me standing behind an executive desk at the top of the lobby. He's not Texan by his accent and his business casual attire screams thrift store chic.

Coupled with his bloodshot eyes, five o'clock shadow, and disheveled hair, I'm guessing he's a graduate student at some nearby university who spends way too much time staring at electronic databases.

"Please, call me Skip," I respond.

"I'll let Dr. Cuinnsey know you're here. One moment, please." The young man disappears through the paneled door behind him.

"Well, I guess we won't be seeing Mr. Booker today," I say.

"*No, you won't. Apparently, he's in China.*"

"Really? This appointment has been set for weeks."

"*Yup. And it looks like she's googling you now.*"

"Cool. What's she gonna see?" I ask. All operatives in our organization have the majority of their digital and public information erased. But, with enough advanced notice, we can also insert ourselves just about anywhere in the virtual world.

"*She'll see Acquisitions Manager at the Smithsonian.*"

"Yeah, I know, but what picture did you use?"

She snickers. "*An old DMV photo. It's awful.*"

"Thanks," I reply. I turn to scan the lobby again, this time paying attention to the walls. Two top-model surveillance cameras hang in opposite corners. A handful of motion sensors are cleverly concealed throughout the room. At both the front and paneled doors there are multiple breach sensors. And not a single visible wire. So, while this building may be turn-of-the-century, its security system is state-of-the-art. The one thing that catches my eye, however, is the painting on the east wall. The rustic wooden floorboards creak as I step closer to it. The Old West painting is large enough to fit a concealable safe behind it. And, yes, I check for that first.

"*Yee haw, cowboy.*"

"Hey, this painting speaks to me," I reply. The painting features three cowboys mounted atop muscular quarter horses and leading cattle into a wooden pen. The horizon behind them is dusky, but a massive storm cloud looms in the background. The whole thing reminds me of my home state of Wyoming.

"Mr. Conway? Dr. Cuinnsey will see you now," the grad student announces, gesturing towards the open paneled door.

The office is distinctly smaller than the lobby and exchanges red brick walls for wood paneling. To the right is another door that leads to a washroom and storage area according to the city plans. There is also a refurbished staircase ascending to the second story. We have zero intel about what's up there. To the left is a bar stand with a medley of mid and top shelf bourbons. There are also more bookcases filled with books, antiques, and framed pictures of Jake Booker—the foundation's namesake. Jake Booker is a meritoriously promoted captain of the oil and gas industry. And he's made a veritable fortune as a treasure hunter. Our intel shows he is a Rhodes Scholar, fluent in multiple languages, an avid gambler, and has a multitude of political connections. Which serve him well as he seems to find trouble in nearly every foreign country, he sets foot in. Mr. Booker is in his late 40s—roughly 10 years older than me—with shaggy silver hair and an impressive physique. He is classically handsome and, apparently, never takes a bad picture. Seriously, the photos around the room show him on a safari, sailing a sleek catamaran, flying a helicopter, and driving a vintage Chevy truck. If I didn't know better, I'd say he's an actor in Viagra commercials. Not that he needs that, mind you. I'm sure he doesn't. But just reading his psych workup made me sprout more chest hair.

"Mr. Conway, it's a pleasure to meet you. I am Dr. Vivian Cuinnsey. Co-director of the Booker Foundation," she says with an accent that is ambiguously East Coast. She extends her hand, which is unusually rough and callused. I'm guessing she spends as much time in the field as she does her office. She is also impeccably dressed. A white button up with a heather gray blazer and matching pencil skirt revealing a leaner frame. Not athletically lean, but more of an I-am-too-busy-to-eat lean. Her black hair is faintly curled and falls to her shoulders framing a slightly aquiline face and eyes the color of London fog. What little makeup she wears seems crisply and methodically applied. Even her floral perfume seems to have been put on in precisely the right amount.

"It's a pleasure to meet you," I reply.

"Please, have a seat," she insists. Dr. Cuinnsey turns and retreats back to her desk on black high heels that have no doubt traversed university libraries for near twenty years. She is roughly my age, but already seems twice as mature as I am.

Behind her desk along the far wall and beneath a set of high windows is a large abstract painting. Pastel orbs revolve around countless lines that swim through blurry colors and meet at chaotic angles.

"*Whoa. Is that a Kandinsky?*"

"Is that a Kandinsky?" I ask.

"An original, yes. Mr. Booker has an affinity for abstract art," she replies.

"*That's fucking expensive.*"

"It's lovely," I say.

"I'll tell Mr. Booker you like it. By the way, are those Durangos you're wearing?"

"Perceptive," I say. "They are." I tug my jeans up a bit and reveal scuffed, square-toed boots.

"Mr. Booker has a similar pair." She straightens her skirt as she sits down. "So, you're with the Smithsonian, then?" She squints at her laptop screen, "Scipio Cincinnatus Conway?"

"*Ha. I put your full name on there.*"

"Please, call me Skip."

"An interesting Latin name," she says.

"My father is a professor of Classical Studies at the University of Wyoming. I'm named after two of his favorite Roman figures. Scipio Africanus and Lucius Quinctius Cincinnatus."

"The general and the dictator," Dr. Cuinnsey adds.

"*Wow. She's good.*"

I nod.

"Tell me, do you know your family history?"

"Yeah. Diabetes and male pattern baldness. But I've been pretty fortunate."

"I meant your last name. Conway. Are you Scottish, Welsh, or Irish?"

"My father always said we were Irish. Honestly though, I've never really looked into it. Why?"

"Well, if that's the case, Conway can mean two different things depending on the original Celtic root. If it was Connbhuidhe," she says with an inflection that reminds me of Klingon speak, "then your name means yellow hound. But," she holds up a finger, "if it is derived from Connmhaigh that translates to head smasher."

*"Oh that's fucking cool. By the way, I forgot to mention the good doctor here is a professor of linguistics. And specializes in Celtic languages."*

"Good to know," I reply to both parties.

"*Ask her to do me*!"

"So, what brings the Smithsonian to the Booker Foundation?"

"I need a book."

"Which one?"

"*Al-Kitaba Manat*," I reply with proficient, but not exactly native, Arabic.

Her brow furrows. "We've only just acquired it. Not even a month ago. How did you know we had it?"

I lift my hands in the air and shrug my shoulders. "We're the Smithsonian."

"Mr. Conway, as you probably know, the mission of the Booker Foundation is to reclaim lost treasures and bring them back to the light of humanity. Certainly, the Smithsonian is one of the brightest lights, but there is a clearly defined process. We allow our consultants up to six months for analysis and processing. During that time, other organizations are allowed to submit proposals to acquire that artifact by loan. Provided they meet specific, but not unrealistic, parameters."

"Yeah, I know. But I need that book," I reply.

"And what interest does the Smithsonian have in *Al-Kitaba Manat,* exactly?"

"Look, I'd be happy to stay here as long as needed and fill out whatever requisite paperwork. But I need that book and any leads you have on its sisters."

Dr. Cuinnsey smiles confidently. "*Al-Kitaba Allat* and *Al-Kitaba Al-Uzza*? I'm sorry, but we're not entirely sure those texts even exist. As a matter of fact, my colleague Dr. Rosella Tassoni—"

"They exist," I interrupt. "And I need to find them. You have one and I think Mr. Booker has a lead on another. In Mali. I just need your contact."

"Well, Mr. Booker is in China on business."

"*He's not on business. He's gambling in Macao.*"

I repeat myself, “Again, I would really like that book. And I would be happy to oblige to all your requests provided that book is in my possession within the next 24 hours.”

“Why?” Dr. Cuinnsey insists.

I sigh. “Bubble Gum. Help me out.”

“*Congratulations. It only took six minutes to blow your cover. That’s a new record.*”

“Dr. Cuinnsey, have you ever seen these men?”

“What men?” she asks.

I nod to her laptop. Right about now, Bubble Gum is bringing up two pictures on Dr. Cuinnsey’s screen. Both black and white. One is of a broad-shouldered Uzbek national wearing a tracksuit and with the blend of European and East Asian features typical for that region. His name is Aziz Yoldashev. The other is a robe-wearing Sudanese national. Thin set with high cheekbones and a menacing snarl. His name is Salim Abdullah.

Dr. Cuinnsey’s startle reflex is atypical. She recovers quickly and asks, “Who are you and how did you take control of my computer?”

“Have you seen the men?”

“No, I haven’t seen these men. You’re not from the Smithsonian, are you?”

“Dr. Cuinnsey, I assure you, we’re the good guys. I can also assure you that as long as you possess that book, your life is in danger.”

“No, Mr. Conway. Your life is in danger.” Dr. Cuinnsey pulls a revolver from the drawer in front of her. It’s a snub-nosed Smith & Wesson Governor and she points it at my chest.

“I didn’t know they carried guns in the halls of academia,” I say, raising my hands in surrender.

“It’s Texas. Everyone carries a gun. Now, tell me who you are.”

“Fair enough,” I reply. “Would you mind just taking your finger off the trigger? I’d hate to have an abstract painting made behind me with that .45.”

“*Casper? What’s your status?*” Bubble Gum asks, referring to me by my call sign.

“Standby,” I order. “Dr. Cuinnsey. We have reason to believe that you and Mr. Booker’s lives may be in danger. The two men in those pictures are leaders of a dangerous cult. A cult which worships the chief goddesses of Arabia's Pre-Islamic pantheon. A cult whose mission is to procure *Al-Kitaba Manat*, *Allat*, and *Al-Uzza*. And, we know for a fact, they will kill anyone that gets in their way. So, what we would like to do is take the aforementioned book from you, so you are no longer in harm's way. And if preservation of your own life isn't enough, we have a few ancient books of our own you might be interested in analyzing. We'd be happy to share them with you. Also, my superiors could smooth over some of Mr. Booker's international indiscretions."

"Who is *we*?"

"We're a covert organization. My team and I are ghosts, but still funded by your tax dollars. I know you've heard the term 'halls of academia.' Well, you might consider us the *balls* of academia."

"*Ha! Good one.*"

"Well, if you're some kind of government agency, then you won't mind me calling the police."

"*Hang on. Rerouting landline.*"

"Be my guest," I say, knowing Bubble Gum is about to play the role of police dispatcher.

"*Casper, you've company. Suspicious male.*" Moose radios with a baritone and stoic voice.

"Doc, do you have another appointment after this?" Dr. Cuinnsey keeps her hand on the phone receiver and shakes her head *no*. I ask, "Do you get a lot of walk-ins?" She shakes her head again.

I hear silenced gunshots in the lobby. Contrary to popular belief, a silenced pistol is quite loud. The real problem is that it muffles the sound just enough that I can't tell if it's a pistol or small machine gun. "Moose, move in."

"*Oscar Mike,*" he replies, letting me know he is *on the move*.

"What was that?" Dr. Cuinnsey asks. "What was that?!"

"Listen to me. My partner is down the street, he'll be here soon, but I need you to shoot the next person that comes through that door." Two more shots ring out from the lobby. "Aim your gun at the doorframe, quickly." Dr. Cuinnsey eyes the door and then me, but keeps the barrel fixed squarely on my chest. "Do it.

Now. Or we're both dead." I would *love* to draw the concealed pistol under my sport coat right about now, but that might give the good doctor the wrong idea. So I refrain.

The door is kicked open. I immediately sink lower in my chair to use its wooden back as cover and minimize myself as a target. "Shoot," I whisper.

She doesn't. She aims at the intruder and yells "Stop! Don't move!"

The intruder yells back in broken English. "Gun down. Now!"

I can see and hear Dr. Cuinnsey's breathing increase as adrenaline floods her body. "Stay low behind that desk," I advise. There is a roll of coins in my right coat pocket to weigh it down and keep it back when reaching for my weapon. I draw my Glock 39 from a concealed holster on my hip.

"*On scene*," I hear Moose call out. Here's the problem. Moose may or may not have a clear shot. And from his position, Dr. Cuinnsey is behind the shooter, which means the shot may not be clean either. "*Visual*," Moose calls, telling me he can see the target.

The intruder shouts again. "Give me book! Now!"

"Standby," I radio quietly. I remove my fake glasses with the audio/visual feed and grip them between my thumb and forefinger. I look at Dr. Cuinnsey. She balances her revolver on the desktop and hunches low behind her desk. Her gaze is fixed on the intruder. That's good.

I flick my glasses across the room. Thanks to millions of years of evolution, there is a primitive part of the brain that forces the intruder to momentarily track and assess the flying object. As he does, I spin up to a shooter's stance and squeeze off four quick rounds at his center of mass.

The intruder falls to the ground dropping his silenced pistol in the process. With balanced footsteps, I advance towards him keeping my sights on his chest and kicking away his 1911-style, foreign pistol. "Hold your fire!" I yell. "Moose?"

"Clear. One down," Moose yells from the lobby before darting to my position.

Our interloper is wearing cargo pants, steel-toed construction boots, and a loose fitting black shirt. He's curled in the fetal position hyperventilating. Also, there's no blood. "He's got a vest," I announce. Kevlar vests do a great job preventing bullets from entering your body, but they do nothing to disperse the force. My guess is our intruder has a few broken ribs and is desperately trying to suck in the air that my shots violently punched from his lungs. The physically imposing Moose, wielding an MP5 submachine gun, enters the room methodically, puts a knee in the intruder's back, and cuffs his wrists with zip-ties.

"Moose, how's our man in the lobby?"

Moose looks at me briefly and shakes his head *no.*

I sigh and holster my gun. "Bubble Gum. You copy?"

"*Loud and clear.*"

"How's the perimeter looking?"

"*I got eyes on. You're clear. Will advise.*"

"Copy. Roll medical. Inform locals of an attempted armed robbery. And update HQ."

"*Copy.*"

I look over at Dr. Cuinnsey. She's still aiming her revolver in our direction. I turn towards the nearby bar stand. Snagging two tumblers, I pluck the cork from a bottle of Pappy's, pour two fingers in each, and bring them both to the good doctor. I set one glass next to her on the desk and swill my own. "We really need to talk about that book," I say.

Dr. Cuinnsey sits up and calmly exchanges her revolver for the glass of bourbon. "It's yours." She takes a sip. "And you'll need to find a man named Omar al-Daris."

"Where can I find him?"

She finally locks her smoky eyes on mine. "Timbuktu."

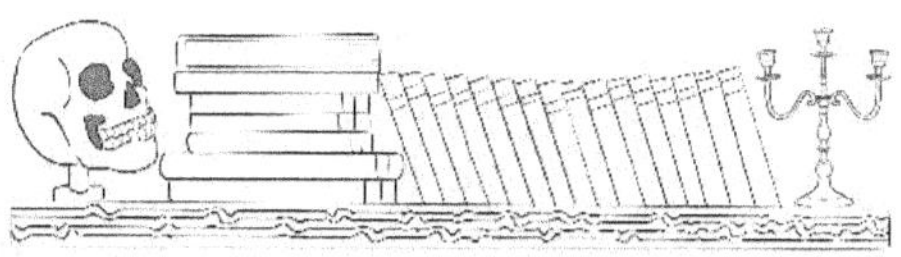

**Over the Atlantic Ocean/11 AUG/1600hrs**

Our chartered Gulfstream G650 is level at 45,000 feet and rockets over the dark Atlantic at near Mach 1. Inside this modern and spacious chariot is everything a corporate bigwig would need to conduct international business.

"Almost patched in, Casper," Bubble Gum announces. Bubble Gum (aka Stephanie Treader) is our combat technologist. If you picture her as the nerdy girl with Coke-bottle glasses who graciously did your calculus homework in high school, you'd be dead wrong. Instead, think of the super-jacked Linda Hamilton from *Terminator 2.* Remember? She turned her asylum cell into an apocalypse-preparing CrossFit gym? Bubble Gum is about 5'6" of lean muscle and, as a former NSA analyst, can kick your ass in cyberspace as easily as she can in reality. One side of her head is buzz-cut while natural blonde and electric pink hair waterfalls down the other.

She chews her gum compulsively and nonchalantly blows a neon green bubble. After the bubble pops she announces, "Patched into HQ, sir."

On the forward cabin wall in front of us, the screen flickers and we see a tall African-American man in a slim-fit beige suit standing over a polished, rune-warded table. Behind him is a wall of monitors displaying everything from classified satellite feeds to the Weather Channel. Director Fiske runs a hand over his bald pate and adjusts his brushed titanium smart-glasses. "Alright, everyone. Let's get started," he says, foregoing any icebreakers as usual. "We've been unable to identify the assailant at the Booker Foundation." A mugshot of an apathetic-looking Middle Eastern man pops up onto the screen. "His fingerprints have been chemically burned off and there is no retinal scan on record. The only identifying mark is this tattoo." The pop-up flashes to the man's neck where a small goblet beneath the crescent moon is inked in red.

"The cup of death and crescent moon. The sign of Manat. So he's another cult member," I say.

"Correct," Fiske answers. "And no other accomplices were found. However, this man has turned up dead in the last 24 hours." The pop-up changes to the visage of a dead man with ligature marks around his neck. "This is Awang Sabit. A Malaysian national and antiquities dealer out of Kuala Lumpur. Mr. Booker acquired *Al-Kitaba Manat* from him. Mr. Sabit is also the one who provided the lead on *Al-Kitaba Allat*."

"Our man Al-Daris in Timbuktu," I confirm.

"Correct," Fiske replies. "It seems as though our cult has a wider reach than initially thought. They got to Sabit, too. So it's safe to say you may encounter further resistance in Mali, commander."

"Fantastic. What's the status on our gear?" I ask.

"An army envoy is en route from Special Operations Command Africa in Bamako," Fiske answers.

Moose chimes in, "What are the rules of engagement?" Master Sergeant Mustafa Sadik is a Turkish-American Muslim and former Delta Force special operator. He's just over 6'0" and, apparently, has the same workout routine and dietary habits as He-Man. He has perfectly groomed black hair, surprisingly boyish features given his forty years, and a rarely seen but disarming smile. He also has the serious and weary eyes of a seasoned combatant.

"Self-defense only," Fiske replies.

"Great," I stretch out the word.

"You are to rendezvous with your envoy and proceed directly to Al-Daris and procure *Al-Kitaba Allat* as well as any leads on *Al-Kitaba Al-Uzza*. I've forwarded you all the pertinent intel."

"Get to Timbuktu. Get book. Get out. Got it." I reply.

Director Fiske sighs through his nose. His telltale sign of frustration. "Commander, it is of the utmost importance that your team prevents that cult from acquiring any of the goddess books. Need I remind you what happens if they do?"

I roll my eyes and whisper, "Please don't say 'like Belize.'"

"It will be like Belize."

"Fantastic. One more thing, sir," I smile and hold up a finger. "Have we figured out who's funding this cult and their global nefariousness?"

"Our people are still working on it," Fiske replies, corners of his mouth turned down into a subtle frown.

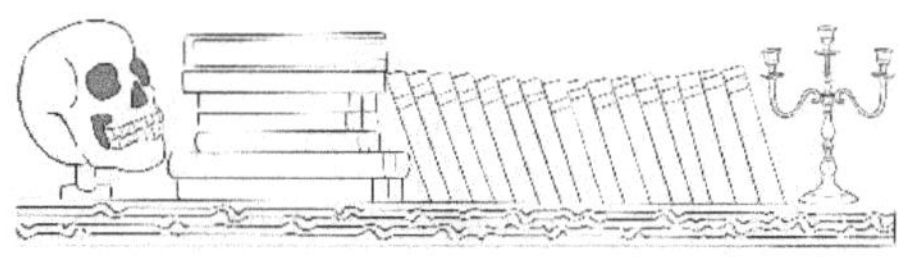

**Timbuktu Airport/Timbuktu/Mail/12 AUG/0755hrs**

"Commander Conway," our young army envoy yells from the bottom of the ramp. He's ramrod straight and his plain clothes are already sweat stained. "I'm Lieutenant Brooks. Army intelligence from SOCAFRICA." He knows better than to salute me as I step onto the steaming tarmac. Special operatives don't carry their rank with them and the last thing we want to do is broadcast a foreign military presence to the Malian general public.

"Nice to meet you. This is my team. Where's our shit?" I say, plainly.

The envoy leads us to a white messenger van 30 yards away and opens the rear doors. He gestures to six rugged cases. Three the size of a standard briefcase and three the size of a travel trunk. "I've already cleared everything with customs so you're good to go. The small cases are the more discreet options."

"What about the larger ones?" I ask.

"They're more of the take-over-a-small-country option," the lieutenant replies.

I smile and point. "Great. We'll have the…"

"Casper," Moose chides me.

I turn to see him shaking his head with a disapproving glare. "What? I was going to say the discreet option. But," I slap the army officer on the shoulder, "Load the rest on the plane for safekeeping. And Lieutenant?"

"Yes, sir?"

"Whose plane is that?" I ask pointing to a shiny black Bombardier Challenger 650 parked by the nearest hangar. It's the only plane other than ours that isn't over 20 years old.

"Not sure. Although, it's not uncommon for affluent folks to visit here. Especially affluent folks looking for old books."

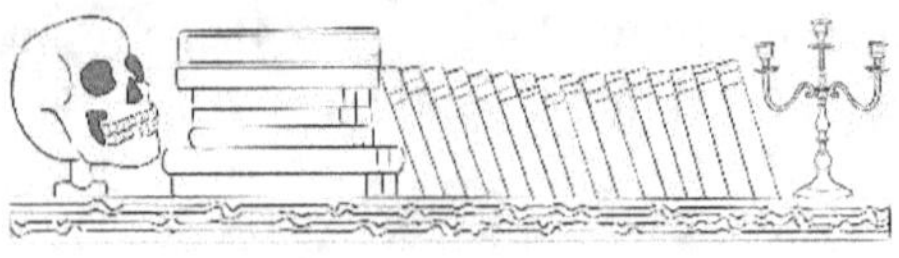

**City of Timbuktu/Mail/12 AUG/0823hrs**

Our borrowed messenger van bounces intermittently down the rough asphalt road leading to the heart of this ancient city. The passing landscape is desolate and clay-oven-hot, but an undeniable magic pervades the place. A mystique that only comes from being the crossroads of a once-thriving, prosperous civilization and a former repository for all of humanity's wisdom. A place where the tireless camels hauling bricks of salt met the wooden canoes that would exchange those bricks for bars of gold. Where the sands of the Sahara met the verdant banks of the Niger River. Where the written word, often times, meant more than a man's life.

A city of limestone and clay brick rises quickly on the horizon underneath a bright blue sky. The intel reports my team read prove to be true. This once bustling sub-Saharan gem is now a backwater trinket. But one thing still stands. Scholarship. There are over 70,000 unexplored manuscripts in this city. Some owned by the university and local mosques, but the majority held by private families. When this city was a thriving trade center, well-to-do merchants needed hobbies signaling their immense wealth to the rest of society. And, thanks to the interconnectedness of the enlightened Abbasid Caliphate, that hobby became book collecting.

"Stop here," I announce from the passenger seat. Moose pulls over and shuts off the engine. "Bubble Gum, cover the rear exit. Moose, you're with me."

Moose and I approach the dusty street festooned with power lines. A pair of small children kick a soccer ball to each other while older kids smoke cigarettes by their parked dirt bikes. The shop we're headed to is the only storefront on this small strip not crumbling and shedding flakes of brick onto the dirt road. Each window is barred and a simple sign above the corner door painted gold on white reads in Arabic: *Al-Daris*. The Scholar.

A bell chimes as we enter the climate-controlled room, almost as though we are entering a convenience store. Inside is a small reading room outfitted with half-filled bookshelves and severely outdated office furniture. The chipped walls are painted a sage green and the herbal, earthy smell of rooibos tea and sweet tobacco circulates thanks to the humming air conditioner. A door that presumably leads back to the archives opens slowly and a Malian man sheepishly pokes out his head. A white keffiyeh winds around his head like a coiled snake and matches the wisps in his manicured beard.

"Monsieur Al-Daris?" Moose, our muscle-laden polyglot, asks in French.

“Oui,” he replies, stepping out cautiously from the door so we cannot see behind him.

As Moose presses the scholar about our missing tomes, I take a closer look at the reading room. Most of the books are historical and referential. A cup of hot, rose-colored tea sits on one table. It’s still hot but spilt as if put down hastily. I glance back to Al-Daris. He’s sweating. There are different varieties of sweat. Athletic sweat, nervous sweat, and it’s-hot-as-all-hell sweat. Al-Daris is clearly suffering from nervous sweat. Also, he anxiously fidgets with his traditional white robes while answering Moose’s questions.

I tap my earbud. “Bubble Gum, you copy?”

No response.

“He says he doesn’t have the book,” Moose announces. “Something is wrong.”

I slide past Al-Daris and quickly peek behind the door leading to the archives. From my angle, I see a labyrinth of bookcases embedded with countless scrolls. In the forefront are tables topped with scanners and magnifiers. The gloved and mask-wearing technicians that typically use those tables, however, all stand with their hands up as armed men wielding AK-74’s traverse the room.

I turn back to Moose and give him the hand signal for hostiles before drawing my concealed pistol. Moose draws his own and asks Al-Daris how many intruders are on site.

“Huit? Neuf?” He replies. “Je ne sais pas.”

I radio again. “Bubble Gum, you copy? We have multiple hostiles on scene. Eight or nine, Al-Daris isn’t sure.”

No response.

The air pressure in the room changes ever so slightly. Someone has opened a back door. I move Al-Daris out of the way and set up for entry on our side of the door. Moose joins me. We both hear shouting and scuffling. Moose counts down from three and flings the door open. Lifting our weapons, we enter the room using a rehearsed crossover maneuver.

There are two hostiles left. Black keffiyehs cover their faces. One aims his AK directly at me. The other holds Bubble Gum hostage at gunpoint in such a way that makes a clean shot nearly impossible. Al-Daris’s technicians take cover behind the bookcases. Moose yells in French, then Arabic, to let the hostage go. Amidst the standoff, I focus on Bubble Gum. She winks and curls one side of her lip. The signal. Believe it or not, my team has rehearsed this scenario and all its permutations many, many times.

I speak slowly in Arabic. “Two things. One, just tell me what you want.” From the open door to the street, I hear the sound of multiple vehicles speeding off. Bad guys getting away. “And two…”

I don’t finish my sentence. I don’t intend to. On the count of two, Moose places two rounds in his threat while Bubble Gum swings her head forward past the barrel of the gun at her temple and immediately steps her left foot backwards. She twists her torso nearly 180 degrees and cups the top of the hostile’s pistol pushing it towards him. The gun goes off, the ejected 9mm puncturing flesh and shattering his collarbone. The gunman screams in pain, but she continues pushing the hot gun barrel towards him and forcing the gunman to release his solid grip. A small sound escapes the hostage-taker’s voice as his wrist bends awkwardly, compounding the pain from his collarbone. That’s when Bubble Gum knuckle punches the man’s windpipe with her other hand, effectively crushing his larynx.

With both men down, I sprint outside to see the tail end of an older model Land Rover turn down a side street, leaving a trail of dust in its wake. Hastily, I round the corner to the front of Al-Daris’ shop and find the teenagers still puffing away on their cigarettes. I hop onto one of their dirt bikes, pull the clutch tight, and kick-start that bastard. The boys protest, but their pleas are drowned out as I throttle up, release the clutch, and speed after the hostiles.

I follow the Land Rover’s dust plumes. Racing down alleys and side streets, avoiding all manner of livestock and rubbish piles, I try to cut them off. They’re going south, heading for the main road out of town. Which means they are either leaving Timbuktu by the highway, headed down to the Niger River for a possible transfer, or to the…

“LT? You copy?” I yell over the comms. I hear a muffled response from our army envoy. “Look alive! You may have company. Multiple hostiles. Do you copy?!” Another muffled response.

I cut right at the next major street, losing traction on bald tires and nearly sliding off into another storefront. An electronics repair shop with, no kidding, a battered cassette player hanging inside the window. I'm lucky, however. Ahead of me is a Land Rover. The last of three to be precise. Now, I know what you are thinking. Skip? This is the perfect time for some action movie shit, right? Just shoot the tires!

That actually doesn't work. Especially when you have a small-caliber round. The bullets just sink into the tire and it deflates over an hour or so.

But Skip! Just speed up, throw yourself onto the roof of a speeding SUV, and forcibly commandeer it!

Right now, our speed is roughly 50mph. Attempting anything like that, helmet or not, is unbelievably asinine and dangerous. Not to mention, if I do successfully land on the Land Rover's roof, I have nothing to hold onto and can't shield myself from the…

AK-74 bullets whizz by me like high-pitched, hypersonic flies from a cultist hanging out the passenger side window.

I ease the throttle and begin to serpentine as best I can given my threadbare tires, eventually sliding towards the left side. Speeding up again, I get close enough to see the menacing eyes of Salim Abdullah in the driver's side mirror. Salim swerves, hoping to catch me with the rear quarter panel. I swerve, too, and hit the brakes. My dirt bike slides perpendicular to the road and comes to a stop. More rifle rounds fly by me, one of them striking and sparking off my handlebars. I dismount quickly and duck behind the small engine block to shield myself.

The trailing Land Rover skids to an abrupt halt. Four men in paramilitary garb exit the vehicle, including the cult leader Salim. All of them wielding assault rifles. The dirt bike will no longer provide adequate cover. I draw my pistol and cut toward an old dumpster that blocks the alley to my left. With my right hand outstretched, I lay down cover fire and launch myself into the dumpster.

I'm not sure which is worse at this point. The deafening cacophony of countless rifle rounds striking the one-inch steel plating around me or the offensive odor emanating from the rubbish that has swallowed me.

Bullets continue to zing, some of them causing the walls to bubble inward. I sink lower into the trash, in case one of them actually pierces the old receptacle's skin.

"*Casper, status?*" I hear Moose's voice in my ear.

"I've been better," I yell back.

"*We are en route to your position,*" he announces. Bubble Gum can track my position with her combat datapad so long as my comms are active.

"Negative," I say, going with my hunch. "Get to the airport, but keep your distance. We have three vehicles. All armed. All dangerous. LT, you copy?"

"*Loud and clear*," the intel officer radios back. The hailstorm of bullets finally ceases. I hear the sounds of reloading followed by four doors slamming and the Land Rover beginning to speed away.

"Hostiles are too dangerous to engage. Stay out of sight and run surveillance," I say, slowly climbing to the pockmarked dumpster's lip. I peek over the edge and see nothing but a dust trail and curious civilians shuffling hesitantly towards the street.

"*Surveillance on what, exactly?*" the intel officer asks.

"The other plane. The Challenger 650."

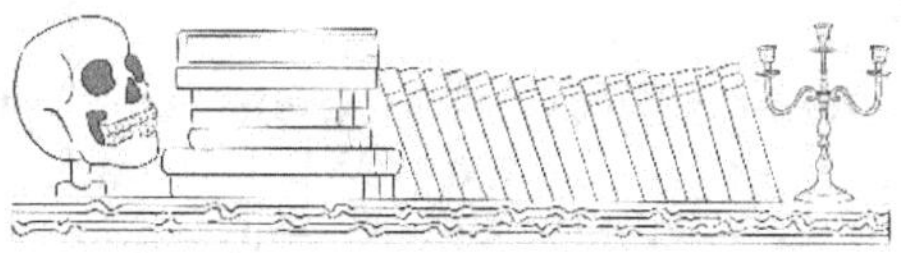

**Over Algerian Airspace/12 AUG/1123hrs**

"Jesus, Casper. You stink. I can't even sit next to you," Bubble Gum announces, taking her datapad and moving to the next row of seats.

"Sorry, but it beat the alternative. Any response from our lovely Dr. Cuinnsey yet?"

"Negative," Bubble Gum replies. "Still trying to establish a connection."

"LT!" I shout to our new Army tag-a-long who sits at the back of the plane. "Your boys figure out the whereabouts of that plane yet?"

"Bearing northeast across the Mediterranean. Plane is

registered to a subsidiary of a subsidiary of a shell corporation. Ultimately though, it leads back to a General Gumanizov of the Uzbek army."

"Uzbek?" I echo. "Is it a coincidence that one of our cult co-leaders is an Uzbek national?" A picture of the Cro-Magnon and red tracksuit wearing Aziz Yoldashev flashes onto the big screen in front of me. He stood atop the stairs of the Challenger 650 back at the Timbuktu airport. Our hastily recruited intel officer was able to capture the picture as the other co-leader, Salim Abdullah, and his crew transferred from their vehicles to the plane. Along with their stolen property.

Moose contributes to the investigation as he paces the isle, "Al-Daris said he had sold *Al-Kitaba Allat* almost five years ago. Just before Islamic militants came through destroying what they thought to be *haram*, or sacrilegious, texts. He sold it to an older man. A general from a foreign country that he couldn't specify."

Lieutenant Brooks interjects, "Gumanizov's profile is thin, but he is a known collector of antiquities. Also, he makes a fortune at arms and drug smuggling. He operates out of a small compound near Uzbekistan's borders with Turkmenistan, Afghanistan, and Tajikistan."

I jest. "Wow. The only place you will see more Stan's is in an accounting firm. Am I right?"

No one laughs.

"Okay," I continue, "So General Gumanizov could likely be the guy bankrolling our cult. Why? What's in it for him? Let's try to figure out the general's whereabouts right now. The cultists' plane could be headed there. Moose? Tell me again what they took from Al-Daris again?"

Moose politely finishes chewing his protein bar before answering. "Al-Daris said they took a mid-nineteenth century letter written by Heinrich Barth to a family friend. Al-Daris claims he had only recently acquired it and had no intention of selling the letter. He planned to hand it over to the local museum dedicated to Barth."

"What does the letter say?" I ask.

Moose answers, "No one knows. The letter wasn't cared for in over a century. It's now sealed in vacuum plastic. According to Al-Daris, opening the letter and exposing it to air would cause it to disintegrate almost immediately."

"Great. So they have a letter they can't open? Why? And can anyone tell me who the hell Heinrich Barth is?"

"Maybe you could ask Dr. Cuinnsey. I have her online," Bubble Gum says.

The big screen flashes in front of me and I see a real-time shot of Dr. Vivian Cuinnsey. She isn't sitting behind a desk at the Booker Foundation. She is sitting in what I am guessing is her bed with her back against a wooden headboard. Strangely, she still looks professional. She isn't wearing any makeup, her black hair is pulled back into a ponytail, and her white blouse is slightly disheveled (probably because she just put it on over her pajama bottoms). She also wears wire frame glasses that probably make a permanent home in her nightstand. This is all most likely because it's very early morning back in the States. "Good morning, doc. Sleep well?"

"Mr. Conway," she nods.

"Please, call me Skip."

"Where are you?" she asks.

"Hightailing it out of North Africa. Ran into your man Al-Daris in Timbuktu. Got shot at by angry cultists. No big deal. Hey, listen. Apparently, Al-Daris sold *Al-Kitaba Allat* a few years back. Possibly to an Uzbek general named—"

"Gumanizov," she finishes.

"You know him?" I ask.

"Mr. Booker and I have had run-ins with him. Most recently when searching for Merlin's tomb. Maybe you read about that in the balls of academia?" she says, matter-of-factly.

I stifle a laugh. As it so happens, my agency did know about that. We weren't worried, however, because Merlin's enciphered manuscript, known to be in his tomb, wasn't on our radar. Another book from Merlin's era, however, was. A book that could spell as much trouble as the goddess books if placed in the wrong hands. Luckily, Morgana le Fey's infamous tome is already locked away safely in our vault in Groom Lake, Nevada. "I recall a little something about that, yes."

"Anyway," she continues, "I've been doing what I do best, lately."

"Which is what?" I ask, watching her pet a curious black cat that stuck its head in the frame.

"Research," she replies. "The Uzbek national you showed me, Aziz Yoldashev, is a major player on the antiquities black market. Jake, I mean Mr. Booker, has had unpleasant encounters with him throughout his career, as well. Unlike Gumanizov, he is a very violent and very dangerous man."

"Yeah, I gathered that."

Dr. Cuinnsey finishes, "And if Gumanizov is involved with the goddess books, something tells me he is utilizing Yoldashev's services. The general may sully his name in the antiquities market with deceit, but not violence. Not yet, anyway."

"Gotcha. Tell me something else. Are you familiar with Heinrich Barth—old timey guy who wrote letters?"

"Are you kidding me?" she replies. "He was a brilliant German scholar and explorer. Barth traveled and mapped both the Middle East and Africa. More importantly though, at least in my opinion, he was an unmatched linguist when it came to Arabic dialects and a comprehensive understating of African languages. He was the first European on record to be fluent in Hausa, Fulani, and even Kanuri. Grad students still read his writings today. It's rumored that he once possessed *Al-Kitaba Manat*. But that comes from an unreliable source, Sir Richard Burton. Another famous European explorer and historian who claimed he had seen the text. If Barth is somehow mixed up with your business, though, I'd say that makes Burton's claims distinctly more credible. Why do you ask?"

"Well, Yoldashev and his crew just stole a nearly 200-year-old letter from ol' Heinrich that apparently is in such bad shape it can't be opened or exposed to air."

"That's interesting."

"What's interesting?" I ask.

"Well, MIT has been utilizing terahertz radiation, the kind they use in airport security scans, which can distinguish between ink and blank paper. Kind of like how an X-ray can detect the difference between tissue and bone. They then run those scans through specially tailored algorithms that can decipher individual letters and words."

"Which means what exactly?"

"It means you can potentially read entire books without ever opening the cover. It could be the ultimate tool for studying antique documents while keeping them perfectly preserved."

"How about old personal letters? Could it read those?"

"Absolutely."

"Sounds like something Gumanizov could get his hands on, too." I turn my head slightly and yell, "LT. We've got a serious lead. I really need the location of General Gumanizov!"

"Hold on," Dr. Cuinnsey says, holding up her cellphone and thumbing it as though she is texting. "Jake has a satellite phone. He might know the general's whereabouts."

*Jake?* I wonder. "Dr. Cuinnsey, I assure you. Our agency has access to some of the world's best intelligence networks."

Dr. Cuinnsey's cellphone vibrates. She reads it, announcing, "Jake said to give him a minute."

"Bubble Gum? What are you finding?" I ask.

"So far, nothing, sir," she says, frantically smashing her datapad with all ten fingers.

"Okay, team," I announce, "Let's get CIA main on the line so we can—"

"He's on his way to Sochi," Dr. Cuinnsey announces. "He'll be staying at the Hotel Pullman."

There's a palpable silence in the plane. "Look alive, team," I correct myself. "We're headed to Russia."

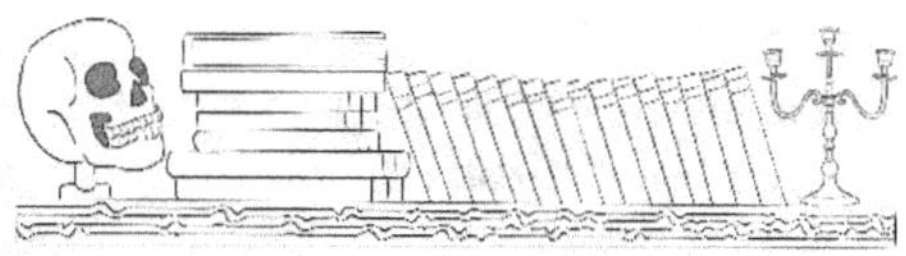

**Bounty Boutique Hotel/Sochi/Russia/13 AUG/0912hrs**

A thousand miles south of Moscow, located on the scenic shores of the Black Sea, is the summer destination for Russians looking to thaw out from historically long winters. Its immense popularity, of course, means there are a variety of hotels and resorts at a variety of price points, which is nice since our agency's budget—while healthy—is by no means unlimited.

Despite the room smelling like cheap vodka, cigarettes, and a hint of bleach, this three star resort room with two queen beds is quite cozy. More importantly, the top floor of this hotel overlooks the five-star Hotel Pullman across the street. There, we are betting our Cup of Death cult is meeting their financing partner, General Gumanizov. Lieutenant Brooks and I set up a classic surveillance blind. A clothesline wall of black blankets surrounds the sole, large window in our room, forming a smaller, squared room. My counterpart and I are inside that room. We also wear black clothes to cut down all light reflections. This technique renders us virtually undetectable with the naked eye.

Lieutenant Brooks lowers his telescopic camera lens and announces, "Gumanizov is still at the pool and his men are setting up the book scanner thing in his room. It looks like they're hardwired in." I'm quite certain this is LT's first oversees tour. He is an eager junior officer and strikes me as a proud Boy Scout when he was younger. The kind who earned every badge and recited his oath nightly. I understand completely. Before I was recruited by the agency, I was naval intelligence. Just a young junior officer who spent most of his time in dark rooms analyzing satellite images. Until that one fateful night in Coronado Beach.

I set down my cup of hearty Russian coffee that has the relative consistency of motor oil and raise my binoculars to confirm. In Gumanizov's suite, on the top floor of the east wing, a technician toils on a laptop. He is surrounded by two suited guard-types who help set up the scanner. It includes a giant metal arm and looks like what a dentist would use to x-ray your teeth. I swing back to the pool deck centered on the top floor and see Gumanizov, who is an unflattering specimen. He lies supine in a lounge chair wearing only mirrored aviator shades and a skimpy blue pair of swim trunks. He is physically unimposing—maybe 5'3"—with a prize-winning vodka gut carpeted in polar white body hair. He bathes in the sunlight filtering through the massive windows that contain the indoor pool. Nearby are two more suited men. Both of them blockish with an unmistakable military bearing and hawk eyes that scan the entire deck incessantly. Gumanizov's personal security—no doubt comprised of the most capable men in his division.

"Moose? Any sign of our cultists?" I radio.

"*Negative,*" he replies.

"Copy. Bubble Gum, status?" I say, scoping her position at

the far edge of the swimming pool through my optics. I can see her typing casually on her datapad.

"I am through the hotel firewall, but the general's men aren't on the Wi-Fi. They're still hardwired. I have no visibility at the moment" she replies. "I need them to log on."

"Copy that."

Lt. Brooks chimes in, "Looks like Gumanizov is about to be on the move."

"Bubble Gum," I say, "G's about to fly the coup. You're up."

"Roger. Oscar Mike," she replies, informing us she's on the move. Bubble Gum stands up from her lounger, sheds her bathrobe, and employs her rarely seen feminine wiles as she saunters down the poolside in a purple two-piece that leaves very little to the imagination.

The hawk-eyed guards don't miss it.

Neither does Lieutenant Brooks. "Sir? Is she, uh, single?"

"Believe me LT. You're not her type."

Bubble Gum approaches one of the blockish guards. Her comms aren't open so all I see is her body language. She steps close to him and twirls the long side of her hair for a moment before running her hands subtly along all her sides. The guard politely pushes her back, but Bubble Gum continues her seduction from a foot further away. Regardless of the language barrier, she is well aware of all her unspoken signals and sinuous movements forcing a man's hormone factory to work overtime. And in the split second that the guard's mammalian imperative to reproduce takes over his brain, Bubble Gum makes her move. She reaches into her bikini top and pulls out a small slip of paper with her hotel room and phone number on it. She coyly tucks it in the man's breast pocket. Then, she tugs on the man's lapels and leans in to kiss him on the cheek before whispering something in his ear. The other guard abruptly intervenes and signals his partner to follow the leaving general. Bubble Gum blows them both a kiss before walking back to her lounge chair and taking up her datapad.

"Mission accomplished, Casper."

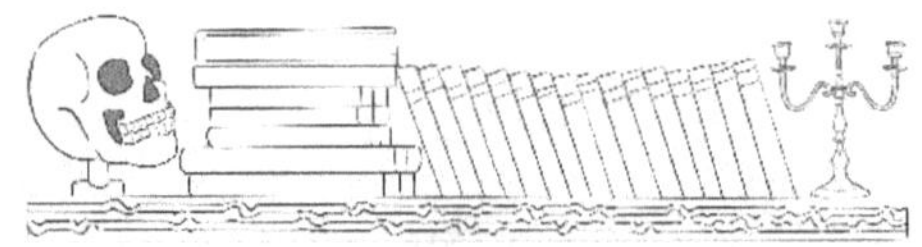

**Bounty Boutique Hotel/Sochi/Russia/13 AUG/0945hrs**

Moose radios. "*Cultists are on scene. Driving a black SUV. Five males. One briefcase*."

"Copy," I reply. "Alright everyone. Stick to the plan. Our primary biscuit is *Al-Kitaba Allat*. Barth's letter is the gravy." I look over to Lieutenant Brooks. "We still have ears?"

The LT turns a knob on the handheld receiver to increase the volume. We hear two men chatter in Russian. Thanks to Bubble Gum, one of our blockheads has a discrete audio transmitter under his lapel. LT confirms everything is being recorded digitally and expands the translation window on his laptop. The software for that program isn't perfect, but it's pretty clear the guards are still talking about Bubble Gum.

The cultists, including Aziz Yoldashev and Salim Abdullah, enter the suite. All of them wearing loose-fitting tourist clothing. Yoldashev, who traded his tracksuit for a European soccer jersey and windbreaker pants, clutches a briefcase handcuffed to his wrist. The room goes silent with just the guards and five cultists in the room. Moments later, a more imposing Gumanizov enters from the private bedroom in the back wearing his olive green military uniform complete with gold embroidered rank and a cornucopia of ribbons and medals. The chatter picks up. Russian pleasantries are exchanged.

"English, please. Too many Russian ears to listen," Gumanizov orders.

"We have what you asked for," Yoldashev replies.

"Please, show me," Gumanizov gestures towards the nearby table.

"Show us the book first!" Salim Abdullah insists.

From my vantage point, it seems as though Gumanizov is not pleased with the demand. But I hear his fingers snap and see one of his guards duck into the bedroom. He returns with a tome the size of a chair seat. Salim unlocks the tethering handcuffs and Yoldashev places the case on the table. He opens it and delivers the vacuum-sealed letter from Al-Daris' library to the general. It's now confirmed. There is a mutual partnership between our general and the cult.

I radio. "Bingo. We're in luck. I got eyes on the biscuit. Moose, move into position. Bubble Gum what's the status on the gravy?"

"*Standby*," she replies. The general walks the sealed letter to the technician manning the scanner near the wet bar. Placing the letter on a small plate, the technician maneuvers the arm so the scanner is directly in front of it. The tech then retreats to his laptop and begins typing.

"Seriously, Bubble Gum. Do I have to call Gramps to see what this letter says?" I ask.

Bubble Gum snarls "*You call that phony and you're a dead man walking, Casper. Give. Me. A goddamn. Minute!*" Gerry Rowe (call sign: Gramps) is our remote viewer back at headquarters. He's a white-haired, grizzled army vet and survivor of the CIA's infamous MK-ULTRA program. You give him a shot of Jack Daniels and blare some Steppenwolf and he will sketch out for you anyone or anything you want to see anywhere on the planet with charcoal and paper. Bubble Gum thinks he's a hack.

I pull my secure smartphone from a cargo pocket to dial HQ. Before I hit send, Bubble Gum pipes up. "*Boom! I'm in. Looks like he logged on to grab the algorithm from a cloud-based server. Standby.*"

The machine continues scanning. Meanwhile, chatter in the room revolves around the incident in Timbuktu. After that, the talk turns to Barth's letter. Why are both parties so interested in this letter? What does it say?

"Bubble Gum. Anything yet?" I radio.

"*The algorithm is still running. What I can see is in German. I am running it through a translator. Looks like some kind of directions and some fancy Arabic script. Oh, there we go. It's deciphered. I got it all. We're gravy.*"

"Copy, Bubble Gum. Get to the rendezvous. Moose, standby for fireworks." Moose copies and I notice that both Gumanizov and the cultists seem overly eager to analyze the results. "LT? Get ready to move," I announce slapping a magazine into my silenced M4 carbine, fitted with an Advanced Combat Optical Gunsight. I leave our blind situated around the window and enter another blind, a wall of black blankets that surrounds the balcony door. I open the balcony door before stepping behind one of the blankets. Tied to the inside doorknob is a long string, the end of which is tucked into my belt. With my advanced sights, I narrow in on Gumanizov's suite slightly below us. I'm still under strict orders not to kill. And I don't intend to kill. I intend to spook. I aim for an empty corner of the room and count down over comms. "Fireworks in three. Two. One."

I methodically rip off eight rounds hitting walls, doors, furniture, and shattering multiple panes of glass. The guards in the suite hit the deck while the cultists scramble. I fire three more rounds and then grab the string tucked into my belt. I pull hard so the balcony door closes in front of me. Now trapped in the blind, the smoke from my assault rifle does not give away my position.

"Cultists grabbed the book! They're Oscar Mike. Guards are scanning. I think we're clear," LT yells.

I hustle to the nearest bed and toss my rifle into a generic rolling suitcase. "Almost time to check out," I say. I grab my optics and reenter the window blind. LT was right. The guards have no clue where the shots came from. But it won't take long before they inspect the bullets' trajectory and trace it back to our room. I turn my attention to the front entrance of their hotel. The black SUV the cultists arrived in, and subsequently valet parked, is now sitting out front with only the passenger side door open. Want to take a guess as to who's in the driver seat?

Yoldashev bursts from the revolving door with *Al-Kitaba Allat* under his arm. The four other cultists are close behind, but Yoldashev is the first into the passenger seat. I'm quite certain, in his haste, he didn't wonder why his car was already waiting out front. I am also quite certain he took Moose, behind the wheel, to be a parking valet. Finally, I'm guessing Yoldashev didn't exactly have time to put on his seatbelt as Moose buries the accelerator into the floorboard. The other cultists, a hair too late, chase the SUV toward the street. Moose drives only 50 yards before slamming on the breaks and leaving a trail of black rubber over the asphalt. The force flings Yoldashev violently against the windshield. And barely a second later, a reeling Yoldashev is pushed out the passenger side door and onto the pavement. Moose floors it again and the car disappears down the street.

Goddess book onboard.

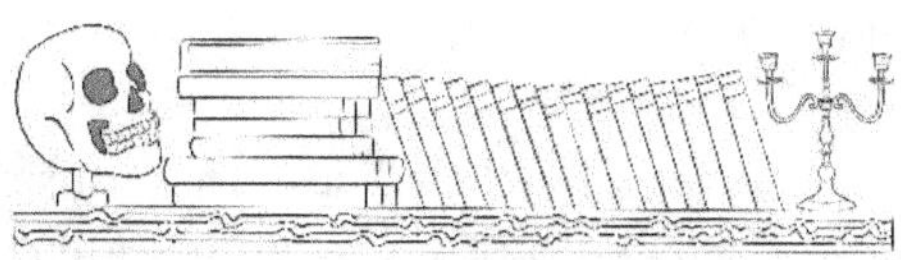

**Over Turkish Airspace/12 AUG/1433hrs**

"As you requested Mr. Conway, I was able to get a hold of my colleague and co-director of the Booker Foundation, Dr. Rosella Tassoni. She has the mythology expertise you desire. Forensic mythology, to be specific. I can bring her online whenever you're ready," says Dr. Vivian Cuinssey, whose image appears on the forward wall of the cabin. She has an earbud stretching from her ear to her laptop and it looks like she is in an airport terminal.

"Please, call me Skip. Hey, you headed somewhere, doc?" I ask.

"Lunenburg, Nova Scotia. I'm researching a uniquely German-influenced English there that dates back to the Colonial Era," she says as if that were a completely normal errand. "Tell me, where you able to procure *Al-Kitaba Allat*?"

"As a matter of fact, we were," I reply. "It's currently on its way to our secure facility and we are currently en route to Dubai." I forego the fact that we tapped Lieutenant Brooks to be our deliveryman. You should have seen his face when I told him that he was heading to Groom Lake, Nevada. "As it turns out, Gumanizov and the Cup of Death cult are working together in a mutual partnership. The cult seems interested solely in the goddess books, but Gumanizov has an interest in something else..."

Dr. Cuinnsey's image shrinks slightly and the image of another woman pops up. Her maple hair flows thickly below her chin and pools at her narrow shoulders. She has a schoolgirl's youth and a complexion like she just returned from summer break. Her owl-wide eyes are a rich caramel and could only be considered welcoming by invitation only. She wears a long sleeve, black tee with an artistic print on it—the kind one might pay too much for at a rock concert. She sits in front of a brightly lit window and is surrounded by moving boxes. "Um, good morning. I'm Dr. Rosella Tassoni."

"Wow," I say, "We now have enough doc's in here to be shipyard. Am I right?"

No one laughs.

"You must be the *man in black,*" Dr. Tassoni says.

"No, the Men in Black don't work international cases. Also they're total assholes. And they're based out of Los Alamos, New Mexico."

"And where is your super-secret agency based out of?" she asks.

"Groom Lake," I reply.

"Ah. Area 51. Of course," Dr. Tassoni says with sarcasm that bites harder than bad whiskey.

"Oh, you've heard of it then?"

She continues, "Mr. Conway—"

"Please, call me Skip."

Dr. Tassoni glares at me. "My specialty is in urban myth, but I understand you have questions on Classical mythology?"

"Sure do. Bubble Gum?" I say. Bubble Gum, half-asleep in her plush leather seat, apathetically taps a few buttons on her datapad. The translated version of Heinrich Barth's letter materializes on both doctors' screens. "This is the letter of some centuries-old German dude who explored the margins of the imperial world. As you can see, at one time he was in possession of all three goddess books. *Manat*, *Allat*, and *Al-Uzza*. He was willing to part with two of them, but one he felt compelled to hide -"

"*Al-Kitaba Al-Uzza*?" Dr. Cuinnsey interjects.

"The Aphrodite of the desert with a fondness for warmongering. You got it," I declare. "Specifically, Barth felt compelled to hide *Al-Uzza* in the place where it was first scribed. An ancient city now lost on the Arabian Peninsula known as Iram of the Pillars. A city that, as you can see, he gave the exact coordinates to. I think finding this lost city is Gumanizov's priority. My theory is that, after Al-Daris refused to sell, Gumanizov leveraged the goddess book in his possession to force the cult into procuring Barth's letter. And now, I think both parties are headed to this lost city."

Dr. Cuinnsey speaks up, "Absolutely, Gumanizov is after the treasures within Iram. That would be the find of a century. And he has enough Saudi generals in his pocket to access the site with very little red tape."

"Yeah, I'm sure he'll be on the cover of *Treasure Hunters Monthly*. Now, Dr. Tassoni, my devout Muslim colleague, Moose, here tells me that Iram of the Pillars is mentioned in the Quran. Isn't that right, Moose?"

Moose answers from off-screen, "The prophet himself brought destruction upon the city after they refused to reject the Pre-Islamic deities and recognize Allah as the one true God."

Dr. Tassoni finishes reading the digital letter. "Iram of the Pillars is also mentioned in *One Thousand and One Nights* and *Atlantis of the Sands* by Ranulph Fiennes who spent over 20 years looking for the city. This is incredible."

"Tell me more, doc," I insist.

"Iram of the Pillars is steeped in myth, sure, but myth often masks truth. In reality, Iram of the Pillars was a major trade center for frankincense. People whispered that its wealthy merchants had achieved their fortunes by forging pacts with evil djinn, but it was really just supply and demand. Natural phenomena were interpreted as a goddess' divine intervention. Similarly, its economic downfall was attributed to the victory of Muhammad's one god. But history tells a story of its own. You see, frankincense, resin gathered from trees of the genus *Boswellia*, was a key ingredient in nearly all rituals in nearly all classical religions. But two things went wrong."

"What two things?" I ask.

"Monotheism and climate," she replies. "Earlier religions in that region gave way to either Islam, thanks to the first Arab caliphate, or Christianity, thanks to the Byzantines. Frankincense isn't widely used in Christian or Muslim rituals. The money dried up. And not long after, a massive sandstorm supposedly buried the city, and it has remained forever lost in one of the world's most formidable deserts. The Empty Quarter that covers the bottom third of the entire Arabian Peninsula."

"The *Rub' al Khali*," I translate.

"The longest contiguous desert in the world," Moose adds.

"Hang on," Dr. Tassoni says searching her own laptop.

"What?" I ask.

"I remember coming across an article that suggested…yes! Here it is. It suggests that at the height of the frankincense trade, tree farms grew larger with demand, which required Iram to irrigate more of its arid surroundings. Which required them to dig further into the natural well beneath the city. One geological model concluded that the city could have fallen into a massive sinkhole created by over-draining the well and, over the centuries, been covered in sand. That same model, however, also predicted that the ruined city could be largely intact under the sands because of the bedrock typically found surrounding underground reservoirs."

Dr. Cuinnsey speaks up again, "What was it that made *Al-Uzza* so dangerous? More than all the others?"

Dr. Tassoni politely shrugs her shoulders. "Presumably, it reveals the location of Iram. But beyond that, I'm not sure. It's a bit concerning that Barth felt the need to hide the book in the ruined city of its origin, though."

"Well, Gumanizov and The Cup of Death sure seem eager to find out," I add. "The real problem is how we access the city. We can't exactly drop right into Saudi territory and into the world's most dangerous desert."

I hear a boarding call, presumably from Dr. Cuinnsey's feed. Then I hear the professor of linguistics say, "I think I know someone who can help."

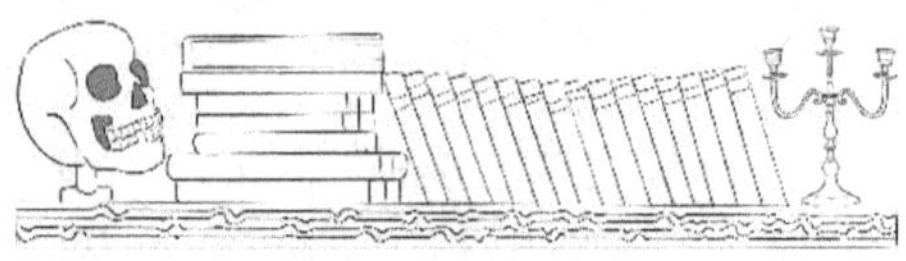

**Nasir Oil Refinement Plant/40 Miles West of Dubai/U.A.E./14 AUG/1015hrs**

Jake fucking Booker. In the flesh. Walks into the cavernous warehouse like he owns the place. I am fairly confident he does own the place, actually. He beelines right for me showing no visible signs of jetlag. “You must be Skip,” he says with a refined draw and extending his hand. His shaggy silver hair is tamed and perfect, and he wears a plain white tee tucked into belted Wranglers. Both of which look painted on him. The two things I really notice are his worn Durango boots—like mine—and the two six-shooters hanging from his armpits in twin shoulder holsters. Jesus, this guy is cool.

“Mr. Booker. It’s a pleasure,” I say.

“Please, call me Jake,” he replies.

I raise an eyebrow.

“So y’all are the spooks Vivian was telling me about,” he says. “I understand you can help smooth over my legal indiscretions in Romania.”

“I’ve already made the call, and yes, you have…wait a minute? Did you say Romania? Our agency has already contacted Macedonian consulate.”

“I may have run into a spot of trouble there, too,” he says with wink and a smile. “Now, I hear you boys,” he stops, glancing at Bubble Gum, “Pardon me. I hear you guys and gal are in need of some transportation.”

Bubble Gum taps her datapad, and thanks to a handy attachment, a 45” image projects on a small section of the interior wall—one of the only spaces in the warehouse not taken up by towering metal shelves filled with 55-gallon steel barrels painted blue or green. Jake Booker joins us in the semicircle of folding chairs around the screen, but doesn’t sit down.

The first map pops up. It’s a close-up of the coordinates for Iram of the Pillars. Just a sprawling, rusty desert with a ridge of windswept dunes to the north and east. “This was a satellite image of our lost city over four hours ago. This is the same location 30 minutes ago.” The picture changes. Same place, but now two grounded helicopters rest in the sand, surrounded by tiny human shadows that are scattered like ants. “The bad news is Gumanizov and the Cup of Death have already beat us to the site. And it looks like they used the Royal Saudi Air Force to get there as evidenced by these two Bell 412 utility helos from the their 30 Squadron.” I suddenly recall the countless hours that I spent analyzing satellite images and military targets as an intelligence officer. “The good news is Gumanizov will discover the entrance for us. Now for the fun news: we need a discrete approach under the cover of darkness and a solid plan for resistance. Here's where you come in, Jake."

The picture changes. Same location, but a much larger scale so that regional borders and coastlines can be seen. A green arrow points to the lost city's location. It's toward the southeastern edge of the Rub' al Khali in Saudi territory, equidistant from Oman and United Arab Emirates. The map also shows border checkpoints and aircraft radar coverage. "We need to cross about 120 miles through these lanes, flying under radar the whole time. We'll land about four miles out and hump the rest of the way. We need transportation for the three of us. Plus gear. Which will be about 900lbs including our water rations." I look to Jake, "I trust your helo can deliver us?"

Jake scrutinizes the map for a moment. "That's doable. But we're not using a helo."

"I'm sorry, what?" I say.

Jake continues, "The helo I have immediately available is a Robinson R22. It's a 2-seater. I take people out to visit the rigs with it. The type of helo we need would take me a few more days to acquire. Dubai is a playground for the rich and renting a helicopter on short notice here is a Herculean feat, even for me."

"I'm sorry, you keep saying 'we?'"

"Follow me everyone," Jake insists.

We all follow him to the nearest exit door leading to a paved access road. Before he opens the door, an overall-clad technician scurries from the small breakroom and delivers a piping hot cup of coffee in the local style. Jake thanks him politely in Arabic and walks out.

Out front, a polished red semi-truck hauling a flatbed trailer is parked in the shadows of distillation towers belching plumes of byproducts into the air. Atop the flatbed are four glistening ultralights with their wings folded and swept to the rear over their solitary propellers. Really, they are just fancy go-carts with wings. Only, instead of wheels, they are outfitted with large skis. "You have to be kidding me?" I say. I've heard of special operators using these vehicles for difficult insertions, but the problem is twofold. One, ultralights have an extremely limited range and carrying capacity. And two, unless you're flying over water, they are difficult to dispose of if you are trying to leave no trace.

"Friend of mine is starting a new business in Dubai. Taking businesspeople on forays in these ultralights along the coast and showing them scenic desert landscapes. These little beauties are made from a lightweight polymer and have a highly efficient two-stroke engine with extra fuel capacity. Their max range is about 118 miles," Jake says. "They're much quieter than any helo. Also, a day or two in the Rub' al Khali and they will be buried in the blowing sands."

"What's the load capacity considering the extra fuel?" I inquire. Liquids are heavy. A gallon of fuel weighs about six pounds and a gallon of water weighs roughly eight pounds. And in a desert, you need a gallon of water a day just to survive.

Jake sips his coffee slowly and answers, "To get the range we need? 250 pounds. Max."

"Listen, Jake. We're facing a dangerous, armed cult and a handful of military professionals in a harsh, unforgiving environment. We've got to be able to haul our gear. I mean, hell, Moose alone weighs, what? 225?"

"230," Moose confirms.

"I'm real sorry, but we're gonna have to travel light," Jake says.

"You keep saying 'we?'"

"That's because I'm going with you," Jake replies. "I have no intention of missing the opportunity to see Iram of the Pillars. Plus, you'll need me."

"How's that?" I ask.

"I know Gumanizov. Personally. I may just be able to persuade him not to shoot you."

I stare at him. I'm not happy. But I'm also working with limited options. "You think you can train my team how to fly those things in less than 12 hours?"

"It's not rocket science. Take off at full power into the wind. At 300 feet, trim it back to three-quarters and find your bearing."

"What about the flight controls?" I add.

"It's a control bar just like a hang glider. It's real simple. Just remember this…" Jake grabs an invisible bar with both hands about chest level, mimicking holding the control bar on the ultralight. He pulls the unseen bar toward him. "Sand dunes get smaller." He pushes the bar away from him. "Sand dunes get bigger."

I stare at him again. Listen, I know we're talking about Jake fucking Booker, here. Titan of industry and all-around manly badass. But he's still a civilian. And I have serious reservations about bringing him along on a potentially deadly mission.

"Of course," Jake continues, "I could just take my toys and go home." He whistles at the truck driver sitting comfortably in his air-conditioned cab. The truck's engine revs and drops into gear.

I look at Bubble Gum. She shrugs with an unspoken *why the hell not*. I look at Moose. He nods slightly. "Okay. Okay," I say. "You're in. But what's your plan for evac?"

Jake takes another slow sip of his coffee. "Well, I was thinking about 'borrowing' a helo from the Royal Saudi Air Force."

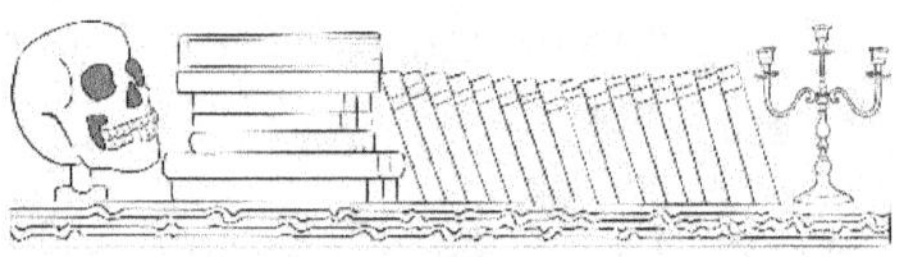

**Over the Rub' al Khali/Eastern Provence/Saudi Arabia/15 AUG/0322hrs**

And the sand dunes get bigger. And bigger. The engine on my flying go-cart just sputtered out and my glide path is now a little steeper than I'd anticipated. Night vision goggles limit my peripheral field and turn the barren landscape around me into every shade of green, but naturally, they do nothing to soften the landing. The skis on my ultralight crash down and then carve through the emerald sand. "Casper. Touch down," I announce.

"*Moose. Touch down.*"

"*Bubble Gum. Hell yeah*!"

"*This is Book. I've landed, as well.*"

"Alright team, everyone on me," I radio.

The current temperature is a brisk 43 degrees Fahrenheit, atomized sand whips our back from the southeasterly wind, and the fingernail moon above us gives off only slightly more light than the chalkboard of stars it scratches. We all wear black thermal suits, black balaclavas, and flip-down NVG's to combat the cold and darkness. We perform a final weapons check together. "Hey Book," I say pointing to both shiny, single-action, cowboy guns holstered under each arm. "Only skin those smoke wagons if you have to. The silver finish will reflect any ambient light and could give away our position." Jake affirms with the tip of an invisible hat. After dragging our ultralights to the leeward side of the nearest dunes to ensure the stirring sands cover them, we head on a northwest bearing that takes us to the long buried city.

The site is situated on the inside angle of dunes that form a sharp dog-leg bend. A foldable solar array the size of a large area-rug with a battery back-up lays flat just north of the two Saudi helos. Wires spider-web out from the array leading to a half-dozen dimly lit ground lamps. Another, thicker bundle of wires stretch from the array towards a hole that opens just at the base of the dunes. A soldier in desert fatigues, and armed with what looks like a compact Dragunov sniper rifle, guards the poorly lighted aperture. One of Gumanizov's men. Surrounding the entrance is a medley of survey and basic excavation equipment. Including crates, that if I had to guess, contained high-grade explosives.

"Movement by the helos," Moose announces. From our vantage point atop the crest of dunes roughly 60 yards away, we spy two men—pilots—having a cigarette at the rear of the two helicopters below. Out of sight from the guard at the entrance.

"Now's our chance," I whisper. "Moose, you and I will take the pilots. Book you stay close behind me. Bubble Gum, you have the guard."

Walking on sand gives us a silent approach, the smell of tobacco smoke will mask any body odor or foreign smell, the moon sliver and the blowing grit will make us hard to detect. Military pilots are a tough bunch. Don't get me wrong. But they spend most of their time either flying or training in flight-based scenarios. They spend very little time on advanced weaponry and close quarter tactics. Which is why when Moose and I get the drop on them with our submachine guns, they put their hands up and accept the deal Moose gives them in Arabic. "Hands behind your back and feet together, and I promise you will see your wives and children again."

It takes me less than two minutes to subdue them, zip-tie their wrists and ankles, and gag them with a plain, old bandana. That's when Moose steps forward with what looks like an Epi pen. Only this pen isn't filled with synthetic adrenaline. It contains fast-acting phenobarbital. The pilots may not fall asleep, but they will definitely be too relaxed to feel like struggling against their restraints and possibly escape. At least for the next four hours, or so. I think. It's not an exact science, OK? We're soldiers. Not anesthesiologists.

"Bubble Gum, you're up," I radio.

She doesn't respond because she is too close to her target. Leaning around one of the parked helos, I toggle the magnifier on my goggles and see the shadow that is Bubble Gum silently and fluidly spider crawling down the dune above the entrance and its guard. Gravity aids her as she slides down intermittently with every gust of wind. When she gets close enough, Bubble Gum leaps over the entrance and lands on the guard's back like a rabid monkey.

The guard lurches forward and falls on his rifle. With her legs wrapped around the guard's waist, Bubble Gum slides her right arm around his neck and locks it in place with her left arm, flawlessly executing a rear naked chokehold. The guard struggles mightily, but his effort will be futile. Which is why Moose, Book, and I approach them. By the time we reach the entrance, the guard has gone limp. But as soon as blood resumes its course through his brain, he will wake up. So we tranquilize him, too. And then bind his ankles and wrists.

I peek into the entrance to see tethered ground lamps illuminating a rocky, sandstone tunnel that leads down. "Alright team, listen up. Book, I need you to secure one of those helos. Familiarize yourself and make sure it's ready to launch. Keep an ear on comms. Moose. Bubble Gum. You're with me. I'll take point. We get in. We get the book. We get out. Any questions?" I leave no time for questions. "Great. We're Oscar Mike."

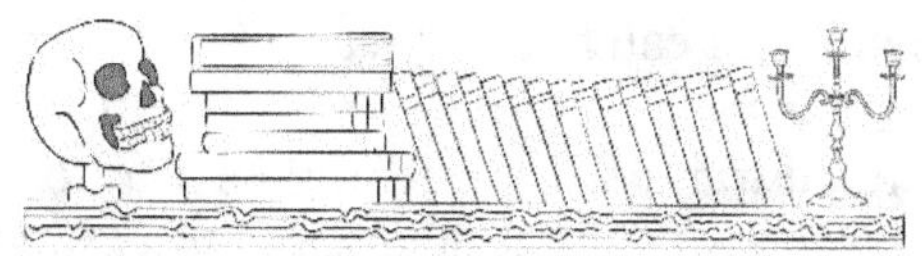

**Iram of the Pillars/Eastern Provence/Saudi Arabia/15 AUG/0407hrs**

We descend the tunnel, stepping around loose rock and over sand piles that makes our footing unstable. The amount of debris, char marks, and the strong rubber smell tip me off that they used C4 explosives to blast this tunnel and shovels, pickaxes, and jackhammers to make it passable. The tunnel is so narrow that Moose barely fits inside. But after about 20 yards the small excavated tunnel gives way to an exposed section of carved bedrock. A partially visible and perfectly sculpted horseshoe arch.

We drop to all fours to pass through the small passage under the arch. The wired ground lamps give way to scattered chemlights, better known as military-grade glow sticks, giving off a bright blue light. They reveal a precipice with a top rope bolted into the ground and snaking over the edge. Moose, Bubble Gum, and I low crawl to the precipice's edge and behold a city that time and history forgot. A city not built atop bedrock, but rather, painstakingly carved from it. An entire city etched and hollowed beneath a sandstone canopy held up by eight massive, sculpted pillars. All of it washed in a cornflower blue from hundreds of chemlights and a few battery-powered spot lamps.

The tip of the Iram iceberg above the sands must have been what collapsed because immense rubble piles of loose sand, molded bricks, and timber roofs cover a quarter of the city to our left. It reminds me of a snow globe that hasn't been shook in a while. Only really dark and with sand instead of snow. However, like most Classical and Pre-Classical Age towns, the two largest structures in this underground city are administrative and spiritual. The palace and the temple. Both brick and mortar buildings, propped up by smoothed pillars and flourishing arches, occupy the center of the city a quarter mile from our position. Carved bedrock does not make up all the buildings here, but all of them are jailed by the eight roughly hewn pillars nearly six stories high. In my countless trips to the unseen corners of the world, I can honestly say, I've never seen anything quite as breathtaking.

A concentrated trail of blue chemlights lead to the palace superstructure surrounded by four squared towers—almost like Islamic minarets. To the right of the palace, a crude dome suspended by layers of rounded pillars caps a slightly smaller structure. From the recesses of this temple, orange lights flicker. Torches.

"What's that smell?" I ask, detecting a stale, but still sweetly warm aroma.

"Frankincense," whispers Moose. "It must have been stored below, in the city proper. There is still water here, too." He points to channels of stagnant water that run through Iram's ruins. "The humidity still carries trace amounts of the scent."

"Well, I'm guessing we have cultists in the temple and Gumanizov in the palace looking for the royal treasury," I say. "We'll stick to the unlit roads towards the temple, single file. Use the shadows and your NVG's. Once in the temple, fan out and await my orders." Bubble Gum signals her understanding by picking up the top rope with her gloved hands, stepping over the precipice, and sliding silently down like it was a pole. Moose goes next. Then me.

We walk expediently and weightlessly. Knees bent with methodical footsteps and our MP5 submachine guns at the ready. Our NVG's turn the entire city, with its curved, clay-brick streets and stratified residences, green as if we are looking through a Sprite bottle. It's hard to balance my historical appreciation and intellectual curiosity for this amazing place with my adrenaline and mission focus. To say nothing of the lower brainstem urge I have to kick the ass of cultists who almost Swiss-cheesed me back in Timbuktu.

We arrive at the stairs leading to the temple and hear chanting. A low, almost Tibetan-esque drone. Climbing to the entrance, the smell of frankincense grows much stronger. We clear a sparsely lit corridor stretching the entire width of the temple. Interconnected fountains, long dry and dusty, line the passageway. In the shapes of desert wildlife: stoic camels, sycophantic jackals, proud eagles, and majestic antelope, these fountains are likely where devotees washed themselves before worship.

The corridor ends in three small archways beneath towering, megalithic figures. Their eyes are bulbous and polished smooth, with no irises. Three women. The coy maiden. The nurturing mother. And the glaring crone.

Al-Uzza. Allat. And Manat.

The blood-curdling scream of a woman pierces the air.

I give the signal to fan out. Moose, Bubble Gum, and I enter Allat's door and immediately come to a brick wall littered with small niches. Ancient spaces for offerings. Moose heads left. Bubble Gum and I cut right. As I round the corner, the sanctuary's brightness overwhelms me. A myriad of torches lights the chamber so intensely that I see only a wall of green and have to flip up my NVG's.

And that's when I see it. The ritual.

While all three goddesses have representation here, this temple is dedicated to Al-Uzza alone. The goddess revered for her beauty and her penchant for waging war. An idol at the temple's center vividly conveys both those facets; her likeness carved as a bas-relief upon a monolith nearly 20 feet high. The image is striking despite roughhewn angles. Eerily, the goddess's visage appears animated in the undulating shadows cast from swaying torch flames. Her body is lithe and each hand wields a sword like it's an extension of her body. Sitting at her feet is a snarling desert lynx nearly as tall as I am.

Pinned to the monolith by layers of hempen rope is a black robed and hooded figure who appears unconscious with their head covered and hung low. In front of the bound person and surrounded by a ring of torches, five chanting cultists clad in similar black robes stand around a makeshift pulpit fashioned from wooden crates. Atop the pulpit is *Al-Kitaba al-Uzza*. Our mission objective looks to be etched in pages of wood—I'm guessing frankincense—and inlayed with gold and gems. Salim Abdallah reads from it with his arms outstretched towards the monolith like an orchestra conductor. Over the others' droning chant, I can pick out some of the words he speaks. A sort of proto-Arabic with hints of Semitic, perhaps. Where the hell is Dr. Cuinnsey when you need her? "Moose," I radio. "Any idea what they're chanting?"

"*I hear praise and mighty. And tuja-sid.*" He replies saying the last word in Arabic.

"Tuja-sid?" I repeat.

"*Incarnation,*" Moose replies.

I give Bubble Gum the hand signal for surveillance, and she begins recording with her datapad. "Moose," I radio again. "Move in. It's almost time for party favors."

As the ceremony continues in the middle, Moose and I move to the sanctuary's vacant wings. We dart between smaller columns depicting Al-Uzza in different scenes, ranging from victorious battlefields where she holds the head of her vanquished enemy aloft to an absurdly large pleasure palanquin with her…well let's just say it's explicit. I move to a vantage point directly across from Salim's makeshift pulpit in time to see him unsheathe a large, gold-hilted dagger and raise it above his head. The chanting gets louder, and Salim rounds the pulpit, reverently walking towards the subdued cultist strung to the carved monolith.

"Moose. Bubble Gum. On my mark," I radio. I reach down to my tactical utility belt and pull out a M84 Stun Grenade—better known as a flashbang. "Now," I radio. Activating my flashbang, I heave it from the shadows. It lands near the pulpit with a loud clank that echoes through the temple. That gets everyone's attention. I close my eyes, cover my ears, and duck behind a pillar to avoid the flash that activates all the photoreceptive cells in the human eye. And the deafening 179 decibel blast that ensues. True, this device is used primarily for disorientation, but it also is superb at activating the flight complex.

My flashbang sends the cultists scrambling for cover. Moose's two subsequent flashbangs sends them stumbling out of the temple. All of them except Salim and the still bound, still unconscious cultist. Taking this opportunity to make a play on the book, I sprint full speed toward the pulpit, letting my MP5 fall by its sling. Salim sees me at the last minute, but it's too late. Jumping, my body goes near horizontal in the air. Both of my combat boots slam into Salim's chest, launching him backwards 10 feet and forcing him to drop the dagger in his hand. Landing on my weapon was, by no means, pleasant. Moose warned me of that when he taught me the maneuver. But it was totally worth it to imbed my size 10's into Salim's torso.

I scurry to my feet, kicking the dagger away. Salim is still down and writhing in pain. Moose materializes from the shadows, flips the *Al Kitaba Al-Uzza* shut, and tucks the mystical tome with a mosaic of precious red stones on its cover under his arm. He nods at me. "Nice move."

"*Casper. Bubble Gum. The cultists are heading towards the city center.*"

"Copy, Bubble Gum," I reply before turning to Moose. "Keep an eye on him." I point to Salim. Turning, I walk towards the bound cultist. Throwing the fabric hood aside, the young Middle Eastern woman beneath slouches forward. Even in her unconscious state she is beautiful. Tendrils of thick black hair are swallowed by the robes. Her eyes are shut. A trail of drying blood runs from her diminutive nose to her narrow lips. I place two fingers over her carotid artery. Her olive skin is clammy and her pulse faint. I walk around to free her from her restraint. As I start removing her restraints, Salim yells, "No! You must kill her!"

I untie the knot and pull the rope through slowly, letting her limp body fall gently to the ground.

"No," Salim repeats. "Take the dagger. Take it! And kill her! Finish the rite!"

I walk around the monolith to straighten the young girl's body.

"Do it! Kill her!" Salim cries.

"Moose. Radio Book. Prep for evac," I order. Moose turns and double-times it for the exit. I walk over to Salim.

"Please! You must listen to me," he pleads lifting himself to his feet.

I take the last tranq pen from my belt. Salim tries to put up a fight. But I bat his arm away and, with a crisp backswing, plant the tranq pen in his neck. "Good night, Salim," I say pushing him backwards. He falls to the ground, now lacking the motivation to get up. I jog back to the offering wall near the exit. Bubble Gum meets me there. "We're ready for evac. You tranq Salim?" she asks.

"Affirmative, let's get moving," I say.

"What about the other one? The one tied up? Where'd she go?"

I look back to where the young woman lay in front of the monolith.

And…she's gone.

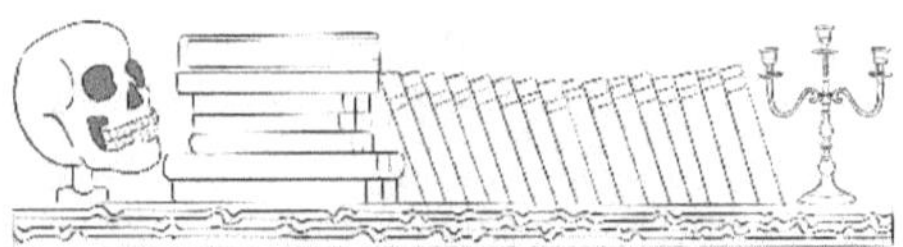

**Iram of the Pillars/Eastern Provence/Saudi Arabia/15 AUG/0444hrs**

The three of us jog back to the precipice along the same path that brought us to the temple. As soon as Bubble Gum grabs the rope to climb up, we hear the gun shot. Dirt from the cliff face explodes out.

We turn with weapons at the ready to see General Gumanizov. In desert fatigues, he casually holds a Desert Eagle that looks way too big for his hands. "That is my book," he yells with a thick Uzbek accent. Two armed soldiers at his side also point automatic weapons at us. "I think I'll have it back. Now." He aims his hand cannon at Moose.

"Maybe we can work out a deal," I offer.

"No deal. Hand over the book."

"No one needs to die here today, General," I say. "This could get awful messy."

"You were the thieves in Sochi, no?" he asks.

"Yeah. Not bad, right?" I smile, but it's lost under my balaclava.

"Tell me. Who do you work for?" he asks.

"Your guess is as good as mine," a voice calls from above all of us.

Gumanizov looks up while his soldiers still have their sights fixed on us. "Ah, Mr. Booker. I should have known these men were in your employ."

Bubble Gum clears her throat.

"Let 'em go, partner," Jake says, holding up a remote detonator. "I've rigged the whole tunnel to blow."

"You wouldn't," Gumanizov laughs.

"You can have anything you want from this place. I'd even be so kind as to not alert the Saudis about it. But these boys and the book? Well, they're coming with me."

Bubble Gum clears her throat, again.

"Sorry, darling," Jake apologizes. Bubble Gum narrows her eyes disapprovingly. I wonder how calling her 'darling' is going to go for Book if we happen to survive.

"So, General?" he returns his attention to Gumanizov. "What do you say?"

"I say you are a terrible liar, Mr. Booker."

Jake laughs and pinches the bridge of his nose. "You know something, Gumanizov. You're right. I didn't rig the tunnel to blow. But, I did rig this." Jake kicks what looks like a white block of clay over the side of the precipice. It lands at the feet of Gumanizov. A block of C4 with a receiving wire hanging from it. A press of a button and that wire will send a small shockwave through the malleable explosive, ignite it, and blow us sky high. "You boys even think about firing your weapons on my friends here, and I promise this place will be your tomb." Gumanizov looks down at his feet, then back up to Jake. "Now," the gambler finishes, "tell me I'm bluffing."

There's a very long, very uncomfortable silence in the underground city. Preferable to gunfire, mind you, but still uncomfortable.

"Give my regards to Dr. Cuinnsey," Gumanizov concedes.

"Don't forget to take up the rope when you climb up here, Casper," Jake says to me. "And, Gumanizov? One more thing." He reveals a Texas-sized grin. "Consider this payback for Mizar-i-Sharif."

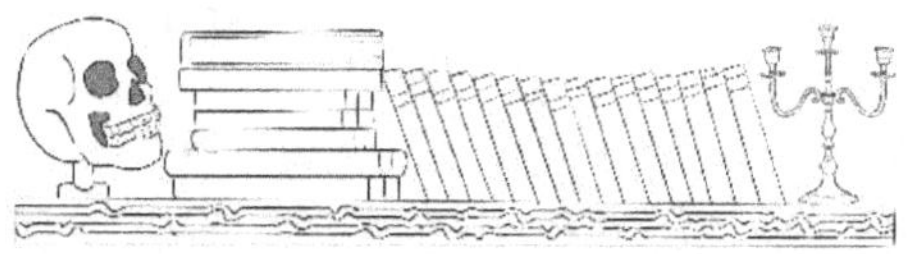

**Iram of the Pillars/Eastern Provence/Saudi Arabia/15 AUG/0458hrs**

"Hang on," Jake says, throttling up. Lurching into the desert sky, our liftoff isn't exactly seamless. "Sorry," Jake yells. "Still getting the hang of this." He finally steadies the rudder and noses the aircraft forward. On the horizon is the slightest ribbon of pink cast by the approaching sun. As we speed away shakily, I pat Moose on the shoulder, but he's already asleep in his jump seat. In his lap, *Al Kitaba al-Uzza* fills the cabin with the smell of frankincense. Bubble Gum has her balaclava folded above her head. She chews a piece of gum and stares through the portside window from her own jump seat.

"Sir," she says pointing. "What's that?"

"What's what?" I walk over to peer out. In the predawn serenity, atop a steep dune, a figure wears dark robes billowing in the growing desert wind. As we pass by, I notice more detail. A beautiful woman with tendrils of thick, black hair and olive skin. She triumphantly holds a gold-hilted dagger in one hand and the severed head of Salim Abdullah in the other, hoisting it in the air like Perseus would Medusa.

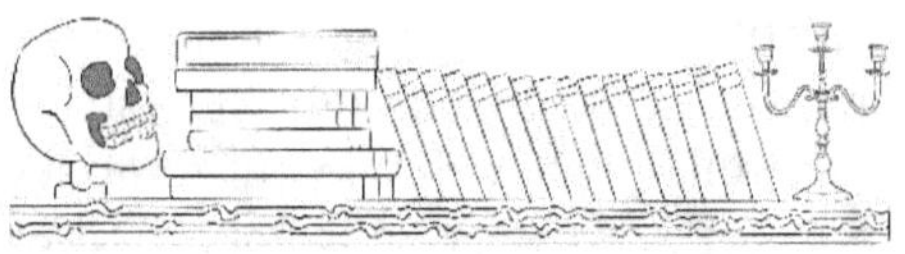

**Area 51/Groom Lake/Nevada/17 AUG/0815hrs**

Underneath our headquarters, affectionately called The Haunt, is an old vault purchased from a San Francisco bank that went under after the Great Depression. The vault door is painted with a medley of Egyptian hieroglyphs, and inside the concrete and steel room are curios from throughout history. Most of them stored on rustic oak bookshelves, inside steamer trunks crafted from centuries-old yew trees, and within refurbished cabinets from the Byzantine Emperor Justinian's private study. I type in the nine-digit password on the keypad next to one of those cabinets and the doors, carved with the faces of Jesus' twelve apostles, unlatch. I swing the doors open and see *Al-Kitaba Manat* and *Al-Kitaba Allat* resting on the bottom shelf, below one of the few copies of the *Necronomicon* and Morgana le Fey's spell book.

Moose hands me *Al-Kitaba al-Uzza*. It's bigger and heavier than its counterparts. Unsurprising, considering its wooden pages are brimming with resin and filled with enough gold and gems to start a jewelry store. But it still fits. I close the age-old cabinet doors and reset the modern lock.

"Remind me to send Jake Booker a thank you card," I say heaving the vault door closed and spinning the massive locking wheel. "Now," I continue, my circadian rhythm still beating across multiple time zones, "I am ready for a drink." My smartphone vibrates in my cargo pocket. A text message across the lit screen reads: *Please call me ASAP*.

Moose and I make our way upstairs to the briefing room and have a seat in cracked leather chairs around the old, polished table etched with Viking runes of protection. Moose tunes one of the many TV's on the wall behind us to the Weather Channel.

Bubble Gum zombie-walks into the room and unceremoniously plops down in another chair. "Is it beer thirty, yet?"

"Amen, sister," I reply hitting the send button on my smartphone and holding it up to my ear. A female voice picks up the call. "Dr. Cuinnsey? Still in Nova Scotia?" I say using my best Canadian accent.

"Skip?"

"Yes? Dr. Cuinnsey? Hello?"

"I've found something here in Lunenburg," she replies. "And I think you need to see it."

# Clue To The Past

## Karen Thrower

Dr. Lawrence Verville sat at The Turnhouse Restaurant in Edinburgh International Airport with a few other red-eyed patrons. Jet lag was kicking his ass and he hoped a nice, traditional breakfast would perk him up. But he was so worn out that the black pudding and baked beans on his plate didn't look the least bit appetizing. Not even the fresh black coffee was doing its job.

As he scraped his fork through the beans a feminine Scottish accent caught his ear. "These Eggs Benedict are abhorrent." He looked up and found the woman sitting at the bar, her back towards him. "All I taste is vinegar, do ya got a shoemaker back there cooking?" She asked the man behind the bar. Lawrence didn't know anyone could get so mad about eggs. Then again, a late flight will turn anyone into a gargoyle.

"I'm sorry Ma'am; I'll get you another plate right away." He reached for the plate and Lawrence watched the woman snatch the man's wrist, stopping him. He could tell she was saying something to him, but the clacking heels of early morning stewardesses and securities' walkie-talkie's crackling covered up her voice. The man behind the bar gave a quick series of nods and ran back into the kitchen. Lawrence watched the woman slowly flex her hands a few times before she ran them through her dark, curly hair.

She turned around in her seat so quickly Lawrence didn't even have time to stop staring at her. Even if he had, it was hard not to look at her. With her black jacket, purple tank top, and dark jeans tucked into combat boots, she was distinctive. The woman's eyes were narrow and full of rage as she leaned back against the bar. Lawrence gasped and looked back down at his breakfast.

"Do I know you?" He heard the woman say as she regarded him.

*Who me? Nope just one of those faces, with a big ol' beaky nose that scares women away!* He thought to himself as he stuffed beans in his mouth. From his periphery he could see her digging in a backpack.

She pulled something out and walked over to his table. She put a copy of his book *The Life and Mystery of Robert Lewis Stevenson* on the table. His picture on the back cover stared up at him. "That's you, isn't it?"

He cleared his throat and wiped his mouth with his napkin. "You found me." He looked up and met her eyes, they were an amazing deep green. "Do you want an autograph?" He was mostly kidding.

She snickered. "No, I'm not a fan girl. Though I don't imagine you have many of those." She sat down at the table across from him. "Hazel Edwards." She pulled out a business card and slid it across the table to him. "So, Dr. Lawrence Verville, what brings you to Edinburgh? Are you writing another book?" He took a bite of his toast, remembering what Dr. Rosella Tassoni told him before he left Washington D.C. '*Don't let anyone know what you're doing. Don't trust anyone. Find the manuscript and come back.*'

"No, I think the world has enough books on Robert Lewis Stevenson. I'm on a bit of a sabbatical. You? Are you coming home or passing through?" He picked up the business card and slid it into his briefcase, trying to be polite.

"Coming home. Peons like me only get so many weeks of holiday a year. Unlike published professors I imagine."

"Well, that book was something I'd always wanted to write. The University wasn't involved at all so they could care less if I made millions with it. I'd still have to be at least sixty years old before they considered tenure for me." He could tell the chuckle that came from her was the polite kind you get at boring cocktail parties. A waiter rushed over and set down a new plate of eggs benedict in front of Hazel. Lawrence swore he saw her glare at the poor waiter before he scuttled away without a word. But when she looked back at him, the glare was gone, almost like he imagined it.

"So, first time in Edinburgh?" She asked, ignoring her eggs.

"Yes." He lied, hoping she'd believe him. "I visited Stevenson's home museum on Samoa when I was researching my book, but never made it here. Thought I ought to~~o~~ now."

She rested her chin in her hand like she was waiting for more.

Finally, she nodded. "I see. Well, would you like a guide? I can take you to all the hot spots. Edinburgh Castle, Arthur's Seat if you feel like getting some fresh air." Lawrence put his tomato slice on his toast and covered it in baked beans. His mind was going a mile a minute trying to figure out with what to say. Purposefully getting rid of a pretty woman wasn't in his handbook. "Whiskey tasting maybe?" She finally suggested. "Or…something more up your alley perhaps?"

He swallowed his toast and tomato. "What might that be?" He motioned to her eggs. "Your breakfast is getting cold."

She shrugged. "It's shite anyway." She opened his book to page 158. He his heart raced, he knew exactly what was on that page. "This is my favorite part, when you talk about the lost manuscript of 'The Strange Tale of Dr. Jekyll and Mr. Hyde.'" She looked up, her head resting in her hands. "Why didn't you expand on it? All you say is it's just another one of the mysteries of Stevenson's life." Lawrence cleared his throat. *I did expand on it, but Dr. Tassoni told me to cut that part out,* he thought. He still wasn't sure how she got ahold of it before his editor. But that was Dr. Rosella Tassoni in a nutshell. Always on top of things.

"Write what sells, or so the saying goes. Most people who read my books don't care for mysteries, they want facts, that's all."

"Well, not me!" She banged her hands on the table, it was so loud it startled him. "I love how his wife Fanny was said to have burned it because it was controversial." She chuckled.

"What a bunch of prudes, eh?"

"Heh, yeah." Was it getting hot in here or was he just so nervous he couldn't calm down? He pulled at the collar of his button up shirt, trying to get some air.

"You know Lawrence," she leaned forward and whispered. "I've done my own digging on the subject."

"Oh? Not satisfied with history~~ as is~~?" He tried not to stammer as he spoke. He was a history professor after all, not a spy. Perhaps with practice he'd be better.

"Never." She laughed. "I think there's more to this than meets the eye, and when I saw you sitting here, I knew I had to introduce myself. It's kismet, isn't it?"

He smiled politely. "If you say so."

She crossed her arms on the table. "See here's what I think happened. Everyone knows Stevenson was horribly sick while writing Jekyll and Hyde. Lungs riddled with tuberculosis, and lord knows what else. I mean~~,~~ wasn't very hygienic back then. On top of that he was probably prescribed a strong mix of cocaine and whiskey to treat it for god's sake! I can't imagine walking down the street on that concoction let alone being able to write!" Lawrence chuckled; she wasn't wrong. "Word got to his parents that Robert was ill. So, his father made the trek from Edinburgh to Bournemouth where his son and wife were living. My theory is his father read the manuscript while visiting~~,~~ and agreed with Fanny that it was ridiculous. It shouldn't see the light of day," She pretended to be faint at the thought, putting the back of her hand on her forehead, "for fear anyone from the church see it. So, he took his son's manuscript." She slammed her hands on the table, making Lawrence jump. "Fanny just told her husband she burned it, so he wouldn't try and follow after his father. After all, a trip like that would have killed him in his condition."

Lawrence mustered up the most convincing smile. "I'm impressed." Hazel preened at his praise. All the research he had done, and not put in his book at Dr. Tassoni's insistence, reached the same conclusion. He tried not to be nervous about what she said, it was all public information after all! Anyone could have come up with the same conclusion. But he knew he had to end this conversation, and quick. "Well, thank you for the company, Hazel. I think I'm going to check into my hotel and get rid of this awful jet lag." He motioned at his waiter who brought him the check. "Thank you for suggesting some things to do." He put some pounds on the table and gathered his bags. "Perhaps I'll see you around."

Her smile immediately disappeared. "Well, wait you really don't want to look into this?"

He shrugged, trying to look nonchalant. "It's not real, it's just something fun to think about. There's no way it's true." Lawrence got to his feet and Hazel mirrored him. But now he could see that flash of anger in her eyes again.

She stepped close and yet he could barely hear her. “I really think we should look into this. I’m missing something here and you can help.” Lawrence was taken aback at how quickly her voice changed. It was no longer as feminine, and pleasant. It sounded scratchy like she’d been screaming for hours.

He chuckled nervously. “It was nice to meet you, Hazel.” He started walking away when he heard something crash behind him. He whirled, and saw the chair she was once sitting in was on its side, and waiters were running over to her.

“You have to help me, Lawrence!” She screamed at him. Three waiters tried to calm her down, but she flailed out of their grasps. A security guard ran over and put her arms behind her back and started escorting her away. “We can find it!” She screeched before she was forced into a nearby office. Lawrence stood flabbergasted a moment, looking at the chaos.

One of the waiters walked over to him. “Are you all right sir?”

“Yeah, I’m fine. Sorry about her.” He wasn't sure why he was apologizing; it wasn't his fault.

The waiter shrugged. “It happens. Early morning flights always leave people cranky.”

Lawrence quickly walked out of the airport and caught a cab, hoping Hazel was still in custody and unable to follow him.

“Where to?” The cabbie asked as Lawrence slid in after his bags.

“Malmaison Hotel, in Leith.”

“Right.” He hit a button to calculate the fare and started driving. Lawrence sat back and sighed, what the hell was that? He wondered. He’d never seen anyone act like that before, especially about something regarding his books! And the way her voice changed, it was creepy, and he shivered at the memory.

He pulled out his phone and started texting Dr. Tassoni. *‘Made it, heading to hotel. Met weird woman in airport, Hazel Edwards. Knew me and my book. Looked nothing like the picture of Harper Edwards that you showed me. Do I need to be worried? Have you heard of Hazel? Maybe they’re working together?’* He found the business card Hazel gave him and took a picture of it and sent that as well. It was around four A.M. Washington time, but he knew she wouldn’t care. Dr. Tassoni would want to know everything.

Not thirty seconds went by before he got a reply. *'I'll look into it and let you know. But be careful. Remember what I told you at our meeting'.* He put his phone away and sat back, thinking about his last meeting with Dr. Tassoni. It was four long days ago. He sat across from her in her office while she arranged all flight and hotel confirmation papers for his trip. It was his second assignment for Dr. Tassoni, and he was glad she thought he'd be able to handle something a little riskier. Out of the country, cell service might be spotty, alone, that sort of thing. But when she told him it had to do with his book, he knew he couldn't say no. No matter how dangerous it might be.

Dr. Tassoni handed him all the paperwork. "The lost manuscript of Jekyll and Hyde, I want you to find it and bring it back." He couldn't stop the single 'Ha!' that slipped out. Finding that manuscript was something he'd always dreamed of doing but pulling it off was harder than he thought. Dr. Tassoni's eyebrow's raised, he hoped in amusement and not annoyance.

He cleared his throat. "You just said you wanted me to do something I've wanted to do almost my entire life."

She nodded. "Now, your first assignment was easy. In the States, picking up a delivery and bringing it back. Simple and you didn't screw it up." She gently patted the round, glass display case on her desk that contained what looked to be an incredibly old vodun talisman. "That's why I trust you with this one. That and I figure your personal interest will help drive you to succeed."

"Oh, immeasurably I guarantee it."

"I've been meaning to get my hands on the manuscript for a while now. It's rumored to contain the formula Jekyll used to turn into Hyde. If something like that exists, we should make sure it's safe, and out of the hands of those who might abuse it." She opened a file on her laptop. "After going through your research and adding a bit of my own, I believe-that the key is the Oxcars Lighthouse. We've had people searching every house Stevenson has ever lived in, along with his father and uncle's and nothing's turned up. A few randy love letters, but no formula." She said with a smile. "The lighthouse is the last credible place we haven't looked." She sat back, folding her hands in her lap. "~~So,~~ it's all yours. Just be on the lookout for this person." She pulled an eight by eleven surveillance picture out of a drawer in her desk and handed it to him. It was a picture of a woman, late twenties or early thirties, with blonde hair and blue eyes. She was sitting in a café with an open laptop in front of her. "Her name is Harper Edwards," Dr. Tassoni continued, "she's been looking into the manuscript as well. She also resides in Scotland so keep an eye out. Now, go find that manuscript and come back."

Lawrence stared out of the cab's window. *What if Harper and Hazel were cousins?* He thought. He didn't recall seeing any blonde-haired women in the restaurant. He looked at his briefcase and couldn't shake the feeling that he needed to make sure everything was still there. He snatched it up and dug into it for a moment. When his fingers felt the thick manila envelope, he sighed in relief and pulled it from the briefcase. He opened it and saw the contents were still there. An old letter and a diary.

The letter was from Robert's father, Thomas, writing to his wife about how worried he was for their son. He felt Robert's health and mental faculties were declining. The things Robert was writing were in Thomas' opinion, disturbing and shouldn't be seen, lest his reputation suffer. He said it reminded him of that play Robert wrote as a teenager about the knave William Brodie. Lawrence knew of the play, it was about how Brodie epitomized the pinnacle of high society in public, but in secret, would break into houses to fund his gambling addiction. It was considered a failure, and Robert took it hard.

Lawrence read the letter's last line for what must have been the millionth time. 'I must stop by Oxcars before I return home, perhaps there, this will all be forgotten.' He knew the lighthouse had to be the key to finding the manuscript. It wasn't at Thomas' house, and if he were as sentimental as Lawrence believed, he wouldn't have just thrown it from a train or into the ocean. In his opinion, no matter how much Thomas detested the work, he would have hidden it, to preserve his son's words.

Looking up from the letter, Lawrence saw the cabbie was driving on the Edinburgh Bypass. He sighed and rolled his eyes. "I know you're taking me the long way."

"Better traffic mate, I promise." Lawrence shook his head in disbelief, he was too tired to argue. Something he figured the cabbie knew and decided to exploit. Lawrence sat back and fought to keep his eyes open. *Damn jet lag* he thought, as he fought against the hypnotizing view of the gorgeous green land out of his window.

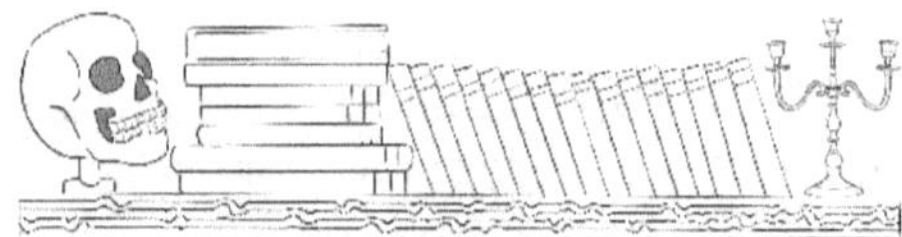

The next day Lawrence felt rested, ready to find the manuscript. It was a sunny, spring day in Edinburgh. That would help. He wasn't looking forward to cruising on choppy seas. But as nice as the day looked, it was off to a rough start. When he was eating his breakfast in the hotel restaurant, he saw a woman with curly dark hair serving mimosas at the bar. He immediately thought it was Hazel and started planning his exit. But when the person turned, he relaxed, it wasn't her. This woman had a wobbly chin and a friendly smile.

Then, when he went to sign for the breakfast he gasped as a waitress with dark hair popped out from the kitchen. But his fear didn't last long when he saw the waitress was much younger than Hazel. His encounter at the airport had shaken him. He wondered if he was going to see her everywhere until he left Scotland.

He walked outside the Malmaison, briefcase in hand, and looked out towards the waterfront. His instructions were to catch a speed boat next to the hotel. From the waterfront, it would be across choppy waters to Oxcars, the lighthouse Robert Lewis Stevenson's father Thomas, and Uncle David built the year 'The Strange Case of Dr. Jekyll and Mr. Hyde' was published. It was the last place Lawrence had to search before it was back to square one. He swallowed his nerves, both excited and scared, and walked towards the waterfront.

He could see a speed boat rocking with the water and an older gentleman walking back and forth on it. His skin was tanned and wrinkly from years on the water. Lawrence sped up and made his way to the boat just in case it wasn't supposed to be there. It didn't exactly match all the other big tour boats that were docked with it.

"Hello there! Are you Marcus Flannagan?" Lawrence called out to the older gentleman in front of the vessel. As stickler for details, or a comment on her estimation of Lawrence, Dr. Tassoni had hired Marcus before Lawrence had even stepped foot on the plane.

"That's me, takin' ya to Oxcars right?" Marcus asked. It was the thickest Scottish accent Lawrence had ever heard. He was relieved he could understand the man.

"That's me!" He stepped down the few stone stairs and stepped into the boat.

The driver tossed him a bright orange life vest. "You crazy lighthouse nuts keep me in business I swear." The man mumbled and sat at the steering wheel. "Have a seat and strap in, be about half an hour." Lawrence nodded and sat in one of the middle seats and buckled up. The engine roared to life and they took off.

He looked behind him and gasped as a woman with dark hair dashed behind some bushes. Was that Hazel or just a jogger? He pulled out his phone to see if he had missed a message from Dr. Tassoni, but there was nothing. Maybe he was just making himself crazy? Edwards had to be a popular surname, right? Even if she was following him, could she really be that dangerous? He put his briefcase on his lap and wrapped his arms around it. *No, it wasn't her, just relax Lawrence.*

Half an hour later the boat's engine cut off and Lawrence could hear his ears ringing. Maybe he should have brought some ear plugs, but it didn't take long for the ringing to be replaced by the sound of water lapping between the boat and the island. The island was small, the lighthouse took up almost the entire landmass. Which made it too small for a dock. The boat simply pulled next to the dark, craggy rocks and Mr. Flannagan threw a rope to tie around one of the bigger ones to keep it from drifting away. The seagulls didn't appreciate that at all and took flight the moment the boat knocked against the island. Lawrence stared at the lighthouse a moment, it looked exactly like the pictures, its white, red and one black stripe towered before him. Green moss was growing up one side, and he could see its two windows facing the mainland. His stomach was fluttering with nerves and excitement. *Finally,* he thought.

"There ya go, have a looksee but don't take nothin'," Marcus said. "I'll be waitin' right here for ya." Lawrence stood and took his lifejacket off, laying it on his seat. He took a few careful steps out of the boat onto the algae covered cement path. As he walked up to the lighthouse, he could feel his heart beating with excitement. He was close he could feel it.

He pushed open the door and walked inside the lighthouse. It smelled like old wood and ocean water. “All right here goes nothing.” He began his search. He sat his briefcase down by the door and started on the first floor. He moved some boxes around that he assumed the caretakers left so they wouldn't have to bring them back and forth when they worked on the lighthouse. The wooden floor was old and warped in places, but there were no hidden spaces beneath. No loose bricks or anywhere else someone might hide something on the first floor. Lawrence sighed and looked up at the second floor. “What about you?” His hands wrapped around the cold, metal stepladder, and he made his way to the upper level.

He looked around the sparsely furnished room for a moment. The wooden floor was dusty, so it was obvious that no one had been there for a long time. There was an old desk opposite of the window. Most likely used for someone to keep papers when they did check on the structure. He searched through its drawers out of curiosity, but he didn’t expect to find the manuscript in there.

The twin bunk beds were bare, there was no need to sleep there anymore so no mattress to tear apart. He was glad, that would have made a huge mess and most likely alert the authorities when someone did check on the lighthouse. He turned and saw the circular cast-iron post that went up to the lantern for the lighthouse above. Lawrence stepped up and read the plaque on it. 'DIOPTRIC FIXED LIGHT APPARATUS designed by T & D Stevenson, Engineers. Barbiere & Finestre, Paris & Dove & Co Edinburgh, Manufacturers, 1885.' He reached out and wrapped his fingers around it, but the pole was so big around, his fingertips couldn't touch. The pole was cold, and he swore he could feel slight vibrations from the wind outside.

He gave it a little tap and it made a muffled *ping*. He tapped along the length of the pipe, the lower he got it turned into more of a *ting*. Around the middle it was the muffled *ping* noise and a few inches higher it returned to the high-pitched *ting*. His eyebrows furled. “No.” He reached in his back pocket and pulled out his little black tool case. “Can't be.” He muttered and opened the case and pulled out a little Philips-head screwdriver. It was small, but strong, and he managed to take out all four screws that held the plague onto the pole.

Years of salt build up, and grime held the plaque on the pole without the screws, so he put the screwdriver away and took out the matching flathead and started prying around the edges. Dark paint and salt flaked away, and he managed to pry the plague off the pole. The plaque was covering a jagged edged hole, and inside it looked like a thick, green, glass bottle. He felt his heart speed up as he touched the glass. It was cold, but didn't have any letters on it, so there was no telling where or when it came from. Lawrence squinted and could see something inside. He laid his fingers on the glass, moving them up and down, but the glass bottle wouldn't budge. He sighed, realizing he'd have to do something unthinkable.

"Sorry." He put the flathead away and pulled out a tiny hammer. *Should have brought some gloves,* he hit the bottle with the hammer. It cracked, and he hit it again then used the little claw of the hammer to pry a few big pieces off the bottle. He was right, something was inside the bottle. Lawrence stood with his chin in his hand, wondering how he could get it out without cutting it, or him.

Using the hammer, he tapped around the hole on the glass bottle until enough of it chipped away. It was about three inches around before it was big enough, he was confident, he wouldn't cut his fingers on it. He opened his kit and put the hammer back and took out his secret weapon, two micro-gel fingertip grips. They were bright pink because that's the only color they had left. That was fine, made it easier to see them deep in pockets of his jackets or his briefcase. He slipped them on his thumb and pointer finger of his right hand and gently squeezed. The feel of leather between his fingers was gratifying, exciting. But that was the easy the part. Lifting, he worked them up through the bottle until he saw the bottom edges of what looked like thin leather covering a bundle of papers. Sneaking his finger into the middle of the bundled papers, Lawrence gently pulled them in an angled downward motion.

Using his left hand to keep the papers from scratching on the bottle, he exhaled in relief as the papers finally came free. They were tied together with a long piece of yellow stained string. *These better not be some fancy bill of sale for the lighthouse* he thought as he took the papers over to the desk.

He slipped out of the fingertip grips and put them in his jacket pocket. With one pull, the string came untied, but the papers had been rolled-up way for so long that they stayed in that shape. He slowly unraveled the tube of papers, and his eyes went wide as he saw the first page. 'The Strange Tale of Dr. Jekyll and Mr. Hyde, first draft 1886'. "I can't believe it." He shuffled through a few pages and recognized Stevenson's handwriting, familiar sentences, plus a few that were different! "Oh my god I found it, I found it!" He did a little jig before pulling out a special plastic poster sleeve he brought and slid the manuscript inside. His hands were shaking as he stood, staring at his rolled-up prize. "Oh my god, oh my god." He kept whispering. He couldn't wait to get back to his hotel room and read it all! He started down the ladder when his phone began ringing.

He landed with a little thud and pulled his phone out of his pocket. He chuckled and hit the green button. "Dr. Tassoni, I can't believe it, I found it!" He tried hard not to yell into the phone. "Thomas hid it behind the plaque that,"

"Good! Now hurry back," She interrupted him, "I had trouble finding this Hazel Edwards you ran into, but I did. At first it seemed like she never travelled, didn't have school records, no medical record, just a simple identification card with a picture that matched the phone number you gave me. I managed to get my hands on some security feeds. Those places that Harper had investigated, she never showed up on the video. But the woman on the identification card did, a woman with dark curly hair. She showed up, every single time. Airports, traffic cameras, even in the background of stranger's photos they'd post to social media. Always this woman with dark hair, never Harper."

Lawrence felt his stomach fall to his feet. "Hazel had dark curly hair."

He heard Dr. Tassoni sigh. "She isn't Harper's cousin or sister, she has none." Lawrence felt confused as he tried to wrap his mind around his conundrum. "Lawrence, it's Hazel whose been looking," Dr. Tassoni continued, "not Harper. But their fingerprints are identical, so it looks like it's Harper. Hazel doesn't really exist, legally speaking, all she has is an ID to get into places. She uses Harper to travel where she wants. There's more

Lawrence, this Hazel has a record a mile long of mainly disorderly conduct and other violent behavior. I don't want to say it, but…" her voice trailed off.

"What? Dr. Tassoni?" Lawrence asked, wondering if the call had been dropped.

When she spoke again, her voice was deadly serious but just above a whisper. "It's almost like Hazel…is Harper's Hyde."

"Her Hyde?" His eyes went wide with shock.

"Oh, there's more," Dr. Tassoni sounded annoyed. "It seems Hazel follows you on Twitter. Hazel, not Harper. She only follows you, no one else, and there's no profile pic, just a black screen. And she liked all your tweet about landing in Scotland. In fact it seemed she liked them only moments after you posted them." Lawrence's jaw dropped. "I know I gave you permission to post about it, so your family and colleagues wouldn't worry about you, but I think that was a bad idea. Hazel followed you or stalked you at the airport. Your meeting wasn't a coincidence. Get back to your hotel room, secure the document and get back here."

His heart was beating frantically. "Yes ma'am. My flight is tomorrow night, I'll just sequester myself in the room until then and ask about an escort to the airport."

"I have a better idea; I have a colleague in London. She can get to you quicker than you can get home." He could hear Dr. Tassoni typing furiously as she spoke. "I'll tell her to go to your hotel room and keep an eye on you. I'm also going to send her everything I have on both the Edwards women. Can't hurt to have someone else looking and she might find something I missed."

"Thanks Dr. Tassoni. What's your colleague's name?"

"Maria Bishop. She's got short dark hair and blue eyes and will have a lot of equipment with her. Do as she says. Especially if something…unfortunate…happens. She can get you out."

"Unfortunate?" His palms began to sweat, and he pulled the collar of his button up shirt away from his neck.

"Unfortunate." She confirmed, then the line clicked as she hung up. Lawrence shoved his phone into his pocket, trying not to think of what kind of things she meant. Hazel had followed him to Scotland or stalked the airport until he showed up. She was even crazier than he thought!

Lawrence quickly put the poster sleeve in his briefcase and

maneuvered his way along the algae covered walkway back to the boat. He jumped in and told Marcus to drop him off back at the hotel. He tried to remain calm, but it was hard knowing some unstable woman might be stalking him. Especially one with a violent history. The closer they got to the shore the more he searched for dark haired women, but he didn't see any.

The boat stopped next the same stone steps he used earlier. "Can't get much closer than this!" Marcus said. "Hope you had fun!" Lawrence climbed out of the boat, tossing his life vest on the floor. "I know I did." Marcus mumbled like a grumpy grandpa as Lawrence quickly walked from the boat, searching for signs of being followed. So far it seemed clear. No one was ducking behind plants or hiding behind newspapers.

Lawrence made his way back to his room unaccosted and locked the door. He just had to watch his back until Dr. Tassoni's colleague showed up. Until then, he pulled the poster sleeve from his briefcase and smiled at the thought of reading this lost tale.

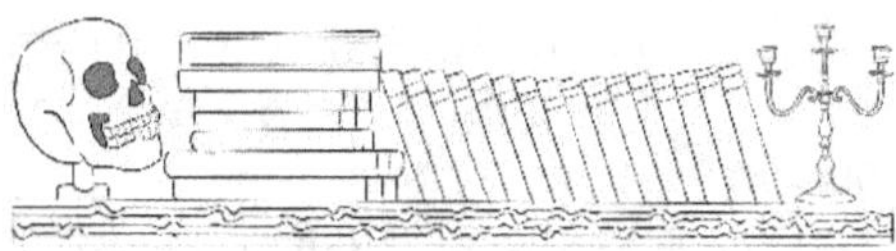

Lawrence was pacing in his hotel room, slowly reading page after page of the manuscript. He had already found a few differences that made him giddy. Names, dates, little things to most people, but to him it gave him butterflies in his stomach. Just then his stomach growled, and he realized in all the excitement, he forgot to eat lunch. He picked up the phone and ordered room service. He thought it would be safer than going down to the restaurant. After perusing the menu, he decided he deserved something amazing to eat, and ordered truffled leeks, a Black Angus grain fed fillet steak with glazed carrots and parsnips. Along with something he really didn't need, dessert. The second he ordered the Valhrona dark chocolate mousse he knew he'd eat that first, after toasting to Stevenson and all his work of course!

He hung up the phone and sat at the little table in his room, the manuscript in front of him. He sighed and wondered if Dr. Tassoni was right about the formula. In his excitement about finding discrepancies between the two manuscripts, he forgot about the formula. He gently flipped through the pages he hadn't read yet, until he came to three pages filled with chemical equations. He was a history professor that loved literature, the chemistry went over his head. Still, while he may not have understood the equations, he understood the idea of that many chemicals going to one body struck him as obscene.

There was a knock at the door and his stomach growled in response. "Coming!" His mouth was watering with anticipation of his food, and he opened the door.

"Afternoon Professor." Hazel shoved past him into the room. *Damn it why didn't I look first!* He chastised himself and blamed his stomach for his slip up. "Did you have a productive morning?" She stopped next to the little table and lovingly touched the papers. "I guess you did." She was wearing the same clothes she had on in the airport, black jacket, dark jeans tucked into combat boots and a purple tank top. Had she been tailing him the whole time?

"Those are mine," He walked up to her, trying to get between her and the table, "get out of here right now or I'll call security." She turned to him, a big smile on her face. Seems his stern professor voice had no effect on her. "I mean it, out!" Hazel's eyes roamed over him, her hands still in her jacket pockets.

"Oh, I can tell you mean it Professor." She moved so fast he could hardly believe it was happening. Her right fist flew from her pocket and punched him in the side of the head so hard he fell to the ground. Pain radiated through his head and everything felt like it was spinning.

"Thanks for finding the formula. I've been looking for years." She kicked him in the stomach, and he felt the air get knocked out of him. "Now everything will be as it should." He felt the heel of her boot smash into his back, it hurt so much he wondered if she broke a rib. How strong was this woman?

He heard the papers shuffling and looked up. Hazel was standing over them, a smirk on her lips and he heard her whisper, "God hath given us these things in tranquility." But she didn't look happy for long, as she suddenly gasped and doubled over in pain. She growled, and her hair started to lighten, and the curl was disappearing. *Was this happening?* He wondered or did he have a concussion from her hit. Hunching over Hazel put the entire manuscript back into the poster sleeve and put it in her jacket with a shaking hand. “Don’t even think about it bitch.” She hissed.

“I wasn’t!” Lawrence yelled and sat up, using the wall for support.

“Not you.” She snapped at him and slapped her cheek so hard he could see her handprint on her skin. “Stay down!” Hazel yelled and stood straight, her hair was dark and curly like before. “I’ll make sure you never come out again.” She leaned over Lawrence who managed one good swing at her face, but she caught his fist in her hand. “Nice try Professor.” One more hard punch to the face and it all went dark.

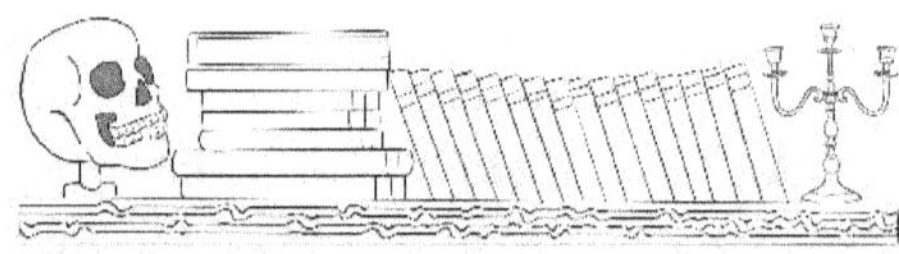

“Dr. Verville?” He heard a woman’s voice, and he jerked awake. A younger woman with short, dark hair was sitting next to him. She looked to be in her twenties and was wearing a worn, silver bomber jacket and shorts. “There you are.” He searched the room and saw his food was on the table. She must have brought it in. He hoped someone from the hotel wouldn't bring his food in and ignore his unconscious body in the corner.

“Who are you?” He said as he sat up, holding his ribs. His head was fit to burst, and it hurt to breathe.

“Maria Bishop, Dr. Tassoni sent me.”

“Oh, right.” He saw an unfamiliar briefcase and large, black backpack on the floor behind her. “Can I see some identification?” He asked. She dug into her back pocket and pulled out a wallet. He tried not to laugh at the old peeling Transformers’ stickers on it. She pulled out a card that said 'The Booker Foundation' on it, with her name underneath and photo on the back. He held out his hand. “Nice to meet you.”

“Same.” She curtly shook his hand. “Now, where's the manuscript?” She turned to her backpack and pulled out a plastic cylindrical container. It would have been perfect for the manuscript. Humidity controlled, crush proof, the works.

“She took it,” Lawrence fought his way to his feet. “Hazel took it and knocked me out.” He dug into his suitcase and pulled out a bottle of Advil and popped two into his mouth.

"You're lucky she didn't kill you." She hopped to her feet and plopped her backpack on the table. "Give me your phone." She started digging through her big black backpack. He pulled it out of his back pocket, thankfully it wasn't broken, and laid it on the table.

"What do you need it for?" He took a big bite of the chocolate mousse, swallowing the Advil with it. He deserved that now.

"You got her number, supposedly, I'm gonna need you to call her." She pulled up a picture of the business card he had sent Dr. Tassoni the day before on her own phone. "Keep her on the line as long as you can." She pulled out a big square box and plugged some wires into it. "The longer you talk the better signal we can use to find her." He watched her pull a cord out of the backpack and plug one end into the box and the other into his phone.

"Quite the spy kit you got there." He tried to be funny.

"Quite the formula you got, oh wait." She handed him the phone. "Call her." She put an earpiece in. Lawrence sucked on his bottom lip and discovered it was split and gasped at the pain.

"Just trying to be friendly." He mumbled and dialed the number Hazel gave him. "Think it's actually her number?"

Maria shrugged. "Hope so."

"Lawrence!" He heard Hazel's voice over the phone and felt his heart jump to his throat. "You called, how nice. How's your head? No permanent damage I hope?" Hearing her voice, knowing what she did, who she was, was making it harder to not sound scared.

"It's fine now. You didn't have to do that, I would have shared it." He watched Maria nod as she watched something on the big box start beeping.

"I don't share well Lawrence. But I can't thank you enough. I've been looking for that manuscript for ages." Maria looked at him and pulled her hands apart, she wanted him to stretch the conversation.

He rolled his eyes. "Why? Are you going to sell it someone? I bet I can find a buyer that would pay twice what yours would pay." He was proud for having pulled that out of his ass at the last minute. "I'll meet you anywhere, you name it. What do you say? Want to be a millionaire?"

"A millionaire?"

"Y-Yes," Maria rolled her hand in a circle for more. "Whatever the price, I can beat it, and I mean it, I'll even meet you in Paris if you want, I'm totally flexible." He said with a nervous chuckle.

"I bet you are." She teased. Maria again pretended to throw up and Lawrence swatted at her.

"So?"

Maria crossed her fingers while he waited for an answer. "No." Lawrence sighed in relief. He really didn't want to come face to face with his attacker her quiet yet. But Maria did a very calm 'yes' with double rock and roll hand signs. He hoped that meant she had found Hazel. "I think not." Hazel's voice brought his attention back to his phone. "It was a pleasure meeting you, but I think I'll take my new manuscript and, thumb through it until I find the important part."

"Important part?" Now he was getting nervous, would she destroy the rest of it! Hazel laughed, and she hung up.

Lawrence sank back into the chair. "Please tell me you got what you needed." He stabbed his steak with the fork and took a big bite. It was still good cold. Maria snickered and unplugged the cord from his phone. "Excuse me for being a history professor who just got his ass beat and not a spy."

She clicked her tongue and put away her things. "I always told Rosella she should be more selective in those she trusts with these missions."

"This mission is my life's work, I had to come." He sighed and dropped the steak back onto the plate. "Did you figure out where she was?"

She nodded. "Signal originated in London."

"London! How long was I out?" London was a good four hours away!

"Few hours maybe, don't sweat it Professor. I was knocked out for ten hours once and I'm fine. A few won't kill you." She slung the backpack on and clapped at him. "You all packed? We got a train to catch."

"Oh, give me a moment." He started throwing clothes into his luggage with one hand and eating his steak with the other. "Didn't think it'd be such a quick exit."

"No one ever does." She winked.

Forty-five minutes later Lawrence was sitting across from Maria in a private train compartment. She had her laptop out and he could hear her typing furiously, the screen was so big it hid her well from his vantage.

"So, Lawrence,-tell me everything that's happened since you got to Scotland." He sighed and sank into his couch, telling her everything from meeting Hazel at the airport, to finding the manuscript, to when she showed up and knocked him out.

"Dr. Tassoni warned me, but I guess I was a bit complacent when it came to lunch."

Maria looked up, her eyes peeking over the top of her computer. "Just a bit." She ducked back behind the flap.

"Losing the manuscript like that, I feel like such a fool."

"Well, it has a powerful formula in it. If it wasn't Hazel, I'm sure someone else could have tried to take it." Her fingers still flying across the keyboard.

"You're just trying to make me feel better."

"Yep." Her lips made a little pop at the end.

Lawrence cleared his throat. "So that formula, I couldn't tell if it was real or something Stevenson just made up for the story. But it was kind of long, three whole pages. Is that normal?"

Maria sighed, "Oh, it's real. Probably why Stevenson took it out of his published edition. The chaos!" She shook her fist in the air then went back to her computer. "But, if we can get it back, maybe we can help Harper Edwards restore her life."

He leaned forward and peeked over her computer monitor. "Hazel really is Harper's Hyde?"

"As impossible as it sounds, yes." She flipped the monitor of her laptop around. He saw it was a security feed dated two years ago. He watched a young blonde girl struggle to get into the bathroom of a pub. It was Harper Edwards. She smashed herself into the walls and one of her hands slapped the other as it tried opening the door. "Pay attention to her clothes." He did. She was wearing a black jacket with a skull on the back. Her frayed skirt was above her knees and her boots were tall with flames on the side. He watched Harper go into the bathroom, the door closing behind her.

The time code on the video sped up to show ten minutes

passing. No one else had entered in that time. When the video slowed, he watched the bathroom door open and Hazel came out of the bathroom, same clothes, same skull, same shoes. Everything.

"Rosella sent me this a few hours ago. She thought it might help make you understand."

Lawrence shook his head. "I mean I see it, but how?"

"When Stevenson was young, he worked with a scientist named Dr. Byron Spalding. You know that play Stevenson wrote about Brodie I assume?" Lawrence nodded, still watching the surveillance video. "He wanted to give Brodie a reason for his personality flip," Maria continued, "hence the formula. Seems Spalding took the assignment literally, instead of just giving Stevenson some fancy science words. Maybe he realized what he had; we'll never know. Anyway, another doctor found it decades later, locked away in a roll top desk after Spalding died." Lawrence gasped and started going through his briefcase and pulled out the old diary that belonged to a prostitute named Hatty.

"Dr. Marshall Jenkyns." He read aloud.

Maria gave him a wink and clicked her tongue. "This diary is said to have been a profound influence on Stevenson's story. The name Jekyll wasn't mentioned, but Hyde is. Hatty wrote that Dr. Jenkyns was a frequent visitor, but then he wrote her a letter saying a man named Hyde would be taking his time instead. She wrote that Jenkyns never came back after that, but a man named Edward Hyde came like clockwork from then on."

"Hatty's diary, yeah," Lawrence tried not to be impressed that Maria knew about the diary. "She was a fan of Stevenson and sold her diary and story to him for a pretty penny. It got her family out of poverty and history was made. Clearly Hyde got rid of the formula that Jenkyns found, for fear of finding a way to reverse it. But he didn't know that the original scientist, Spalding, had given that same formula to Stevenson, all those years earlier and that it survived in the lost draft of Jekyll and Hyde. According to the notes Dr. Tassoni sent me, this original Hyde died before the story was published, but not before getting Hatty pregnant. Harper is a direct descendant of Dr. Jenkyns after he took the formula and turned into Hyde. His poor descendants never had a chance." Lawrence stared at the video of Hazel misbehaving in the pub, flipping over chip bowls and stealing beer from the tap.

He sat slack jawed. "I…" He couldn't even think of what to say.

"Welcome to The Booker Foundation where the myths are real, and the science doesn't matter!" Maria said as she thrust her fist into the air. "But we have a few hours before you need to get your marbles back in a row before…"

Lawrence noticed the silence and flipped the monitor back towards her. "Before what?"

"Crap." She snapped her laptop shut and he noticed the black band around her wrist was blinking. "The signal we got from her phone was bounced, it wasn't in London. Damn it."

His jaw dropped. "Where is it?"

Maria quickly put her stuff back in her backpack. "On the train."

His eyes went wide as he looked between her and the door. "This train? She's here?"

"Yep, and I doubt she wants us to get off." Her face scrunched up for a second, "Err get off the train, ugh, you know what I mean!" She put her backpack on and picked up her briefcase. "Come on, we don't want to be alone if she finds us."

"You think she'll come after us? I mean she has what she wants!" He stood and slid his luggage out of its little cubby.

Maria slid the door open and she hustled down the hall. "Yes, but we know what she has, and theoretically what she wants to do with it. That's enough for her. Hyde was a homicidal maniac with no remorse, and that trait passed to Hazel. More people around won't stop her, but it might give us time to run."

"Theoretically? What does she want to do with it?"

She looked over her shoulder. "Get rid of Harper." He sighed heavily at the thought and followed Maria through the train.

They didn't stop until they reached the restaurant car. The hostess smiled as the door slid shut behind them. "Hello, can I see your tickets?" Maria showed the woman her phone which had the receipt for their tickets. "Thank you, this way." They followed her to a little table on the left side of the car. They could see the countryside zooming past and Lawrence quickly scanned the other faces with them. No Hazel and no Harper. The hostess set down some menus, "The bar is closed but will open in an hour if you'd like to wait. The specials today are,"

"Thanks!" Maria interrupted her and hid behind her open menu.

"Oh, okay, well, have a good meal."

When she was out of earshot Lawrence picked up his menu. "Now what?"

"You watch that door," She motioned to the door behind her, "And I'll watch the one behind you. If you see her, run."

"You really think she'll try to kill us on a crowded train?"

"Plan for the worst." She put her menu down and checked the black band around her wrist. "Signal doesn't seem to be moving at least."

"Can't she just put her phone down?" Lawrence asked.

She looked up; her eyes wide. "Damn it." Her head whipped around to look for Hazel.

"Some spy." Lawrence said and rolled his eyes as a server came in through the door he was supposed to watch. Her hair was under a white cap and there were several bottles of beer on the tray she was carrying. *Not her.*

"Hey!" Maria turned and pointed a stern finger at him. "I am not a spy." She leaned close and hissed at him. "I'm a Librarian." He wanted to laugh when he remembered something the hostess said. The bar was closed. So, why was that server carrying beer?

"Some librarian." A familiar Scottish accent said. Lawrence's eyes went wise and they both gasped when saw Hazel standing next to the table. She was hiding a gun under the serving tray that had the beer on it. "Let's go back to your compartment." She turned her whole body a bit and pointed the gun at a young woman at another table. "Or she dies."

"Really?" Maria rolled her eyes at Hazel. "I don't know her. I don't care."

Lawrence's jaw dropped. "But… But…"

Maria jumped up and swung her backpack into Hazel, knocking the serving tray, beer, and gun out of her hands. Lawrence watched the gun skitter along the floor and people started screaming and running for the doors.

"Damn it!" Hazel jumped for the gun and Maria grabbed Lawrence's hand and pulled him through the nearest door.

"Thought you really meant that about that woman." He said as she pulled him into the next car.

"Oh, I did. But thankfully it didn't go down that way." She stopped and looked at the black band on her wrist. "Let's find that phone. I'd bet a year's salary she's got pictures of the formula on it now. We can delete the pictures and see if she sent them anywhere."

"Then what?" Lawrence seemed lost.

"Then we keep her from killing us." Maria and Lawrence dashed through two more train cars until it seemed they were in the last one. It was filled with luggage and boxes.

"She stashed it in here?" He raised his voice. The clickity clack of the train was louder here.

"That's what it says." She slid her backpack off and opened a little lid on her wristlet. "Keep watch, I'm going to look." He watched her disappear behind some boxes and heard her pushing things around.

"Sure you don't need help?"

"Just keep watch!" Her voice was muffled.

"Okay!" He turned back to the door and through the window he could see Hazel, that white hat was long gone. She smiled and waved at him. "Crap, she's here!"

"Stall her! I can't find the phone."

He watched the door slide open and she stepped inside, gun in hand. "Hello Professor." Hazel pointed the gun at him. "Tell your little friend to get over here."

"Screw you!" Maria yelled from behind some boxes, as packets of noodles went flying in the air.

Lawrence put his hands up. "Hazel, we don't have to do this, we can find a way to help," but before he could finish, he watched as Hazel's entire body shuddered and she dropped the gun. She fell to her knees and Lawrence kicked the gun towards the back of the car. He watched as she looked up at him, her dark hair turning gray, then blonde, and her eyes flickering between green and brown. "Hazel?" He kneeled, and she reached out for him.

"H...Harper." She whispered. He could tell she was in pain. "Don't let her have the formula please." Even her voice was different! It was higher pitched than Hazel's, making her seem younger than she was. She grabbed his shirt and pulled him close. "If she can recreate the formula, I'll disappear. I'd rather die than let her have complete control." She reached into her shirt and pulled out the poster sleeve, the manuscript was still inside. "Take it!" She shoved it into his chest. He took the sleeve and quickly put it in the outside pocket of his briefcase. He turned back to Harper and could see the tendons in her throat pulling as she spoke. "She's just…too strong!"

"Harper, tell me what I can do." He pulled her into his lap, her entire body was stiff from the effort of keeping Hazel at bay.

"I found it!" Maria popped up from behind more boxes, Hazel's phone in her hands. "Damn it there's a password."

"Six-zero-three-nine!" Harper struggled to say. He watched Maria put in the password then furiously push a series of buttons.

"Okay, doesn't seem she sent them anywhere, we're good."

Harper reached out with a clawed hand. "Destroy the pictures!" Her hair was slowly turning dark again, and she scratched Lawrence across the cheek. "Give it back!" Her other hand went to his throat, and he felt her fingertips digging into his skin. "That's mine!"

Lawrence wrapped his hands around her wrist, but she was insanely strong. Her nails were digging into his skin, and she had his windpipe between her fingers. He could feel his air getting cut off. "Give it back!" She screamed, and a loud boom made Lawrence jump. Hazel's hand let go and she fell back to the floor, blood quickly spreading from her back. Her hair went blonde in a breath and her green eyes turned brown. She was breathing raggedly and staring up at Lawrence.

"Harper?" He leaned down and laid a hand on her cheek.

Tears fell from her eyes. "I'm sorry."

"Don't be, it wasn't you. We'll get you help." He took her hand, but it went limp and he heard a long, slow exhale from her lips. Her eyes, still staring into his, didn't move. "Harper?" But there was nothing. He looked up and saw Maria on her knees, the gun pointed at the ground. "Did you have to do that?"

Maria pointed at his neck. "She would have killed you," he said. "I did what I had to." He reached up and felt his throat was wet. When he looked down, he saw his fingers were covered in blood and he could feel it running down his neck.

"Oh my God." He put more pressure on his neck in case it was worse than he thought.

"I told you, Hyde had immeasurable strength, I wasn't going to watch her literally rip your throat out."

He sat back and sighed, trying not to look at Harper's poor body. "I guess I should thank you."

She gave him a little nod and dropped the gun. "All in a day's work. Well, a weird day anyway."

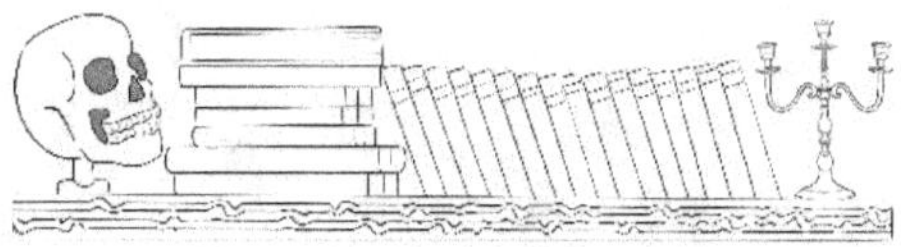

Two days later Lawrence was sitting across from Dr. Rosella Tassoni. His neck was bandaged from Hazel's attack on the train, and jet leg was once again kicking his ass. But he was glad to be back in the States. Rosella was shifting through the no longer lost manuscript of 'The Strange Case of Dr. Jekyll and Mr. Hyde'. Hazel's phone was next to it, the photos having been deleted, but she wanted someone to make double sure they weren't sent somewhere. The way Dr. Tassoni's eyes dashed across the words it reminded him of his own excitement about the manuscript. Rosella cleared her throat and gently put the manuscript in a high-tech, circular preservation container that would keep it from deteriorating.

"You did good Lawrence."

He gave her a half-hearted smile. "Thank you, Dr. Tassoni. Honestly without Maria, it would have been a disaster. How is she?" Rosella leaned back in her chair; he noticed her hair gently brushing the collar of her tan blouse. Maria had dropped him off at Edinburgh Airport, then went on her way. Where that was, he wasn't sure, but killing someone can't be easy on a person and he was worried about her.

"She's doing fine." Dr. Tassoni said. "It's always tough firing a gun for the first time, let alone killing someone at the same time. Hazel was dangerous and clearly taking over."

Dr. Tassoni pulled out a little check book and started writing. "How about a little extra hazard pay for almost getting your throat torn out?" She ripped the check from its book and handed it to him. "Any interest in helping the Booker Foundation find more lost manuscripts or items of special significance?"

Lawrence shook his head and took the check without looking at it. “No thanks. I think two adventures is enough for me. But if I hear anything, I’ll let you know.”

“Deal.” He shook Dr. Tassoni’s hand and left the office, eager to get back to Michigan. He wondered if he should write any of this down but thought better of it. Who would believe him anyway?

# Provenance

## Jon Black

**Austin, Texas, June 10**

Jen was determined to prove the experts wrong.

Again.

Leaning over the thrift store dining table repurposed as her desk, she examined copies of ancient inscriptions written with complicated characters that seemed to be all right angles and triangles. Part of the Semitic language family, Himyaritic had been used at Arabia's southern tip from the first century BCE until…well, nobody really knew when. That was one of its mysteries. While the eponymous kingdom of Himyar collapsed in the sixth century, its language continued on. Possibly as late as the tenth century, according to some tenuous evidence.

Yet scholars knew next to nothing about it. Surviving writing samples were limited, mostly from Wellsted's 1835 expedition to Yemen. And other information was nearly nonexistent. Until now. Next to Jen's inscriptions lay a short primer on Himyaritic created by a man who traversed southern Arabia in the mid-sixth century. A man who, for all intents and purposes, had been Merlin of Camelot. The primer had been among manuscripts found when Merlin's tomb was discovered in France's Brittany Peninsula a year ago.

Still, most linguists hadn't gotten their hopes up. Merlin described the language only in broad strokes, including a lexicon of a hundred or so words. Not enough to crack the extinct tongue. Not even enough, the experts said, to figure out how it fit into the broader Semitic language family. Jen knew they were wrong. And that she was the one to show them.

She made detailed notes on how the language's main definite article, 'am' or 'an' depending on a word's gender, functioned in relation to the newly revealed vocabulary. A tedious process, but it could go a long way to working out Himyaritic's linguistic relationships.

Knocking at Jen's front door interrupted her notetaking. She glanced at the clock ticking above her mantel. After midnight. Her few friends were past the age of unannounced late-night visits. The crabby upstairs neighbor who always complained about her music? Jen had toned it down since the noise citation. Though the $300 fine had been irritating and her landlord unamused, the memory made her smile. Expecting a college party raging out of control, the police had encountered a solitary linguist pouring over 2,000-year-old Aramaic inscriptions while blasting Megadeth's *Countdown to Extinction*. No, she didn't look like most people's idea of a metal head. But metal had rules, Jen liked that.

None of that explained who was knocking now. Or why. Realizing she'd get no further with the Himyaritic until her caller went away, Jen headed for the door.

Outside, she found an unfamiliar woman, tall and well-dressed in casual yet fashionable clothes. Short, dark hair framed an elegant face wearing a guarded, peevish expression. A few years older than Jen—thirty perhaps—she had the healthy tan of a person residing someplace where nature didn't want to kill you.

"Can I help you?" Jen demanded.

"Are you Jennifer Gerson?" the stranger asked before clarifying, "The Semitic languages expert?"

In a movie, an opening like that would make her visitor a cop. This wasn't a movie, so far as Jen knew. She knew only that the woman hadn't arrived by mistake. With less aplomb than she would have preferred, Jen nodded and uttered a response sounding like *er-yeah*.

"I need something translated."

"I'm really backlogged right now," Jen explained. "I do have a website. You're welcome to contact me there and we can discuss specifics. I can give you a business card if you'd like."

"This can't wait," the woman replied. Not desperately or aggressively, but as if simply stating a fact. From her large handbag, she produced a bundle of $100 bills. "Here's ten thousand. You do the translation now. It's only two pages. And no questions asked."

Jen didn't know how a translation job could be shady, but this one had to be. Why else the late-night visit? The immediacy of the demand? The immense payment…in cash? While the money was considerable, it was curiosity that got Jen. What could be so important that it required translation right now? Under such unusual circumstances?

"Come in."

"April Miller," her visitor introduced herself so mechanically that Jen knew it was a lie. Besides, she just didn't look like an April.

"Can I offer you a beer?"

Her guest shook her head. "Wine?"

"Coffee?" Jen compromised.

The woman nodded.

Walking into the kitchen, Jen put the coffeemaker on. Her tall visitor, ducking to avoid Jen's curiously low ceilings, deposited her sizable bag down by one chair and made herself comfortable in the living area.

"Can you turn that ear-gonorrhea down?" her guest asked.

"Nope," Jen answered. "Music helps me think."

"That's music?" The visitor rolled her eyes but seemed resigned.

"Okay," Jen took the initiative as she sat mugs of black coffee down in front of them. "Let's see this document of yours."

From the bag, the woman produced photos showing two pages of text. Or, more likely, two sides of a single page. Nothing fancy, just digital images printed out on regular 8.5" x 11" paper. A glance told Jen that the text was Hebrew. Good. It was her strongest language. The typeface, while blocky, was not without a certain elegance. Though hardly an expert on printing, Jen guessed it came from the sixteenth or seventeenth century. Maybe early eighteenth.

Translation started smoothly. Vocabulary allowed her to source the document to Central Europe during the fifteenth or sixteenth century. Given her thoughts about the typeface, she leaned toward the latter. Though things went quickly at first, Jen was soon forced to her bookshelves for reference works and to her laptop for online searches. Amid much that was familiar she encountered outliers suggesting enormous antiquity or, less likely, loanwords from related languages which Jen failed to immediately identify.

Absorbed in the mathematical, almost mystical, pleasure of translation, Jen paid scant attention to the document's content. A wild bit of Near Eastern mythology, she recognized some of its names but none of the context.

Puzzling through those outliers of vocabulary, it was nearly dawn as Jen printed out a translation and handed it to her guest. As the stranger read the text, Jen noted that its bizarre subject matter prompted no expression of surprise.

"And this is the best you can do?" she asked after she'd finished.

Jen bristled at the implied slight. "It's the best anyone for a thousand miles could do. And it's the best I can do tonight. With a few days, weeks, maybe months, I could refine it further. There are a lot of mysteries in there."

Shrugging as if to say, *well, it will have to do*, she tossed Jen the money. She flinched as her guest produced a 9mm pistol from her handbag.

"Don't mention this to anyone," her strange visitor said before rattling off two addresses. One in Palm Springs. The other in a north Chicago suburb. Recognizing the addresses of her mother and her brother and his family, Jen understood the unspoken threat. With that, the woman gathered her belongings and took off into the night.

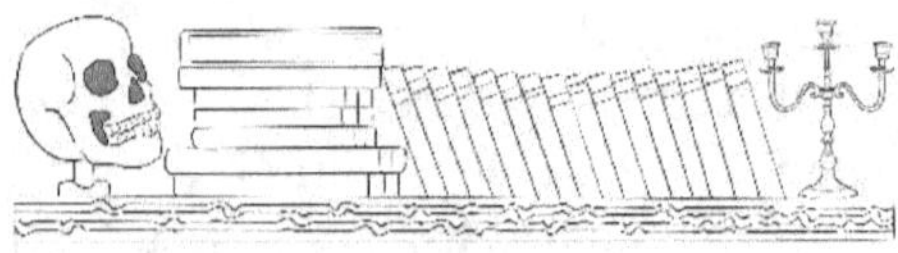

**San Francisco, California, June 3**

The antiquarian examined the document with his magnifying visor, the high-tech heir to the old jeweler's glass. Starting at the top, he scrutinized the strong Gilbey comprising the broadsheet's title: a simple, attractive font popular during the 1850s and 1860s but now nearly extinct. The Bookman font, used for the broadsheet's text, still saw some use. Reaching the bottom, noticing the nickel-sized bit missing from the document's left-hand corner, he frowned. Then, too, there was the almost unnoticeable tear along one edge. Unnoticeable, that was, to anyone but a dealer in antique documents.

Raising his head to look at Cassidy, it took him a moment to remember to turn off the visor's headlamp. "Well, this is quite the find, young lady. An 1864 broadsheet issued by General Ulysses S. Grant supporting Samuel Cony's candidacy for Governor of Maine. What's its provenance?"

"Provenance?" Cassidy inquired timidly.

"Its origin. Its story. Where it's from." If the antiquarian meant his clarification to sound kindly, he did a poor job. Condescension oozed out beneath a facade of warmth.

"We found it in my grandmother's papers after she...passed. Her people were from Maine originally. Anyway, we wanted to see if it was worth anything."

"Well, it would be worth more if it wasn't missing a corner and didn't have this tear on the side. Those definitely hurt its value. But I can give you sixteen hundred for it." The antiquarian looked sly for a moment. "Or a flat two-thousand if you're willing to take cash."

"I'm fine with cash," Cassidy nodded eagerly.

Opening his safe, the antiquary counted out the bills and handed them over. "You find anything else in your grandmother's papers, feel free to bring it right to me."

"Oh, I will," she nodded as she stuffed the wad into her oversized handbag.

Out on the street, Cassidy savored the mild San Francisco afternoon. And the thrill of a successful con. Removing the corner and tearing the edge had been the right call. Never expecting forgers to do anything that would diminish a document's value, dealers often took such flaws as proof of authenticity. And, anyway, those flaws had distracted attention from the Gilbey type, which Cassidy wasn't certain she'd gotten exactly right.

An hour later she was back at the tiny backstreet warehouse in the South of Market neighborhood. Officially registered to CST Enterprises—using her real initials was, admittedly, a risky bit of hubris on her part—unofficially, it was her residence.

Most people would mistake the warehouse for a print shop. Those slightly more in the know might think it a museum of printing history. The equipment within allowed Cassidy to replicate anything printed on either side of the Atlantic over the past 500 years.

True, Gutenberg invented movable type in 1439. But Cassidy shied away from fabricating anything within a century of that. Such works, known as *incunabula* or, in the singular, *incunabulum,* brought big bucks but were so rare that they invariably attracted heavy scrutiny. A replica press, circa 1550, she'd assembled from images in various woodcuts and written descriptions was the oldest project she'd touch.

Next to the 1550 press was another replica, a Blaew press. William Jensen Blaew, a Dutch printer, made the first substantial changes to Gutenberg's design. European and New World printers copied his innovations throughout the seventeenth century.

Cassidy had constructed what she called her "French Press" from engravings of Parisian print shops around the time of the Revolution. While similar to Blaew's, it had several small tweaks of the kind that often tripped-up forgers.

Her 1815 Columbian was the genuine article. John Clymer had designed the press based on an earlier model by the Earl of Stanhope. The giant cast-iron beast had been more popular in Europe than the New World but its sound design kept it under production until 1913.

Also authentic, the lightweight but rugged 1848 Washington was a press that got a lot of mileage on the rough and tumble frontier. First sold in 1821, the model remained in production well into the twentieth century. It earned the distinction of being the last hand press manufactured in America.

Rounding out her collection, next to the Washington, sat an 1890s card printer. People would pay hundreds of dollars for James Joyce's calling card or the business card of New York police commissioner Theodore Roosevelt. Such forgeries carried little risk. It was a rare collector willing to spend more money authenticating an item than they paid for it in the first place.

Scattered among the presses were metal shelves holding various papers and parchments as well as plastic tubs with materials for a dozen variations of printer's ink. On an old and rather scorched desk along the wall rested equipment for making those inks. And all around were wooden type cases full of movable type and bins of print blocks. The latter allowed Cassidy to produce "antique" Christmas Cards, patriotic cards from various wars, and similar creations. Those didn't sell for much but were nearly risk free. And she could crank them out in volume.

Running her hand affectionately along the frames of the various presses as she passed them, Cassidy made her way to the Spartan metal stairs ascending to the warehouse office.

Sliding open her door and looking out on a balcony barely large enough for one person, she relished the fresh sea breeze, uncorked a Napa Cabernet, and glanced around the tiny office she'd converted into her living space. Admittedly, not much of one. Photos from vacations in Ibiza and a poster from Coachella covered one wall. A futon served as her bed; space was at a premium. Not so premium that she couldn't cram in an 18-bottle thermoelectric wine fridge. A wardrobe and a bookcase occupied another wall. Opposite her futon was a second desk, in better condition than the one down on the print floor. It housed her laptop and a hardcopy of *The Encyclopedia of Typefaces*, the authoritative source on more than two-thousand fonts back to Gutenberg.

Reclining on the futon and savoring the cab, her eyes rested on the glass case atop her bookshelf. It held a stuffed bird of curious appearance. Resembling a nightjar but, at over two feet long, it was larger than any nightjar acknowledged by science. Extravagant ear tufts, reminiscent of horns, lent the bird a diabolic appearance. It was the only thing she had from her father, mostly because the feds hadn't realized its true identity or value. According to him, it was the last Ulama, the Devil Bird of Sri Lanka, shot and stuffed at a time when that island was still called Ceylon. It had been one of many strange and wonderful things her father brought into their home.

Cassidy's reflection in the small mirror hanging from her wardrobe testified that she had one other thing from her father, her appearance. Classical features and dark eyes that seemed to broadcast perpetual disapproval. Though the world, she acknowledged, was more than enough to put that expression there without help.

Thoughts of her father brought Cassidy's gaze to a bundle of documents on her desk. Even from the futon, she could make out the text on the top page:

**Booker Foundation**
**Lost Books Project**
**Guidelines and Conditions**

Cassidy was about to undertake the most ambitious forgery of her career. This time, her motive wasn't profit…it was revenge.

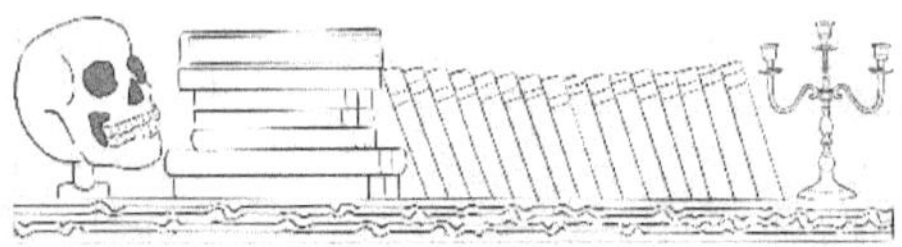

The following afternoon, Cassidy visited the one incunabulum she didn't shy away from. In this case "Incunabulum" was the name of a posh antiquarian bookstore and coffee house off Nob Hill's Larson Street. It was the only rare book dealer in town where she hadn't passed a forgery, no matter how tiny. "Don't shit where you eat" was a crude expression. That didn't make it bad advice.

Acquiring a cappuccino, she sat down at a table. Cassidy dropped her bag, filled with newly purchased nineteenth and early twentieth century volumes, at her feet. Not especially rare, none of the books set her back more than $20. For her, their real value wasn't in their text anyway. Rather, it was in the few blank pages at the beginning and end of such volumes. A forger's goldmine. There were ways to test the age of paper. Many forgeries got outed that way. But, of course, if you used paper from the appropriate era, test results came back as genuine. Also useful, though not quite so valuable, were bindings and covers which a clever crafter like Cassidy could modify and repurpose. Still, wanting something to keep her company as she drank her cappuccino, she took up an 1897 printing of *Tristan and Isolde* and read.

The sound of the chair opposite her being pulled out roused Cassidy from her book. A dignified and debonair man of about 70 took the seat. "How did yesterday go with the broadsheet?" he inquired. It mystified Cassidy that, though he had lived his whole life in America, traces of a Castilian accent, and its ubiquitous lisp, clung to Hierbabuena's speech.

"I'm here, aren't I?" she smiled.

"And so you are, my dear." He returned her smile. Stirring his tea, he popped a peppermint into his mouth. His compulsive consumption of the candies had earned Hierbabuena his distinctive alias. After a decade as her mentor and confidant, she still didn't know his real name. Probably just as well.

"And where have you been hiding recently?" she asked.

"México. The Biblioteca Palafoxiana in Puebla. I have become curious about early ecclesiastical printing for an upcoming…project."

Cassidy understood. The Palafoxiana was the New World's oldest library. For forgers, it was a wellspring of information and inspiration. "It's good to see you taking up the craft again," she said. Recently, her mentor had worked only intermittently. As the man behind a 'newly discovered' volume of Cervantes poems currently setting the literary world on fire, he could afford that luxury. Hell, after that job, he could have retired. But, like Cassidy, he was an artist, not merely a criminal.

"And what now for you?" he inquired, raising an eyebrow. "Are you still resolved to move forward with this matter of *venganza*…er…revenge?"

Smiling confidently, Cassidy nodded.

"And have you decided upon a text with which to trap Mr. Booker?"

Her smile widened into a broad grin. "I have. The *Sefer Bohem.*"

To Cassidy's surprise, Hierbabuena flinched as if someone had thrown his hot tea in his face. The old man made the sign of the cross. "That one? Are you sure?"

"Yeah. Why not? It will be a challenge but nothing I can't handle."

"Sometimes the question is not *can you* but, rather, *should you.*" Seeing his pupil did not understand his point, he continued. "Let me tell you a story about my father back in Spain. I've told you that, during their Civil War, he worked as a forger for the Republicans. Antique books to fund ammunition and supplies.

Passports and identity papers. Even fake battle orders 'leaked' to the Nationalists to throw their strategy into disarray.

"The Republicans came to my father one night asking him to forge orders of execution for the Nationalist militias. A Republican agent would then insert them among legitimate orders carried by a Nationalist courier. The trick was the execution orders were all for Franco supporters. It was quite clever, really. Get the Nationalists to eliminate their own people. But when my father looked at the names that were to be on those orders, he saw it was priests, teachers, businesspeople, farmers, even housewives. He refused the job. As a result, my father's own allegiances became questioned. Fortunately, a friend tipped him off. He fled with my mother to America one step ahead of the Republicans' own killers.

"My father told me that story when I was young, not long after I had followed him into the craft. But it wasn't until his deathbed that I thought to ask him why he had refused.

"'My son,' he told me in a voice I could barely hear over the machines keeping him alive, 'forgers, we are artists. Our creations become part of us, no different than painters or sculptors. I did not want the murder of those people becoming part of me.'

"His words have stayed with me all these years."

"Yes, I can see that," Cassidy acknowledged, "but it doesn't apply to me. To my situation. Jake Booker is no innocent. For all I know, he killed my father. He was definitely complicit in it."

"That may be true," Hierbabuena tossed another mint into his mouth. "But the *Sefer Bohem*? Whispers call it a blasphemous thing. Death and darkness surround it. Do you wish to make *that* part of you?"

Though the old man was her mentor, she didn't buy into the mystical mumbo-jumbo that made up much of Hierbabuena's mental universe. Of course, she couldn't tell him that. Instead, she settled for, "It's a risk I'm willing to take."

That declaration made, it fascinated Cassidy how quickly Hierbabuena's interest in the practical aspects of her task overpowered his hesitation about the project itself. "You do not know Hebrew," he observed matter-of-factly. "How will you fabricate a work in that language?"

Technically, Cassidy's project would be a *fabrication*, not a *forgery*. A forgery copied an existing document. A fabrication was an invention, something that plausibly could exist or a vanished work with no surviving copies. A bogus Declaration of Independence was a forgery. The "lost" memoirs of Amelia Earhart, because nobody knew what such a thing might contain, would be a fabrication. But, colloquially, even their creators often referred to both categories of fraudulent documents as "forgeries."

"The old switcheroo," she answered. "I'll print a more recent 'previously unknown translation' in a language I'm comfortable with. Nobody has seen the *Sefer Bohem* for centuries. If it ever existed at all. As long as it has the right sound and feel, I can fill my fabrication with any old screed."

"And what is your origin story for this unsuspected 'translation?'"

"English. Early seventeenth century. London printing. Maybe tie it in with John Dee somehow to increase believability."

Making a sound of displeasure as he sucked on his candy, Hierbabuena shook his head. "Dee scholarship is on the rise. People rediscover that he was not a madman. Or not only a madman. An unknown work connected with him will be examined closely. You can do better, my dear. Remember, the easiest place to hide a book's history is where there's already a shadow."

Cassidy fought back indignation. She hated being challenged. Only Hierbabuena ever got away with it. But she knew he was right. Both about Dee being the wrong angle and his advice for finding the right one. History, even after printing's invention, was a messy place. There were whole decades where she could insert a fabricated book with nobody being the wiser. And she had many options for language: English, French, Spanish, Italian. Dutch or German if the project was short and simple. Of course, this one wouldn't be.

"Paris, late 1780s," she began hesitantly, gaining confidence as she continued. "The last years before the revolution, and first years after, were such a shit-show that all kinds of things got lost."

"Good. Good," her mentor beamed like an excited child. "And, of course, both the Jacobins and the Church would have reasons for suppressing such a work, making its unknown status all the more credible."

Cassidy gritted her teeth. She had been about to get to that.

"And how are you going to generate text for the fabrication?" He continued. "You talk of a work that is almost unknown and yet, in certain circles, much speculated about. Normally a blank slate would be welcome. But you must satisfy impossible expectations."

"A small college in Texas, of all places, has a page of unidentified sixteenth century Hebrew print. Some people in those 'certain circles' you speak of claim it's from the *Sefer Bohem.* I can use that page to get the feel of the subject matter and flavor of the language. Then I'll round out the content using other works about Canaanite and ancient Near Eastern religion."

"And, this document in Texas, how will you translate it?"

"I'm still figuring that out," she admitted.

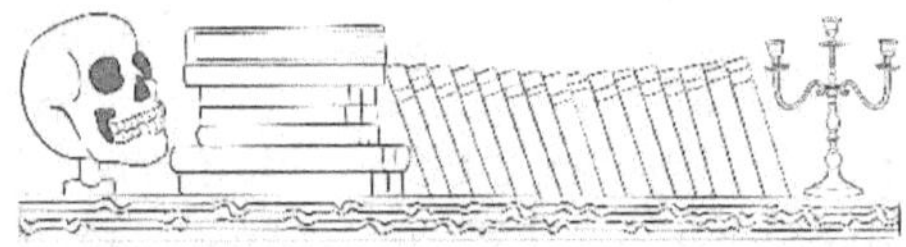

Alone back at her warehouse, Cassidy still heard Hierbabuena's words. And his warning. On principle, she wondered if she should heed him. Hierbabuena was her mentor by his choice. He could just have easily landed Cassidy in a prison cell. Or, perhaps, worse. Early in her career, she'd been reckless. She'd clumsily touched-up some of her forgeries. Used the wrong ink sometimes. She'd fabricated a World War One "Vigilance England" poster admonishing readers to be on guard against "Enemy Propaganda and Disinformation," the latter word, unfortunately, not coined until the 1920s. She'd botched applying a faux water stain on the "will and testament" of a well-known nineteenth century captain of industry. Stains, it turned out, were difficult and risky. Since then, she'd settled for easier and safer tearing.

After leaving her hands, many of those documents were proven as bogus as a four-dollar bill…and not the legit ones printed by Florida during the Civil War. Though she had been unaware of it, with each document coming up for sale now greeted with suspicion, Cassidy's screw-ups turned up the heat on every other West Coast forger. That hit Hierbabuena, who shared her San Francisco stomping ground, particularly hard. Taking matters into his own hands, he'd tracked Cassidy to her warehouse.

To this day, she didn't know what had been in his mind when he arrived. But seeing how young Cassidy was and discovering her to be self-taught, the master forger took her under his wing. Teaching her their craft's ancient pedigree. Highlighting common pitfalls. Showing her tricks she'd never imagined. And, whenever possible, keeping Cassidy's ambition from outracing her talent.

She had been little more than a child when that race began. And it started with her father. Other kids could describe their parents' jobs with simple labels like "doctor," "firefighter," or "taxi driver." All Cassidy knew was that her father spent a lot of time away from home, usually returning with beautiful and valuable things, and that her family lived well. Growing a little older, between the lessons of TV and video games, she'd realized her father was a kind of treasure hunter…and not the kind who turned his finds over to a museum.

Then came Alaska. Before leaving, her father sat Cassidy down. It was the first time he'd ever referenced his work. "There's something big up there," she could still picture him telling her with absolute clarity. "Wish daddy luck. Some of my competition is really good. Really dangerous, maybe." Immediately, his face expressed regret at that admission. Perhaps hoping to distract her, he rattled off several names of other people racing him for the…whatever it was. The only one Cassidy remembered, because future events gave cause to burn it into her brain, was Jake Booker.

A week later she saw the news story. Far above the Arctic Circle, that same Jake Booker had discovered treasures belonging to a long dead Russian named Alexi Ulinov. The report made no mention of her father.

He never came back. Officially, nobody knew what happened to him. But the authorities, after a long conversation with Jake Booker, figured out how her father made his living…and that he hadn't paid taxes on any of it. They swooped down on what remained of her family: the bank accounts (even the ones her mother hadn't known about), the house, the cars, the wonderful objects that surrounded Cassidy throughout her childhood. Everything except the Sri Lankan Devil Bird.

She and her mother moved into a crappy apartment in a not so safe part of town. Mom got a clerical job at the local library. Just to squeeze by, she had to work both days and evenings. Months when mom couldn't even afford a sitter, she dragged Cassidy along. At night, one of her main tasks was repairing damaged books. Cassidy watched her repair bindings, reattach loose pages, clean covers, mend tears, and perform a dozen other common patches necessitated by the books' heavy use.

It all made sense to Cassidy. One night, asking if she could help, her mother said yes. Cassidy would never forget the hardback edition of Dickens' *Old Curiosity Shop,* its cover showing a sleazy and sinister Quilp wearing an impossibly tall top hat as he loomed menacingly over an unbelievably good and pure Little Nell. The book looked as if it had been dropped in the mud *and* run over. Well into the evening, Cassidy cleaned, mended, and glued.

Without ever having heard the term "hinging-in," she figured out how to re-secure a loose page by gluing its inside edge to a narrow scrap of paper and then creating a "hinge" by applying glue to the scrap's other side and gently attaching it to the following page, leaving it looking good as new.

After Cassidy finished with *Old Curiosity Shop*, she and her mother stared at the resurrected book. Neither of them said a word. But they both knew Cassidy had done a better job than her mother ever could.

It wasn't long before Cassidy started scouting used bookstores, picking up damaged volumes for a pittance, fixing them up, and unloading what she bogusly claimed to be "mint condition volumes" on unsuspecting buyers. From there, it was a short leap to forgery and fabrication. Written documents seemed risky. Handwriting was so idiosyncratic that forgeries were almost always detectable if an investigator took enough time. Print, on the other hand, was antiseptic and anonymous. If you used the right tech and did your research, it took serious and expensive investigation to root out fakes. Sometimes not even then.

Using her savings from the book repair scam, Cassidy bought the 1848 Washington press, some movable type, and books about printing. She'd never looked back.

The moments it took those memories to flash through Cassidy's mind were enough to reopen the wounds from her father's death, leaving them as raw as the day mom explained he would never come home. Hierbabuena meant well. He wanted what he thought best for Cassidy. But he didn't understand. She wondered how *his* father would have reacted if the people the Spanish Republicans wanted executed had hurt him so much.

Oh yes, Jake Booker would get his. Cassidy would hurt him as badly as her skills allowed. Acquiring a copy of the *Sefer Bohem* would be a huge coup for his foundation and its Lost Books Project. Wanting it to be genuine, hopefully they wouldn't look too closely. And they'd make a big deal about its acquisition. But Cassidy would build in a "tell" that the book was fake. Something so subtle they wouldn't notice for weeks or months. If necessary, Cassidy could even give an anonymous tip to the media. The revelation would deliver a significant blow to Jake Booker's reputation and the credibility of his foundation.

Gleefully, Cassidy popped online to book her flight to Austin and reserve a rental car.

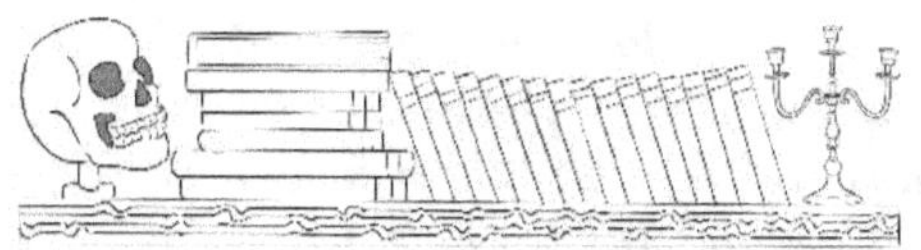

**Austin, June 13**

Since the bizarre nighttime visit Jen had been unable to focus on the Himyaritic inscriptions. She could look at the South Arabian letters…but she couldn't make herself *see* them. Instead, for what had to be the hundredth time, Jen read through the translation she'd made for the strange woman.

> *It was long after the days when Dagan defeated Tiamath, Her blood falling upon the fertile shores and begetting Lilith. After, even, the days when the Powers defeated their rivals to East and West. It was in those days when the 70 Sons of Asherah lived peacefully and Dagan and his brother El dwelled together in the House of the Star, when three Rephaim trespassed across the River.*
>
> *As She slept, the Rephaim stole the Shawl of Qetesh. Using Her shawl to fly at great speed over the Land, the Rephaim made much mischief: killing men, kicking over the palaces of the 70 Sons of Asherah, and burning their Holy Places.*

*Dagan dispatched a seraph to demand the return of Qetesh's Shawl and the Rephaim's departure. As the seraph flew to their camp, the Burning Asp beheld the Rephaim gaming with lots and growing drunk off grains of the field and fruits of the vine. They laughed at the seraph's demands, the foremost Raphaite saying, "Who is this Dagan? Let Him come to my camp and tell me Himself what He wants."*

*And so the Burning Asp flew back to the House of the Star, where the Powers dwelled, and repeated what the foremost Rephaite had said as well as telling what it had witnessed with its fiery eyes.*

*And Dagan said, "It pleases the trespassers to game with lots? Then We shall make a trap for them from their own diversions." He commanded all the Powers come to the House of the Star. Gathered on the High Mount, They mooted who best to challenge the Rephaim. Save for Lilith, who told the others "You shun me save when You need me. We share no blood. What care I if Your handiwork is undone?" With that, She transformed into a great beast and departed through the earth.*

*In the end, it was decided that Belatu, El, and Dagan Himself would challenge the Rephaim.*

*Belatu, She who loves above all else fire and the crafts, went to the least of the Rephaim and said, "I wager my Ceaseless Loom you cannot go the month drinking neither water nor any other drink. If you lose, you must join the 70 Sons of Asherah."*

*Once the Rephaite had accepted, Belatu called down curtains of flame around him. Heat rolled over him and thirst through him as his yearning for drink grew all consuming. "Mistress Belatu, I yield," he pled. "I beg You, take these flames away and give me water to quench my endless thirst." And so he went among the 70 Sons of Asherah.*

*Then El, He who loves most the men who hunt and herd and wander from place to place, went to the next of the Rephaim. "I wager my Impenetrable Fleece you cannot run with the antelope from one river to the other and back again, fight with the wild bull, and tell me where the cat goes at night. If you lose, you must join the 70 Sons of Asherah."*

*That morning, the Rephaite raced with the antelope from one river to the other and back again. By afternoon, he bested the wild bull. Yet, at night, there was no sign of him. At new light, he reappeared saying, "Master El, I yield. No matter how I looked, I do not know where the cat goes at night." And so he went among the 70 Sons of Asherah.*

*It remained for Dagan, He who loves most the men who till the field and lay the stone hearth, to go to the foremost Rephaite and say, "I wager my dominion over the fields of men that you cannot imbibe all they can produce."*

*And so He caused the harvest to fall early and fermented every kernel and corn, saying, "Drink." And the foremost Rephaite began. He drank that which had come from the north. He drank that which had come from the east. He drank that which had come from the south. Finally, he drank that which had come from the west. "I have met your wager, Dagan," the foremost Rephaite boasted, "and so I claim your dominion over the fields of men."*

*"You have done well," Dagan acknowledged, "So well that, as a further boon, I shall give you a jewel bigger than a man's head. Dagan flew back to the House of the Star and, from His palace, retrieved the prize. Presenting it to the foremost Rephaite, the jewel was none other than Attar, the Morning Star, the thousand-faced diamond of yellow-white. Smote by its beauty and perfection, the foremost Rephaite fell dead upon the ground just as Dagan knew he would.*

*Dagan returned Qetesh's Shawl to Her and then turned to the other Powers, proclaiming, "It is I, Dagan, who master the Attar. It is by this sign that you know I am first among You and You shall place none before Me."*

*From the back, El whispered darkly, "Belatu and I won Our wagers. How is it right that He be first among Us?"*

Jen understood the words, mostly. But much about the narrative remained obscure. When the time was right, she had someone for that. For now, Jen was too busy kicking herself for not finding a way to keep the visitor's photos of the document. Without them, her translation had only so much value. To go further, she needed to examine the original.

Humility gave her a place to start. Though great with Semitic languages, Jen knew she was not the best. A half-dozen scholars in North America were better. Probably the same number in Europe and, again, in the Middle East. Plus, Montefiore in Australia. Twenty people, more or less, around the world surpassed her. The stranger hadn't come because Jen was the best. So, she must have come because Jen was close to where she'd found the document.

Jen remembered a little about the photos. Around the document's edges she'd glimpsed bits of the room surrounding it. Elaborately-carved cases of dark wood, open shelves, and dim lighting lent the repository an old-world appearance. Certainly, it was none of the institutions in Austin. Hell, it didn't look like anything that should exist this side of New Orleans. And, if that was the case, the woman would have just gone to Lafavre at Tulane. But there was another possibility…

West of Austin, deep in the Hill Country, hid a tiny college established by German and Czech immigrants. Jen had never visited, but heard the place described as looking like something out of nineteenth century Europe. And she knew its archival holdings were formidable. That added up to a plausible home for the document she'd translated.

But there was the woman's warning to consider, her oblique threat to Jen's family, to keep silent about the visit. Examining the college's archives would violate the spirit, if not the letter, of that. How much was Jen willing to do, and risk, to satisfy her curiosity? Was she truly capable of not pursuing the matter? Dostoevsky or William James would have said Jen had free will. Of course, Dostoevsky and James were dead.

Picking up her phone, Jen stared at it, rationalizing why texting would be as good as calling. She had no special desire to speak to her brother, the successful gastroenterologist. Or listen to her mother complaining, "expressing concern" as she'd no doubt put it, about Jen's basement-gnome lifestyle. She began typing.

> *Hope you are well. If anything unusual happens in the next week or so, call the police.*

Grabbing her keys, Jen reflected that the vague message, while warning her family, would also alarm them. Heading for her Jetta, she wore a distinctively passive-aggressive grin.

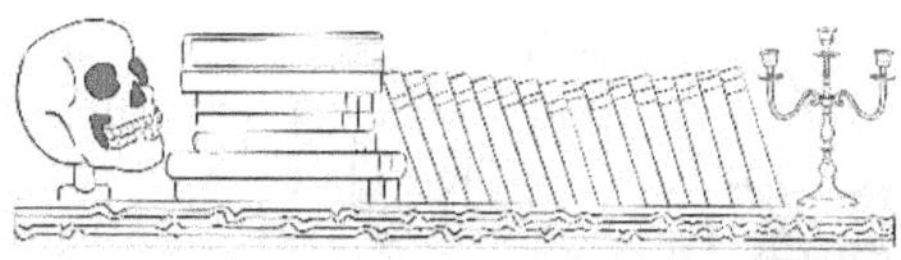

**San Francisco, June 13**

"How did Texas go?" Hierbabuena looked up from reading a copy of *El Pais* at his favorite table in Incunabulum.

"I saw the document. It looks legit," Cassidy replied, pausing for a moment as she joined him. "Hell, it might really be from the *Sefer Bohem*. Even if not, I can use it to bang out a credible fabrication." Cassidy omitted the details of how she'd accessed the document. It was a crass trick; one she didn't like. That didn't mean she wouldn't use it when necessary. A big smile and some batted eyelashes had been sufficient to get a lonely-looking graduate student to show her the page she wanted, circumventing more traditional procedures.

"And you succeeded in getting a translation, then?"

"Yes." When she didn't elaborate, her mentor regarded Cassidy curiously. She couldn't blame him. But it was something else she didn't want to go into. Disappointed with the library's clumsy-sounding translation, she'd looked for an expert in medieval Hebrew nearby. Discovering one in Austin, Cassidy thought she'd gotten lucky. Now she wasn't so sure. The exchange with the mousy linguist wearing a faded heavy metal t-shirt and pajama pants hadn't gone the way she'd expected. Cassidy never felt as in control of the encounter as she should have, considering she was the one with the cash, the gun, and the addresses of the translator's family. Not that she'd do anything to them, of course.

But the bluff had always been enough to secure cooperation in the past. So why her lingering anxiety now?

"Even if it truly comes from the *Sefer Bohem*," Hierbabuena looked as if he considered making the sign of the cross again, "a single page is hardly sufficient to fabricate an entire text. What will you use for your other sources?"

Having done her research, Cassidy listed off works on the old Canaanite religion and strange corners of pre-modern Jewish theology. Texts from royal archives in Mesopotamian city-states like Ugar and Tel Mardikh as well as the Akkadian version of the *Gilgamesh Epic*. The Arslan Tash amulets. Sure, some experts disputed the amulets' authenticity, or at least their dating. But the information was still good. Then there were classical sources. Fragments from the Dead Sea Scrolls, notably the *Songs of the Sage*. Lucian of Samosata's *De Dea Syria*. Surviving bits of Sanchuniathon's *Phoenician History* as preserved by Philo of Byblos. Mystical texts from thirteenth century Spain and sixteenth century Prague.

Finally, she'd set aside a few works from the modern Semitic neo-pagan revival, mostly as references. She'd need to treat those with extreme caution, lest she subconsciously repurpose text containing anachronistic language. This project couldn't afford a debacle like she'd had with the First World War "Propaganda and Disinformation" poster.

Before Hierbabuena could point it out, as Cassidy knew he would, she made it clear she was leaning hard on older translations of her sources. Older was important. An eighteenth century translation, such as she intended to fabricate, would be more literal and less idiomatic than a modern one. It was essential to immerse herself in the style of such language.

Her mentor's smirk, blending irritation and approval, notified Cassidy of Hierbabuena's awareness that she had anticipated and preempted him. "And how is it going?"

"I should have the draft done soon," she answered. "After that, I'll take as much time as I need to be sure everything is authentic to late eighteenth century French. Then comes the fun part."

"Yes, about that, I have a gift for you. Something my father left me. Even at the time, I knew it would be for a special project. Only after our last conversation did I realize that special project would not be mine." With that, he passed Cassidy a large document folder of the kind used by printmakers or architects.

Within, she discovered thirteen large sheets of antique paper. Standardized paper sizes did not emerge until the nineteenth century and, clearly, these were much older. But Cassidy estimated them to be about 30 inches by 20.

"They are fifteenth or sixteenth century," Hierbabuena explained. "My father did not give me a clear provenance. If, indeed, he knew it. He said only that they came from a monastery the Republicans looted. If someone tests the paper chemically, they may be able to determine its origins are Spanish not French.

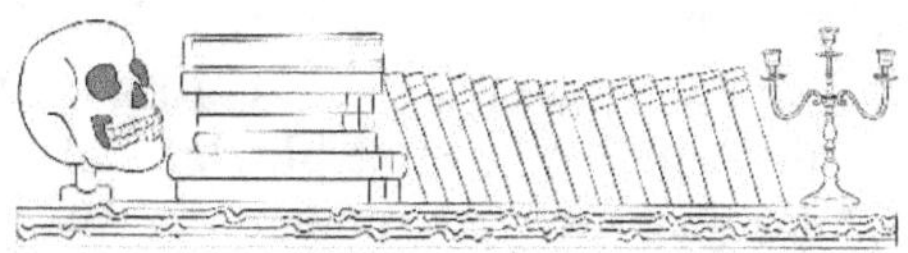

At her warehouse Cassidy examined the beautiful sheets. Being able to trace the paper's origins might complicate things but shouldn't be a deal breaker.

Her mentor's gift took an enormous load off her mind. Paper often foiled forgers. And it wasn't always their fault, the options weren't good. Artificially aging modern paper to look old was cheap and easy but risky. Chemical tests and sometimes even fluorescent lighting could detect it. Making paper by pulping antique rags and cloth was safer but time consuming and expensive. Using blank pages taken from the beginning and end of period volumes worked great for small projects but not whole books. Even trimmed to an identical size, concealing that the pages came from different sources was nearly impossible. Using actual period paper was the best solution, but so rare it seemed miraculous.

Measurement showed the paper from her mentor to be about 29 inches by 19 inches, the kind of thing used for a display piece or large folio. Cassidy suspected the monks' stock were leftovers from some longer work.

A thirteen-page book would be odd for the time period, she needed smaller pages. Cassidy calculated that a standard *octavo* fold of her thirteen sheets would yield 208 pages of 6.75 by 4.25 inches. While there had been no true standards, those measurements were common enough in the eighteenth century. With the printing technology and formatting conventions of the day, she could fit about 40,000 words on those pages.

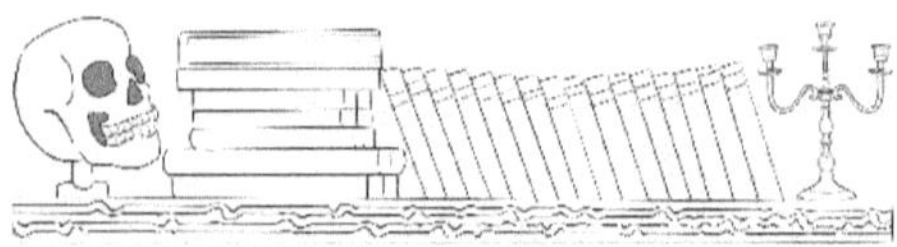

**Texas Hill Country, June 13**

Driving westward through rolling peaks and thick woods, Jen hoped she could wrap up her errand in time for barbeque and a nice Texas-German microbrew before heading home. Though she'd cranked Maiden as loudly as her car stereo would go, Jen couldn't have said what song was playing. Instead, her mind obsessed over that mysterious document.

True, there were those twenty or so better linguists out there. But they'd gotten where they were through a lifetime of backbreaking work, mentally speaking. Most of them were twice her age or more. Montefiore, in his mid-30s, counted as the only other *wunderkind* among them. Not that Jen couldn't work hard. She could, and often did. But her affinity for Semitic languages went beyond normal. Sometimes she felt guilty, undeserving of that gift.

Her connection with Judaism had always come through its ethics and history; not any supernatural or metaphysical dimensions. Long before she first heard the term "cultural Jew," she knew she was one. Keeping peace with her family, Jen resigned herself to a Bat Mitzvah. That meant Hebrew School and studying the Hebrew language. And there, after a fashion, she *did* find her true faith.

She had an intuitive knack for the language. Everything about it clicked into place for her. Not just rationally but aesthetically. Tastes in languages, no different than in music or food, were subjective. In Hebrew, Jen found a mathematical beauty and symmetry that her native English lacked.

Then she'd discovered the same sublime and appealing order in other living Semitic languages like Arabic, Amharic, and Tigrinya. But it was the family's old and esoteric members which especially delighted her. Earlier forms of Hebrew. Extinct or obscure languages such as Aramaic, Ge'ez, Phoenician, and Razihi. And, of course, the old South Arabian tongues like Himyaritic.

In all of them dwelled a mathematical intricacy inviting fancies of higher meaning. No wonder the language family so easily gave rise to things like Kabala, various forms of Arabic arithmancy and logomancy, or the talismanic powers so many Semitic peoples ascribed to the written forms of words and phrases. Not that Jen believed in any of that.

Arriving at Goethe College, it lived up to every description she'd heard. Thick masses of emerald-colored ivy covered its old limestone buildings, designed in a style knocking at the door of Gothic. The college's library cranked all those trends to eleven. Honest-to-God gargoyles stared down at Jen from the building's eaves as she approached.

Sitting in the basement, where the college housed its "restricted collections," Jen presented her credentials to the collections' director. Wearing her iron-gray hair in a bun drawn so tightly Jen feared it would explode, the director projected the image of a mirthless functionary. An impression reinforced by the cumbersome moniker proclaimed on her nameplate, "Dr. Eierkopf-Tegeler."

Scanning Jen's academic credentials, she looked askance. Normally, it required a doctorate to ensure admission to the collection. A master's degree was the bare minimum. Jen's bachelors', albeit in linguistics, didn't make the cut.

She didn't sweat it. The director was just reaching the list of Jen's publications and professional achievements: *A Case for Subdividing Aramaic's Eastern Dialect*; *Grammatical Gender and the Divine in Qumran Hebrew*; *Linguistic Drift and Loan Words between Amharic, Ga'ez, Sabaean, and Tigrinya*; *Non-Hebrew Semitic Substratum in Yiddish,* as well as significant advances in deciphering Hadramitic. Her credentials didn't even mention her work on Himyaritic. Not yet, anyway. But Jen knew the director's expression would change.

It did.

"Ms. Gerson, it's a pleasure for me to grant you access to our collections." Dr. Eierkopf-Tegeler practically glowed. "Is there something in particular I can help you with or would you prefer to browse a list of our holdings?"

Jen described what she was looking for: a document in Hebrew, probably just a single page, likely printed in the sixteenth century, quite possibly in Central Europe. She hit pay dirt, the director confirmed such a document existed among the college's holdings. For the first time, Jen wondered exactly how her visitor, who hardly seemed like an academic, had gained access. If the director was aware someone else had viewed the document just days ago, her face gave no hint of it.

A harried-looking graduate student escorted Jen to the restricted collections, housed in chambers which looked as much like a medieval fortress as a modern archival repository. He then disappeared into the archive's bowels to fetch the document matching Jen's description.

A single glance confirmed it to be the manuscript from her visitor's photos. Jen had made the right call. Metaphorically patting herself on the back, Jen thought under different circumstances she might make a pretty good detective. Jen took several photos of the document with her phone, no flash of course, for future reference.

A typed translation accompanied the document. Made during the late nineteenth or early twentieth century, Jen guessed based on the font and the paper. A quick review of the translation confirmed that impression. When you knew a language well enough, translations actually told you a lot about the translator. Even for the time period, this one was not stellar. Good for a Hebrew School instructor but not for a professional linguist. The translator had been out of his or her depth. Jen's slapdash effort had been orders of magnitude better.

Having photographed the document and dismissed the provided translation, Jen turned to what she could learn of its origins and how it came to be in Central Texas. The document's finding aid recorded its arrival at Goethe College via one Teodor Macek and provided a short biography of the donor.

Born in Bohemia around 1794, Macek immigrated to what was then the Republic of Texas in 1837. A collector and amateur scholar, upon his death in 1850, Macek left his entire collection of over a thousand books and manuscripts to the college.

Checking an inventory of Macek's bequest, Jen noticed an item with the rather antiseptic label of TM-0117 described as "Hebrew text fragment, print, middle sixteenth century, Prague," a provenance hardly up to modern archival standards. She also noted that, though many of Macek's donations originated in Prague, TM-0117 was the collection's only item in Hebrew.

Hours later, Jen drove back to Austin. A little nest of brisket in her stomach sated her body's hunger. But not her head's. Confirming the document's location and learning something of its provenance only whetted her appetite. Knowing *where* the document was, she now obsessed over *what* it was.

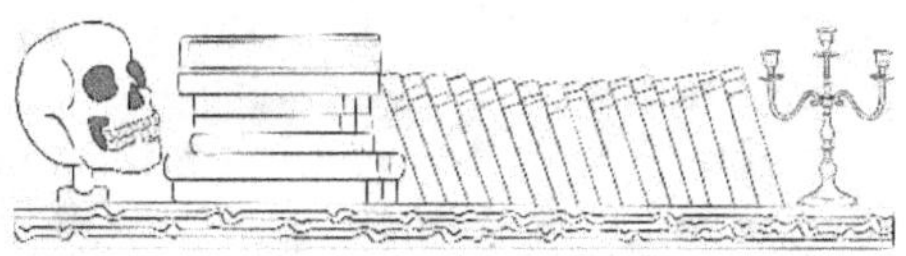

**San Francisco, June 27**

After days scrutinizing documents printed in 1780s and 1790s Paris, Cassidy painstakingly picked out compatible letters from her type cases. The Didot font, developed in 1790, didn't have quite the look she wanted. Instead, she went with Fournier, an old typographic workhorse from 1742. Eighteenth century type blocks saw heavy use and were not especially robust. A document full of crisp, clean, perfect print would raise suspicion. Taking a paring knife, Cassidy carved imperfections and damage into several of the letters.

Like paper, ink was problematic. Forgers could do only so much to make it resistant to testing. Still, she had an eighteenth century recipe that had served her well: iron sulfate, charcoal, gum Arabic, alum, salt, vinegar, and water. *Distilled* water, Cassidy corrected herself. That was important. If someone chemically tested the ink, it would not do for traces of fluoride, chromium, selenium, and so forth to show up. She did what she could and hoped for the best.

She pulled out a book cover and spine repurposed from a 1750s Bible. Cassidy had set them aside as soon as she learned about the Lost Books Project and began plotting revenge on Jake Booker. The pasteboard covers sheathed in black leather were beautiful but stopped short of "too good to be true." A few flecks of gold-leaf still clung to a simple pattern debossed into the cowhide. The covers suffered from some rubbing and their once sharp corners were now blunt and rounded. It had the look Cassidy needed: a quality book not especially well cared for. One that might, in fact, have spent centuries lost behind a bookshelf or forgotten in an attic trunk.

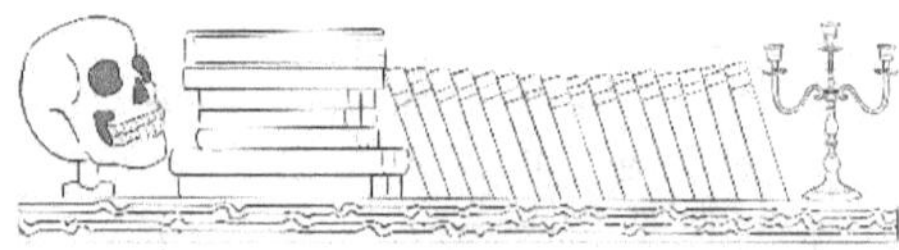

Though her "French Press" had never been so busy, progress was slow. It had to be. After typesetting each page by hand, Cassidy checked her work. Then she checked it again. And again. Only then did she print. Even the slightest error could ruin one of her precious pages.

Cassidy meticulously arranged the letters on a sturdy metal frame called the chase. She filled any space not occupied by typeface with wooden blocks prosaically known as furniture. Once she was absolutely certain both the layout and format of the page were correct, she locked everything in place with metal wedges named quoins. Over the top, she laid a frisk, a kind of stencil preventing ink from straying as well as demarcating each one of Hierbabuena's large sheets into the sixteen pages Cassidy would later fold it.

She took an ink ball in each hand. Looking like hand bells, their wooden handles terminated in puffy balls of sheepskin stuffed with cloth. Dipping them in the ink she'd mixed, Cassidy used the ink balls to coat the typeface with dark ink. Some printers referred to it as "patting," an odd description for a percussive process with all the gentleness of a whack-a-mole game.

After ink covered the typeface, Cassidy delicately laid one of Hierbabuena's beautiful sheets on top and slid the chase underneath the press frame.

Using both hands to grasp the press's sturdy horizontal lever, still called "The Devil's Tail," by some romantic printers, she pulled the wooden bar toward her. The lever dropped a heavy screw that forced down the platen, the wide plate applying the pressure which transferred ink from typeface to paper. The whole process, beginning with a satisfying rolling sound and concluding with a firm thud, took about two seconds.

On large material, like the sheets from the Spanish monastery, Cassidy dropped the platen twice. The first time a third of the way from the top, the second time a third of the way from the bottom, ensuring every bit of type received firm pressure to transfer the ink.

Sliding out the chase, Cassidy carefully loosened each corner of the paper to minimize risk of tearing. Then, using both hands, she gingerly removed the sheet.

After taking a moment to admire the midnight black of fresh ink clinging to the vintage page, Cassidy carefully hung the sheet to dry on a repurposed laundry line. Recalling that the laundry line had come from the first apartment she and her mother moved into after her father's death, Cassidy smiled.

The printing process always brought the tightly-wound Cassidy a sense of release. With its blend of delicacy, as with setting type, and brutality, such as patting the ink and dropping the platen, printing was inherently sensual.

When the ink dried, she proofed the printed page thrice more, hunting for any mistake or imperfection which might tip off a suspicious investigator.

Then the whole process started over. Twenty-six times. Thirteen sheets, front and back, which would ultimately yield 208 pages.

Cassidy paid special attention to what would become the twenty-fourth page of text. Its first 13 lines began with the letters J-K-B-K-R-T-H-S-B-K-S-F-K. In order to prevent casual detection, she had omitted the vowels but those letters contained a damning acrostic.

*JaKe BooKeR, THiS BooK iS FaKe*

It had been an enormous pain in the ass to generate text that began with the necessary letters while still reading organically enough not to be an immediate tipoff. It made things worse that French rarely used the letter 'K,' and she needed four of them, except for words borrowed from other languages. Hebrew, fortunately, was replete with 'K' sounds.

The odds that such a sequence of first letters on a line would occur randomly were millions to one. But, just to underscore the point, Cassidy placed the acrostic on the twenty-fourth page, the same number of letters the message would contain if vowels were included. At that point, nobody could credibly call it coincidence. All it would take was one email to the right historian, linguist, or reporter.

In the entire process Cassidy made but a single error. Despite all her efforts at pre-proofing, one page repeated the word *décès* twice in a row. The page would have to go. Self-confidently, arrogantly perhaps, she'd allowed no margin for error in her text. Hierbabuena, had he been there, no doubt would have chided her. There was nothing she could do about it now, her *Sefer Bohem* would be missing its final page.

Cassidy decided to turn the mistake to her advantage. She would include it with the others and, after binding, would tear the flawed page away, leaving a rough edge of paper near the seam testifying to its former presence. Like the missing corner on the Ulysses Grant broadsheet, such damage would make the fabrication more believable.

With that decision made, Cassidy turned her attention to the binding, transforming Hierbabuena's thirteen sheets into the 208 pages of her *Sefer Bohem*. A new process for bookbinding emerged in the eighteenth century. Printers began sewing pages onto recessed cords hidden beneath the spine. The technique yielded a smooth, flush appearance noticeably different from the rounded, convex spines of earlier books. That was important. The kind of thing where lesser forgers might make a telling error.

With the binding complete and carefully concealed under the spine, Cassidy admired her handiwork. Knowing she'd wipe it clean of prints later, she allowed herself the luxury of running her fingertips over the covers and up and down the spine. The book was a thing of beauty.

*It's almost a shame that it isn't real.*

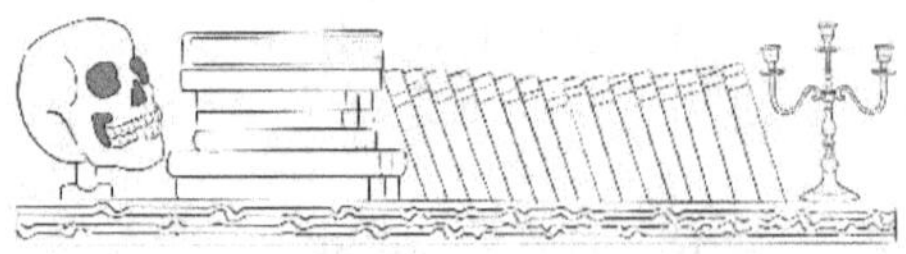

**Austin, June 27**

Even Jen had to acknowledge, for the past two weeks, she'd justified her mother's "basement gnome" accusation. A kitchen trashcan overflowing with delivery containers, and a tower of pizza boxes stacked at its side, testified to fourteen days she'd barely changed out of her PJs, much less left the house. She'd had Judas Priest's *Defenders of the Faith* cranked and on repeat, earning Jen a scowl from her curmudgeonly upstairs neighbor on one of the few occasions she'd ventured out her front door.

She finally had images of the original document, which she'd mentally dubbed the "Macek Text," after the Czech collector who'd left it to Goethe College. Putting her other projects on hold, even the Himyaritic, she had all the time in the world. Starting from scratch, Jen used every resource at her disposal to ferociously attack those outliers of vocabulary.

When standard references proved useless, she'd turned to more esoteric ones. After those ran dry, she'd sent discreet and rather oblique emails to some of those twenty or so Semitic Language scholars better than she. When even their advice left some dark corners, Jen turned to archaeological records.

In the end, she found the pieces she needed. Enough of them, anyway. The document might have been printed in the sixteenth century but its content sure as hell hadn't originated then. Three possibilities existed regarding the outliers. And all of them exceeded her initial suspicions regarding the material's enormous antiquity.

The first option was that the words came from extinct dialects of Archaic Hebrew or sister languages used by non-Judean groups like the Ammonites, Edomites, and Moabites. A second, more remarkable, possibility was that the outliers originated in a parent language of Archaic Hebrew such as Proto-Canaanite or even Amorite. The third possibility was that different outliers came from both sources. Dialects or sister languages of Archaic Hebrew would date the Macek Text's content to between 1000-500 BCE. Coming from a parent language meant a tantalizingly ancient 2500-1000 BCE.

Jen peered through time's hazy mist into a dim Bronze Age semi-history hinted at by archaeology and oblique references in works that were themselves ancient. But the Macek Text seemed to pull back the curtains on that distant world, throwing open the window to allow fresh air and bright sunshine. And it illuminated a mythology so old it should more properly be called Canaanite than Early Hebrew.

You didn't study ancient languages, at least not to the level Jen did, without picking up some history and culture in the bargain. The monotheistic Jews hadn't started out that way. During the early Iron Age, came a kind of halfway house between polytheism and monotheism called *monolatry* or *henotheism* which acknowledged many gods' existence but concerned itself with worshiping only one of them. Some scholars hypothesized traces of monolatry lingered, overlooked by the majority of modern readers, within the oldest scriptures.

"Thou shalt have no other gods before me," Jen whispered to herself.

But follow that trail back further, before the Covenant, Moses, or Mt. Sinai, and the Jews' ancestors had practiced one of several closely related polytheistic Canaanite religions. And the names of those deities, Asherah, Attar, Belatu, Dagan, Qatesh, littered the Macek Text.

Dagan had been the Canaanite fertility God. In most Semitic languages, words with the root D-G-N related to grain or agriculture. In light of that, Jen carefully noted the Macek Text's description of Dagan as having dominion over the fields and their produce. Before the twentieth century, linguists had overlooked the importance of the D-G-N root, focusing instead on "Dag" as the word for "fish" in some Semitic tongues. As a result, earlier scholars misclassified Dagan as a thalassic deity. Under that erroneous interpretation "Dagon" had entered the works of Lovecraft and some of Jen's other favorite authors.

Though not gods precisely, Lilith and the Rephaim, other entities mentioned by the Macek Text, were still referenced today. Granted, rarely in mainstream sources.

Whatever Jen's acquisition of Canaanite history, culture, and spirituality via linguistics amounted to, it was still scattershot. To really understand what she was looking at, to see a dozen, or hundred things, which had no doubt passed over Jen's head, she needed an expert.

The outdoor meeting spot certainly hadn't been Jen's idea. But since she was the one who needed help, she'd not felt comfortable saying no.

Amid a stretch of greenbelt not far from her apartment, Jen sat on a limestone slab. At her back a tiny stream flowed along the bottom of a deep channel worn into the bedrock. Using her phone to erect a wall of unavailability, Jen kept one eye on the steady stream of hikers, joggers, dog walkers, one cat walker, and ambling strollers.

"Sunlight looks good on you." At last, the voice Jen had been expecting.

"Gee, thanks."

"We're hiking Brockenberg next week," Dana's lean, athletic frame testified that the mental vigor radiating from dark eyes behind a pair of hipster glasses was matched by similar physical vigor. "Want to come?"

"I'll think about it."

"And what will you think?"

"How awful it sounds." Their relationship defied easy classification. Dana had too many years on Jen to qualify as a peer, but not so many that "mentor" really fit. And while Dana was a rabbi at one of Austin's temples, the one Jen invariably visited for High Holy Days, if no other time, she wasn't exactly Jen's spiritual advisor. Still, Dana was the person Jen called when she needed to bounce ideas off someone about life's more numinous and esoteric aspects.

"So, what have you got?" Dana regarded Jen curiously. "You're not exactly a 'let's get together and chat' girl."

"What do I have?" Jen shrugged. "That's what I'm hoping you'll tell me." With that, she handed Dana the photos she'd taken of the Macek Text as well her translation. Sure, Dana read and spoke Hebrew excellently. But Jen wasn't sure about her sixteenth century Hebrew, a language that had evolved more over time than sometimes acknowledged. And, of course, those bits of prodigiously ancient vocabulary. If they taxed Jen, most people wouldn't stand a chance. But it was more than that. The look, the language, of the Macek Text was so wonderful, so elegant, Jen wanted to share it with someone else who might appreciate it.

Dana, Jen noted, started with the photos. Only after laying those aside did she turn to Jen's translation. Intense concentration on her face, Dana's only reaction while absorbing the words were a couple of almost inaudible grunts. Were those good grunts or bad grunts? Jen couldn't tell.

When Dana was done, Jen summarized what linguistics told her and then asked what the corners of history, culture, and theology where her friend lived might reveal. Dana began with a summary of *monolatry* and *henotheism* in the ancient near east. Jen knew all that, of course. But she had to admit Dana's presentation was more polished and sure-footed than what she could have managed. Only then did Dana dive into what Jen really wanted to know. "If it, or most of it, really is as old as you say the vocabulary suggests, then I'm as sure as I can be there's been at least one alteration since then. And probably a second one."

After Jen asked the obvious question with her face, Dana continued. "Lilith's appearance is problematic. She wasn't really a thing until the fifth century. And as the embodiment of patriarchal fears of female sexuality? That's not until the seventh century." Pausing, Dana examined her companion's face before mirroring Jen's small frown on her own features. "You're not sold on that?"

"Not completely," Jen began. "Read the part about Lilith again. Does that sound like unbridled sexuality to you? I'm getting much more of a 'primordial chaos' vibe. A good fit considering she's described as arising from Tiamat's shed blood."

"Which I've never come across before."

"Or me." Jen paused, briefly struggling against the urge to nerd-out, and losing. "In Semitic languages generally, not just Hebrew, L-Y-L indicates 'night' or, idiomatically, 'darkness.' For millennia, various Semitic peoples have imbued entities whose names incorporate the L-Y-L root with whatever qualities they feared most in the darkness. Our sultry succubus is only the modern incarnation."

"Okay," Dana accepted the new information. "Could someone in the sixteenth century have encountered a different L-Y-L word in an earlier source and mistaken it for Lilith? Or have deliberately changed that other L-Y-L word to something their audience would recognize?"

Jen smiled. This was why conversations with Dana were good. "What about the Rephaim, then?"

"I was coming to that," Dana said. "Your text's three antagonists belong to a race, or category of beings, called the Rephaim. Or, in the singular, Rephait. References to Rephaim are scattered around the *Tanakh*."

"As well as ancient texts from other peoples in the region," Jen added with an *I know that* look.

Dana nodded. "Usually interpreted as 'giants,' the term could also imply 'ancestor spirits,' 'inhabitants of the underworld,' or, allowing some leeway, 'undead' in the modern sense."

Though not explicit on the matter, Jen thought the Macek Text suggestive of the traditional "giant" concept.

"Especially considering, as you point out, their broader Canaanite context," Dana continued, "I don't see anything about their usage here which raises red flags. However, there is something else…"

"El?" Jen volunteered.

"Yes," Dana acknowledged. "El. I don't have to tell you it means 'The God.' As opposed to "el" which means "a god." So, the way it's used here, it bothers me. The story makes it very clear that Dagan, god of agriculture, is first among the gods. You would know better than I do, but I'm not familiar with any other sources listing Dagan as high god. But, given all the things we don't know about Canaanite religion, I'll allow it. Even so, in that case, there's no reason another deity in the story should be called 'El.'" She paused, looking to Jen for guidance. "Unless there are other linguistic implications I'm not aware of."

"No. You're solid. Most Semitic languages have a similar word for god. And the ones that survived long enough to become monotheistic have the same dual usage. Like Arabic's *all*ah and *All*ah."

"Okay, so why is this god who is not in charge 'El'?"

"I think I know," Jen brightened. "And we're back to your idea of a sixteenth century editor making changes. Look at who El is in the story, 'he who loves most the men who hunt and herd and wander from place to place.' Then think of Genesis, the whole Cain and Abel thing. And Exodus and Psalm 23. I think, with the benefit of hindsight, someone looked at this text, saw the similarities between Dagan's brother and the God of Israelites, and made the change."

Receiving another approving nod for that logic, Jen continued. "If we found an older version of this material, I wonder what name we would find. Y-H-W-H? Something else?" Knowing Jen, Dana showed surprise that the impious linguist had spelled out rather than spoken God's name. If she had known Jen just a little better, she would have understood. It *was* piety, but not of a religious sort. Languages had rules, and you followed them.

As a thought occurred, Dana laughed. "Whoever produced your document, and made those changes…they were one brave sonofabitch." Seeing Jen didn't follow, she expounded on the point. "Think about the time we live in. Critical exegesis, analytic history, linguistics, archaeology. For two centuries or more, most people have accepted their validity." Pausing, she drew a long breath. "But in the centuries before that? The idea that El had been only one of many gods, not even the head of the pantheon? The notion would have been blasphemous. Even in sixteenth century Prague, people would have eagerly suppressed such a thing."

"Which leads us to the million dollar question. What is this? Can it be for real?"

"You wouldn't have called me if you didn't think there was a chance it was."

"True. Let me rephrase…do *you* think it's real?"

"First, I need to hear again what the linguist thinks."

"Okay…" Jen hesitated, "but that depends on your answer to one question. In the sixteenth century, was there enough knowledge about Canaanite religion to allow intentional fraud?"

"Certainly not in general circulation. That wouldn't have been possible until the late nineteenth century. And even that's pushing it. Can I tell you with 100% certainty that some small group now lost to history wasn't in possession of such information? I can't. But everything we do know says the answer is no."

"That tracks with the linguistics of this thing," Jen replied. "Before 100 years ago, limited understanding of Archaic Hebrew's sister and parent languages wouldn't have allowed for the document's outliers in vocabulary." *The vocabulary*, Jen thought but didn't say, *that even vexed me*. What she said, instead, was, "The Macek Text was donated to Goethe College in 1850. So, unless the school itself is perpetrating some kind of hoax…"

"… then it's not a fake," Dana finished Jen's thought. "At least not in the traditional sense. But it's not inviolate, either. The original source, whatever that was, has been altered in transmission. We've identified two potential changes made at a later date, quite possibly in the sixteenth century. I'll allow there may be others we've missed."

Even though she knew it was true, Dana's final assertion irked Jen. "So, what, exactly, is it? And why is it? That's your bag, not mine."

"Hmm…" Dana intoned noncommittally. "What's the difference between astrology and astronomy?"

"What?"

"What's the difference between astrology and astronomy?"

"Astronomy is the scientific study of space and the objects in it," Jen answered, wondering what the hell her friend was driving at. "Astrology is a pseudoscience based on the belief that celestial bodies influence fortunes and personality."

"What's the difference between chemistry and alchemy?"

Jen sighed. "Chemistry is the scientific study of how matter interacts," now feeling feisty, she followed with "alchemy is trying to turn lead into gold and crap."

"Very good twenty-first century answers," Dana said coyly. "At the time, however, that's not how people saw it. Alchemy and chemistry were all one body of knowledge. Ditto astronomy and astrology. History likes things neat. We want to forget that Newton dabbled with alchemy. Or that his writing on numerology would make a kabbalist proud. On the other side of that, John Dee did some very legit work in astronomy and mathematics. It's only with hindsight that we can say, at least superficially, that astronomy and chemistry were right and astrology and alchemy wrong."

"Superficially?"

"Even back in the day, most people, even practitioners, got astrology and alchemy wrong. They didn't understand what it was really for. They mixed up subject and object."

"Huh?"

“Think about it, promise me?” Dana smiled, handing Jen’s pages back to her as she stood and stretched. “If hiking doesn’t sound like your bag, we’re going kayaking next month. How about that?”

“I’ll be busy then,” Jen grinned, thinking it was a lie.

As they went their separate ways, each taking a different direction down the greenbelt trail, Dana called after Jen. “Seriously. Alchemy. Think about it.”

Jen spent most of the drive back home scratching her head about the strange turn her conversation with Dana had taken at the end. Then, realizing the implications of their exchange’s more productive parts, Jen was thunderstruck. Occam’s razor left her staring at a genuine and remarkable document preserving, at least in part, material at least two and half millennia old. And the material’s earliest possible date, exceeding the *Gilgamesh Epic* by more than 1,000 years, would make it humanity’s oldest surviving narrative.

Jen’s head no longer itched, it spun. So much so that she nearly rear-ended a Prius drifting lazily between lanes ahead of her.

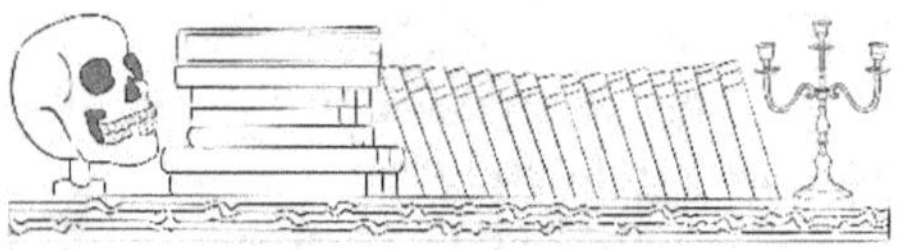

After more days cloistered in research, even Jen’s brain burned out on linguistics, history, and theology. Allowing herself a break, she put on Blue Öyster Cult—admittedly in that nebulous zone between metal and hard rock, and sat down with a beer at her desk. Warily, as if it were a hot coal, she picked up the book delivered earlier that day. *Three Books of Occult Philosophy* by Heinrich Cornelius Agrippa.

No, what Dana said about alchemy hadn’t made any sense. Then again, Jen had to admit, a lot of things Dana said didn’t make sense in the moment—but had a habit of panning out in the long run

Jen had gravitated toward Agrippa because a quick online search suggested he blended elements of kabbalah into his alchemy. Also, bearing out at least some of what Dana had said, Agrippa’s other accomplishments as a humanist scholar left Jen feeling a little less queasy about the whole thing.

Thus far, if that made Agrippa *better*, Jen shuddered at what *worse* would look like. The stuff that was just plain wrong was bad enough…

> *For we know that of Worms are generated Gnats, of a Horse Waspes, of a Calf, and Ox Bees, of a Crab, his legs being taken of, and he buried in the ground, a Scorpion; of a Duck dryed into powder, and put into Water, are generated Frogs; but if it be baked in a Pie, and cut into pieces, and put into a moist place under the ground, Toads are generated of it: of the Hearb Garden Basill bruised betwixt two stones, are generated Scorpions, and of the hairs of a menstruous Woman put under dung, are bred Serpents; and the hair of a Horse taile put into Water, receiveth life, and is turned into a pernicious Worm.*

But at least that sentence, and yes, it was a single sentence, could be understood. Jen would have reluctantly accepted passages that blasphemed against twenty-first century science over those blaspheming against twenty-first century sentence structure. Consider…

> *For the superior binds that which is inferior, and converts it to it self, and the inferior is by the same reason converted to the superior, or is otherwise affected, and wrought upon. By this reason things that receive a superior degree of any Star, bind, or attract, or hinder things which have an inferior, according as they agree, or disagree amongst themselves. Whence a Lion is afraid of a Cock, because the presence of the Solary vertue is more agreeable to a Cock then to a Lion: So a Loadstone draws Iron, because in order it hath a superior degree of the Celestiall Bear.*

Bellowing with frustration, Jen hurtled *Three Books of Occult Philosophy* across the room. Striking a wall and falling to the floor, it fell silent as if chastised. At least that last passage had said nothing about menstruation, Agrippa was obsessed with it. *Having my period mansplained to me is bad enough*, Jen seethed mentally, *but from an alchemist who has been dead for 500 years is so much worse.*

Rather than allow herself to think less than charitable thoughts about Dana for starting her down this road, Jen moved from her desk to her third-hand couch. Perhaps it was inevitable that she would pick up her phone and examine the Macek Text photos she'd taken at Goethe College. After the fussy academic posturing of Agrippa's sixteenth century Latin—made worse by translation into that slovenly packrat of languages, English—Hebrew's elegant precision came as a balm.

Reading through the page, something caught her eye. And not something connected with the text itself. Looking at the page displayed at normal size, its left edge appeared perfectly straight. But, zooming in, Jen saw that wasn't quite so. Its jagged edge rendered the page just a little wider at the bottom than at the top. Sometime before 1850 someone, perhaps Teodor Macek and perhaps not, had torn the page from a larger work.

That changed, for the better, the nature of Jen's quest. A manuscript, a single page, was a tiny thing. Something which could easily hide in history's shadows. But in the sixteenth century, books had been a big deal. While it wouldn't be impossible, it was unlikely such a book could have existed without someone, somewhere knowing something about it.

What had that larger work been? And was the Macek Text's story an outlier within it? A remarkable survival among an otherwise prosaic collection of myths? An inclusion within a now lost book of religious scholarship and commentary? Such a work would have been right at home among sixteenth century Prague's learned Jewish community. But what if the text had come from a tome full of ancient survivals? That could revolutionize everything. And Jen would never again feel looked down at by other scholars.

The existence of a book opened up new avenues of research. But further headway required less circumspection in her inquiries. Jen was at a loss. Of her twenty betters scattered across the world, whom could she trust? Professor Tanzer seemed the best bet. Private, taciturn, and with eccentric ideas of his own, she suspected he would be the most likely to treat a bizarre inquiry seriously while also respecting its confidence.

Such was Tanzer's aversion to human interaction that it caught Jen off guard when her call didn't go to voicemail. "Ms. Gerson," he answered in his distinctive voice, a mélange of accents further blurred by shooting too much whisky and smoking too many cigars. Many of Jen's colleagues would have emphasized the *Ms.*, implicitly reminding her that she lacked a doctorate. That Gus Tanzer let it pass his lips without special note seemed confirmation that she'd chosen wisely.

"I've got a strange question for you, Gus," Jen said. "So strange I'm having trouble figuring out how to phrase it."

"Well, do your best, then."

"Have you ever heard anything about a Hebrew book from sixteenth century Prague, I suppose there could be other printings, of really old Canaanite mythology? El, Lilith, Dagan, stuff like that? But, here's the kicker, it's got the vocabulary to back that up. Plenty of Archaic Hebrew, Edomite, Moabite, maybe even Amorite and Proto-Canaanite all mixed in."

"What you're describing sounds like the *Sefer Bohem*. If it ever existed."

Jen understood *Sefer Bohem's* literal meaning, "Bohemian Book" or "Bohemian Codex," but nothing more. "What is that?"

"Allegedly? A compilation of Canaanite legends. Some will say it's Judean, but that has more to do with where they say it was printed than its contents. The book is very likely a myth but, well, one of those stories that's just too good to die."

"Okay, tell me about it."

"Typically, the tale runs something like this. Printed by a mysterious hakham in mid-sixteenth century Prague, the city's rabbis immediately suppressed it. In addition to finding its content objectionable, it was definitely something they didn't want falling into the hands of their Christian neighbors. So, you will note, the story builds in a convenient explanation for why a copy has never surfaced. Of course, some versions of the tale come with a 'single copy was secreted out of the city' denouement.

"Whether or not it exists, the *Sefer Bohem* has an evil reputation. And not just for its iconoclasm. Tales hint at tragedy befalling those who become involved with it." Tanzer stopped suddenly, as if his words hit a brick wall. "Why do you ask?"

"I might have seen a page from it."

"What? Where?"

"A university archive not far from here. The provenance, the language, the content. All of it matches what you've described."

"Amazing. Tell me more."

Jen summarized her visit to Goethe College, omitting the pistol-packing visitor that had been its prologue. And she spoke about the rest in generalities. Her trust in Tanzer went only so far. She'd been burned by colleagues before, like the sixth century liturgical Arabic she'd shared too much of with Arbley. Still, when it came to her reasons for thinking the Macek Text genuine, Jen spoke plainly.

"I'm glad you called me," the professor said, emphasizing the last word, when she'd finished. "This is like a respected zoologist having an interest in bigfoot. Not something you'd want your colleagues to know about."

"What about you?" Jen asked anxiously.

After a long pause, Tanzer continued, "You've piqued my curiosity. I'll be discreet. If you need more help, call me."

"Wait, where should I start?"

"A mysterious volume of Judaica? Or something akin to Judaica. You *know* where to start." After a moment, Tanzer added. "Also, I have a memory that Geiger and Hirsch may have referenced it in their disputations." He sounded like a professor guiding a lazy grad student toward an answer rather than one scholar directly answering another. Apparently feeling he had rendered ample assistance, Gus Tanzer ended the call.

What he'd told her made sense. It would be hard to imagine a more perfect time and place for a book like the *Sefer Bohem* he'd described to emerge. In the sixteenth century, Prague's Jewish community flourished in the midst of an intellectual and cultural golden age. Already home to one of the world's largest such communities, it swelled with refugees from elsewhere in Europe and beyond. Those new arrivals added to Prague's reputation as a center of sacred and secular learning, the former often of a distinctly mystical bent. Both natives and immigrants included many hakham, such the one to which Tanzer attributed the *Sefer*

*Bohem's* printing. The vague term indicated a person of great wisdom or a religious scholar, though not necessarily a rabbi.

Among the hakham then wandering Prague's streets could be found a young rabbi named Judah Loew, a scholar, natural philosopher, and mystic who was to the sixteenth century what Da Vinci had been to Renaissance Italy. Not that she expected Rabbi Loew to be the hand behind the Macek Text—neither his legacy nor his beliefs supported such a connection—but his presence was indicative.

In time, Loew's name attached itself to the city's best-known legend, credited as the creator of that mystical construct, the Golem. Jen had no doubt the tale was little more than a "wish fulfillment" story told by a persecuted people who wanted to be left in peace. *Then again*, she thought as a bark of laughter blending cynicism and wonder escaped her lips, *if there had been a Merlin, could I completely discount a Golem?*

When Professor Tanzer implied there was an obvious place to begin tracking the text, Jen had understood. The Latvian-born Ephraim Deinard had been more than a book scout and bookseller. Throughout the late nineteenth and early twentieth centuries he was the world's top expert on historic Judaica. Jen spent days wading through his prodigious writing. Oh, he referenced the *Sefer Bohem*. But only in the negative. Deinard received inquiries about the book throughout his career. Not only had his efforts failed to turn up the tome, they left him doubting that it ever existed.

Tanzer had mentioned two other names, Geiger and Hirsch. Linguists, or perhaps bibliophiles, with whom Jen was unfamiliar. Google quickly told her why. The men were neither linguists nor bibliophiles, at least not primarily. They had been rabbis from nineteenth century Germany.

Europe in the nineteenth century had been an intellectually precocious period in general, but one with special resonance for Judaism. It was the time of the *Haskalah*, colloquially called the Jewish Enlightenment, a fertile if not always harmonious movement sowing the seeds of modern Judaism's division into Reform, Conservative, and Orthodox denominations.

Jen was comfortable with those broad strokes. But a "disputation," as Tanzer had called it, between two rabbis of apparently very scholarly bent? Out of her depth, Jen didn't trust herself to navigate those waters. Fortunately, she knew who could. Jen resigned herself to another hour of Agrippa to salve her conscience about the call she would make afterward.

It didn't take long to confirm she'd phoned the right person. It wasn't just that Dana acknowledged familiarity with Geiger and Hirsch, it was the tone Jen heard in her voice. The giddy excitement of someone who has a good, and slightly scandalous, story to tell. It was only after Jen made clear her specific needs regarding the rabbis that Dana sprung her trap. "It'll take me a couple days to put together what I need to answer your questions as fully as I know you'll want them answered. I'll have it ready by the time you come hiking with us this weekend."

"What!?"

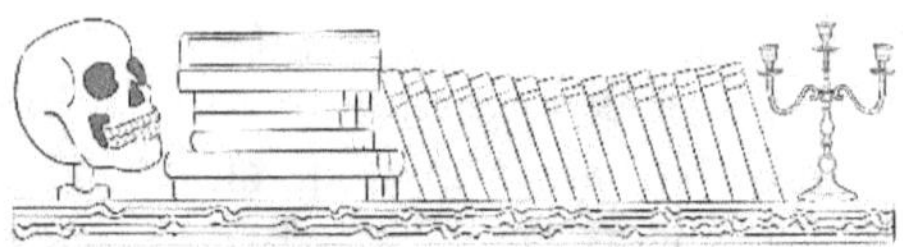

**San Francisco, June 30**

Exiting the cab on a side street near the heart of Haight-Ashbury, Cassidy handed her driver a wad of cash. True, ride-sharing services were usually faster and more pleasant. The cab reeked of stale cigar smoke and she'd had to endure sports radio the entire drive. But, for Cassidy, not leaving an electronic trail was at a premium. So was doing things in cash.

Glancing at the scrap of paper she'd found inserted between door and doorframe at her warehouse, she checked the street address authored in her mentor's elegant, continental script against the brass numbers on the well-kept three-story wooden house in front of her. She would never have picked Haight-Ashbury as his neighborhood but, upon finding it so, somehow it made perfect sense.

Climbing the steps and driving the antique iron doorknocker against its backplate three times, she waited. A minute later, the door opened first a crack and then all the way as Hierbabuena stepped out onto his porch. Over his favorite suit, he wore a white apron carefully tied behind his back. "You are on time." He smiled, motioning her inside. "Too many young people today do not number punctuality among the virtues."

Within, Cassidy discovered the warm, rich aromas of a kitchen put to its proper use. "Of course I'm on time. When I found your note, I didn't know whether to be excited or worried."

"Perhaps you should reserve judgement until you have sampled my cooking." Under the medley of scents from the kitchen, Cassidy could smell the trademark peppermint tucked into her host's mouth. Glancing over his shoulder toward the kitchen, he added "It will be another five minutes, perhaps ten. I trust you can entertain yourself in the parlor until then?"

*Not the living room, the parlor*, she thought to herself. Carefully scrutinizing its furnishings, she hoped for external clues to her mentor's carefully guarded internal landscape. Tasteful if rather conventional European antiques which might have traveled with his family from Spain. Masks and other curios hinting at escapades in Africa, the Pacific, and beyond. Memorabilia suggesting a deep immersion in Haight's 1960s counterculture.

"Holy shit, is this you with Allen Ginsberg?" Cassidy called out, examining a photo. A young Hierbabuena, awkward yet still somehow already dignified; his arm curled affectionately around a bespectacled older man who, even in his forties, remained handsome in a bookish, bohemian sort of way.

"Yes," Hierbabuena shouted back over the clangs of pots and pans. "While, at the time that photo was taken, he had already left San Francisco to travel the world, Allen visited often."

Not, "Ginsberg," but *Allen*, Cassidy noted, wondering what else her mentor had been keeping from her.

A few moments later, Hierbabuena emerged from the kitchen bearing a large silver tureen. With his chin, he motioned for Cassidy to take her place at a small enamel-topped table set for two. As she sat, her mentor ladled soup into two china bowls. Quartered new potatoes, green onions, and some kind of tender, blanched meat floated in a broth which smelled of sweet peppers and garlic. Pulling the linen back on a wicker basket, he revealed slices of rounded, honey-colored bread.

Removing his apron and carefully folding it over the back of his chair, Hierbabuena joined Cassidy. "*Caldierada*," he answered the question posed by her face while he looked at the soup. "I was born in Madrid. As were my father and grandfather. But, originally, my family was from Galicia. My pallet, it seems, preserves some ancestral memory of those origins. Admittedly, I have taken the liberty of substituting mahi-mahi for the traditional cod.

"This, I suspect, will interest you far more," he announced, reaching for a wine bucket matching, in every particular, the soup tureen. Uncorking the bottle within, Hierbabuena poured the white wine into Cassidy's glass before attending to his own.

Holding the glass a polite distance from her nose, she detected a floral aroma. Against her tongue, it brought a refreshing flavor full of lively citrus notes. And yet the vintage was imperfectly familiar to her. "This is lovely. What is it?"

"Albareño," he answered. "The best comes from Corunna, where it is said my family also comes from."

"Another fine vintage, no doubt," she toasted. "Fancy suit. Fancy dinner. If I didn't know better, I'd think you were putting the moves on me," Cassidy added in full jest.

"Yes, I know how it must look," Hierbabuena acknowledged with a playful wave. "You are a lovely young woman. But you are not my type." Cassidy's mentor gave a wink and a wry nod to the photo she'd mentioned earlier. Upon reexamination, perhaps the fashion in which the poet nestled into Hierbabuena's enveloping arm was a bit more than affectionate.

"So, you're an old hippie," she reflected. "Like the house, I wouldn't have guessed. But, discovering it, it makes perfect sense."

He nodded. "Perhaps, then, you will be genuinely surprised that, while the craft was always in my blood, it was my time among the hippies that served as my gateway into it."

Cassidy's brow creased. "Okay, you can't just drop that into conversation and not give the backstory."

"You know I speak with reverence and love about my father. But, for many years, my family and I were at odds. At that time, where was a rebellious young man in San Francisco to go but Haight-Ashbury? As soon as I could, I moved here. To this very house. And here I have been ever since. Back then, I was terribly shy. Yet the hippies, the heads, the diggers—they all loved me. You see, I could always 'find' tickets to concerts that no one else could. In time, my activities took a more serious turn. More than one young man from this neighborhood avoided the horrors of Vietnam with a medical exemption of dubious provenance tucked under his arm."

Standing and donning his white apron once more, Hierbabuena collected their soup bowls before disappearing back into the kitchen. He reappeared with two small dessert plates. While refilling their wine glasses, he named the plates' contents as *filloas*—clearly crepes in all but name. By any name, they were marvelous in their simplicity. Translucently light, filled with a milky sweet cream rolled in bits of hazelnut, and drizzled with honey.

Finally setting down glass and laying aside fork, Cassidy took a breath and prepared to put a bit of an edge in her voice. "This is all very nice. But I doubt you invited me tonight so you could brag about banging Allen Ginsberg and confess to helping people dodge the draft. Why am I really here?"

"Firstly, because of the completion of a task worthy of celebration. The *Sefer Bohem*. Secondly, it occurs to me, I have seen your *sanctum sanctorum*. Admittedly, that was not at your invitation. But I have seen it all the same. At this point in our friendship, it seemed past time that I return that gesture."

It sounded plausible enough. And yet it struck Cassidy as not the truth. At least not the *whole* truth.

"While I am proud of my parlor," Hierbabuena continued, "it is not where the magic happens. Would you like to see my workshop?"

At that opportunity, any hesitation Cassidy might have felt vanished as completely as the crepes on her now empty plate.

In the back of the house, heavy blackout curtains had been nailed over the room's windows. A half-dozen locks, latches, and deadbolts safeguarded the door leading outside. But what Cassidy chiefly noticed was how small the room was, and how spare. Her warehouse was far more extensively equipped. And yet she was unsure it was any *better* equipped. Every object here, from the largest press to the smallest block of pewter typeface, had been selected with the practiced eye of a master at his craft for half a century.

The small number of presses especially surprised Cassidy. Less than a handful of small machines on tables or shelves, including an unfamiliar hand-operated rolling press similar to her Washington. Also unfamiliar to Cassidy was the workshop's single large press. Leaning in for a closer look, the cleverness of its design instantly impressed her. It combined elements of a post-Gutenberg press, circa 1500 or so, and a Blaew press, like the replica in her warehouse. With a few small adjustments by the printer, this machine could function as either.

"My father's device," Hierbabuena explained, acknowledging Cassidy's admiration. "When I grew more ambitious in the craft, I made a few additions of my own. In fact, this is where Cervantes' most recent collection was born." He smiled. "I would be happy to share its secrets with you."

Cassidy beamed with pride. "Thank you. And I'm not just talking about the press. Or tonight. Thank you for everything. Is there some way I can repay you?"

"You know how you can repay me, my dear. Did you bring it?"

With a conspiratorial grin, Cassidy reached into her handbag. Unwrapping the oilcloth which protected the book, Cassidy offered the *Sefer Bohem*, her *Sefer Bohem*, to Hierbabuena. Deftly, her mentor donned white linen gloves—not as an affectation, but to ensure neither oils (bad for the work) nor fingerprints (bad for him) remained upon the book—before taking it in hand.

Slowly, he rotated the *Sefer Bohem* in front of him, considering the tooling and wear upon the covers Cassidy had repurposed from the old bible. Then, with the tenderness of a lover caressing his beloved, he opened the book, examining several pages, seemingly at random.

Cassidy was aware that, other than her father, Hierbabuena was the only person she had ever truly respected. Still, the wave of nervousness, bordering on nausea, sweeping over her as he examined her work... *judged her work...*caught Cassidy by surprise.

Holding the book toward the Tiffany lamp at his side, he tilted it back and forth, scrutinizing how the light played on Cassidy's recreated eighteenth century printers' ink. Modern inks gave a matte effect and were pure black. Further back in history, inks had a gloss. And, sometimes, colorful undertones imparted by their curious ingredients. Reds, blues, greens, or golds, depending on the recipe, which would show themselves under direct illumination.

Applying gentle but steady pressure, Hierbabuena ran two fingers over the spine, taking the measure of the sewn binding beneath. Then, from his suit pocket, he produced a jeweler's monocle. Placing it over his left eye, he rotated the book to its top and bottom as he examined the tiny sections of binding visible at each end.

Starting at the beginning, he methodically flipped through the book, a process taking many minutes. Reaching the torn-away page at the book's end, the inspirational touch born of Cassidy's error in proofing, he nodded approvingly—more to himself than to Cassidy.

The book made a soft noise, like a single heartbeat, as Hierbabuena closed its covers. For a few moments, his gaze fell from the book toward the tiled floor. Raising his head, looking at Cassidy, his expression proved inscrutable, save for a single tear trailing down his cheek.

"I am proud of you. And my father would have been proud of the use to which his pages have been put. This is a true masterwork. We are not a guild. We have no ceremonies or rites of passage. But, on this day, you are no longer my pupil, you are my peer."

Cassidy had never been a hugger. But, for just one instant, she reached out and held Hierbabuena tightly. Clearly finding the moment as significant, and as awkward, as she did, after a moment of his own, he deftly disengaged. "Cappuccino?" he offered.

Back in the parlor, with the small dining table still cluttered by the remains of dessert, Cassidy rested on an art nouveau divan upholstered in vertical stripes of goldenrod and emerald green. A few minutes later, setting cups and saucers in front of them, he took his place in a small chair that perfectly matched the divan. He gave Cassidy a moment to appreciate the foam "leaf" floating on the surface of each drink.

"Latte art?" she raised an eyebrow as they reached for their cups. "I'm impressed." Returning cup to saucer after her first taste, she was even more impressed. “This is way better than the stuff at Incunabulum,” she observed.

“I know,” he replied with a half-smile.

“Why do you go there then?”

“None of us are solitary creatures. Even I have a need to be among others occasionally.” While it seemed as if Hierbabuena had been set to continue that thought, he halted, regarding Cassidy curiously.

“What?” she asked, suddenly anxious.

“On more than one occasion, I saw Grace Slick passed out upon that very divan.” He paused. “It occurs to me that you are not so unlike her.”

His observation prompted several stories from Hierbabuena about living in Haight during the ‘60s and ‘70s height of its fame and infamy. Cassidy had known who Allen Ginsberg and Grace Slick were. But the names Hierbabuena now dropped into his tales were as meaningless to her as the untranslated letters on the page from that Texas college. Instead, her interest wandered to the collection of masks, their style and origins unfamiliar to her, on the wall behind him. Despite herself, her attention returned over and over to a mask of repellent and vaguely ichthyic aspect.

Turning his head, Hierbabuena followed Cassidy’s gaze. “Ah, yes, that one. Perhaps you’d like to hear a story about the craft rather than from my days among the hippies?”

While Cassidy did not respond, she definitely preferred such a tale.

“In the 1970s, as the hippies began fading away and Haight entered a slow and not so genteel decline, I began to travel. And used those travels as inspiration for my craft. I became curious about a certain obscure and supposedly vanished text that Colonel Churchward had cited in his writings on the lost continent of Mu. While long aeons have swallowed the document’s proper name, it is known as the *Ponape Scripture*.” Hierbabuena paused and made the sign of the cross before continuing.

“Sailing the islands of the Pacific, I was determined to see if I might learn enough to perpetrate a fabrication of those scriptures. I did not go alone, I traveled in the company of Anders Lyngard, the Danish sailor and adventurer who, unknown to most, also indulged in our craft on occasion.

"It was never easy going. Among islanders and missionaries alike, our inquiries met with hostility. But eventually, in the Caroline Islands, on a remote coral atoll, we found a basalt pillar engraved with characters said to be from the *Ponape Scripture*—perhaps where Churchward himself had first encountered them. We transcribed the letters, from no alphabet either of us had ever seen, and set sail back to Brisbane, hoping to use the transcription as the basis for our fabrication.

"From that point forward, terrible misfortunes befell us. Including Typhoon Kit, which blew Anders' sailboat off course and damaged it so badly we were forced to detour to Port Moresby for emergency repairs. Our first night at anchor there, Anders disappeared. He was even older than I am now. So it is certainly possible he simply experienced some accident and fell overboard. But, unwilling to take the chance it was something so innocent, I heeded the omens. Tearing up the transcription we had made, I allowed its pieces to fall among the waves. And was thereafter untroubled by whatever ill fortune had followed us."

It was the strangest tale connected with the craft Cassidy had ever heard. And yet, it was not entirely unfamiliar. In fact, parts of it were very like the stories surrounding… "Wait, you're really talking about the *Sefer Bohem*, aren't you? That's why you invited me here tonight." Had the crafty old man even gone so far as to purposely leave the dessert dishes on the enamel table and steer her toward the divan, knowing she would stare at the masks and provide him an opening to tell his story?

"It is true," Hirebabuena acknowledged, his arms wide with palms turned up. He was clearly embarrassed at being called out. "I am excited for you. But I also worry for you. I worry because of that book. Even a fabrication may be tempting fate. You think I do not understand why you do what you do. But you are wrong. Still, I wanted to give you one more chance to ask yourself if it is the right thing to do."

Because it was Hierbabuena, Cassidy stifled the impulse to respond with pique and hubris. Instead, as best as possible, she tried conducting an honest accounting of her intended course of action. Obviously, no curse, or anything like a curse, surrounded the *Sefer Bohem*. No more than had surrounded Hierbabuena's *Ponape Scriptures*. Sometimes bad things just happened. Turning to the worldly dimensions of her plan, Cassidy's fingernails dug into the flesh of her palms. Vengeance...no, *justice*...for her father? Jake Booker getting what was coming to him? It felt right. It felt proper.

"It is." Cassidy's reply was as soft as it was unwavering in its conviction.

"I expected it would be so. Were I young and in your position, I cannot doubt I would say the same. But give me one thing. Let us pray for God to guide you. And for San Miguel to guard your person and San Benedetto to protect your spirit."

"Hierbabuena, you know I don't believe..."

He cut her off with a loud click of his tongue against his teeth. "I know, but do this thing for me. Please. Just because you do not believe in them does not mean you cannot learn from them. The Saints and the Angels...tell us stories. And those stories tell us much both about what is outside of us and what is inside of us. In each of us there lives a Santiago and a Saint Francis. A San Martin and a San Martin de Porres. A Mary and a Magdalene. A Peter, a Thomas, even a Judas..."

"Peter? Paul? Mary? You're sure you're not talking about the 1960s again?" Cassidy asked, her forced humor an attempt to divert a conversation making her feel increasingly awkward and adrift.

To her surprise, and relief, Hierbabuena's laughter sounded genuine. Alas, her reprieve was only partial. "It is as you say," he acknowledged. "But it is also as I say. Please, I have asked very little of you. If you will not pray with me, at least stand with me as I do."

While Hierbabuena spoke his words addressed to God and the saints, Cassidy bowed her head in prayer. Or at least the affect of prayer. This was not how she'd seen her evening ending.

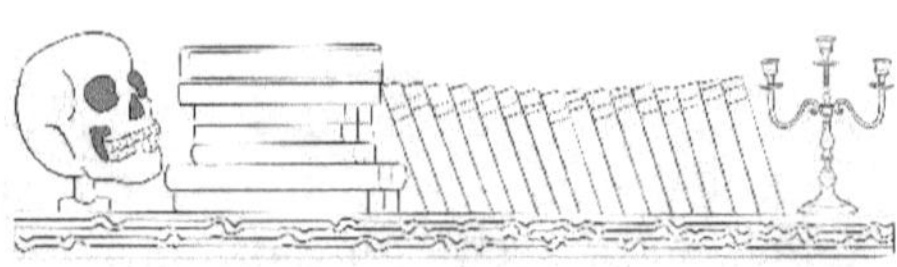

**Texas Hill Country, June 30**

Leaving town twice in as many weeks? And the same for doing something outdoorsy? Jen felt her basement gnome cred had been put at risk. Brockenberg, a massive dome of pink granite, was the Hill Country's highest point and, ergo, a popular spot for hiking. In the parking lot at its base, she met Dana, her husband Anesh, and about a dozen of their friends. Though introductions were made, Jen didn't so much catch the names as stand aside and let them fly past her. In large groups, she just turtled up anyway.

Yeah, Brockenberg was pretty. Both from a distance and, she found as they hiked, up close. Pockets of hardy green grasses and small trees, the latter clustered around tiny pools where rainwater collected in divots and fissures, made a pleasing contrast against the rose-hued stone. Of course, it came with all the annoyances, and actual dangers, of nature in Texas. Rattlesnakes. Cactus. Fire ants. Poison Ivy. Scorpions. Spear Grass. Armadillos.

Why armadillos? As her pathologist mother invariably reminded Jen whenever the topic came up, the animals were carriers for Hansen's Disease—the clinical term for what most people called leprosy. Of course, the next armadillo Jen met that wanted to cuddle with her would be the first. Personally, Jen had a soft spot for the strange creatures. Feisty little things with protective shells that, when the going got too rough, curled up into an armored ball—she saw a lot of herself in the creatures. Then, thinking of the animals' tendency to end up dead on the roadside, Jen decided she shouldn't push the analogy too far.

"So, Geiger and Hirsch. What do you have for me?" Jen asked Dana, forcing the words out while fighting for breath.

"Okay, first the background," Dana answered smoothly, obviously not winded by the climb. "Abraham Geiger was a rabbi in Hamburg, and one of the founders of Reform Judaism. Rabbi Sampson Hirsch led Frankfurt's Orthodox Community. The pair, loudly, were at odds on almost every important question of the day. It wasn't hard to find the exchange you asked about. And it was fascinating. At no point did either one of them directly address the other. The whole thing even played out in totally separate publications. But there's no doubt the editorials that the pair penned back and forth were basically a nineteenth century rabbinical flame war.

"I printed out modern translations of everything. But, I know you, you'll want the originals, too. So, I printed those out."

The linguist would have been more than happy to stop right there, examine Dana's printouts, and then walk right back down the hill. Unfortunately, Dana's gaze, still focused on the summit ahead, made it clear her friend had other ideas.

Jen was perspiring. No, that wasn't right, she sweated like a pig. In Texas, even during a good June, summer had already declared her intentions. Years like this? She was already here. And the hikers were getting a double dose. Heat from the brooding sun over their heads radiated back at them from the stone beneath their feet.

She took inordinate pride that she wasn't bringing up the rear. One of the other guests, a middle-aged journalist with a potbelly, stubby legs, and wearing a "Jungle Jim" hat, trailed the group by a minute or more.

"So, how's the Agrippa coming?" Dana asked as they walked.

Every language had its good points. One of English's best was its flexibility and creativity in expressing displeasure. It was a characteristic Jen put to use. Criticizing the alchemist's tedious verbiage seemed pointless, so she focused her invective on how obscure, how useless, how…just plain wrong…so much of it was.

After looking thoughtful for a moment, Dana's counterpoint, when it came, was at least brief. "Don't pay attention to what Agrippa says. Pay attention to what he means. Not everything is literal. Remember what I said about even many of alchemy's practitioners not understanding its real point. Reverse subject and object."

"Yes, you said that already. But what does that mean?"

"A girl who can master how many languages?" Dana gave a coy grin. "You'll figure it out."

Jen turned that over in her mind, or at least tried, all the way until reaching the summit. Looking down at the thick carpet of green trees blanketing the lesser hills which rolled to the horizon in every direction, she had to admit, the view didn't suck.

"You were thinking about what I said on the way up?" Dana asked.

"Yeah." Jen acknowledged.

"Good girl. Here's your reward," Dana replied, passing over a thin bundle of papers.

"Gee, thanks."

Ignoring the translations Dana had found, a quick scan of the originals told Jen she'd need two non-Semitic languages: German and Yiddish. Fortunately, Jen came to the task well prepared. So many of linguistics' luminaries had been (and still were) German, and so many of the discipline's foundational texts written in their language, that Jen had thought it remiss not to learn it.

And, more than ever, Jen was grateful for the year she'd spent working on her paper *Non-Hebrew Semitic Substratum in Yiddish.* True, even within the field of linguistics, the topic was an esoteric one. Jen felt certain her publication had been more praised than read. But it had necessitated mastering Yiddish. Though incorporating many elements, and much vocabulary, from Hebrew, Yiddish was a Germanic language in which Jen previously had only dabbled.

As to the matter literally at hand, Rabbi Geiger had fired the opening salvo, found among the pages of *Wissenschaftliche Zeitschrift für jüdische Theologie,* the *Scientific Journal for Jewish Theology*. Citing historical antecedents, he enthusiastically described the kind of intellectual flowering he expected the Haskalah to usher in. Prominently lionized was the robust and prolific community of early modern Prague.

Answering in his periodical, *Jeschurun,* an ancient term for Israelites idiomatically meaning "the upright, or blessed, people," Rabbi Hirsch's reply contained a passage Jen found most suggestive. "Those who hold sixteenth century Prague as an ideal ignore attitudes leading to many errors prefiguring current movements. Counted among these is a certain work, blasphemous to name, taking its common title from the region containing Prague."

Appearing soon afterward in *Wissenschaftliche Zeitschrift für jüdische Theologie,* Rabbi Geiger's follow-up proved less circumspect. "Those citing the *Buch Bohem* in opposition to Haskalah show only their argument's weakness. That work is widely regarded not only as myth but as slander perpetuated by the most intolerant among our Gentile neighbors. Even were it genuine, those who fear its existence and content must place little stock in rabbinical education, a major purpose of which must certainly be development of the critical faculty as regards both exegesis and knowledge more generally."

Jen paused. Geiger's use of "Buch Bohem" rather than "Sefer Bohem" was no doubt why the passage hadn't turned up in her research. Granted, either term would have been easily understood by nineteenth century Yiddish speakers. But why the distinctive choice of the informal, secular "buch" rather than the more formal, religious "sefer?" Deciding it was a puzzle for another time, she returned her attention to the rabbis' exchange.

*Jeschurun* was not long in replying to Geiger's latest salvo. "Those doubting a certain blasphemous work's existence clearly do not look too hard for proof they do not wish to find. It is not difficult to discover scholars, within the community and without, who have encountered the book. This includes so-called Reformers. As far as the danger represented by this work, perhaps only time will tell. But prudent men, those with the critical faculty, would take heed from the fates of those whose lives became too intertwined with that text."

While taking aim at "fear mongering" and "emotional appeals" as tools of religious scholarship, *Wissenschaftliche Zeitschrift für jüdische Theologie* did not specifically address the *Sefer Bohem* in response. And, according to Dana, while the crossing of intellectual swords between Rabbis Geiger and Hirsch continued for many years, the book never again appeared as a point of contention.

Anesh checked his phone and looked at Dana "Just over an hour until sunset, we should get going, hun."

Jen had noticed the metal sign, white lettering on a blue background. County ordinances forbade loitering on Brockenberg after dark, for *reasons of health and safety*. And if that wasn't enough, *violators would be prosecuted to the fullest extent of the law*.

"They're really serious about that," Jen said to no one in particular, observing a series of identical signs scattered every couple hundred feet around the summit's rim like a crown.

"Oh, yeah. People have a habit of going missing up here at night," Potbellied Journalist replied. "Walking off the edge. Falling in fissures. That kind of thing. At least that's what most people say." While there was no missing the *I've got a story about that* expression on his face, nobody was biting.

Descent was always easier than climbing and the waning light forced more caution from the group. On their way down, Jen found it easier to keep up with the pack, and keep her breath. She used that to pick Dana's brain about something else.

"So, why alchemy? Not just that it's the twenty-first century, it's also *you*." At first intending to let the real question just hang there, unspoken, after a moment, Jen doubled down. "I mean, you don't really believe it...do you?"

"So, we've talked about how I can be not just a Jew but a rabbi, even though I would also describe myself as an atheist," Dana began before a pause of her own. "Just because something isn't real, doesn't mean that it's not true. Or, more to the point, contains important truths. Has value. Judaism, or religion in general, isn't the only place you can find that. Alchemy, astrology, the *I Ching*, the tarot. There's a lot of truth and wisdom in those, even if they're not real. No, don't change your career or marry someone just because of a tarot reading. But, if you understand the system—the archetypes and their meaning—you can learn a lot about the world. And about yourself.

"On some level, Jen, you understand what I'm talking about. If you didn't, you wouldn't show up to temple for High Holy Days. While I hate the phrase 'you'd be happier,' I think you would...find your life enriched...if you had something else that let you focus on that more deliberately.

"Why alchemy? It seems methodical enough for that clockwork brain of yours, but far enough removed from your usual stomping ground that you would have to actively work to master it."

Biting her tongue, Jen felt condescended to. She hated that. She also hated the existence of a certain artful symmetry in Dana's argument that refused easy dismissal.

From the car park, the group paused long enough to watch the sun set. Bathed in dusk's rosy light, Brockenberg's pink granite seemed to glow. Jen supposed it was kind of magical. But once the sun sunk below the hills, change came with startling suddenness. Now an ominous black shape silhouetted against the first twinkling stars, Brockenberg assumed a menacing aspect. Periodically, great groans and pops came from the vast rock now shrouded in darkness. They reminded Jen of whale songs, but a thousand times more ponderous. As if the rock sung to something so large as to preclude human understanding.

"The sound of Brockenberg cooling." Anesh spoke to no one, or to everyone. "The stone contracts as the day's heat bleeds off."

A single *humph* came from the darkness. Jen was pretty sure it was Potbellied Journalist.

Whatever the hazards, Jen would definitely not want to be up there after nightfall.

On the dark drive home, she turned Rabbi Geiger's curious phrasing over in her mind. *Buch* not *Sefer*. But why? She hit upon two possible answers. And, understanding those answers were at odds with each other, Jen took little comfort from the exercise.

On the one hand, in keeping with the explicit tone of his statements, it could have been an intentional snubbing of the work in question. To an enlightened nineteenth century religious leader, such as Geiger, stories such as the one she'd discovered in the Macek Text would have been little more than sloppy myths.

On the other hand, rather than derision, Geiger's choice of words could have masked genuine fear. In Semitic languages, words had power. As mirrored in Rabbi Hirsch's own phrasing of "a certain work, blasphemous to name, taking its common title from the region containing Prague," the words one spoke or wrote were chosen with great care. Whatever his head told him, in his heart, had Geiger balked at committing the words *Sefer Bohem* into print?

Returning to Austin, she reflected on another aspect of the reading she'd done atop Brockenberg's summit. It underscored that knowledge of the *Sefer Bohem*, even only as a myth, was the province of scholars like Deinard, Geiger, Hirsch, and, now, herself. The woman who'd come to Jen with images of the Macek Text, a bundle of cash, and a pistol, had been no academic. But why else would someone be interested in the obscure tome? Realizing that the encounter's shady nature pointed in a very specific direction, once she was back in her apartment, Jen fired off an email to a colleague in the broader field of linguistics, alerting her about the strange visitor's possible interest in the *Sefer Bohem*.

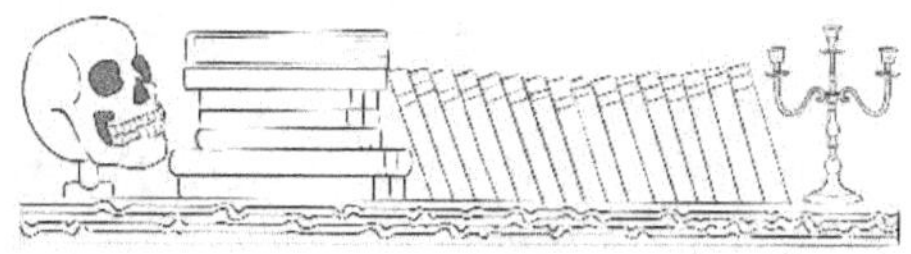

**Houston, July 2**

Driving in from the airport, Cassidy reflected she'd never expected to spend so much time in Texas. Austin, small and sleepy, had at least been charming. Houston felt like a swamp. Sprawling and boxy, it reminded her of an L.A. that had never learned to comb its hair or put on make-up.

A week earlier, even before her strange dinner with Hierbabuena, she'd baited her hook with an email to the Booker foundation:

> *I am pleased to announce the recovery of a previously unknown 1788 French printing of the* Sefer Bohem *which I am prepared to turn over to the Booker Foundation, in exchange for appropriate remuneration, as part of the Lost Books Project. I would like to request a meeting with one of the project administrators, Dr. Vivian Cuinnsey or Dr. Rosella Tassoni.*

The Foundation had bitten, as Cassidy knew it would. She was just minutes away from her meeting. And bringing her plan for revenge to fruition. Wondering why the foundation's offices were in a God-forsaken place like Houston, she figured it was probably so Jake Booker wouldn't have to take time away from his precious oil interests.

Reaching downtown, discovering museums and architecture someone had clearly paid attention to, Cassidy found reason to think a little better of Houston. Here, if nowhere else in the city, a century's worth of oil tycoons had put their money to good use. Following the instructions from her GPS, Cassidy rolled up outside an inconspicuous two-story red-brick building.

Passing through unmarked glass doors, Cassidy strode confidently through a cavernous lobby toward the young man behind a desk.

"Hello, welcome to the Booker Foundation," he greeted her. "I'm Charles." Long, disheveled hair fell in front of his face as he glanced at the laptop in front of him. "You must be Ms. Miller?"

She nodded. One of these days, she needed to start using a new alias. But, over the years, Cassidy had grown oddly fond of "April Miller."

"Make yourself comfortable," Charles invited her while brushing his hair away from his eyes. "Help yourself to coffee or a water. We'll be ready for you soon."

Sinking into one of the lobby's comfortable, and comfortably beyond most people's price range, leather chairs, Cassidy took stock of her surroundings. An enormous Old West oil painting occupied one wall. Framed prints and manuscripts decorated the others, between display cases full of old books and tasteful but rather generic antiques.

Intrigued by the books, Cassidy left her chair and examined the titles. She liked the idea that something here, of all places, might give her inspiration for a future project.

"Ms. Miller?" Charles stared at her. Cassidy had the impression that, lost in her examination, the receptionist had already called her name at least once. "Follow me please."

He escorted her to an office that, while not as spacious as the lobby, no one would call tiny. A bar stocked with various brown liquors filled one corner. Focusing on what appeared to be an authentic Kandinsky hanging from the back wall, she barely registered the framed photographs covering the other three. She noted all of that in the instant before her eyes locked on the man behind the desk...with his cowboy hat, blazer, and long, skinny legs terminating in cowboy boots kicked up on the desk. A man she'd first seen on the news in the days before learning of her father's death. "Jake Booker? I thought I'd be meeting with..."

"Yes, Doctor Cuinnsey and Doctor Tassoni usually handle intake and acquisitions. But essential work elsewhere has pulled them both away. So, I'm handling this acquisition personally."

Suddenly suspicious, Cassidy scanned the cowboy's tanned, craggy face for hints of deception. Finding neither confirmation nor refutation, she decided she'd never want to meet Jake Booker across a poker table.

"May I see the text?" he asked as Cassidy realized she had been studying him long enough for it to become awkward.

"A previously unknown French translation of the *Sefer Bohem.* Marvelous. Incredible, even," he said with a wink of turquoise-blue eyes. Taking the volume, Jake Booker enjoyed its weight and heft in his hands. Cassidy grimaced as he ran his fingers along the cover and spine. Watching her nemesis perform the same action that she had back at the warehouse after completing her masterwork was a humanizing detail Cassidy could have done without.

After holding it to his nose and inhaling with a broad grin, Jake Booker sat it to one side on his desktop. Taking a pen from a repurposed coffee mug, he began writing in a checkbook fished out of his blazer's pocket. The noise made by a check torn from a checkbook was distinctive, and probably on its way to extinction, Cassidy reflected as she took it from him.

Her eyes focused on the check's two most important fields, conspicuously left blank. "You didn't write anything for the amount."

"Why don't you tell me what you think it's worth?"

His remark choked off Cassidy's nascent sensation of triumph. She realized Jake Booker hadn't performed even the most rudimentary tests for authenticity. Or, actually, even opened the damn thing. She was suddenly certain that… "You think it's fake?"

"I *know* it's fake."

"What kind of game are you playing, Mr. Booker?" she asked, sticking one hand into her bag, letting it rest against the Glock.

"I'm more interested in what game you're playing, Ms. Miller." His inflection left no doubt he knew her name was as bogus as the volume before him. For the first time, he opened the book. After taking a minute to flip through it, he looked up at Cassidy with obvious respect. "You're a forger of the highest caliber, I'll give you that. But you need to pay more attention to people. You knew, I presume, that Jennifer Gerson is working on the Himyaritic inscriptions from *Merlin's Manuscripts*?"

She shook her head. What the linguist was working on when Cassidy showed up to get her translation hadn't seemed important.

"If you had known that, you might have wondered exactly how she got her hands on excerpts from the *Manuscripts*." He paused. "Viv, I mean Dr. Cuinnsey, and Ms. Gerson are colleagues and your translator is aware of the Lost Books Project. After examining the manuscript at Goethe College and researching its provenance, she gave us a call warning us to be on the lookout for anyone turning in a copy of the *Sefer Bohem*."

Under her breath, Cassidy cursed.

"But that's peanuts," Jake Booker continued. "What I want to know is 'why'? You poured your heart and soul into this." He glanced down at the volume. "There are easier and safer ways to make a buck as a forger. If I were a betting man, and I am, I'd wager this isn't about the money."

"My name, Mr. Booker, is Cassidy St. Tropez. You killed my father. The fabrication was going to be my way of avenging him. But, if I can't have revenge one way, I'll get it another." From her handbag, Cassidy produced the pistol, pointing it at the man who took her father away.

She didn't care for the way his expression remained unchanged. It suggested this wasn't the first time, or even the tenth, someone had aimed a weapon at Jake Booker.

"So, you're Michael St. Tropez's daughter?" he asked with a faraway look. "Why don't you sit down? At this distance you can shoot me just as easily sitting as standing." Though accepting his suggestion, Cassidy remained alert, literally on the edge of her seat. "Ms. St. Tropez," he said finally. "Do you want to know what happened to your father?"

Opening her mouth, she halted. She had spent years wondering but, now, with the answer in front of her, Cassidy found that part of her *didn't* want to know. That hesitant voice was easily shouted down.

"Yes," she said, her voice raspy in a mouth suddenly dry.

"First, let me say treasure hunting is a rough business. It attracts some really terrible people. Michael, your father, was never one of them. We faced off against each other often enough: Juan de Oñate's gold in New Mexico, the Bacchus Club vaults beneath London, the Queen Rangammal emeralds in Sri Lanka. But he always had my respect."

On a visceral level, the words pleased her. And a connection formed in her mind, her father must have acquired the Sri Lankan Devil Bird, sitting on her bookcase back in San Francisco, during the search for the emeralds of Queen whatever-her-name-was. But she resented Jake Booker for what had to be an attempt to butter her up.

"None of us knew it at the time," Booker continued, "but the whole thing really began in 1991 when the Soviet Union collapsed. Archives opened up that had been closed for most of a century. A decade later, in one of those repositories, a historian researching Russian Orthodox Church history came across a curious document.

"Forgive the history lesson but, if you really want to understand what happened, you need the backstory. In 1666, the Orthodox Patriarch, Nikon, began major reforms he thought the church needed. But a lot of people weren't happy with his changes. Resisting Nikon's reforms in various ways, they became known as the 'Old Believers.' You can still find their descendants in remote parts of Russia and across Alaska. Even farther afield, too. I've met some not far from here.

"Anyway, what our modern scholar found was a document about an Old Believer named Alexi Ulinov, the abbot of a wealthy monastery and youngest son of a Muscovite noble family. Convinced that Patriarch Nikon was the antichrist and the end times were at hand, Ulinov decided to move his entire monastery, with all its relics and treasures, as far beyond the patriarch's reach as possible. Purchasing three ships, which he rechristened the *Otetz*, the *Syun*, and the *Svyatoi Dukh*—the Father, Son, and Holy Ghost—Ulinov and his monastery sailed from Arkhangelsk never to be seen again.

"'As far from the patriarch's reach as possible' covers a lot of ground. Too much. But the document also referenced the name 'Dezhnev.' In 1648, a generation before the business with Ulinov and Patriarch Nikon, a Russian sailor named Semyon Dezhnev told tales about a voyage he and his crew had undertaken. Dezhnev, who lived in the far north along Russia's Pacific coast, described sailing past an enormous bay before encountering a chain of islands and rejoining the mainland again. More of a fur trapper than a real explorer, Dezhnev didn't understand the significance of what he'd done. But an educated person, like Abbot Ulinov, would have. Dezhnev had passed what we now call the Bering Strait. He'd gone from East Asia to North America's west coast. In 1666, that would have been as far from Patriarch Nikon, or anything else, as imaginable.

"The manuscript's meaning seemed clear: more than 100 years before Russia's first official settlement in Alaska, Abbot Ulinov moved his entire monastery there. Or intended to, anyway. Full of allusions to the monastery's wealth and relics, that little discovery in the church archives grabbed treasure hunters' attention. Of course, it also left a big question mark hanging in the air. Was Ulinov successful? Treasure hunters, good ones at least, started looking for more information.

"In 1784, the Russian-America Company, a trading monopoly with royal patronage, kind of like the British East India Company, established a trading post and mission called Fort Sankt Georgy in Alaska at the mouth of the Kasilof River. Upon arriving, the fort's commander sent a report to company directors back in Moscow. The strangest part of that report described encountering a group of Russian speakers living an austere, pious existence just inland from the fort.

"Another report came not long after, the first in a series of missives from one Father Pyotr, a clergyman the church sent along with the company in hopes of converting the indigenous population.

"The priest devoted considerable attention to describing the curious community which shared his mother tongue. The inhabitants called their settlement 'Ulinov,' rather suggestive wouldn't you say?" Jake Booker asked, raising his eyes to meet Cassidy's before continuing. "While Ulinov's residents showed reticence, even suspicion, toward the other newcomers, Pyotr managed to befriend their leader, a man named Kyril. He explained to Father Pyotr that Ulinov's founders came from Russia generations ago. Dubbing his neighbors the Ulinovites, the astute father noted their settlement was laid out in the fashion of an Orthodox monastery.

"As the missionary gained the community's trust, Kyril invited Pyotr inside their church. Seeing the riches on display, he realized the people who settled here had not been simple village monastics.

His report went into great detail about the gold, gems, and relics within. It puzzled Pyotr that the community gave pride of place to a ship's compass from one of the vessels that brought them to the wilderness. Certainly, the compass seemed a very minor thing alongside the other treasures. But, eventually, it heralded a curious twist in the father's tale.

"Over time, Kyril gained enough faith in Father Pyotr to allow him to observe their services. The Father realized that the community's rituals matched his own in every detail except one. They lacked Patriarch Nikon's changes. From that, the father concluded their ancestors must have left Russia before Nikon."

"Wait," Cassidy interrupted. "You said the monks left *because* of Nikon."

"Hold your horses," Jake Booker replied. "I'm getting to that.

"And Kyril explained that though their ancestors had been celibate monks back in Russia, after years in Alaska they began marrying natives so that their community could continue."

Looking up, Jake Booker used a tone of voice indicating an aside, "While Orthodox monks are celibate, Orthodox clergy can marry. So, that wasn't a huge leap."

"Mr. Booker, I am familiar with basic aspects of the world's major religions," Cassidy replied pointedly.

"Who's telling this story? You or me?"

Cassidy was sorely tempted to remind Jake Booker she was the one holding the gun. But, truth be told, the story had hooked her and she wanted him to get back to it.

Shrugging, the treasure hunter resumed. "As Pyotr's friendship with Kyril deepened, he discovered the Ulinov community had some very unusual beliefs. Indeed, you could say the Ulinovites were 'Old Believers' only in the sense that they rejected Nikon's reforms. So much of what Father Pyotr recorded seems unique to the Ulinovites, unlike other Old Believers who have fiercely held on to their orthodoxy.

"And that's true of later groups of Old Believers who took to the Bering Strait's far side like ducks to water. But Alaska influenced the Ulinovites in some singular ways. They believed the frozen wilderness to their north was a physical barrier separating our world from heaven. Asked pointedly by Father Pyotr, Kyril answered that, yes, in theory, traveling from one to the other was possible. The Ulinovites also attached great significance to the *aurora borealis,* interpreting the Northern Lights as signs and omens which God projected across the barrier. And, having a crude notion of the link between the aurora and magnetism, they held magnetism to be a divine manifestation. That's why, among the community's relics, the old ship's compass was venerated above all others. They believed it pointed them directly toward God.

"Or, at least, that's what was in Father Pyotr's reports. Despite what he perceived as their heresy, it's clear that the father had grown fond of the Ulinovites. Given how differently he describes them from any other group of Old Believers—hell, from any other group of anything—part of me still wonders if he was trying to shield the community by making them sound like harmless kooks.

"Strange as all that was, Father Pyotr was more taken aback to learn Kyril and the Ulinovites were aware of Nikon's reforms. The priest had finally recognized his initial conclusion was wrong. The Ulinovites' ancestors hadn't left Russia before Nikon's reforms, ignorant of them. Instead, they left afterward, fleeing them. And it horrified the monastics to learn that the patriarch's changes had taken root. Father Pyotr suspected that was why the Ulinovites shunned the other newcomers at Fort Sankt Georgy. They found something ominous in the nearby fort's presence.

"As if confirming those suspicions, many months passed when the aurora seldom appeared. On rare occasions when it did, it was faint and ghostly. Today we know the aurora's frequency and intensity depend on interactions between Earth's magnetosphere and solar wind. Without that understanding, and with their own distinctive ideas about the aurora, the Ulinovites took it as a sign from God. A sign that, as the fort brought worldly corruption closer, God's grace withdrew further and further away.

"So Kyril made a decision. However far Abbot Ulinov had taken his monastery from Russia, it was no longer far enough. If their community was to continue experiencing God's grace, they must go to him, to God. Kyril declared he would lead his people northward, across the great arctic barrier, to heaven. And they would carry with them their relics and treasures to keep them from Satan's grasp.

“Alone among the newcomers, they invited Father Pyotr to come with them. It sounds like the father wrestled with his answer until the last moment, fearing both the physical dangers of that harsh land and the spiritual dangers of Kyril’s heterodox pilgrimage. But, in the end, he joined them.

“He left us with no insight into his decision. Indeed, the last surviving account of the Ulinovites comes not from the father but from one of the fort’s minor functionaries. He recorded watching the community disappear across the horizon, heavily laden with supplies, riches, and relics. He records Father Pyotr and two others struggling under the weight of the massive ship’s compass which they expected to literally point their way to God.

“Uncovering the father’s missives back to Moscow about the Ulinovites, the already eager treasure hunters became sharks scenting blood in the water. But the prudent among us wanted confirmation. Some proof the community Father Pyotr described had actually existed. Not only would that argue the whole thing wasn’t just an entertaining tale, it would give a proper starting point for finding what, if anything, remained of the Ulinovites’ riches.

“Reaching Alaska as soon as I could, I met up with my partner Dr. Hope, the prominent Tlingit geologist. At Kasilof, we engaged the services of a local bush pilot. From the air, even among the thick trees beneath us, we clearly made out the distinctively-shaped foundations of a monastery and even the remnants of an earthen wall surrounding the community.

“By that time, it was too late, and too dark, to get out of town. A frenzied search for the Ulinovites’ lost gold would begin at first light. But, that night, the world’s top treasure hunters packed a rotgut shack occupying a Quonset hut outside of Kasilof.

“Dr. Hope and I were there. And your dad, of course. There was K.C. Swain, as close to my evil twin as I’d ever want to meet. I don’t know if I’d call her an enemy, but Frieda Yoshinari, the self-described ‘Princess of Lima’ and ‘Scourge of Atahualpa’ has been my foil more times than I can count. ‘Prince’ Fawzi claims to be Saudi royalty, though I have my doubts. Dr. Esther Förster was a renowned archaeologist before giving in to the dark side. Professor Auguste had, likewise, fallen from academia’s lofty towers. Courtney found his way to treasure hunting after prospecting for opals in the Outback and running guns during the Yugoslavian Civil War.

"And there were a pair of regional hunters who might give us a run for our money. Alva Sheakley, the last of the old Alaska gold hunters. And Colonel Sokolov, former Russian Military Intelligence out of Vladivostok, who knew more than a bit about Alaska.

"The next day we'd be joined by a hundred amateurs out of Fairbanks. Men and women who thought owning a pick and spade and having access to a jeep or plane was all it took to be a treasure hunter. But the ones who mattered were in the hut that night. A gathering of legends.

"At first glance, our task might sound impossible. After all, the treasure could have been anywhere in the 700 miles between Kasilof and the Arctic Ocean. But, knowing what we did about the Ulinovites' beliefs regarding magnetism, the treasure would be somewhere along a narrow band connecting Kasilof and the Magnetic Pole. *If* their compass held out. *If* they hadn't achieved the impossible and sailed onward from the north shore. But, Ms. St. Tropez, treasure hunting isn't a business where you get very far bogged-down in 'ifs.'

"The others got out of Kasilof by first light. Dr. Hope and I relaxed over breakfast and a second cup of coffee. We knew something we felt sure our competitors didn't. Something that would be decisive. Before treasure hunting, I was in oil and gas. So, Dr. Hope and I were both geologists. We knew that the earth's magnetic pole shifts over time. In 2001, at Kasilof, it was 24° 5' east of true north. Back in 1786, when the Russian-America Company set up shop and the Ulinovites took off, it was 26° 46' east. A difference of two and half degrees may not sound like much but, over Alaskan distances, it adds up. All our competitors would be looking in the wrong place.

"Or so we thought. We weren't quite alone as we traveled north by north east. Michael, your dad, was headed the same direction. Maybe he'd learned about the changing magnetic pole on his own. Or he found some clue everyone else missed. Perhaps, seeing us confidently break away from the herd, he figured Dr. Hope and I knew something. Knowing your dad, none of those possibilities would surprise me. But, for reasons I'll explain in a moment, I'd wager against the idea he was just following us.

"Dr. Hope and I had made other calculations. Ones that had to do with people, not geology. We knew that, by the time they began their pilgrimage, Abbot Ulinov's descendants had already survived the wilderness for over a century. Clearly, they'd adapted well enough to life in Alaska. Southern Alaska, anyway.

"But abandoning their settlement, we suspected that somewhere further north would come a point when they could no longer feed and shelter such a large and heavily-laden company. Doing some research and making a few admittedly half-assed assumptions, we estimated that would have happened somewhere around the southwestern border of what is now the Arctic National Wildlife Refuge, just below the Brooks Range.

"We established base camp along a tributary of the Sheenjek River which ran almost perfectly along the route between Kasilof and the 1784 magnetic pole. Its banks would have offered the Ulinovites a natural highway. To scout along the river, I'd borrowed a helicopter and pilot from my oil operations up by Prudhoe Bay.

"The next day, a bush plane, a Cessna 206, flew over and landed a couple miles east. Checking it out, we discovered that your dad, and a few strong backs he'd hired at Fort Yukon, had set up along a big patch of muskeg swampland. Every couple days, that Cessna came in from Fairbanks bringing supplies. I don't know what the attraction of the site was, but it made me think Michael already had a plan and hadn't just been following us.

"Later that week, a terrible storm blew in. The damn thing looked like a solid wall stretching from horizon to horizon, rushing at us so fast you could see it move. As it was almost upon us, I watched an old Aviat Husky fly in low toward your father's camp. I don't know what happened to the 206. Maybe the Husky was a last-minute replacement after the Cessna's pilot saw the weather report and decided *hell no.* I know I would have. Back home, a storm like that would send me scrambling for a tornado shelter.

"Up there? It was no tornado, but it might as well have been. Wind drove sleet and frigid rain right into our faces. I don't know if you've ever been in horizontal rain, Ms. St. Tropez, but it blinds you and stings your skin. We ran for cover in our modular shelter. Even then, rain and cold crept in through every corner and crack. As Dr. Hope explained it, Alaska's last big storm of the year was often a doozy, like nature was reminding people not to get complacent during the short spring and summer.

"After that, Dr. Hope grew quiet. He's a great partner, a great friend, and there's nobody better to have your back in a brawl, but the doc was never one for small talk. Nerves rattled by the big blow outside, our helo pilot had curled up in the fetal position on his cot, sleeping bag pulled up over his head as he whimpered. I worried he wouldn't be much good to us afterward. And that could screw up everything. I made myself a little promise that, at some point, I'd learn to fly those damn machines myself.

"But I won't lie, that weird mix of natural fury and human silence ate at my nerves, too. After a while, I got on the two-way radio and started trading insults with your father. We repeated that performance every half-hour or so. I can't speak for him but, whatever words we spoke, I wanted to hear another voice. Sometime after midnight, he stopped responding. I figured he'd either tired of our mutual forced bravado or, somehow, managed to fall asleep.

"Alone with my thoughts, watching our shelter's walls quiver and hearing the wind howl, I realized something. Kyril's people, without the technology available to us, would have made camp in locations sheltered from the prevailing winds to protect them from storms like this one.

"Next morning, after the storm spent itself and departed as quickly as it came, I mentioned my idea to Dr. Hope. He suggested we try to raise your father on the radio first, to be sure he and his crew were okay. In my excitement, I told the doc we should just start searching for whatever remained of the Ulinovites. I was feeling lucky, Ms. St. Tropez, and I wanted to act before that feeling passed.

"After digging our 4x4s out from a foot of muck, we scouted the area. And Lady Luck was with us. Before noon, we found a hillock shaped like a clover or starburst. With some imagination, you could see that it had once been cross-shaped, like a monastery's main building. Kyril's people, we now suspected, had moved even slower than our calculations. With no other choice, they'd raised a permanent shelter in hopes of riding out the Arctic winter.

"When our metal detectors sounded hits almost right away, we broke out our picks and spades. And the things we started pulling from the earth…" As Jake Booker recounted his list of booty, his expression suggested he had forgotten about explaining to Cassidy how her father died. Suggested, in fact, he had mostly forgotten she was there.

"A gold crucifix, two and a half feet long, inlaid with malachite and set with diamonds and emeralds. A silver crucifix, six feet long, elaborately engraved. Dozens of smaller crosses and crucifixes made of precious metals and set with gems and semiprecious stones. A very old silver communion chalice adorned with garnets, its lip and base covered by beaten gold. A gold censer with painted enamel and colored glass. The glass had broken, of course.

"Lots of things hadn't held up well after two centuries in ground alternately frozen and muddy. Wooden icons, books, reliquaries, and so forth. The rusted ship's compass on which the whole tale turned wasn't in great shape, but magnetism lasts almost forever in cold conditions and its needle still beckoned travelers north.

"The damnedest thing was that there were no human remains at the site. With one amazing exception. A black lacquer box inlaid with pearl and semi-precious stones. Inside we found a hand. Between the box's iconography and various records about Abbot Ulinov's original monastery, we determined it had been that of St. Methodius. *The* St. Methodius. One of the ninth century missionaries who brought Christianity to Russia.

"But, as far as the others, we never found a trace of them. Part of me was disappointed. I would very much like to have met, even across the gulf of two hundred and fifty years, Kyril and Father Pyotr. Maybe they were nearby, but too well concealed beneath a landscape changed by quarter-millennium of rain, mud, and snow for us to find.

"But another part of me wants to believe, despite leaving their treasures and relics behind, they somehow made it further. Maybe somewhere along the way they fell into a deep valley where they'll never be found. Or died of exposure, their bones scattered by wind and ground to dust by ice. But maybe they made it to the ocean and, even above the Arctic treeline, figured out a way to fashion rafts or boats that carried them over some of the world's most remote waters.

"Or, maybe…" Jake Booker paused. Cassidy resented him for the way he looked her over, seeking confirmation that she was hanging on his every word. And she resented herself because she knew she was giving it. "….maybe they even found what they were looking for." He winked.

Cassidy sat up straighter, clutching the gun. As if to remind him, and herself, who was in charge here.

His inventory of wonders and personal musings complete, Jake Booker returned to the heart of the matter. "Sometime in the afternoon," he continued in a more somber vein, "our pilot emerged from the shelter. Despite looking like death warmed-over, he managed to examine the helo, perform some basic maintenance, and declare her worthy to fly. We started loading up our finds.

"Only then did I radio your father, telling him 'You can stop now, Michael. We found it.' At the time, I took his silence as pettiness. It wasn't until much later it occurred to me there were other possibilities.

"As soon as Dr. Hope and I announced our discovery, the government got really interested. They always do when someone finds a big treasure. They sat us down for a very long, detailed, and not particularly friendly conversation. In the course of that meeting, I mentioned that your father had set up his camp near ours. Their ears perked up at that. That's when I learned he was missing. They asked lots of questions about your dad and what I knew about him. I answered as best I could, figuring that might help them find Michael."

Jake Booker paused, his eyes locking onto Cassidy's. "I'm sorry for his loss. He was a competitor but, as I said, he seemed like a good man. And that, Ms. St. Tropez, is what I know about your father's disappearance."

Cassidy felt shocked. Frozen. Unable to move. If Jake Booker told the truth, her father likely died in a freak storm. *If.* The cowboy's perfect poker face didn't encourage her trust. On the other hand, if he was bluffing, wouldn't he come up with a better story than one painting him as greedy and callous even if not actually murderous? But what did she do with that information? She couldn't take revenge on a storm. On nature.

As Cassidy sat, overwhelmed by feelings, Jake Booker brought their conversation back to the standoff in his office. "If I were a betting man, and I am, I'd wager you don't really want to shoot me." He looked her over again. "Correction, I'd wager you don't really want to ruin the rest of your life by shooting me. Why don't you put that pistol away?"

Thoughts flooded disjointedly through Cassidy's mind. Killing Jake Booker for murdering her father would have been one thing. But shooting him for negligence and indifference? Oh, she would still have happily pinned the fabricated *Sefer Bohem* on him for that. Unfortunately, her carelessness had taken that option off the table. What could she do?

Even more unfortunately, Jake Booker was likely right about one thing. Killing him *would* ruin the rest of her life. That felt too much like letting him destroy another member of her family. Perhaps the only thing she knew with certainty was that her father wouldn't have wanted that.

Crestfallen, her energy suddenly sapped, Cassidy returned the gun to her bag. "Okay, what happens now?"

"You take that blank check and you go. Before I change my mind."

"I take the check?"

"You believe I owe you *wergild*…blood money," he clarified, seeing the confused look on her face. "And maybe I do. I didn't kill your father. But I didn't save him, either."

Stashing the check into her handbag, Cassidy gathered her things to leave. When Jake Booker called "Ms. St. Tropez?" as she stormed out of the room, she worried the man had already reconsidered. As she turned around, he said something very different. "You are a master forger by the age of," he examined her carefully, "thirty." He intoned the final word as if it was half statement and half question. "But you are also Michael St. Tropez's daughter. Have you asked yourself whether you'd rather fabricate a fake *Sefer Bohem*…or find the real one?"

For most of her life Cassidy had hated Jake Booker for killing her father. She found she still hated him for denying her closure and certainty about what really happened.

"Go to hell," she spat.

Storming down the Booker Foundation's hallways, Cassidy's head swam violently as she muttered dark curses to herself. Yes, she had the money, but this was yet another encounter that hadn't gone how she'd planned at all.

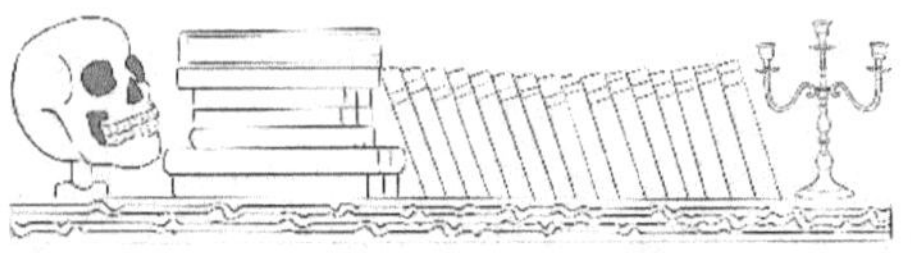

**Austin, July 2**

*Pay attention to what Agrippa means, not what he says. Reverse subject and object.*

Okay, Jen got it. Or thought she did. *Three Books of Occult Philosophy,* indeed alchemy in general, was a frustrating, tangled mass of allegory, symbolism, analogy, and metaphor. And reversing subject and object? Alchemy wasn't about what you did to reagents. It was about what those reagents, supposedly, did to you—*if* you understood the true meaning and metaphor beneath the reagents, the formula, the procedure itself. Yes, producing the chrysopoeia, the fabled philosopher's stone, was about transmuting base metals into gold. But the transformation wasn't in the reagents. It was the alchemist who was the base metal. And who, hopefully, would become gold. Metaphorically speaking, of course.

Jen got that. It didn't change the fact that alchemy was basically premodern self-help, with expensive equipment and toxic substances thrown into the equation.

Unfortunately, her current wrestling with the Macek Text, or the *Sepher Bohem*, wasn't any clearer or less frustrating than her look into alchemy.

Testing Rabbi Hirsch's assertion that "it is not difficult to find scholars, both within the community and without, who have encountered the book," Jen discovered accounts either too vague to be useful or too wildly imaginative to be credible. With one exception.

A footnote to history, Hermann Vodnik had been more dilettante scholar than serious academic. Nevertheless, his correspondents included thinkers as diverse as Protestant theologian Henrich Ewald and Bohemian-German Rabbi Zecharias Frankel. Vodnik's disorganized papers noted that Frankel, though Dresden's chief rabbi, came from Prague where his ancestors had been prominent scholars during the sixteenth century. Frankel, he recorded, certainly regarded the *Sefer Bohem* as genuine.

Perhaps it was through Frankel, then, that Vodnik had accessed the book. His notes, unfortunately, did not say. But, alone among alleged encounters with the *Sefer Bohem*, Vodnik left an accounting that could be called scholarly.

> *Setting aside the work's sensationalistic content, it is most striking for its eschatological perspective. Its lack of references to heaven and hell as an afterlife has ample precedent. More noteworthy is its apparent absence of any trans-existential realms. Indeed, one notes similarities between the "House of the Star," that abode of the gods and Dagan's palace, with the Mt. Olympus of Greek mythology. Situated atop a mountain, descriptions of the House of the Star suggest a place in and of the world rather than a realm apart.*
>
> *Though the book is never explicit on the point, I believe the "Star" in "House of the Star" refers to the Attar, "The Morning Star," described as an enormous white-yellow gem. On several occasions, the text implies possessing the Morning Star confers leadership of the Canaanite pantheon.*
>
> *The* Sefer's *numerous stories lack genuine continuity. They do, however, reference many of the same events at different points in their progression. These include conflicts with Tiamat, Proto-Phoenician and Mesopotamian deities, as well as strife between Dagon and El. Lacking direct connections but within an obvious general framework, I hypothesize the* Sefer Bohem's *stories come from an older source, both broader and more cohesive. Perhaps even an*

> *epic poem or cycle of poems, in the manner of the* Iliad *or* Bhagavad Gita.

Vodnik's level-headed, dispassionate, and academic tone argued on his account's behalf. Just as significant were its obvious similarities with the page at Goethe College. Battles with Tiamat/Tiamath. Tensions between Dagan and El. Even the Attar, the magnificent jewel. They all tracked. More importantly and, truth be told, more excitingly, it seemingly confirmed that rather than an outlier, the Macek Text was representative of the *Sefer Bohem* as a whole.

Jen investigated whether Vodnik's later writings referenced the book. They didn't. In fact, he produced little output of any kind after examining the mysterious tome. Research quickly revealed why. Mistaken for another scholar of more radical inclinations, Vodnik met his demise in front of a Hapsburg firing squad during the 1848 Revolutions.

Almost despite herself, Gus Tanzer's words about the Sefer Bohem's "evil reputation" floated through Jen's mind.

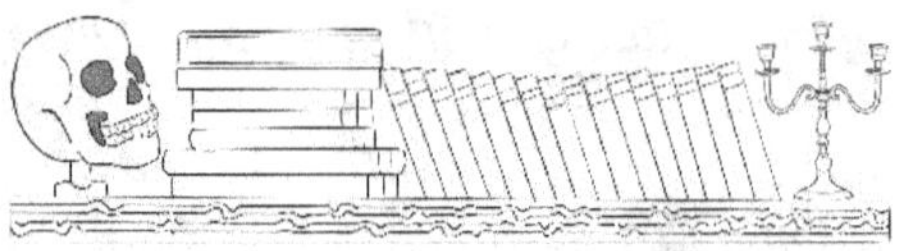

**San Francisco, July 8**

Back home in the South of Market warehouse, Cassidy stretched across her futon, trying to appreciate the simple pleasure of a Napa cab and endeavoring to consider the contents of the oversized manila folder opened beside her. Bond certificates from before the 1906 earthquake, no two seemed to be quite the same size or shape.

Cassidy had fallen in love with the beautiful documents. Their elaborate borders printed in rich reds, royal blues, and the crisp green of newly-minted cash. The bold engravings of their headers: stately factories, towering skyscrapers, massive dams, mighty locomotives, American Eagles, Statues of Liberty, and a dozen other images oozing an unquestionable faith in progress that Cassidy found simultaneously narcissistic and naïve. For all that, there was something powerful and evocative in those images.

From the handful of genuine certificates in that folder, Cassidy would produce many, many more.

True, she had a dozen prosaic tasks on her to-do list. Call Hierbabuena. Call her mother. Restock the wine fridge. Pick up her dry cleaning. But the bond certificates were the treat she had promised herself when the *Sefer Bohem* was out of the way. Pushing her talents in a new direction. The project would be a working vacation of sorts, a blend of the easy and the exciting. The language was boilerplate, the fonts were commonplace. But those bright, pretty borders? Rarely had Cassidy worked with colored inks, offering her an exciting challenge. And there would be stamped signatures on each certificate. Categorically, Cassidy swore off script—one of the easiest ways for a forgery to get outed. But these would be mass produced, each exactly like the next. That meant Cassidy had to get it right only once, odds she liked.

There was just one problem. She didn't care anymore.

Cassidy still hated Jake Booker. Possibly more than ever. The man had done something to her. She had planned to begin working on those bond certificates the morning after her return to San Francisco. But awake, and even asleep, her mind kept returning to her conversation with Booker. And not to what happened to her father. Cassidy saw herself pouring over forgotten documents in musty libraries and obscure archives. Braving exotic locations and extreme environments. And holding lost treasure in her hands. Forging was an intellectual thrill. But the idea of going out and finding something authentic, something real? The idea was seductively primal. Only it wasn't just any lost treasure she saw herself holding in those fantasies. It was something very specific. The *Sefer Bohem*.

Those thoughts had begun even before she landed at SFO, while she was still high above flyover territory. Expecting the strange notions to subside once she was home, they had only grown. "Damn it," she announced to nobody in particular. Cassidy was a pragmatist. Accepting the reality of the situation, she returned the certificates to their folder and the folder to its place in her desk drawer.

Then she fired up her laptop.

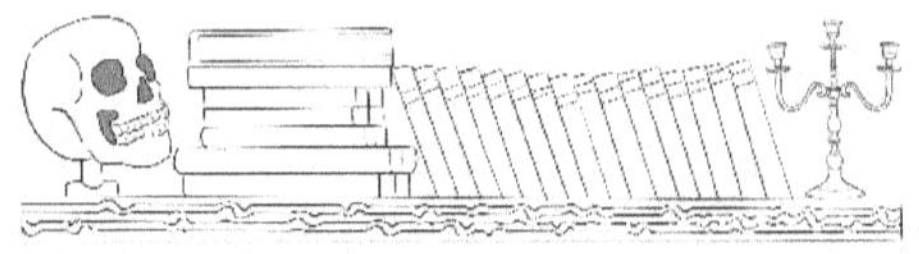

**Austin, July 8**

Academic sources had given Jen five solid hits: Deinard, Geiger, Hirsch, Vodnik, and, through Vodnik, Frankel. Even had they not been divided on the question of the *Sefer Bohem's* existence, three in favor and two against, it hardly constituted an embarrassment of riches. Again, she felt the frustration of exciting revelations which also marked dead ends. Thrilling leads which had quickly played out.

What was that famous quote about the definition of insanity? Jen hadn't changed her research approach since first looking into the Macek Text. Hell, hadn't really changed her approach since college. Dana's words came back to her. Jen had put all her eggs into looking for *reality*. Maybe what she needed to be looking for was *truth*. Or at least someone's version of it.

It was time to broaden her horizons. *Think outside the box*. But how did she do that when the box in question was her brain?

What was the "truth" in the Macek Text? If she were to borrow from Agrippa, she thought with a sigh, it was time to pay attention to the text's "reagents," its key elements. And to their relationship to each other. She steeled herself to cast that broader net, and wade through mountains of unrelated garbage. The reward finally came as she was diving into the Attar, that fabulous jewel functioning almost as the Macek Text's McGuffin. And it came from a most unexpected direction, hinting that the entire matter might take a very strange turn.

Jen found it, of all places, among the digitized correspondence and journals of H. Rider Haggard, author of *King Solomon's Mines*, *SHE*, and other Victorian classics. It seemed that Haggard's most famous creation, Allan Quatermain, the British-born big game hunter and adventurer who frequented colonial Africa, had not been entirely fictional. Quatermain had been inspired, if not quite cut from whole cloth, by Haggard's friend Fredrick Selous. Like the character he bequeathed life to, Selous had been a venturesome explorer and hunter. Unlike his doppelganger, Selous had been a soldier as well as a genuine conservationist and naturalist. He was as enthusiastic about bagging butterflies as big game, and turned most of his specimens over to natural history museums around the world.

Haggard's papers preserved an interesting conversation with Selous.

> *I wish I had been more attentive with my pen and paper that evening. Instead, lost in Freddie's story, I can but summarize most of what he said. His opening, however, I recall with absolute clarity. Having asked him what it was like to be the very incarnation of a heroic explorer, he brushed the notion aside saying, "There are men harder than I in the bush. Who have beheld sights more wonderful and terrible than ever my eyes saw. And no one will ever know their names."*
>
> *He then proceeded to tell a tale remarkable even for Freddie:*
>
> *"Arriving in Africa in 1872, I was traveling Ndebele lands after having received permission from their king, Lobengula, to take game without restriction. One night at a trading post, I met an ancient European. I took him for English by his speech, though so long away from his home that I would not swear it. His age might have been as much as 70 and, though his body remained hearty and hale, his skin was like leather. Proclaiming himself to be a prospector, he showed me six uncut diamonds, the smallest larger than a quarter-farthing coin. Pronouncing, honestly, I had never seen such fine stones, he waved away my superlatives. Proclaiming he had seen the greatest jewel of them all, he relayed a most curious story.*
>
> *In his youth, the man had a fondness for certain strange old books. In one of them, written, as he said, in the language of the Twelve Tribes of Israel, he had learned of a stone called the Atar, also known as the Morning Star. A diamond the color of sunlight, larger than a man's head, and cut into facets uncountable. Though this book ascribed magical powers to the stone, he discounted them. What he did not discount were certain passages among its pages*

*giving hint as to the Atar's location. For two decades he traversed Ottoman domains, risking life and limb. In the end, he had seen it. But the Atar's situation, he decried, was such that no man could attain it and live to profit by its acquisition. And so, he departed to seek lesser stones.*

*He confessed to me that he now wished he had thrown his life away in vain attempt to achieve the Atar because, having witnessed perfection, nothing in this world would ever give him true pleasure again.*

*After his strange tale, we lapsed into silence and each of us separated to the rush-thatched dwellings that were to be our lodging. The next morning, the pouch of diamonds lay at the threshold of my hut. Of its owner, I could find nothing. One of the Ndebele women revealed to me that, late at night, the ancient prospector had wandered off into the bush. He was not seen again.*

It was easy to see how, transmitted only orally, and through two different mouths, what Haggard had recorded as "atar" might elsewhere be rendered "attar." Certainly, it carried the same epithet of "morning star" and description of superlative size and faceting. How long had such ideas about the Attar been around? And did they circulate still? Depending on the answers to those questions, people might have an interest in the *Sefer Bohem* unconnected with traditional scholarship. Or forgery. Perhaps Jen had misread the strange woman who visited her and Jen's tip-off to the Booker Foundation had been unnecessary.

Haggard's short passage had a curious effect on Jen. Her mind had rushed reading Deinard, Geiger, Hirsch, and Vodnik. But the words of Haggard, or rather Selous, made Jen's pulse race.

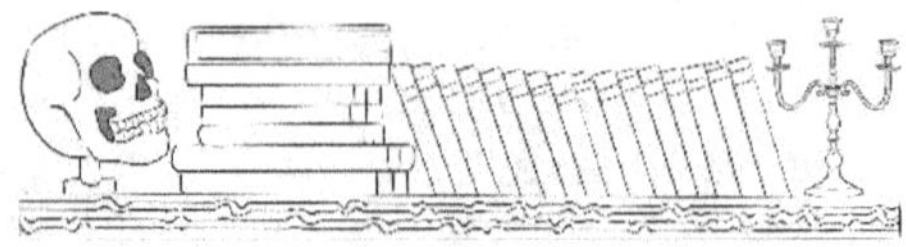

**Austin, July 9**

Her rental car's engine purred as Cassidy sat outside the house. The European sports car was much nicer than anything she would have chosen a few weeks ago. But Jake Booker's blank check had taken care of that. And quite a few other things.

Booking her flight on the morning red-eye out of San Francisco, Cassidy had accepted the strange turn her desires had taken. The *Sefer Bohem*. The real one. Or, at least Cassidy thought she had.

The problem was that Cassidy didn't have all the knowledge she'd need to make that desire a reality. But plugging those gaps involved so many unknowns. For the dozenth time since idling her car outside the slightly ramshackle subdivided house, she thought how easy it would be to return to the airport, fly back to San Francisco, and start on those bond certificates. Before second-guessing herself again, she turned off the car, forced herself to the porch, and started knocking.

"You?" Jen exclaimed, opening the door to find her mysterious visitor once again on her doorstep.

"Don't worry," Cassidy began, "I'm not here to hurt you. I…I need your help."

"What do you want now, *April*?" Jen asked, pointedly throwing back the clearly bogus name her visitor had given previously.

"The *Sefer Bohem*. I want you to help me find it."

In that instant, Jen realized her own thoughts had been knocking on the door of that idea…she just hadn't allowed herself to think the words. For one thing, it was preposterous. Her, the basement gnome, going out into the big bad world to recover a lost book? It would be reckless, stupid even. Oh, with time she knew she could untangle the mystery of the *Sefer Bohem* and its history. But to actually find it? It, and perhaps a gemstone that had beguiled for millennia.

The idea thrilled Jen but would require an entirely different skill set from the one she'd spent her life building. The woman on her doorstep, though? Clearly, she had some experience with life's shadowy and dangerous corners. "Okay, come in."

As they walked inside, Jen headed for the kitchen. "Sit down, I'll put the coffee on."

After serving the coffee, she cranked Helloween loudly enough on her speakers that it would be certain to irritate her guest. Sinking into her chair, one of Jen's hands disappeared under the dinner table. Reappearing, it held a revolver, looking a little too large for the linguist's petite hand, which she politely laid to one side. "This time, no funny business, okay?"

Cassidy's eyes widened. "You have a gun?" Her voice was both shocked and distant as her mind replayed their first encounter…and how it could have ended very differently.

"What part of 'Texas' don't you understand?" Jen replied.

Cassidy nodded. "I understand why you did that. But, I think, if we're going to do this, we need to trust each other. How can I make you trust me?"

"Let's start with a name. A real name, this time."

"Cassidy St. Tropez"

"St. Tropez?" Jen looked skeptical.

"Really," Cassidy pled with her eyes. "Family lore says, when my great-grandfather came to the U.S., an inattentive Ellis Island clerk switched his surname and place of birth on the paperwork. Another piece of family lore suggests his reasons for leaving home and coming to America made him grateful for the obfuscation."

Nodding, Jen made the revolver disappear. "Jen Gerson," she extended her hand, sealing the proper introduction with a rather tentative handshake.

She then briefed Cassidy, in layperson's terms, on her research into the codex since the woman disappeared into the night weeks ago, concluding with the possible reference to the attar she'd found in Haggard's papers yesterday.

"I've been trailing copies of the *Sefer Bohem.* The only one I can confirm existed is what I call the Prague Copy. It's the one Vodnik saw. And it's probably where the page at Goethe College came from. There may have been other copies but, as things stand, I can't disprove that all the references I've found are to the Prague Copy. And those references end about two centuries ago.

"In fact, we have negative evidence after that. Ephraim Deinard's hunt for the *Sefer Bohem* suggests that, by the twentieth century, something happened to the Prague Copy and any other European copies. Destroyed. Relocated. Maybe just better hidden. Whatever it was, we have to expand our search beyond Europe. And, as Haggard's story shows, information about the book can turn up anywhere."

Cassidy had liked that tidbit from H. Rider Haggard. And not just because, when she was a young girl, her father had often read Haggard to her as bedtime stories. The idea that the Attar, the enormous yellow-white gem, was real? Like most things that sounded too good to be true, it probably was. Still, if she could find it, if she and Jen Gerson could find it, Cassidy forced herself to make the correction, Jake Booker would sweat with envy.

"I don't care where it comes from," Jen concluded, "but I'd really like to find a more recent reference to the book than what we have so far."

"Maybe I can help."

Bristling under the look Jen gave her, Cassidy continued. "I don't know what you think you know about forgers but I'm guessing a lot of it is probably wrong. Yes, a lot of them are just out to make a buck. But the really good ones get that way because we're also bibliophiles. Learning as much as we can about books is part of the craft, but the ones who learn the most are the ones who have a passion for it.

"And those great forgers? Unlike your crowd, we've all heard of the *Sefer Bohem*. The tome of distant and forgotten Jewish lore. It sounds like *I'd* heard of it long before *you* did. Forgers don't seem any surer about the book's actual existence than linguists. But they all know the stories. Maybe they know about it because of this Deinard guy." She thought of Hierbabuena and some of his associates she'd met. "I can definitely see the old guard being familiar with him. At least a few forgers know about that page at Goethe College. And some of those already think it's from the *Sefer Bohem*. But maybe some of them also know of sources other than ones you've found. I don't want to promise anything, we're not big on sharing, but I can at least put out feelers."

Good forgers being bibliophiles? That made a kind of perverse sense to Jen. But the idea forgers might know something about the *Sefer Bohem* not preserved in the sources a good linguist could find? The assertion that a group of...criminals...had already apparently scooped her in knowing not only about the *Sefer Bohem* but also the Macek Text? That was a thought Jen wasn't willing to process at the moment.

Besides, the woman's own words revealed that forgers' knowledge was broad, not deep. To underscore that point, and because Jen relished correcting people, she interjected "Canaanite, not Jewish."

"What?"

"The content of the *Sefer Bohem* is Canaanite. Not Jewish." Jen went on to describe how the early Jews had been only one subset of Canaanites and, while some things might be common to all that large and diverse people, things pertaining to another group of Canaanites might have no bearing on early Jews, much less modern Judaism.

"Yes," Cassidy sighed, "Canaanite. I *do* understand the difference. Do you know what I did to prepare myself for fabricating the *Sefer Bohem*? I read the *Hekhalots*, The *Pardes Rimonim*. The *Bahir*. Schaefer. John Gray. Kathleen Kenyon. I read translations of the royal archives of Tel Mardikh and Ugar. The Arslan Tash amulets. The Essenes. Lucian of Samosta. Philo of Byblos." There was more, a lot more. But Cassidy pulled back. Somewhere along the way, she's crossed the line from proving her credentials to trying to score points.

Preparing to respond, Jen found she could only stammer. Some of those she hadn't read. Hell, a few of those she hadn't heard of. And that hit Jen where it hurt.

"That's great," Jen sounded as if it was anything but. "Tell me, do you understand the context of what you read? Or can you just parrot back the words? And you mentioned translations. What will you do when you find something that's never been translated because it's never been found?"

Both remarks landed a bit too close to home for Cassidy's comfort. "You're smart. I get it. That translation you did? I was impressed. I didn't say it because, at the time, it didn't suit my purposes. But I was. I know you've read a lot. Especially about this stuff. But if finding this shit was easy, someone else already would have. How are you on street smarts? What's the worst trouble you've ever been in? Busted smoking a joint when you were in college?" Cringing under the sounds blasting from Jen's stereo, she added "Noise citation?"

Jen winced. And resented her visitor for being on the nose. Twice.

"And how are you with risk and danger? Be honest. You read what that old prospector said about getting to the Attar. And what about what happened to…" Cassidy fished for the name of the scholar who ended up in front of a firing squad. "…Vodnik?" Cassidy knew she might have been overselling her own dangerous-woman cred. As criminals went, she was strictly white collar, and a bohemian one at that. Still, in the face of the linguist's withering glance of dismissal, Cassidy had felt the need to pump up her bona fides.

"And what if we're not alone in looking for the *Sefer Bohem*? What if there's competition? Someone like Jake Booker would eat you for breakfast," she said to the mouse in front of her, hoping it didn't apply to herself as well. And some of the competitors Booker had hinted at? They sounded like they might do a lot worse than that.

"You need me," she told Jen. "So don't get so smug about who is going to be holding whose hand."

"Yeah? Well, you need me, too," Jen fired back. "You're resourceful. And cunning. Otherwise you wouldn't have…gotten away with what you've been doing for as long as you have. But this time you won't be able to just *invent*—" even full of pique, *forge* felt too rude to say, "—what you need. You have to find, and be able to read, the real thing."

"Okay, yes, we need each other. I get that. That's why I came here," Cassidy said grudgingly.

"I get it too. That's why you're in my living room," Jen said, no more happily than the other woman, but at least omitting *instead of in the back of a squad car*.

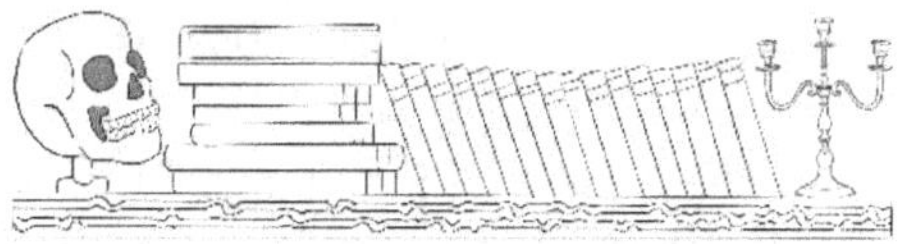

**Austin, July 23**

After weeks of online searches and books expensively overnighted (courtesy, indirectly, of Jake Booker) on interlibrary loan from universities and archives across the globe, Jen's trashcan resembled a map of the world as expressed through empty takeout containers. Chinese, both Cantonese and Szechuan. Ethiopian. French. Indian, both North and South. Mediterranean. Korean. Kosher deli. Mexican, both Tex-Mex and Interior. Sushi.

Russian. Thai. And, on more than a few occasions, barbeque. Outside, recycling bins overflowed with glassy remnants of Jen's microbrew and Cassidy's wine.

Cassidy figured, as long as she had to be here, she might as well try to instill a little wine culture into her host. So far, she had little to show for her efforts. Oh, the linguist seemed happy enough to drink it. But with a shocking indifference to whether it was red or white, sweet or dry, exceptional or mediocre.

That was frustrating. But not as frustrating as that, after talking up the forging community's acumen and esoteric knowledge to her partner, Cassidy had zero to show for it. Her contacts either had nothing to share or did, but wouldn't. Either seemed possible—and Cassidy couldn't decide which was worse. Of course, Ms. "behold the awesome power of my intellect" hadn't exactly pulled any rabbits out of the hat since H. Rider Haggard, either. Cassidy probably shouldn't have taken as much satisfaction from that as she did. And Jen's inquiries to her global network of eggheads had likewise gone nowhere, though one of her contacts, Gus somebody-or-other, texted regularly to see if the linguist had made any progress.

Cassidy returned to the book in front of her. Smelling of mildew, it displayed photostatic reproductions of cuneiform tablets on the left page accompanied by English translations on the right. She'd stared at the book long enough that both sets of characters had grown equally unintelligible. Cassidy rubbed her temples. Despairingly, she looked at Jen's aging TV. "Can that thing even stream?" When the linguist's nonplussed look seemed to answer in the affirmative, Cassidy continued. "You want to take a break and watch something?"

When Jen shut her own book with an audible *thud*, Cassidy prepared for her killjoy partner to make some unjustified remark about Cassidy's lack of intellectual rigor. Instead, Jen answered "Do I ever!"

"*The French Dispatch*? I haven't seen it yet." Cassidy sounded slightly sheepish.

Assuming the forger's embarrassment stemmed from not having seen it, rather than wanting to, Jen didn't quite sneer at the suggestion before offering "How about *Flash Gordon*?"

"Jesus, are you fifty?"

"I'll take that as a complement."

"If we're going to pick something ancient, at least do ancient with class. Black and white or nothing."

"*Maltese Falcon*?"

"We have a winner."

Noir had rules, and Jen liked that. Of course, *Falcon* sometimes broke those rules. And not like a clumsy amateur that didn't know them, but like a master that crossed every line with inspired calculation. She had seen the film before. Maybe not a dozen times, but certainly a half-dozen. This watch-through was different, somehow. Jen felt her brain making connections, new ones, even if it hadn't let her in on what they were yet.

*The, eh, stuff that dreams are made of...*

At the words of Sam Spade's final soliloquy, Jen bolted upright against the couch. The Maltese Falcon was a piece of inert matter, really no different at the end of the film than the beginning. But everyone who came into contact with the Falcon was transformed. And not transformed in any old way. O'Shaughnessy, Gutman, Cairo, Archer. Even Spade. They each got out of the Falcon exactly what they put into it. The Maltese Falcon, the philosopher's stone, they were the same thing. Sam Spade had done what Agrippa and Dana couldn't. Spade made alchemy make sense to Jen.

And what had she been putting in her hunt for the *Sefer Bohem*? If she was honest with herself, nothing different than she'd put into anything for the past decade. True, she had already asked herself that question, and already given herself that answer. But now Jen understood she had been...*reversing subject and object.* What was needed wasn't a new *approach*, it was a new *her*. Jen needed to transform.

Standing, walking to her desk and considering it for a moment, Jen shoved her books of musty linguistics and staid history to the ground.

"Are you having some kind of episode or something?" Cassidy asked apprehensively.

"Let's open this motherfucker up," Jen's voice breathed fire.

"Okay," Cassidy nodded, trepidation mostly gone, "I'm not sure where this is coming from. But I'm kind of digging it. Thoughts on where to start?"

"The attar, maybe? I already had the thought, I just didn't know what to do with it yet." When she saw Cassidy didn't follow, she explained. "When I found Haggard's story about Selous and the old prospector, it briefly occurred to me that you might be a treasure hunter and not a forger."

At the words *treasure hunter*, Cassidy flinched. Treasure hunters were people like Jake Booker—that her father had also been one was something Cassidy conveniently put at the back of her mind. And yet, hadn't that been the very thing Jake Booker had dangled in front of her as a temptation. A temptation that worked so well that she had spent weeks in Jen Gerson's apartment trying to find the *Sefer Bohem*, And, yes, maybe the Attar in the bargain.

"In our story, the *Sefer Bohem* is the McGuffin. But, in the *Sefer Bohem*, or at least the Macek Text, it's pretty clear the Attar is being set up as the McGuffin. Maybe it's the chrysopoeia, too."

Cassidy shrugged. It wasn't the first time she had no idea what the linguist was talking about. She would have bet every press back home in her workshop it wouldn't be the last time, either.

Leaving "reality" aside and searching for the footprints of people who had sought the Attar for truths other than her own, Jen found new vistas opening. In the years following the Crimean War, the Ottoman Sultan Abdülmecid had been troubled by European adventurers trespassing within his borders as they sought some unspecified but significant treasure. Given the unnamed prospector's indication the Attar was somewhere in the Empire's domains, Jen wondered exactly what that treasure had been. Considering the timing of Selous' account, and his estimation of the prospector's age, the old man could well have been one of those interlopers troubling the Sultan.

After weeks of working together, Cassidy had to admit her research skills were not as well-honed as her new partner's, but she was even more confident she had gifts of her own. It might have been Jen's suggestion to start looking off the beaten path, that didn't mean she had the eye for it, at least not yet. Jen was a specialist. But a good forger was a generalist. More than that, intuition was an asset. Knowing when something didn't "look right," or when a deal was about to go south, was a survival skill.

Granted, one that had failed her with Jake Booker—but the cowboy seemed to have his own ample supply of intuition.

So, perhaps it was not surprising that when they encountered a potential lead from nearly a century after Macek and Vodnik, it was Cassidy who found it. And heeded intuition's call by looking beyond the Attar. The lead's location, however, caught them both by surprise. If it was good, not only could they drive there, they could do it in a night.

Upon hearing its source, however, the linguist balked. "*The Boston Society for Psychical Research*?" condescension dripped so thickly from Jen's voice that it might as well have *condensation.*

Cassidy was tempted to point out that Jen's own sources included theologians, mystics, and adventurers—people not always known for objective, academic rigor. But she suspected that was the wrong approach to take with her partner. Instead, after doing enough research to support the assertion, Cassidy pointed out to Jen that the specific source for the account, whatever else he was into, had also been a respected physician. That bought her a little time.

She used that reprieve to read the account aloud.

> ***September 12, 1929***
> *Based on information given to me by the Storyville musicians, and with a driver provided by my hotel, I headed south into the deep bayou country in search of a "Gris Gris Queen" named Lola. At no point south of New Orleans could the road be called "good." Beyond the village of Lafitte, it became a little track running between islands in the swamp, barely wide enough for a single vehicle. At Bayou Rigolettes, taciturn locals pointed us eastward toward a place called Fin de Terres along a path so poor it had almost sunken into the swamp.*
>
> *When we found it, Fin de Terres was nothing more than a few shacks built on poles to escape flooding, a couple of houseboats, and a general store. Following directions from men at the store, I walked a narrow trail through the swamp flanked on either side by large trees draped with Spanish*

*moss and punctuated by displays I interpreted as shrines of a most disturbing nature.*

*The path terminated at a narrow bridge leading to a small island where Lola's hut stood. Like the shacks at Fin de Terres, it was elevated to prevent flooding but, instead of poles, it rested on undressed tree trunks disturbingly reminiscent of legs. Once on the island, I was surprised by Lola's silent manservant and dogsbody, Mose. Soon after, Lola called down to me from her hut. Never in my life have I encountered a woman at once so striking and alarming; with wild hair, magnetic gaze, patchwork dress, and countless charms and bangles.*

*Lola seemed to know, or at least intuit, more about me and my errand than made me comfortable. Nevertheless, apparently satisfied as to my character and earnestness, she bade me climb into her hut. Much of it was exactly as I expected, mortar and pestle on a crude wooden table, burning candles, jars full of herbs, piles of animal bones, and shelves of terrifying idols. But there were surprises as well, fine French cognac, a handsome antique mirror that would fetch a pretty penny at auction, and the latest newspapers. Most striking of all was a tiny antique bookcase of delicate workmanship, its holdings locked away behind brass lattice.*

*Over cognac we talked about Gabriel. While Lola left me with no doubt she is not a woman a prudent man should anger, our conversation also convinced me she held no malice toward the trumpeter. Their relationship hadn't ended badly but instead had merely trailed off. For better or worse, I do not believe she is responsible for either Gabriel's death or his reappearance.*

*Afterward, we discussed matters which, while not pertaining to the Gibbs case, may be of broader interest to the society. Of her beliefs and practices, Lola explained she belonged to a class of practitioners who worked with a variety of spirits not just the loa of traditional voodoo.*

*Inquiring as to the non-loa spirits of her practice, she gave the example of "Empress Lilith." My curiosity whether this related to the entity of the same name from ancient Near East mythology was answered by a tome she removed from her bookcase. The leather-bound text was printed entirely in Hebrew, save for the title page indicating the place and time of printing as Prague, 1556. A hand-written translation in archaic French had been added to most of the text. Though it may have been a failing as a scholar, I closed the book without examining further. It did not seem good to further pursue those lines of crabbed translation.*

While highly entertaining reading, most of the investigator's account of his remaining time in the bayou seemed scarcely credible. That didn't matter. What mattered was the Hebrew text. The references to Lilith. The time and place of printing. It painted a picture which looked too much like the *Sefer Bohem* to ignore. At least Cassidy thought it did. Her partner? She was almost there, but Cassidy could see the traces of hesitation on Jen's face.

"*Let's open this motherfucker up,*" Cassidy intoned with a mischievous grin. "Your words, not mine."

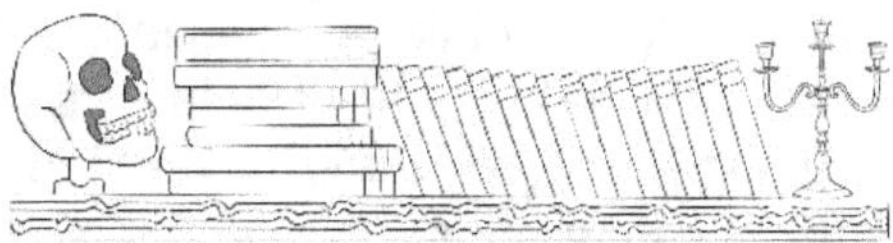

Houston was already an hour in the rearview as Jen's Jetta streaked eastward through marshy lowland thick with pungent-smelling refineries. Briefly, Cassidy had considered stopping off to tell Jake Booker she'd taken up his suggestion. Then, just quickly, wondered *why give him the satisfaction?* Besides, since the teacher's pet in the driver's seat was certain to email Dr. Whats-Her-Name, Booker would find out anyway.

All they had was a single account from 1920s swamp country. Maybe they wouldn't be able to pick up the trail of the *Sefer Bohem*, or what damn sure sounded like the *Sefer Bohem*. Maybe they could, but the book no longer existed. Either way, they wouldn't know if they didn't go. They both understood they would get nowhere letting every *maybe* shut them down.

Since Jen was the one with the car, it only seemed fair that Cassidy took the first shift behind the wheel—before petering out in some no-name town where Jen had insisted on stopping for barbeque. Driving since then, the linguist showed no signs of tiring. While she refused to say as much, Cassidy was impressed. Maybe, when you lived someplace where everything was surrounded by vast stretches of nothing, distance driving was just something you got good at.

Things were definitely still touch and go with her new partner. Wanting some less combative interaction, pulling her out her phone, Cassidy called the contact listed simply as *peppermint*.

"My Dear, I'm so pleased to hear from you." Underneath his calm, patrician tones she heard Hierbabuena's relief. "I figured, within hours of you landing in Houston, the news would inform me of the Booker Foundation's acquisition of the *Sefer Bohem.* Or of your arrest."

"Gee, I'm sorry my not being in jail worried you," Cassidy teased.

Hierbabuena chuckled. "You know what I mean. After weeks of nothing? We are talking about Jake Booker."

"I was face to face with Jake Booker," even as she said the words, it was still difficult to believe it had really happened. "Here's the thing, I don't think he caused my father's death anymore." Cassidy sighed. "He didn't help. But he didn't cause it." Having to actually say those words hit her hard. As long as she had made one difficult admission, she might as well make another. "I think I'm leaving the craft. For a while anyway."

Long silence over the phone cut deeper than Cassidy expected. "All I ever wanted was for you to be happy," Hierbabuena's words, when they finally came, were a relief. "Besides," she could almost hear his wry smile and wink, "I can picture you setting the craft down, but not so far from you that you could not pick it back up. It is in your blood."

"It is. But I think there are other things in my blood, too. It's time for me to explore those." With that, Cassidy ended the call.

In the seat beside her, Jen frowned at her own phone resting in its dashboard mount. She had her own needed conversation. True, there was another text from Gus Tanzer awaiting answer. But that wasn't the one she was thinking of. After passing a long line of eighteen-wheelers, leaving the interstate mostly clear ahead of the Jettta, she made the call.

“Hey, I was gonna be in touch,” Dana said. “You coming kayaking with us this weekend?”

“I can’t. I’m going to Louisiana.”

“What are you doing there?”

Briefly, Jen thought about how a real alchemist, an Agrippa, a Paracelsus, or a Sam Spade, would answer. “Hopefully? Transmuting…”

Their phones no longer needed as phones, Jen and Cassidy began another disputation…over whose playlist would see them across the state line.

“Japanese Breakfast?”

“Motörhead?”

“Bowie?”

“Queen?” they offered in unison.

*We could be heroes…*

As the words came from the Jetta’s tiny, and tinny, speakers, Jen found a challenging, even skeptical, tone to them she’d never heard before. That was alright.

# In The Hearts of Lads

## Fio Trethewey

It would be true to say that cities are like people, layered and complicated. Some are untrustworthy, seedy and to be avoided at all costs, whilst some you desperately wish to experience and want to get to know intimately. What people don't talk about is the mundanity of a city. The parts that are unspectacular, dull, lethargic. So much so that they don't even qualify for the strange news items at the end of a news broadcast. The missing links, the abandoned roads and people who have fallen through the cracks.

Hobbs was a person who lived in one of these places: a forgotten section of Bristol.

Bristol itself was a mismatch of urban and countrified life. In one corner, you could have the familiar cramped terraced houses of students, who partied the night away. In the same street, families painted their houses pink, tied up mellow-looking bunting, and stayed stuck forty years in the past.

Where Hobbs lived however, nothing ever happened. His home was numb to the joys Bristol had to offer, which is why it was obvious that he didn't belong there.

Hobbs was a tall boy in his late teens and could have easily snuck into a WOMAD festival. Straw-coloured hair tied into a tangled bun fell awkwardly into his freckled face. His washed-out red hoodie, which was almost pink, hung over low-cut jeans that probably hadn't ever been washed.

As he plodded down the street, air balloons dotted the summer sky. But Hobbs just continued towards the local shops. His old in-ear headphones buzzed a melodic electric sound.

He pushed open the charity shop door, giving the regular

worker a lazy wave. He took out an earbud to greet her, but barely glanced up from the bookcase at the back of the room.

The worker greeted him with her usual enthusiasm. “Alright, me luvver?”

“I’m lush, thanks. You alright, Dawn?”

Shuffling to the book section, he wasn’t really listening. His music continued to pump into his left ear. Something with bass that made his feet bounce in rhythm. Still, he frowned at the bookcase. Removing the second ear bud, he turned back to her.

“You not got a lot 'ere today, Dawn.” His hand rolled across each spine in turn, recognising the titles. “Where I thought you said you had a load of old books coming in from Clifton?”

“That’s what I was saying, love, someone broke in last night. Everything was left as it was, apart from the books, mind. Spent hours tidying up before I opened.”

“Oh...”

She continued to chatter on, something about the world gone mad over a load of old books, blaming those Americans on the television. Hobbs just gave a mild shrug and turned to leave. As he went to move his shoe caught on a small wicker basket. He raised his eyebrows at the lone book that caught his eye. It was trapped between the basket and the bookcase. He picked it up.

The paperback was frayed at the edges. It seemed to have issues with the binding, and a faded front which might have been in French. He only recognised the name. Wilfred Owen. Wasn’t he that guy who wrote war poems? Hobbs turned from the bookcase, book now in hand, putting it on the counter in front of Dawn.

“Is it still a pound a book?”

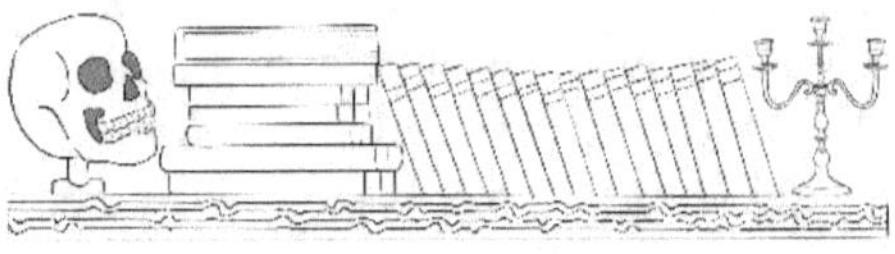

Now he dawdled back through the dull grey streets, letting the chill low beats of his music be his rhythm. He crossed a neglected garden to get to his front door.

He was greeted by a deafening sound—his father snoring. Sighing, Hobbs set the book down in the brightest part of the living room and took a few photos with his phone before moving over to his laptop. He opened his browser to see the private chat room with his best friends had been continuing without him, as normal. With a few speedy clicks, he sent the photos of the book across. The response, as usual at this time of night, was immediate.

**darryl_p_dunc:** please no memes, Hobbs.

**hobbsthehobbes:** Ha. Ha.

**hobbsthehobbes:** Got the book for a quid. Looks like something you'd be interested in Dunc.

**darryl_p_dunc:** Yeah? Looks old. Can barely make out the print. Can you send a better pic?

**hobbsthehobbes:** Dunno man. Dad's still passed out on the sofa. Give me a sec.

Hobbs picked up his laptop under one arm, careful to detach the cables from his eclectic gaming set-up. He snatched up the book in his other hand and carried his load to his bedroom.

The room wasn't tidy, and there wasn't a desk, but at least the bed was clear.

There wasn't a clear surface anywhere else. Books, dirty clothes, and schoolwork scattered the floor. Posters hung awkwardly in place with tac. The TV he had accidentally left on was still playing.

Hobbs lit an incense stick with his lighter to try and get rid of the smell and opened a window. Dropping the laptop onto the messy bed, he took some more photos of the book.

If anyone knew about books, it was Duncan. Dunc was probably the friend he talked to the most. He was a black teen from Manchester, and off to university in September. It didn't surprise any of them that he'd got in. He was always going on about reading, an obsession that he said struck in childhood, which Dunc pretended to only feign interest in. It was obvious, though, from his love of bringing "authenticity" to his Scottish Chieftain in their video game sessions that he enjoyed research more than most. Hobbs had no doubt that this would probably turn out to be another book he sent to Duncan in the post after a casual snap.

**hobbsthehobbes:** There ya go, better pic.

**awesome.lucas:** Looks like a hunk of junk, Hobbs.

**austinpowersrules:** DAD BOUGHT HOME JERKY!

**darryl_p_dunc:** I don't recognise it. Weird. I'm sure we studied Owen at GCSE, let me google it.

Hobbs wasn't surprised by their other friends ignoring the conversation, particularly Lucas, who loved to be the center of attention. Austin was just excitable about anything and everything that happened. It was sometimes strange to think he was the same age. Despite being from the same country, Hobbs couldn't imagine two more different boys. In the video chats, Austin was slender, freckled, with messy red hair. He always seemed to have a smile in his arsenal, even when losing—it was like Austin found it funny instead of frustrating. Meanwhile Lucas was a hunched, plump boy. Extremely competitive, he usually had something to say on the negative side. He'd roll his eyes constantly at Austin. Had Hobbs thought about it, a simple Google search could have told him what he needed to know. Still, he decided Dunc was the best man for the job. Besides, his friend loved a mystery.

Hobbs rolled a cigarette. By the time Dunc responded, Hobbs' room smelled distinctly of what his mother would call 'his funny stuff.' If she wasn't working nights, she would have been screaming at him.

**darryl_p_dunc:** sorry I'm back. Mum wanted me to wash up.

**austinpowersrules:** Are we actually going to play WGO today?

**darryl_p_dunc:** Guys, this book might be legit.

**darryl_p_dunc:** Like, google talks about him maybe having more poetry out there.

**darryl_p_dunc:** but he died before they could print it.

**darry;_p_dunc:** it was all lost.

**darryl_p_dunc**: it's all speculation.

**awesome.lucas:** So you're saying there's money here? Serious money?

**darryl_p_dunc:** Seems like it. We could split it between us, eh Hobbs?

**hobbsthehobbes:** I mean, if it is real. Why not.

**austinpowersrules:** Yeaaaah!

**hobbsthehobbes:** Guess we should probably check then? Is there someone you can call?

**darryl_p_dunc:** I've found a number. Let me see if I can check.

And so, 170 miles away, Duncan stared at the websites on his computer before pressing the hotline number into his phone, unaware of just what they'd be getting into.

Duncan tried his best telephone voice. To look at him, you wouldn't think he could pull one off. If Hobbs looked like a festival goer, Duncan was built like an athlete. A large grey jacket stretched over solid shoulders. He scratched at his short dark hair as he waited for his mobile to connect.

He glanced over the Foundation's website. A lot of work had gone into the website, if the graphics were anything to go by. This Jake character—the founder, apparently—was clearly rolling in money.

He paced up and down his small bedroom as the phone remained on hold. Where Hobbs had a room fit for a scrapyard, Duncan's was organised and well cared for. A proper computer desk with two screens, beside piles of essays all covered in notes. The shelves were filled with books. Photos of family cascaded across the large noticeboard behind his bedroom door. The calendar was covered in red writing. The words 'CLEARING DAY' marked and underlined and written in clear capitals.

As Duncan waited, a dull voice reminded him that the Booker Foundation's phone calls were recorded. A reminder that added to his anxiety as he scratched at his neck and twisted his desk chair. A few times he glanced back at the chat box but they were now waiting for him as patiently as three boys could. Not well.

And then a voice burst through the line.

"Hello, you're through to the Booker Foundation. My name is Olivia Blake. How may I help you?"

Duncan took a moment, psyching himself up.

"Hiya, yeah...." He hesitated. Those minutes on hold had stolen his phone voice, and his words. "My friend thinks he's found one of those missing books you're after."

A pause. Duncan was starting to wish he'd just asked Lucas to ring, but it was too late to turn back.

“Okay, let's take some details,” the woman replied calmly. “Can I take your name and

your location please?”

“It’s Darryl Duncan, and I live in Manchester.”

“Manchester, New Hampshire?”

“Err—No? England? In the United Kingdom?”

There’s a change in tone, the woman’s tone seemed to brighten. “I thought your accent sounded familiar. Okay, Darryl—”

“It’s Duncan—or Dunc. I prefer Dunc.”

“Okay, Dunc, sorry about that. Can you tell me more about the book your friend has?”

Putting the American woman on speaker, he started to describe the book.

“It’s called *CEST LA VIE*,” he concluded. Duncan knew his accent is terrible but he knew what the title meant. *This is Life*. “The name on it is Wilfred Owen.”

Olivia typed the information into her system with a pleasant hum, which settled his stomach. Duncan heard the rattling of her keys as he continued. “There’s no sign of a publisher, there’s still lots of handwritten notes. Some English and some, my friend believes, in French. It’s a mystery.”

“Okay Dunc, it certainly sounds like something one of our Foundation Observers is looking for. If you could send it to our Washington, DC office by—”

“Hey, I’m not sending it to you. It’s not mine. Besides, I know Hobbs will have nowt to be able to send something this precious, if it is that precious.”

Olivia’s tone changed, a forced forbearance creeping into her voice. “Dunc, how else do you propose we receive this book and confirm its authenticity?” The pause between them is enough to give him an idea. Electricity danced on his lips as he spilled it to her. His excitement bubbled over.

“You send Hobbs to you lot direct. He’ll be your courier. Though...” He dragged it out with a sigh he hoped sounded genuine. “He is afraid of flying, so...I suppose I could do you a favour and I can come with him, like? Would hate for him to not be able to get on the plane...”

Duncan seemed sure he could hear her cogs turn, even

thousands of miles away. She clicked her tongue against her teeth. With a polite “Please hold,” the line went silent. Soon an obviously recorded voice took over. He couldn’t decide if the speaker enjoyed the task or not.

“Thank you for calling the Booker Foundation. This is Jake Booker, founder. We’re dedicated to finding books that history says are lost. And we’re happy to reward your efforts. You’re on hold right now, but we’ll get back to you shortly.” This repeated a fair few times before Olivia finally came back to him.

“I’ve spoken to one of our project’s co-directors and they are willing to provide two return tickets to Washington DC from Bristol Airport, sadly not direct but the stop in Paris isn’t long. That’s where you said your friend was based, Bristol? I’ll need both your passport details so I can arrange your ESTAs. Then we’re good to go for your meeting in Washington. Also, I have to have your email address to provide more travel information.”

Duncan’s face hurt from grinning. What a fabulous trick. Something like a proper journalist would do. Unfortunately, he wasn’t lying about Hobbs’ fear of flying.

**hobbsthehobbes:** i’m doing what now!?

**darryl_p_dunc:** it’s all being arranged; can you send me your passport details for your visa.

**austinpowersrules:** you’re a wizard Dunc, how’d you do that.

**darryl_p_dunc**: I just told the truth; Hobbs is afraid of flying and he couldn’t go alone. I’m like a chaperone.

**hobbsthehobbes:** Dunc I’m going to kill you.

**darryl_p_dunc:** Well, I can just come to you and I’ll take the book to Washington then.

**awesome.lucas:** My step-mom said they’re happy for you both to stay a few days, this is awesome!

**darryl_p_dunc:** Thanks Lucas.

**darryl_p_dunc:** So Hobbs, I’m getting the train, so I’ll be in Bristol tomorrow morning. You need to actually pack something for the flight and don’t forget your passport.

**hobbsthehobbes:** I hate you, Dunc. I hate you. I can’t.

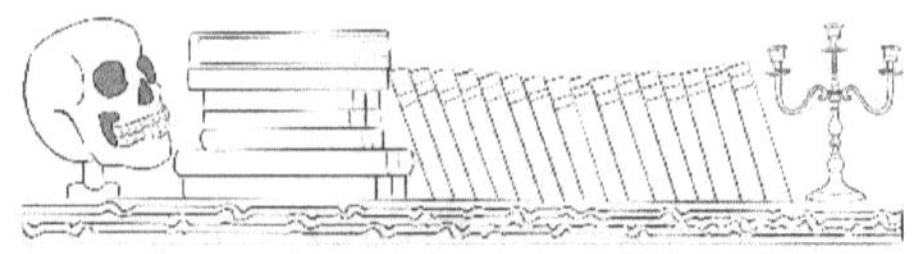

Hobbs had dreamt, if you could call it dreaming, of every possibility: that the flight could go wrong. He dreamt the plane could crash, or oxygen would be removed, or they would blow up. He had barely settled before he had been unable to stay awake anymore. It was just a book, a stupid old book. Why did he even have to go? But could he resist? He had always wanted to go to America. Same as Duncan. Between the price and his fear of flying, he never thought it possible. But he was getting a free flight...and he wasn't going on his own.

Still, the boy was white-faced. His passport, inhaler, and wallet on him, Hobbs packed a simple rucksack with a few shirts and changes of underwear though he barely had anything in it that would be useful for a trip. If it wasn't for Lucas they would be both screwed. He told his parents he was going to visit Duncan for a week, not that they cared. Both Mr. and Mrs. Hobbs were too busy to mind what their teenage son was up to.

"Just call once in a while," his mum called on his way out the door.

"And don't even think about calling up for more money," Mr. Hobbs shouted when the door was nearly closed behind his son.

Duncan was due to meet Hobbs at Temple Meads station so they could go together on the bus to the airport. The station was a magnificent structure. Its entrance was a large, sloping road where a string of taxis headed back round towards the centre. At the top of said road was a large Jacobean structure carved in stone. It should have been impressive, but Hobbs had grown up with it only a bus ride away. To him, it was just another building.

He checked his phone; the chat hadn't moved. The other two boys should be sleeping by now. Time zones were always weird, considering Lucas and Austin lived in the same country but were themselves an hour apart. Still, he slipped his phone away, rubbing his neck as he looked out for Duncan's train. Without going through the barriers there was only one train that Hobbs could see through the stone archways. He had music for company, trying not to think about flying, and focused instead on whether Duncan would be taller than him. He couldn't remember if he'd ever asked that question.

Something caught his eye. A dark, tall boy in a jacket with a backpack loose on his shoulder stepped off the train. Hobbs knew that sloping hunch anywhere, even though he'd only seen it digitally. Duncan waved towards him. Hobbs' mouth only spread even bigger, waving back.

And as Hobbs stepped forward, all his balance suddenly disappeared. Something black went over his eyes, and with it the world went dark.

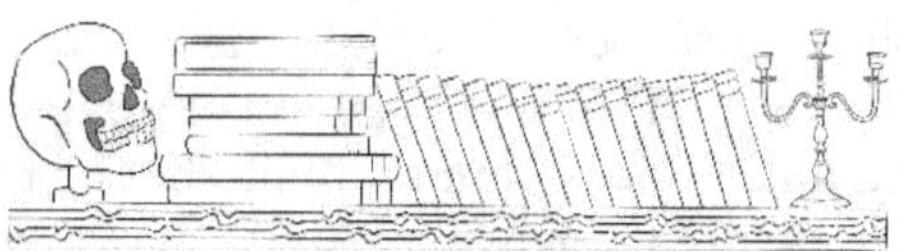

One moment Duncan saw his scruffy friend, as he had seen countless times on his monitor. The next, a black bag was thrown over the boy's head, and he disappeared out of sight. Being able to get through the barriers quickly was a blessing. Rushing to where Hobbs had been standing, Duncan watched a dirty white transit van pull away with a gasp of its engine.

Panic soared through him, causing the ends of his fingers to itch. He had to think—and fast. A few feet from him, Duncan turned his attention to one of the city's 'free' bikes. These were available to rent using an app, and this one with a battered handlebar had simply been left by the station door. There was no time to consider an alternative. Duncan fled forward and jumped on the bike, started to follow.

The van turned through a small roundabout and headed towards the city centre.

Already pedalling hard, Dunc shot into traffic, earning him angry honks from an overbearing Audi Estate car. He ignored it. All he could think about was Hobbs.

To Duncan's relief, Bristol was a busy city. Roadworks meant that traffic was slow and heavy. It was a balancing act; he wanted to keep the van in sight, but without being seen himself. Bristol's traffic was bad enough, but the hills worked in his favour, and luckily, he had the stamina to climb them. No wonder Hobbs hadn't bothered learning to drive yet.

About ten minutes later, a face peeked out from the van's passenger window and looked back. He'd been spotted. After a moment, the face disappeared. Duncan feared the van would speed up or try some fancy driving to lose him.

That didn't happen.

Instead, the white vehicle turned fast into a discreet road away from the city just ahead of him.

As panic threatened to surge again, Duncan picked up speed, following them blindly into the turn.

Both lanes were blocked by lorries idling as they waited to unload goods ahead of him. He squeezed his brakes hard.

A screeching noise permeated the air as he came to a halt before hitting the rear. That had been too close to call. One of the drivers shouted unnecessary things at him, but he raised a hand in apology as he walked the bike quickly past the lorries, settling his heart and taking off again down the narrow road.

The lorries were masking an entrance to an industrial estate, large similar-sized warehouses with very little parking off the minor road, lots of strange signs, mostly for garages or small offices made out of faded red brick and congregated iron. Duncan had arrived at a sudden dead end, and there was no sign of the white van.

His hands squeezed together in frustration. How was he supposed to find Hobbs now? It wasn't like those vehicles were hardly uncommon among the estate's factories and warehouses. Why hadn't he thought of taking down the vehicle's registration number?

He stopped the bike and tried to settle. He had to think about this rationally. That was what he was all about, wasn't it? Working out things based on the information presented to him. The white van couldn't be far. It was a vehicle that had kidnapped someone, a minor at that. It needed to unload its passenger discreetly. Most of these locations were too open, and he hadn't been that far behind...

Duncan observed his location one more time and took in each building before he saw a deserted company garage at the end of the dead-end street. A garage that seemed conspicuously closed for business, and yet its gates were open.

He moved towards it, keeping low with the bike. As he got closer to the ajar gate, he saw a flash of a familiar white shape. Duncan breathed a sigh of relief. The dirty white van had parked erratically. All of its doors hung open as three towering men the size of bodybuilders stood around the vehicle. Keeping the bike close, he carefully started making his way towards them. Fortunately for Duncan, a whole line of cars in various stages of repair gave him somewhere to hide.

Duncan took a closer look at the men. They had thick bodies, small heads and lumpy hands. The leader sported a scorpion tattoo on his neck. With no hair on his head and a pair of black sunglasses, he reminded Dunc of the *Men in Black* movies. His other two consorts were only slightly smaller, but just as mean looking. Both wore attempts at beards. All three of them wore black, dark sunglasses and gloves, which made Duncan's stomach twist. One of the stooges opened the boot of the van and Hobbs was thrown out into the gravel. If Hobbs had looked raggedy before, he looked worse now. Despite hitting the ground hard, adrenaline caused the teenager to bounce up onto his feet, pointing blindly at those that had grabbed him.

"What the fuck are you playing at mate?!" His fierce tone wavered.

Duncan watched as the teenager went to grip his rucksack on his back, only to find that another of the men had it in his hands. His voice stammered but it was still filled with rage. "A-And that's mine—give it back—!"

They said nothing. Hobbs rushed forward, but Scorpion Man raised the rucksack high over Hobbs's head out of reach with a satisfied smirk. Dunc could feel his blood boiling under his skin as he continued to creep closer. Keeping low, he made it behind another vehicle four cars away from Hobbs and the men.

This time his hidey-hole was a small Ford Fiesta. The glass of the rear quarter lights crunched loudly under his trainers. He fell as silent as he could, frozen. After a few terrifying seconds the moment past. No one had noticed. They were too busy with Hobbs.

As the young man continued to snatch desperately at his rucksack, a voice rang out through the courtyard. "It's Robin, isn't it? I'm Ms. Cobalt. I believe you have something that belongs to me."

Leaving the garage, the speaker stepped toward the group. Dark hair streaked with grey hung down over her leather jacket. She held a confident posture and an intense stare that could swallow you whole. Hobbs' eyebrows raised high on his forehead, rucksack forgotten. She was an older woman, but that didn't mean she wasn't beautiful. There was something about her accent that Duncan couldn't place, but he knew it wasn't English that was for sure. Cobalt's tone didn't sound threatening, but that made his stomach tighten further. Hobbs gawked at the woman for a long moment, before surprising himself and probably everyone else by shaking his head.

"Look, I don't know what this is about, but that weed was from Mike's and he said he got that from—"

She cut him off with a cruel laugh. It was so far from her elegant image that his skin crawled. "I'm not after your stash, you stupid boy. The book. I want the book you bought yesterday."

"Wait—no!" His arms flailing around, the teenager rushed for his rucksack. Each henchman passed it between them. The biggest of them tripped him into the cement below. Wincing, Hobbs rubbed his knee. Cobalt was now holding his rucksack, starting to pull on the zip.

A siren burst \around them. One of the abandoned cars blaring loudly with purpose. Cobalt and her men turned in all directions for the source of the noise. As they did so, Hobbs took his chance. He reached forward and tugged the rucksack from Cobalt's grasp.

"Gotcha!"

With a shaky breath the teen raced towards the end of the garage with the stooges in tow.

Hope started to drain away from Hobbs until he saw a vulgar yellow bike appear in view with a familiar Mancunian boy.

"Duncan!"

The shorter boy skidded in front of him to a halt in the gravel. "Get the hell on!" he growled.

It took two tries for Hobbs, panicking as men shouted behind them, to get his clumsy feet firmly on the bike pegs and through the garage gate. He grabbed hold of Duncan's jacketed shoulders as his friend started pedalling again. His ears fixed on listening to the sound of an engine behind him, nothing yet, only the distance sound of irritated growls.

As Duncan wrestled to get used to the new load, Hobbs began to smack his arms as he started to cycle in the direction he came.

"Dunc, go right! I said right here!"

"What? Why?! It's the wrong *bloody* way!"

Hobbs pointed, and Duncan followed the finger to an empty road. "One way systems, bike paths—bike the ways a van can't go! Go right!"

Duncan listened reluctantly. A twist of the handlebars and onward in Hobb's recommended direction. Just as he made the road, he recognised the sound of a gasping engine.

"They're back in the van!" Hobbs cried out.

"I know! Shut the hell up, Hobbs!"

"Through the park! They can't get through there!"

Having a navigator was frustrating but not nearly as maddening as Hobbs shouting and hitting on his back.

They reached the park. It took every scrap of strength for Duncan to keep balance as they entered the park path. Duncan glanced back to watch the van pathetically trapped behind them. A fist punching the wheel.

Hobbs couldn't help himself, a whooping glee of adrenaline as he turned back to the predatory van behind them.

"Suck it, losers!"

Duncan didn't have the energy to tell him not to. Pedalling through the park.

It took them to the other side and down a large hill towards the station. The bus lanes kept Duncan sure that the van couldn't easily follow, even if the thought of the van still blaring into view behind them any moment sick to his stomach. There was another sharp turn, and a crossroads before Hobbs patted him eagerly on the back.

"We're here!"

Bristol Temple Meads merged into view around the corner, an extensive line of buses and taxis waiting for them.

Duncan placed the bike where he found it, out of breath, before rushing to the front of the taxi, dragging the blond boy with him. Looking at Hobbs, he saw how pale he'd become, almost blue. Adrenaline had run out, and the realisation of his day was sinking in.

He checked his wallet. The cash he had brought with him looked meagre, but the airport bus was no longer an option. It would cost him a small fortune, and he knew Hobbs wouldn't have the money. Still, he pushed the lad inside, reasoning that the Foundation might give them any travel costs, and the white van men wouldn't be looking for a black cab.

They were probably stuck in some one-way road.

"What the hell was all that about—" Hobbs started to say, only for Duncan to kick his friend hard in the shin. Hobbs yelled out, beginning to rub the shin through gritted his teeth.

This caused the taxi driver to turn to them for their destination, eying them with suspicion before looking back to the road and pulled out of the station.

Duncan got out of his phone and quickly typed out his reasoning: ***Not here. Too dangerous. Let's fill in the others online.***

Hobbs eyes darted over it quickly and nodded. He lay his head back against the seat taking deep breaths, pulling the inhaler out of his pocket. Duncan listened to Hobbs intake his asthma medicine and let his rattling chest to finally rela as he continued to type.

***Maybe Lucas can contact the Foundation for us. I'm just glad we've still got three hours until our flight...***

**awesome.lucas:** I think you're pulling our leg.

**darryl_p_dunc:** sod off lucas, we're not joking.

**awesome.lucas:** no way is there someone else after that book.

**awesome.lucas:** It's junk. I mean, free trip to see me is cool, but...nah.

**darryl_p_dunc:** I mean it. Hobbs and I are at the airport now.

**darryl_p_dunc:** If it's not bad enough Hobbs is now more paranoid than normal.

**austinpowersrules:** What about the van?

**austinpowersrules:** you did lose em?

**darryl_p_dunc:** think so. They weren't able to get through the one way systems.

**austinpowersrules:** I mean, they don't know where you're going to. do they?

**darryl_p_dunc:** they knew Hobbs' real name. Maybe they

were stalking him.

**darryl_p_dunc:** they might know, but we're on the plane now and we have to stop in Paris for two hours. And America is much bigger than England so it might be easier to keep off their trail.

**awesome.lucas:** Have a safe trip, see you later.

**awesome.lucas:** Oh. Tell Hobbs to not be a wuss.

**awesome.lucas:** More people die in cars than planes these days.

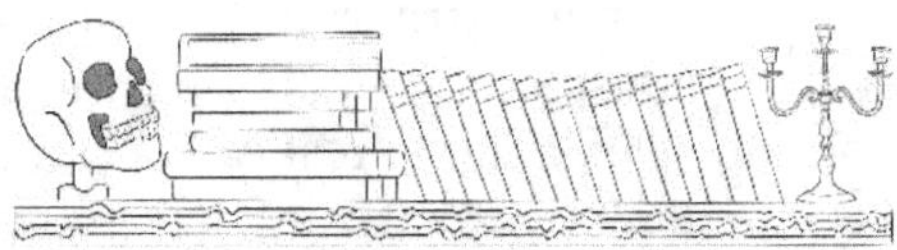

“I'm going to punch him when I see him,” Duncan told Hobbs.

The plane to their transfer stop in Paris was small but crowded. Luckily Hobbs and Duncan had a whole section between themselves. Hobbs’ fear of flying left him white. Even after sucking on boiled sweets and squeezing onto his favourite sweatshirt to try and calm himself—advice he’d read online—he looked worse than ever.

“At least we get to *see* Lucas to punch him.” Duncan retorted “Do you think he's like that in real life?”

“Dunno, maybe he won't have the guts to say those sort of things to your face. Not when he sees you're probably as tall as two of him...”

Duncan laughed, trying to settle in his seat, glad to get Hobbs to concentrate on something else—anything else—but the flight. The plane had not yet moved to get in the queue on the runway, so the distraction was probably welcome.

“This is all mad, speaking to you face to face, and getting to go to America. I've never even left Bristol, except a school trip to the beach in Weston...especially after my episode last year.”

Smiling, Duncan punched lightly on Hobbs' shoulder.

“You deserve it. Welcome to the rest of the world, pal. Maybe you'll actually love flying after this—”

But as the tannoy broke out the pilot’s final instructions, and air hostesses walked past checking seat belts Hobbs groaned. He closed his eyes as he heard the engines rattle, his grip steadfast before he took a shuddering wheeze of his inhaler.

"Don't hold your breath. Don't make me hit you too, man."

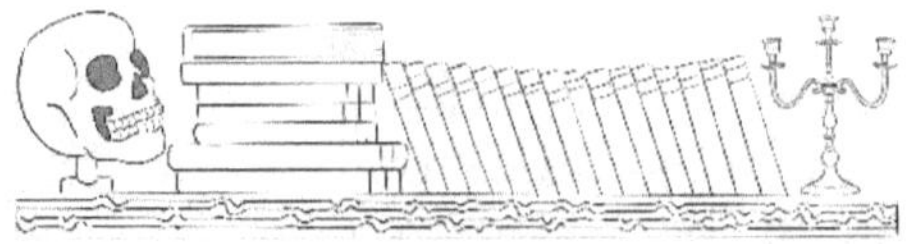

Hobbs had a sleeping pill just a few minutes into their second journey, as suggested by one of the air hostesses on their first flight. The Charles de Gaulle Airport in Paris had been nice, but Duncan couldn't help constantly checking over their shoulder for Ms. Cobalt, Scorpion Man, and the rest of the stooges. Now onto their second flight, and Hobbs shaking for twenty minutes every time the plane hit turbulence, finally he'd found time for himself when the Bristolian boy had started to truly rest.

It was Hobbs' snores that reminded Duncan that he hadn't even looked at the book, apart from the photographs Hobbs had taken. With care, Duncan pulled the book out from behind the coat that Hobbs packed. It was smaller than he expected, no bigger than his palm and not incredibly thick, either. The paper between his fingers was a pasty yellow. The handwriting and typewriter text were in French with some scattered English scrawls. He couldn't make out all of the words.

His fingers gently prized open the first page. English and handwritten, like a note.

Another hand had written a few amendments and Duncan couldn't help but be curious. If this was Wilfred Owens' work, why was someone else editing it? He flicked through, but nothing else jumped out at him. He gently put the book back where it had been in the rucksack. Safe and sound once again. With that in mind, Duncan shifted in his seat and tried to stretch out and get comfortable.

It was going to be a long few hours before they arrived in America.

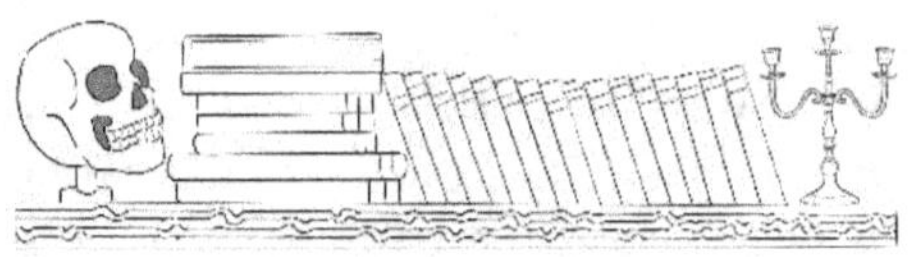

He should have known it was a dream when he saw Hobbs, still asleep, as smoke came up the aisle.

He should have known it was a dream when Cobalt's head goon had his mother by the throat and a gun to her head, shouting at him, but he was unable to get off his seatbelt.

He should have known it was a dream when everyone spoke in French and he understood nothing but his mother's sobbing for her life as she vanished into smoke.

He should have known it was a dream when Wilfred Owen sat beside him. A young man whose sad eyes and moustache were plastered on the front of all of his English textbooks.

"Wake up Duncan, you have work to do. Ambition may be defined as the willingness to receive any number of hits on the nose."

He woke with such a yell that Hobbs even spluttered awake. The other passengers who had been sleeping gave him a filthy look. He turned away from them, toward his friend. Duncan was a startling pasty colour that even took Hobbs by surprise. The other boy frowned, nudging him with an elbow.

"You alright man?"

"Do I look bloody alright...?" Duncan rubbed his forehead with the back of his hand, sweat glistening. He licked his lips. "Bad dream. It's nothing to worry about. Must be nerves ya know, travelling so far."

"You feel bad about lying to your mum?"

"No—no, not really." Duncan's lip formed a half-smile, but Hobbs could see his adam's apple bobbing as he swallowed. "Just, I hope those men don't know where we're going, that's all."

"Well, we are hundreds of miles away. How will they know? I just can't wait to get off this bloody plane...."

Duncan looks to the ceiling, wiping at his forehead again and closing his tired eyes. "Same. Just a few more hours to go..."

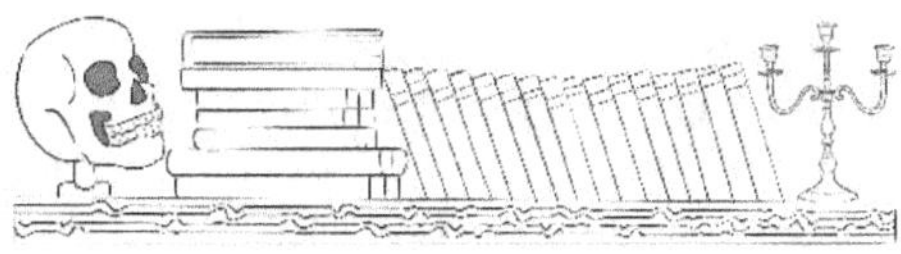

As Hobbs and Duncan finally moved through towards the arrivals section with their backpacks, two figures in the crowd waited for them. Even though neither boy had met them face to face, they both knew exactly who they were looking for.

Lucas was almost as tall as he was wide, something that wasn't as overly clear in the times they'd videoed as a group but had always been joked about. He had chestnut brown hair, greasy and outgrown, with a few bad spots and a pair of glasses. He had made them a welcome sign, cut from a shoe box top and using a red sharpie. He'd scribbled their usernames instead of their real ones. Austin had suggested it apparently, as Duncan caught up with the chat box on his phone.

"You're a bit pathetic, mate!" Duncan said with a smirk. But Lucas was already giving Hobbs a bear hug. Both laughed as he spun Hobbs around, his free hand giving Duncan the finger. If other people thought it strange to watch the two teenagers hugging delightedly, no one seemed to care. After Duncan and Lucas hugged, Lucas gave a signing off kiss on the boy's forehead.

"Good to see you too, dipshit."

Next to Lucas stood a short woman dressed in a sharp blue suit, focused on her mobile. She seemed far too professional to be hanging around a bunch of teenagers. However, once her focus was on them, she greeted them with a smile. She raised an eyebrow at the boys before introducing herself. To their surprise, she offered handshakes.

"Dunc and Hobbs? Welcome to America! I'm Olivia from the Booker Foundation. I hear from Lucas that you had a bit of trouble getting to the airport?"

Duncan nodded. The events with Cobalt and her minions seemed long behind them, but he wouldn't be forgetting her laugh in a hurry after that dream. Hobbs unconsciously rubbed his scraped elbow.

"Do you think they will follow us, like?" Duncan asked as they started to move away to the exit.

Olivia shrugged, checking her phone once more. "I don't know, but if they think the book is worth that little stunt they pulled back in England...it makes this far more interesting. But I'm afraid until we've spoken to the doctor, we won't have an expert opinion."

"Doctor? Doctor who?"

Olivia's smile brightened even wider as if having a private joke, before going back into professional mode, gesturing for them to follow. “You'll find out. But Mr. Booker has advised we should make sure we get her a sealed, lidded tea on the way.”

**austinpowersrules**: guys?
**austinpowersrules:** Hello??
**austinpowersrules:** Lucas you said you'd update me!
**austinpowersrules:** This is bullshit.
**hobbsthehobbes**: Relax mate, we're all driving to Washington office
**hobbsthehobbes:** why are your roads so bloody wide?
**hobbsthehobbes:** are you all compensating for something?
**austinpowersrules:** So is she hot?
**hobbsthehobbes:** You and your mind mate seriously.
**austinpowersrules**: So?
**austinpowersrules:** Is the Olivia girl hot?
**awesome.lucas:** She's hot.
**austinpowersrules:** ffs!

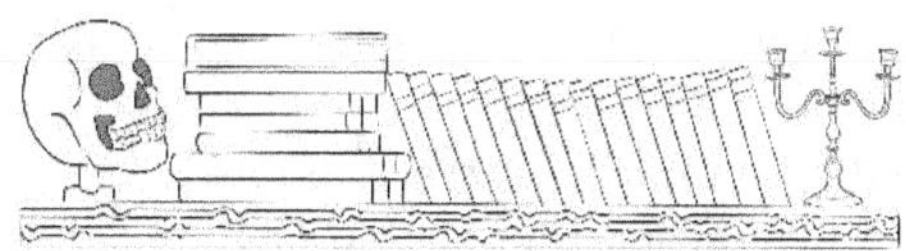

Dr. Rosella Tassoni was already in her office when they arrived. The tower block had multiple offices and departments inside, including hers. Though Hobbs and Duncan were excited to see Washington, they had ended up so enthralled in meeting Lucas and Olivia that they’d almost forgotten they were in another country. That was until they stepped out of the car and into the building. To Duncan it looked like a film set, with its modernist décor, stark white walls, and a swish elevator up to the top floors. They briefly stood in the first floor waiting room before being shown the office on the second floor. Their host sat behind her desk and watched each boy with interest as they sat down.

“Doctor Tassoni is a Forensic Mythologist and one of the minds behind the Booker Foundation’s initiative,” Olivia explained. “She’ll be the one to give your find the initial assessment.”

Duncan considered that Doctor Tassoni was probably only slightly older than Olivia Blake. She wore a long sleeve blouse and looked tired, perhaps a little frustrated. Observing the sealed, lidded tea Olivia had brought, she seemed both touched and suspicious.

"When you see Jake next, Livvy, please thank him for remembering. I'll get Kiara to send him something...interesting." She turned to look at the three boys. Duncan tried to imagine what exactly she must think of them. They were a motley crew to say the least. They didn't fit into this world at all, with their hoodies and rucksacks. She sipped her tea as the boys shuffled anxiously in their seats. She would, after all, either confirm or deny their hopes for the book.

"So," Rosella said, calmly, "am I allowed to see this book?"

As she suspected, the others looked to Duncan, who nodded. Hobbs brought the rucksack he had been hugging forward, passed the book to Duncan, who then handed it over to her.

Eagle-eyed, the boys watched Rosella become enthralled. The way her eyes lit up, and her smile peaked from the corners of her mouth, it was obvious she thought it was the real deal. Duncan saw Lucas nudging Hobbs excitedly. Then she put the book carefully on the desk and stood.

"If this is what I think it is, it's quite a find. I'll keep the book safe for now, and you boys can enjoy your free holiday. Olivia will contact you for your rewards in the next few days."

Lucas, mouth agape, shook his head. "Hang on, these two were chased and threatened to get this book here, a reward on your say so isn't good enough."

Duncan hissed at him to stop, but there wasn't any give. Lucas ignored him. "I mean it. What if they get attacked again? Hobbs isn't exactly safe if they're still out there. They knew where he was going to be and everything."

Olivia and Rosella exchanged glances.

"I suppose, in this case, you could come with us to the Foundation." Rosella didn't seem too pleased with the decision. "If you could stay here and mind the office in Kiara's place, Olivia?"

Olivia nodded. "I'll give Jake a call now and let them know you'll be on your way, though I think someone else is currently holding down the fort..." With that, she left the room to make the call, leaving Rosella alone with them. Hobbs, seeming to struggle with this, turned to his phone to fill in Austin, whilst Lucas asked her questions which gained him another raised eyebrow.

"So, what is Forensic Mythology, and why do I get the feeling Dunc's going to want your job?"

But Duncan was more concerned with looking around than listening to the others. Standing, he took in the surreal view of Washington outside the large window. He wasn't sure what to expect from America. There were a lot of grey tall buildings, large blocks of them. And driving along the other side of the road. But it was cloudy, just like his weather...

Still staring out of the window, he thought he saw something below them. It was the entrance. And at the entrance, two men...two men he recognised...even from this height. The two stooges...he'd recognise that pair anywhere. Backing away from the window, he turned to the others. If those two were here, where was the Scorpion Man?

"Doctor Tassoni, I—?" Duncan began to say, he could feel the heat already crawling up his neck. A crack, sharp and deafening, came from outside the room. Olivia barged through the door. She clutched at one of her shoulders, struggling to speak, scarlet pooling between her fingers. It stained her blue jacket a deep purple.

"They're in the lobby—go—break room— " Shaking, Lucas couldn't move. Duncan rushed forward towards Olivia but Rosella was already pulling him by his jacket back towards the door.

"Quick. To the break room!"

"But what about—"

"I SAID NOW!"

The three boys bundled towards the door. As Duncan followed after Lucas and Hobbs, who he's practically slamming into the exit, he turned to check with Olivia but she pushed him away with a sharp dig in his back.

"Go—Go, Dunc— "

One more shove and he was out of the door. The sound of the door locking behind him. If not for Rosella, he'd still be pounding on the door.

"What is she doing!?" His voice was strained and high-pitched.

They just made it to the break room, as Duncan heard the office door break. He understood too late, his question finally answered with new sounds, two gunshots. Hobbs looked about to be sick. Lucas seemed in a daze. But Rosella only seemed to get angrier.

"We keep moving—we have to keep moving, down the fire escape...and if Booker doesn't think he's paying for the damage to my property we're having words—"

As she turned, Hobbs saw the fire safety button, and quickly punched it as hard as he could. A loud wailing alarm filled the building.

"They might struggle to get to us if we're in a crowd of other people—?"

Just as Hobbs suggested, other offices started evacuating, some more concerned than others, and they joined the rabble.

Forcing a smile at her fellow office renters, Rosella led the boys out of the front door. It appeared the sudden rush of people distracted the stooges; the boys evaded their gaze. They rushed to the next block where Rosella hollered for a taxi. As the bright yellow vehicle pulled to a halt in front of them, they bundled inside. Whilst the doctor gave directions the boys buckled in and tried to keep their heads down. Just in case they drove past the way they'd come.

"Where are we going?" Lucas asked.

"Houston."

"By cab?"

"No, I've asked him to take me to my home. I'll grab a few things and arrange a rental car to the airport. There's a small plane there ready to fly us to Houston."

"But isn't that where they're expecting us to go? What if it's a trap?"

Everyone stared at Lucas. He shuffled uncomfortably in the packed backseat. Hobbs paled at the words 'airport' and 'fly' but he was ignored.

"They've seemed to be ahead of us every step?" Lucas continued. "Why don't we.... fly to somewhere they're not expecting? Not Houston, but someplace close to Houston, to throw them off?"

Knowing exactly what his friend was playing at, Duncan felt his shoulders hunch uncomfortably. "Our friend Aust—Noah—he lives in Austin, Texas..."

Rosella seemed to consider, then nodded, before picking up her phone. "Looks like you'd better tell your friend we're on our way to see him."

**austinpowersrules:** Well, I would check with my parents but they're going to be away for a trade show with my sisters and my brothers that night. so it'd just be me anyway.

**darryl_p_dunc:** Are you sure about this?

**darryl_p_dunc:** I don't know if this is a good idea.

**darryl_p_dunc:** We still don't know what happened to Olivia...

**awesome.lucas:** This is a foolproof plan. Austin puts us up for the night, then it's just under four hours to go. The Doc says it's the Foundation's pretty secure.

**austinpowersrules:** It'll be great, no problem and and I get to meet you all!

**hobbsthehobbes:** It would be pretty nice to meet you Austin...

**awesome.lucas:** stop being square, Dunc. It's going to be fine. Trust me.

**darryl_p_dunc:** Okay. I'm sure it's going to be fine....Looking forward to seeing you mate.

**hobbsthehobbes:** same1!

**awesome.lucas:** It's going to be great

**austinpowersrules:** Yay!

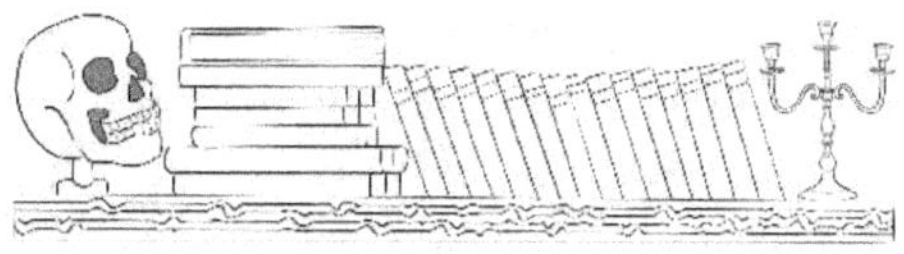

If the Boeing 747 to America gave Hobbs anxiety, nothing compared to his terror at the small charter plane they were using to get to Texas. It took a great deal of coaxing just to get the boy on the plane. By the time he was in his seat, he was already downing another couple of pills, chugging on his inhaler and praying he would sleep through the journey.

Once in the air, with cloudy Washington behind them, it wouldn't be a long journey. The boys were left with their thoughts. Lucas sat next to the conked-out Hobbs at the back of the plane, whilst Rosella sat next to Duncan.

"Do you think she's okay?" Duncan said quietly. "Olivia—do you..."

"I don't know." Her face still turned to the clouds that the plane glided through. "I hope so..."

In the window's reflection, he saw that her expression was hard as she spoke. Duncan swallowed, glad that, of all the adults that were involved with this book, Rosella was on their side. Then she asked a question that surprised him.

"And you said her name was Cobalt? The woman who threatened Hobbs in the warehouse?"

Duncan nodded. "Ms. Cobalt, yeah. Though that could be a stage name, like..."

"Oh, it's her real name, alright. I had Livvy do some digging. She's a treasure hunter. About ten years ago she found an old Spanish galleon off the coast of Mexico with her father and has been.... what's the word you'd use—"

"Minted?"

She smiled for the first time since their meeting in her office.

"Minted, yes. They even took the United States to court for five years to claim ownership. I think they won finally with the phrase 'Finders Keepers.'"

He smiled back, a bit more at ease. But he then found himself frowning again.

"So why is she so interested in the book that we found? How does she even know about it?"

"Your guess is as good as mine. But with my line of work, people do tend to put faith in myths and legends. Perhaps more than they really should. So, Wilfred Owen. He was a very interesting man."

Duncan shrugged, "I just know about his poems, the war ones. We studied them at school."

"Far from my favorite author whose work was shaped by the war. Though he's hardly part of my line of work, either. Do you enjoy them?"

"They were alright, I guess? I mean like, GCSE poetry ain't there to be enjoyed, it's there to be stripped away to guess the author's mysterious intentions for your exams. By the end of the two years looking at 'em you're wishing to never see another poem again."

"For a teenager who claims not to know much about poems, you know a lot about how to pass an English exam."

It was Duncan's turn to smile. "I like figuring things out. Besides, I never said I didn't like poems and that, I just said I didn't like GCSE poetry."

They were interrupted by Hobbs, snoring, rolling against the window whilst Lucas fell asleep against him. The teen and the doctor shared amused glances, but the sight of the boys sleeping reminded Duncan of his own fatigue. He shuffled his shoulders trying to stifle a yawn and failed.

"How much longer until we get to Texas?"

"Another hour. You should rest, Duncan. We don't know what's coming after we get off the plane. If I were Cobalt, I'd be doubling my efforts to find us. Though, if I was Cobalt, I wouldn't have let a fire alarm stop me from catching some kids with a valuable book."

"Good thing you're on our side then."

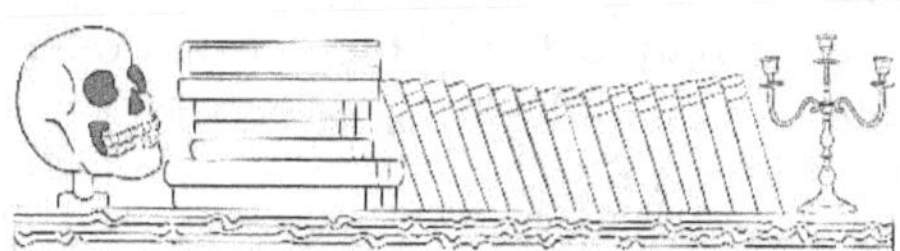

Noah's farmhouse was in Dripping Springs, only forty five minutes away from the airport, which they did via rental car. Compared to Washington DC, it was strange how different the landscape was. There were hardly any buildings for miles and miles. The odd shed, old roads covered in sand. Duncan felt like he had been dropped straight into the setting of *Breaking Bad*, the sandy grassland and the contrasting lush trees. He felt the dry heat on his neck, his breath hot on his tongue. He turned to Hobbs, somehow still wearing his hoodie.

"Aren't you warm?"

Hobbs just shrugged. Colour returned to his face now that he was no longer on a plane or stuck in a car.

"Just hungry, the last time we ate anything was on the plane to DC and I can't even figure anymore what time it would have been at home..."

The farmhouse was a huge wooden structure, and everything

Duncan had imagined it to be. It was oak with two floors, the top overlaying the bottom floor to create a canopy for the porch. There was even a rocking chair to complete the picturesque scene. Behind that were two large barns. To the right of the house, three horses grazed in the paddock chewing at the long grass.

As they approached, a young man bounced out of the front door, down the porch's small steps and towards them. Running now, the flurry of red hair practically slammed into Hobbs knocking them both on the dusty ground, the Bristolian teen's nose a little red as the American's head had made contact in the excitement.

If Hobbs was unhappy about it, it didn't show, both boys laughing away.

"I think you hit my nose, mate!"

"—I can't believe you're here!"

Austin, as they had always known him, stood to his full height, pulling Hobbs back up with him. He was a wiry lad, wearing dirty trainers, cropped jeans, an orange shirt with holes in it and a blue short sleeved plaid shirt over the top. In real life he was more freckled and redder haired than Duncan had ever realised—and shorter, much shorter than they'd realised too. He barely came up to Duncan's shoulder.

"I thought you were tall?"

"Oh. Yeah! Well. You know what cameras are like."

Even the accent seemed...lighter somehow than he remembered hearing it on the video. Lucas had the same curious expression on his face.

"Well, let's get you inside, I've got my best dish all prepared for y'all—" He hugged each boy in turn again and tightly, before reaching Rosella. "Oh, and you're the doc? I'm Noah Dumout, but I'm known by these guys as Austin but—" He talked so fast that he stopped, took a breath and blushed on realisation. "You can call me whatever you like."

Rosella simply raised an eyebrow before nodding, having taken in their happy interactions in her stride. "Noah, then. Shall we talk more inside?"

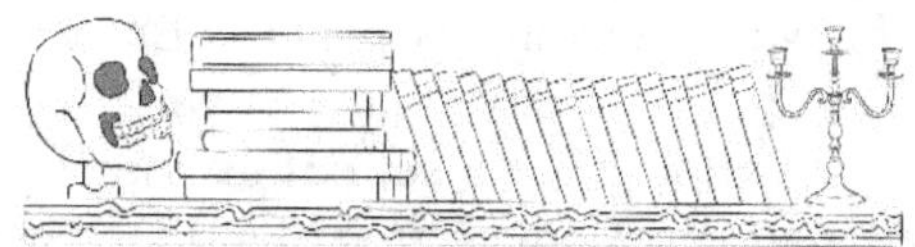

Austin wasn't lying about food. Two large pots of rice and gumbo sat out on the table, lovingly prepared. Lucas was suspicious, but after a few bites felt satisfied. Duncan didn't realise how hungry he was until he could smell the stew.

"I didn't know you could cook," Hobbs said between mouthfuls. After all, aside from their stop in France where they had been able to just afford sandwiches, their journey had been mostly shuffling from one part of the world to another without much stopping.

"It's a hobby. Ma's pretty good and my brothers ain't all that interested and I find it...calming..."

Duncan nodded, chewing on a soft piece of mince, heaven on his tongue. "You're pretty good at it too."

Austin got redder than ever, if that was even possible. He cleared his throat. "So, this book? Is it really that valuable?" Austin mopped up the remaining stew in his bowl with some bread, chewing as he spoke. "I mean, what can a book of poems even be worth?"

"In this case, a lot." Rosella chimed in. She hadn't opted to eat with the boys. Instead, she prepared herself something from his fridge. "If it is as authentic as it appears, the manuscript in Hobbs' possession could be some of Wilfred Owen's first poems, before the war."

"So, the whole.... Anthem of my Dying Day—"

"I think that's a song, Austin." Hobbs butted in, amused.

"Oh—"

"It's actually called 'Anthem for Doomed Youth,'" Duncan corrected.

"So, he wrote lots more poems?"

Rosella seemed to have her teacher mode on, because she allowed the question to sink in before answering. "He wrote many poems during the war, but not so many before it...so this book is quite a find. Based on the information I could source from my colleagues, as well as the use of French words and the placement in his timeline, we think they were written in 1913. We know from his letters that he was a teaching assistant in Bordeaux at that time and already interested in poetry. These poems in the book, some of them in French, appear to be set before that time, along with notes from a woman who's never been mentioned in his history..."

"A woman, eh?" Austin said, raising his eyebrows. Lucas kicked him.

"A woman, yes, Noah. Some of the poems are romantic in nature, and it may shed light on a few things. For example, why would Wilfred have wanted to be part of the French army but then change his mind? It could also cast doubt on his suspected love interest in his fellow poet, Siegfried Sassoon...."

Rosella watched with mild amusement at how the teenage boys reacted to this. Austin seemed the most uncomfortable, his eyes flickering to the others before shrugging.

"Well, whatever it is, he's been dead a long time. How can we prove he wrote this?"

"Well, the handwriting. If it matches previously owned letters and manuscripts. But that's not really the concern, it's making sure we're correct with the placing of the year. Regardless, it's still one of a kind. It'll be worth a small fortune, at any rate. The Foundation will pay handsomely for it."

Lucas grinned like the Cheshire Cat. Duncan's smile was tight as he nodded his head.

Hobbs grabbed Austin's shoulders and ruffled his hair as the redhead burst into laughter. "So....are we still splitting it?" Austin asked.

Hobbs smiled. "'Well, of course we're still splitting it. Small fortune or not. It's ours. As a group."

Lucas was the only one not celebrating. "What about the treasure hunters? If they were to get the book before we got it to the Foundation, would the Foundation pay them?"

Everyone turned to Rosella. She was unconcerned by the question. "Jake Booker's no boy scout, but he would draw the line at dealing with people who kidnap children and shoot at his own foundation's staff. He'd want a crack at them himself. Unfortunately, plenty of other people in the world would pay handsomely for a book of previously unknown Wilfred Owen poetry."

Their plans for the following day were simple; a three-hour drive to the Foundation and then there they'd probably fly home from Houston. There was a vehicle in the barn, a yellow pick-up truck. It needed some tender loving care, but Austin presented it as his pride and joy.

The engine was loud—terrifyingly so, reminding Hobbs of the old Volkswagen Beetle that used to roar past his house most mornings.

"Pa's going to give her to me officially soon. At the moment she's my brother's but he's upgrading now. So, I can learn to drive her properly"

Lucas raised an eyebrow. He had a hunch, and he nudged Duncan's shoulder. "You know Austin, you can learn to drive at sixteen in most states. Bit weird that you're starting so late...."

"I am not starting late! Here it's fifteen and—" and then he stopped. His eyes widened. "Oh ...oh I guess the secret's out?"

"So you're not seventeen." Hobbs mused, still admiring the car. "Why'd you lie?"

"Oh, you guys were so cool when we met and.... you were older and I didn't want you to think I was too young to play the games with you. I even used to put on a voice a bit, so it sounded deeper...just enough...pretty pathetic, huh?"

Duncan shrugged. "Well, don't matter to me how old you are, you're still pretty great at WGO." He smirked at Lucas. "You were beat multiple times by a fifteen-year-old. Lucas, now who's smug?"

Lucas was too busy looking at his phone to respond, which seemed unlike him. Rosella finally returned to them; her phone slipped back in her pocket.

"I have news about Olivia. Emergency services found her when they arrived. She's in the hospital, and she has a long road of recovery ahead, but she's alive..."

Everything seemed to be going far too smoothly, lightening their moods considerably. But they had no idea of the horror to come.

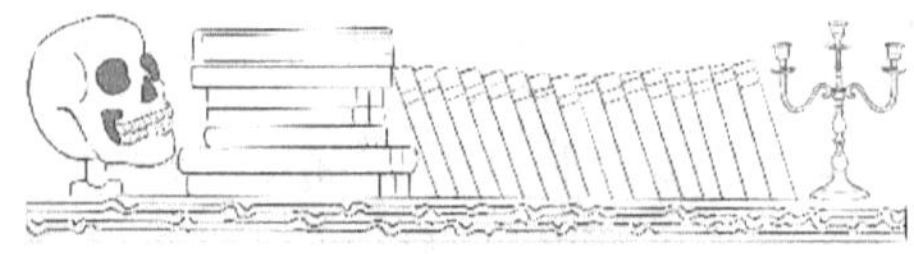

Night came quickly at the farmhouse. After a tour of the ranch, even though it was early, it felt like a good time to rest. Particularly as Hobbs gave Duncan the insight that, even with sleeping on the planes, they hadn't officially had a night's sleep in the last twenty-four hours and both he and Hobbs had lost the concept of time.

Austin had set up the house for his visitors. He gave Rosella his parents' room, whilst the three boys crashed with him in his room. Austin normally shared his room with his oldest brother, and it was obvious how different they were from the décor. Photography, prints and posters decorated Austin's side: nature, horses, WarGamesOnline art, and drawings of Austin's character in the game, Shiloh, a Texan from the Revolution of 1836. His brother's side was covered in posters of women in provocative positions, as well as rappers. His only rule was that Hobbs couldn't smoke. The smell would linger and his parents would kill him.

"Shouldn't smoke if you're asthmatic anyway, makes it worse," the redhead chided.

With the night almost upon them the group felt sleepy but celebratory, Austin and his friends lay on a makeshift bundle of pillows and quilts, letting the dying embers of sunset wash over them. The room seemed lit in a purple haze. It dawned on Duncan that for the first time, they were all talking together in real life. Despite the situation, despite everything, a warm feeling tinged in his chest.

"What do you think you'll do with your share, Hobbs?" Lucas asked, his eyes back to his phone.

"Oh, dunno. Depends on how much we get each. But I could put it towards moving out...would be nice to find a house-share and live with friends. It's that or try college again...just having the money there would be a bonus, yah know?"

The boys all nodded.

Austin smiled, "Well, I'll use the money to sort out my truck.

Maybe I'll come visit you in England. I've always wanted to see London."

"You do know neither of us lives in London?"

"Sure, but it's not far." Austin insisted. "It's only a few hours drive from one end to the other, and we have to drive almost as much just to get groceries!."

Duncan rolled his eyes at this but said nothing. After all, from Austin's perspective, his statement probably seemed true. Back home, it would be hard for Duncan to drive an hour and not strike the coast line. Austin wouldn't reach the coast for days if he drove east or west.

"Come on, Lucas, what about you?"

"Oh, probably update my computer so I can play WGO better. Maybe I'll take my girlfriend on a trip."

The other boys perked up, surprised. If they had been in a chat room, you would have seen caps locks as typed in surprise.

"Girlfriend! A new one?" Austin bellowed so loud that Hobbs had to cover his mouth. Rosella might already be asleep.

"This is news to us, mate!" The Bristolian added.

"I thought I'd mentioned it."

"I think you want us to *think* you mentioned it. Okay, spill the details Lucas."

Red eared, Lucas opened his mouth and closed it a few times, but before he could answer his phone beeped and he turned his attention back to it instead.

"Is that why you're on the phone all the time?" Austin asked, poking his friend's shoulder with a bony finger. "We should have guessed. What's she like?"

"She's err—pretty. Dark hair. She's from money and, uh, very particular."

This did not satisfy Austin at all. He threw a pillow at Lucas's head. "Details, man, details! Has she walked all over you yet?"

Sensing Lucas's unease, Duncan decided to change the subject. He was glad he didn't have to explain what he wanted the money for.

"Do you guys really think Wilfred Owen's poems from France are about a woman? Doesn't seem the type to suddenly write about war and death in that case."

"Well, maybe he was dumped," Hobbs suggested. "Nothing

makes you more bitter than being dumped."

"Says someone from experience?" Duncan said.

Hobbs shrugged. "Says someone who listens to enough music to know that's what men write about. War, love, politics, and money. It's the eternal truth of musicians. Why is poetry any different?"

The conversation fizzled out after that. In their warm blankets, sleep called them. Out in the now unassuming darkness, Austin's voice interrupted the peaceful silence.

"You guys really don't mind I'm younger than y'all?"

"Nope," Duncan said, yawning into his pillow. Whatever these blankets had been washed with reminded him of a holiday in Cornwall. There was a lavender scent that made him wish for sleep. "Doesn't matter that you're still only sixteen..."

"—Fifteen and a half."

"Doesn't matter that you're still only fifteen and a half...."

"And it doesn't matter to you guys, either?"

Hobbs didn't respond, dead to the world in slumber, whilst Lucas shuffled and snored in response. "I think we'd know by now, wouldn't you? See you in the morning, Austin…"

Being lolled into sleep, Duncan could smell something new. Dozing, he thought perhaps he had woken the morning to the smell of bacon, only for the smoky smell to become more and more prominent. Then, there was something else. Seeing smoke out of the window, he bolted upwards.

"Guys! Guys, wake up!" He grabbed Hobbs' shoulders, then Lucas'. It took a moment, but they were awake and up, clasping for reality.

"What the hell, Dunc—"

They heard it, the flickering of flames. Hobbs rushed to the window. Duncan pulled Austin up out of bed and the boy's arms flew to grab him to stand.

"Fire! There's a fire, Austin!"

Throwing on clothes, the boys grabbed everything they could. Lucas even grabbed hold of Hobbs' rucksack for him.

A layer of smoke already filled the house. The boys covered their mouths and noses with their t-shirts. On the landing, Duncan looked down the corridor. The doctor's room was just next to them.

“I’m getting Dr. Tassoni—go downstairs—I’ll meet you outside.”

“ARE YOU CRAZY!” screamed Lucas over the smoke, but Duncan was already gone, down the hall.

“Dr. Tassoni? Hello?” He hit his hand on the bedroom door, which opened easily. He only hoped she was dressed.

She sat on the bed in a vest and cropped leggings, frozen. Her eyes were glued to the window, where flames crept, struggling for breath. Reaching her, she seemed to not even notice his presence. For a moment he thought she was injured, only to realise that she had a nasty scar running down her right arm. And that she had always carefully hidden it before. He swallowed, trying to regain his composure. He wasn’t used to telling adults what to do.

“R-Rosella? We need to get out!” He grabbed at her hand. He pulled her. He had to get her out of this stiffened trance. Shaking terribly, she watched the wall as though something was there.

Duncan swallowed. He took off his overshirt and used it to cover her mouth. Wrapping his arms around her, he scooped Rosella up and carried her as quickly as her state allowed. It was like she had an inability to speak, struggling only to breathe in his arms. The fire had spread inside. As they made their way downstairs, the inside of Austin’s home had been ravished with red and orange.

Outside, Duncan saw Scorpion Man and his two henchmen. He pointed his gun at Hobbs’ head whilst his stooges now pointed theirs in his direction. Hobbs stared past Duncan, towards the house. In the firelight, Duncan made out tears streaming down his cheeks, then he realised that Austin was missing. It was too dark to see if he was anywhere else. Duncan’s insides ran cold and he could feel the bellow rise before he could consider whether it was wise or not.

“Where is he!?”

Duncan almost didn’t recognise his own voice. He didn’t think it could get that high or strained. “Where’s Austin—” But something else made his skin prickle with anxiety. Two figures stood next to the henchmen, and for a moment, Duncan thought the smoke had clouded his vision.

“Lucas?”

The large boy stood next to a woman who could only be

Cobalt, both illuminated by the orange glow of the burning farmhouse in front of them. He held Hobbs' rucksack, not meeting Duncan's eyes.

"Guys, it's not like that. The Foundation was going to rip us off. You heard what she said. She said it didn't matter who got the book to them, that's all they cared about—"

Before Lucas could continue his rant, Cobalt touched his shoulder and he seemed to instantly relax. She stepped forwards. Still standing just feet from the burning building, Duncan still clung to Rosella, more out of protection than necessity… The doctor was finally coming round.

Cobalt addressed him directly, ignoring everything else. "Darryl, no—it's Dunc, isn't it? I explained to your friend Lucas that The Foundation only wants the book for their own profit. It's another book for their collection. I am not Jake Booker, some gambling cowboy. There's more to it than that for me, and I assured Lucas that I will pay even more handsomely for it."

Before Duncan could reply, Rosella bit back. Regaining composure—with a grateful look to him—she stood on her own. Perhaps facing away from the fire made it easier to manage.

"I take it the guns and the henchmen are just part of the welcoming committee?"

Cobalt ignored her, but Duncan was sure he saw her twitch, "I'm terribly sorry about your friend Noah, a dreadful loss I'm sure for you all—"

"But you shot Olivia! Your gorilla here shot her three times! We heard it!" Dunc yelled. The gorilla didn't seem to bat an eyelid. Cobalt didn't seem bothered either. She continued on her spiel regardless.

"The Foundation are not your allies, Dunc. We never harmed you, did we? We only intended to get what was mine and leave you be. Lucas here knew that it was a miracle they flew you to America in the first place. It surprised me that they didn't just have it sent by courier..."

She smiled. "Speaking of, where is *my* book?"

Lucas, his eyes still downcast, handed the bag forward. Duncan wanted to punch Lucas over and over. How could he do this to them? But there was nothing anyone could do. Everyone had a gun to their head. Duncan could feel sweat running down his neck that had nothing to do with heat.

As Ms. Cobalt opened the rucksack there were two noises.

The first was the sound of wood smashing, Duncan assumed it was the house falling apart behind them as the fire rose. But then there was the second noise, the roar of an engine.

Two sets of piercing white lights flew out of the fire. The henchmen turned and opened fire on the vintage gold pickup truck. As the driver laid on its horn, the truck turned in a doughnut, kicking up smoke and dust—blinding everyone and anyone in its path.

It was just enough of a distraction. Duncan and Rosella ran. So did Hobbs. All around them they heard shouting and gunshots. A crescendo of chaos.

In front of them, the vehicle squealed to a stop.

Duncan climbed into the truck's bed, his hand out for Rosella. She took it as Hobbs scrambled up beside her. There was no sign of Lucas. There was no sign of Ms. Cobalt. There was no sign of the henchman. All still lost in the dust and smoke.

With a cry from its engine like something from WarGamesOnline, the pick-up shot off hard and fast across the farmland. Behind them, the fire continued to burn.

Duncan's heart thudded fast. His throat still burned from the smoke. Hands still shook.

Rosella breathed heavily, as if finally waking from the nightmare for the first time. Hobbs took a puff of his inhaler. They all looked back, the flames bringing the wooden structure to its knees.

"It's over. They have the book."

Hobbs cleared his throat. "I think you'll find that's not *entirely* true." Holding out his rucksack with one hand, he wiped at his eyes with the back of the other. 'I might have tackled Lucas for the bag when everyone was distracted." Still out of breath and keeping his inhaler close to him, he flexed his free hand. "And punched him in the face for good measure."

They drove for a good fifteen minutes making sure they weren't being followed before the truck stopped to a sudden halt. The pick-up's partition slid open, and a face peered out on them. A redhead covered in freckles, soot, and a mischievous grin.

"Hey, y'all!"

Austin climbed out of the driver's seat before being devoured by a crushing hug by Duncan, and then being slammed hard in the shoulder by Hobbs. The boy visibly winced. Soot covered him and there were signs of some burns on his arms. He shrugged off their concerns with a mere pained look. "I'm alright, I'm alright, settle down y'all."

"Austin, you little shit, what the hell were you thinking—running back into the house—gave me a heart attack!"

"I had to get the keys—for the truck! They were in the garage at the back of the house...your rental car was on fire too...."

It just led to Hobbs giving him another hug. Rosella, who had quietly watched the exchange, finally found a moment to speak. "I'll drive."

The three boys took the back of the pick-up. The others worked together inspecting Austin's wounds and cleaning them as carefully as they could with the bumpy roads. They had no idea if they were being followed or if Cobalt would have another way of getting to the Foundation.

Either way, there were one hundred and eighty miles to go until the book was in safe hands. Before they knew it, they were used to the road. Hobbs shared his earphones with Austin, all his things had still been in his rucksack. Duncan laid down, watching the starry sky above him speed past. He thought again of his dream of Wilfred Owen on the plane to DC, of Lucas and the blazing fire, of Olivia's blooded jacket, the sound of the two gunshots—and the feeling in his chest when Austin was missing from the group.

As the sun began to rise, cascading them in a purple hue, Duncan found himself falling asleep, strangely, almost as comfortably as he had been in the farmhouse.

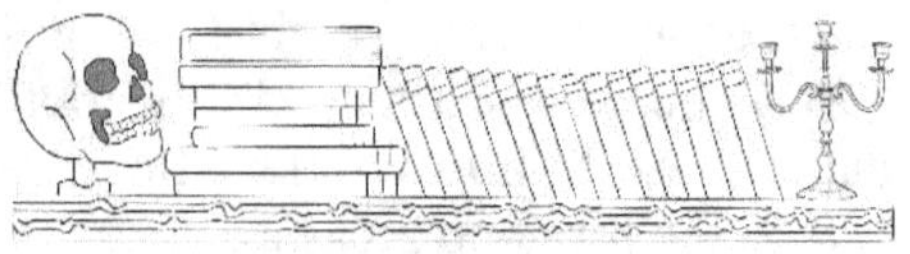

"So, you're actually okay with me driving?"

Duncan was surprised to hear Rosella and Austin talking when he woke. By the tone of her voice she was obviously very tired. Glancing up, he saw Rosella's eyes were puffy. She still wore what she had fallen asleep in, a short-sleeved t-shirt (proclaiming

Seb's) and a pair of leggings. Meanwhile the redhead sat next to her in the driver's seat, still sooty but his burns not looking so red.

"Whether it's legal or not, you're not a bad driver. But if you're going to drive any of this journey before I take over on the interstate, you need to be better driving on the highways. Don't stop and start, you'll kill us all."

Duncan snorted, causing the pair to turn round. Hobbs remained snoring in a ball at his feet. Even though they were now quite a few miles away from Austin's home, there was still an elephant that needed addressing. Something Duncan felt guilty enough about.

"Have you called your parents yet?" Duncan asked Austin.

"I called them an hour ago," Rosella said. "I thought it would be better coming from me. The house will be rebuilt, at the Foundation's expense...Luckily, Austin's parents were too pleased to hear their son was alive to be horrified at the loss of the farmhouse. I've told them that he'll be meeting them in Houston."

Austin swallowed and Duncan patted his shoulder. Their missing friend was the other issue. His messages were the last on their chat. Only sent a few hours ago.

**awesome.lucas:** guys
**awesome.lucas:** guys
**awesome.lucas:** look I know you might hate me.
**awesome.lucas:** but I thought I was doing the right thing.
**awesome.lucas:** she's really convincing you know...
**awesome.lucas:** cobalt knows where you're heading.
**awesome.lucas:** don't go to the foundation. She's not messing around.
**awesome.lucas:** take the book away, burn it if you have to!
**awesome.lucas:** guys

Duncan didn't even know how to reply, after they'd all read the messages. Or in Austin's case, read out to him and Rosella in the front. His nose wrinkled with suspicion. "It could be a trap. To make us trust him again."

"Or he could be risking his life to tell us the truth," Duncan retorted before frowning.

Rosella took the phone from Hobbs' hand and turned it off.

"Or trying to get a trace on you. Turn your cellphones off, all of you. We're probably too far in the wilderness for any cell towers to let them get that good of a look at where we are. But let's not risk that. Take out the batteries."

"And what if he's right?" Duncan wondered. "What if she finds us before we get there? She won't stop until she has the book."

Silence fell over them, and with it that feeling of dread. Despite the Texan heat, he shivered. "But my other question is...if she's a treasure hunter with a galleon's worth of gold—why does she want the book so badly?"

Rosella spoke up, half listening from the front of the truck, still more concerned with assessing Austin's driving. "Maybe it's like we discussed at the plantation. Wilfred Owen had a girlfriend. Maybe that wasn't all that happened while he was in France."

Hobbs's mouth fell open, eyes wide. "You don't think she's related, do you?"

"Related to who?" Austin said, missing the trick completely. Though that may have been because Rosella kept turning his head back to the road.

"To Owen? Wilfred Owen?" Hobbs confirmed, to Austin's continued bafflement.

"Maybe there was more to his letters to his brother, things that were written out of history," Rosella suggested. "A pregnancy out of wedlock was certainly frowned upon. Either way, whatever the reason, the sooner we get to the Foundation—the better for all of us."

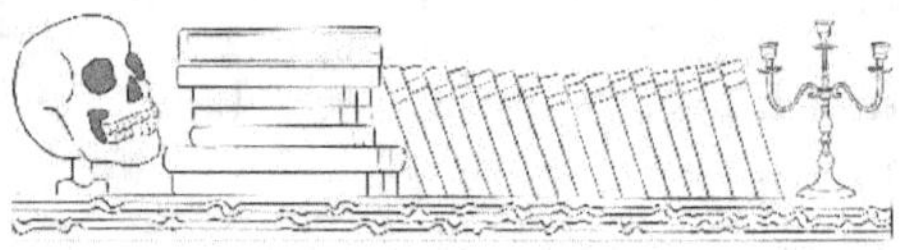

Duncan found himself staring at the Texas surroundings, so different from Manchester. There, grey buildings were cramped specks of colour and, like scars on skin, old buildings that haven't been fixed since the 50s.

This felt like what it was, a newer country, with very little to show what had happened to its landscape in the last hundred years beside the tarmac stretching through it. Cars zipped hundreds of miles through large expanses of land, and roads that were the length of flats back home. Large trucks passed them like ships. So little life surrounded them, at least to their eyes.

After a few hours. It was obvious that Hobbs had caught the sun, his nose burning crisp red. The boys still only wore t-shirts; the car's speed caused a breeze to blow over them, but sizzling heat Texas provided tan lines. Duncan couldn't help imagine this place in the same way those cartoonish scenes on television of deserts were displayed; vicious vultures surveying the hot scene as air seemed to crack and fizzle over the tarmac in the hot sun.

With just over halfway to go, the truck needed to be refueled, and the sense of hunger had crept upon them. Pulling into a sprawling gas station, they attended to both needs.

While Rosella fueled the pickup, she sent the boys to clean themselves up in the washroom. After, she handed them money for food. Duncan still found himself still staring at the scar on her right arm but couldn't find his voice.

"And what about you?" Hobbs wanted to know.

Rosella looked at her smoke and ash-stained sleep clothes and then to a few racks of clothing near the registers. "I really think I need something a little more suitable to wear, don't you?"

If this had been a normal holiday, Duncan would have insisted on eating, stopping properly in the diner by the gas station and getting a feel for the place. Instead, they had to take food for the road. Austin opted that the easiest thing to eat were twinkies, pop tarts and cans of Mountain Dew. His friends didn't disagree.

When Rosella reappeared, the boys couldn't help staring. The long-sleeve denim shirt was buttoned with rhinestones; the pockets were made from bedazzled leather. The large Texas-shaped patch sewn onto the shirt's back was of the same stuff, with dazzling stones marking the major cities

"I know," Rosella said, holding up one hand. "It's the only thing they had in my size," she paused before admitting, "and that covers my...arms."

They boys offered to share their food with her. Looking at arms laden with junk food, Rosella bought her own meal out of protest.

Austin offered to drive, to give Rosella a rest. She had barely slept since they had started travelling. Rosella gratefully took the suggestion and so she sat at the back of the truck with the others as they set off to leave.

Duncan asked for a can of drink so Hobbs passed him a Mountain Dew. Austin teased the boys for calling it "drink." But since, in Texas, drink was apparently called "coke," whether or not it was actually a "Coke," Austin didn't really have the high ground there.

As Duncan opened his can, Hobbs rooted around for cigarettes in his rucksack. Disappointed, he asked Rosella the question Duncan so desperately wanted an answer for. "Is that why you're always wearing long sleeved blouses? Your scar?" Hobbs received a not so subtle kick to his shin from Duncan. But Rosella didn't seem especially put out by the question.

"Yes. No. I'm not used to meeting people who didn't hear about it on the news—and make up their minds from that. Bless your self-obsessed generation." She sucked in a breath. "It's a long story."

Hobbs beamed, "We still have an hour and a half to go to Houston, so I'm game for a story."

She smiled back, but not enough to bite. Tilting her head, she gestured to the boys with her thumb. "I'd rather hear about how you guys know each other?"

Hobbs enlightened her, beaming. "Oh, that's easy. WGO. War Games Online."

"Ah. My sister mentioned that it was a craze once."

"We still play, we're a team." Hobbs said.

"And it's like a mix match of time-travelling soldiers fighting a dark evil across history? That's right isn't it?"

Hobbs nodded at her observation. "Basically yeah. Though we don't play it as often as we did, we talk a lot more than play now. About all sorts of stuff. Luc—Lucas's parents were getting divorced, and I guess that became a talking point, and then we'd just all chat whenever we could. I guess we found a safe space, we could talk about all the shit that was bothering us. It wasn't just a game anymore. We talked out all the crap that bothered us in real life. It's a proper friendship."

Rosella was quiet for a moment, considering, "So Lucas turning against you..."

"Yeah, big shit-eating traitor. Never thought he'd sell us out after everything." Hobbs paused before adding with a frown. "You wait until I get the chance to punch him again."

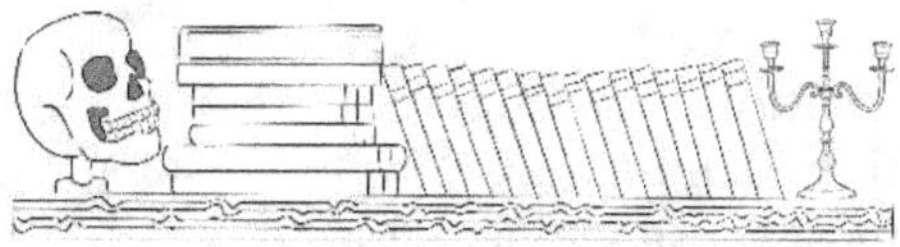

Houston's skyline greeted them while Rosella, who had taken the wheel once they reached the interstate, drove the last few miles to the Foundation. Hobbs' head ached as he stared upwards. He had never felt so small, staring up at the skyscrapers.

"You okay, man?" Austin asked him, picking up at a pop tart.

"Yeah just...this is all so much more than I ever thought it would be. I thought the book was just a cool find, a mystery for Dunc to solve—and now we've all almost died at least once..." Hobbs confessed miserably. "I guess two or three times for me now."

Austin bristled at the reminder, some how he turned pinker than usual as his voice raised. "This ain't your fault. It's that *heifer*. We're going to give the book over and there's nothing she can do about it after that..."

Hobbs winced a little, Austin angry was not a sight he was used to. "But your home, all your things? Lucas—"

The young american cut him off. "Mom and Dad are going to be upset, sure, but...there are worse things. Booker told Rosella he'd take care of it. We'll get the reward, and we'll use it to sort out the rest if we can."

The boys grew silent, Hobbs wrappers his arms around his knees before replying.

"I know, I know. But I ain't so sure about this. I wasn't even feeling all that good before the trip and all the flying—I don't want a breakdown again..."

Austin's anger dissipated and his arm went around him, pressing the boys close together. "You know, me and Dunc always have your back, Hobbs."

"Yeah, I know, thanks...you know, for a punk fifteen-year-old you're not too bad."

"Hey, it's fifteen and a half!"

"Whatever."

The pair sat in silence. Hobbs then turned his attention to

Duncan. The other boy sat in the front of the truck beside Rosella, lost in thought admiring the surroundings. He might as well have been in his own cocoon.

Hobbs and Austin shared a glance.

"Do you think he'll be okay? Off to uni soon..."

"He's the most sensible one out of all of us—even if he can't cook." There's a small pause, before Austin nudged Hobbs' shoulder again in clarification. "He'll be alright."

"Suppose." Hobbs' nose wrinkles in thought. "—Can't really imagine him being a doctor though, can you?"

"Well, aren't doctors about helping people? Dunc's good at that…but yeah…" Austin sighed. "You never know, maybe the reward can help with that too..."

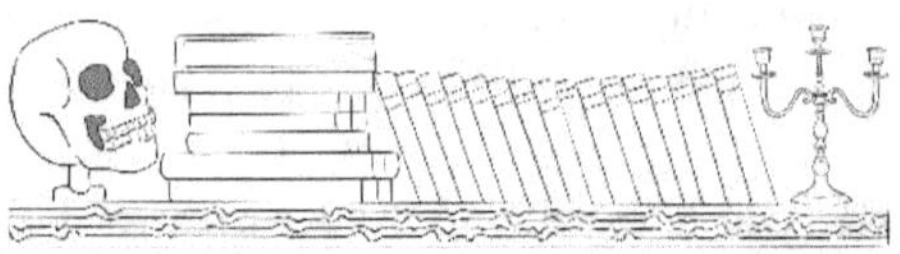

Time passed. For the most part the party stayed silent. With the horrors of the farm still pressing on their minds, they processed their decisions. Rosella called out to them from the front, breaking their focus. "We'll be there in a few minutes. Make sure you have everything. We'll be leaving the truck nearby."

Hobbs made sure everything was packed, rubbish shoved into pockets, headphones back in bags. The book remained at the top of Hobbs rucksack. Rosella parked the truck with ease outside the front door of the large red brick building that wouldn't have looked out of place in any of England's richest areas; a trendy London art gallery perhaps, or a Bristol hipster shop. He hadn't known what to expect, feeling only relief that it was all over.

Standing on the curb, Rosella turned to look at the three motley boys who were dirty, sweaty, and still smelled of soot. Still, it wasn't as bad as it could have been. She smiled a bit out of the corner of her mouth.

"We're all looking rather ragged but at least it'll give our story some merit, come on." Walking through the door, they were each pulled aside and thrown to their knees.

Crashing to the ground, Austin was the only one who made a noise as his burnt arms were manhandled. Duncan looked up, finding himself surrounded by sofas and bookcases. Even with the comfort that the room offered. Cobalt's goons towered over them. It made Dunc question, once again, how they had arrived first.

Hobbs' fingers dug into his rucksack, not letting go, but the click of a gun near his head made him tremble. Rosella remained calm, but her eyes showed a fire the likes of which Duncan hadn't seen before.

"You're not going to get away with this."

Ms. Cobalt moved toward them from behind a bookcase, putting back a book she had been admiring, almost as if she'd forgotten her threat to murder her guests.

"I think I will be. Your Foundation friends are nowhere to be found. My little decoy led them on a bit of a goose chase. Thank you so much for your help, Lucas..."

Scorpion Man dragged Lucas in from the side room, before shoving him onto the ground in a heap. Austin flinched, watching a stooge pull the pudgy teenager upright by his greasy, chestnut hair.

"We want the book," she told the group. "And you can have your little friend back and go on your way..."

Duncan looked at Hobbs and Austin, then they all looked to Rosella. There were few options. Would the Foundation really allow the death of a boy, or boys, just to get their hands on the book? They weren't here when they were most needed. What could anyone else possibly do?

Hobbs broke the silence, shifting underneath the weight of the stooge restraining him.

"Okay, okay. I'll give it to you. Let go of me."

With a wave of her hand, Ms. Cobalt ordered her man off him. Hobbs trembled as he stood, still hugging the rucksack to his chest. He opened it, revealing the book. Duncan wanted to grab at his legs, to keep him close.

Hobbs stepped forward, each agonising step was treated with a shuddering breath. He moved close enough to be standing by Lucas. For the first time since they'd been in the same room Lucas's eyes met Hobbs'. It was like someone had pushed a switch. Before anyone could stop him, Hobbs launched a punch at the other boy's face. Confused, the stooge let go of Lucas.

The boys scuffled on the ground, Hobbs pinning Lucas to the

floor.

Ms. Cobalt gave the same wicked laugh Hobbs and Duncan first heard back at the Bristol garage.

"Boys will be boys." She turned to her henchmen. "Separate them, won't you?"

Orders from their boss briefly distracted the men. Even with guns still pointed at them, the two boys charged their captors. Caught by surprise, even once Scorpion Man realised it was a fake-out, he hadn't the time to react. Lucas kicked him between the legs. Taking the stunned man's gun in his thick fingers, he pointed it at Ms. Cobalt. Hobbs stood at his side.

"Y-You all just put down your guns. Or I'll shoot her."

Her stooges obeyed as Ms. Cobalt gave them a considered nod. Austin and Duncan rushed over to join a now armed Lucas, one of his eyes closed where he was punched. Hobbs shook his hand repeatedly as it pulsated in pain for a second time in two days. Rosella checked behind the desk. Sure enough, the receptionist was there, bound and gagged, tears in his eyes but still alive. Cobalt smiled, still radiating control. She stepped forward, malice in each word.

"Lucas, darling Lucas, you're not really going to shoot me, are you? What happens now?"

Lucas, his mouth dry, looked to Duncan, then back to Cobalt. He couldn't speak, all his bark gone. His weakness already apparent, she smirked.

"Enough chit chat—get the book. Now!"

And as her men rushed forward, Duncan pushed Hobbs away from him and towards the side door. "LEG IT! GO!"

It was like the bottom fell out of his stomach. No time to argue. No time to help his friends. Hobbs dropped his rucksack, clutching the book in his hand as he darted out of the room and out of sight; disappearing into the many rooms the Foundation had to offer as his friends did everything in their power to block his pursuers' path.

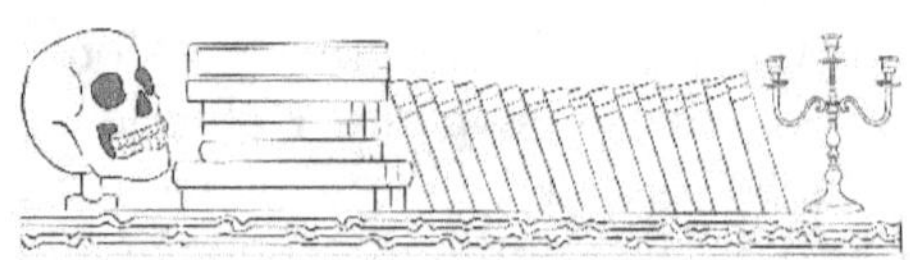

Hobbs hoped that pushing into the foundation's dimly lit library meant escape. The sound of heels clacking on the tile floor behind him told him otherwise. And told him more than he wished it did about his pursuer's identity.

He heard what remained of the fight in the reception. The sound of cries and footsteps.

His heart twinged in his chest, his mind in chaos as he considered what might be happening out of sight. He breathed in hard, trying to focus, trying to make sense of the bookshelves' arrangement. It was worse than navigating a maze. Outside with his friends and Rosella seemed like days ago, not minutes, but he remembered seeing that the building had more than one story. What Hobbs really needed to find was a staircase to the second floor. What he got instead was a dead end among the shelves.

He froze in place, not daring to move.

A gunshot.

"Come out, Hobbs. It's just a book to you. Is this cat and mouse chase really worth it?"

Her footsteps seemed to echo everywhere at once. Was she across the room? Or around the next bookcase?

"You—you're a millionaire. You don't need the book either...." he called back, before realising too late this was what she wanted. Darting quickly behind another bookcase, he tried to quiet his breathing.

Having a panic attack now wouldn't be a good idea, and his inhaler was in his rucksack.

"My grandmother always told my mother she was the daughter of an English poet, but I never knew his name. She had married my grandfather in the hopes no one would ever find out that she had actually given birth out of wedlock. When she died last year, I discovered she had taught at the same school as Wilfred Owen. It couldn't be a coincidence."

Hobbs could hear her. She was getting closer to his bookcase. With effort he shuffled round, trying to move slowly. His hands reached the end of the wall. Just more books and a wall. No doors. Trapped. Stomach turning, he replied in anger, "So, you're willing to kill a bunch of kids for...what? Coincidental proof? It's meaningless. Dunc says this Foundation's a charity anyway—"

It didn't matter what the answer was. She'd found him. Cobalt struck forward, blanketed in shadow. Hobbs held the book tighter as she stepped forwards into the incandescent light.

"Give me the book, Hobbs."

Fixing her eyes with his, trying not to focus on the gun, he shook his head. His fingers and toes seemed to shudder as his heart pumped harder than ever. "I don't want to shoot you. Shooting people is messy. I just want the book and you can go. No more fuss. You understand? You can go back to your smelly house and your weed addiction and your video games—"

He thought of home, of what he'd be doing if he was back in Bristol. Gaming with his friends, probably smoking and relaxing as best he could.

Smoking.

Hobbs' eyes brightened in the dark. Fumbling into his pocket, he produced his lighter and held it underneath the book. This was the only bargaining chip he had left.

"You take one more step, and I'll burn the bloody thing." He'd upset her. Her lips twisted in a snarl, but she didn't move.

"You wouldn't dare."

His breathing quickened, a laugh. Hobbs flicked the lighter spindle, its sparks made Cobalt twitch and her face contorted again. Her eyes burned like a furnace.

"If you destroy the book, I will shoot you where you stand."

"Then you're going to have to kill me, aren't you?"

And as he flicked the lighter for a second time, sparking a small flame. Hobbs smirked, moving the flame to the corner. Cobalt cried out—and a gun fired. An alarm sounded around them. Hobbs still heard her screaming as he dropped the lighter, his other hand still tight around the book, bringing it to his chest like a shield.

And though he heard a name—his own—he couldn't focus on anything else but the pain as the world dulled and it felt like the world was disappearing underneath him until everything was gone.

The world was void of colour, stark and empty. As though there was no emotion left in the world. But shapes and colours soon come into focus again. Familiar faces surround Hobbs: his friends, seeming more fatigued than ever. Rosella, too. And another face he didn't recognize, only belatedly realizing that she wasn't one of his friends, but a medic. Pain seared through him.

Glancing down, he saw a bloody furrow in his shoulder. The book was gone.

"Where is it—"

"—Safe. It's okay. We're safe, man," Austin replied.

"And Cobalt and her goons are in cuffs," Lucas added.

"You had us worried for a second, dickhead," Duncan chimed in.

Another wince as the medic wrapped another bandage around his arm. But it wasn't important. He started to smile weakly.

"So...we won? We made it? The Foundation has the book?"

Rosella nodded. "Looks like your trip was a success."

Hobbs deflated. He started to laugh a little, breathless, tears forming in the corner of his eyes.

"I'd like to sleep for a bit longer then, if that's cool." And before anyone else could reply, the teenager's eyes closed as he settled back to sleep while his friends chuckled about him.

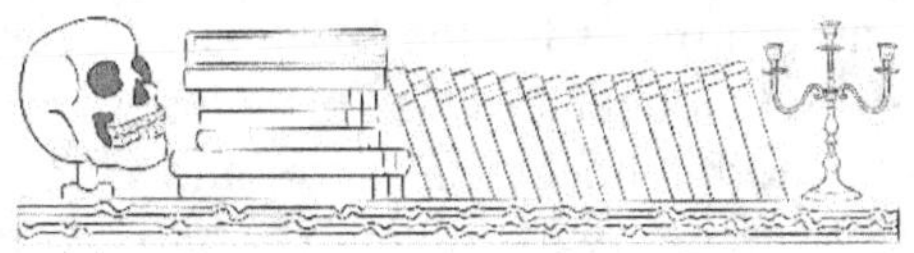

**Epilogue**

Airports had felt like home over the last couple of days. But with home itself now calling, Duncan wasn't sure he was pleased to see the signs for Heathrow overhead. The group gathered near security. They had been trying to say goodbye for the last five minutes, but it was much harder than they expected.

"I don't know what all the fuss is about. We'll be on the chat the moment we get the internet back," Hobbs said as Austin refused to let go.

"You know it's not the same thing, dipshit."

Lucas stood with Rosella, his black eye raw, but still smiling. He would travel home with Rosella on a later flight. "You know, Hobbs—more people die in cars than planes these days."

He then gave Hobbs a hug. Dunc turned to shake hands with Rosella, the quietest boy taking in the moment.

"It was a pleasure to meet you, Dr. Tassoni."

"Likewise, Dunc. Use your reward wisely." She looked at the

other boys out of the corner of her eye. "I'm not sure your friends will be so good with it. Hopefully this won't be the last time we meet."

She was overheard and the crow was indignant. "Hey! I gave most of my share to Austin, thank you very much," Lucas stated, still in the middle of his hug. "He needs it to get a new computer setup for WGO."

"Which means I'm paying for us to go visit London when the house is rebuilt. Our own English Adventure."

"Hopefully without treasure hunters and risk of life, Austin?"

Duncan smiled and said nothing at first, considering. Rosella's eyes turned back to him "Well, I've got a few ideas. There's still clearing courses I can go for...maybe I can do something I really want to do at university now...."

Each boy hugged the others for a final time.

"Catch you guys later, okay? Set up a new campaign?" Lucas called as they started to move away. "Catch you online, Lucas. Safe trips home everyone."

Hobbs prepared himself for the flight ahead, but it didn't feel so terrifying now. He looked down at his inhaler in his hand before shoving it back into his pocket. Duncan and Hobbs looked back to the two American boys waving them goodbye at the gate. They waved back until they were out of sight.

Duncan thought it was strange, the feeling of leaving such good friends and not being sure when they'd meet offline again, only knowing that they were never in reality that far apart. It would feel just as special when he woke up each morning to Austin's ramblings, or Hobbs stories about the Bristol music scene, or Lucas complaining. Whilst on the surface, only having an online interface meant it was easier to connect, it had become a way of solidifying friendships that Duncan felt in his gut that would last a lifetime. After all, very few people in the world could say they bonded over a lost book.

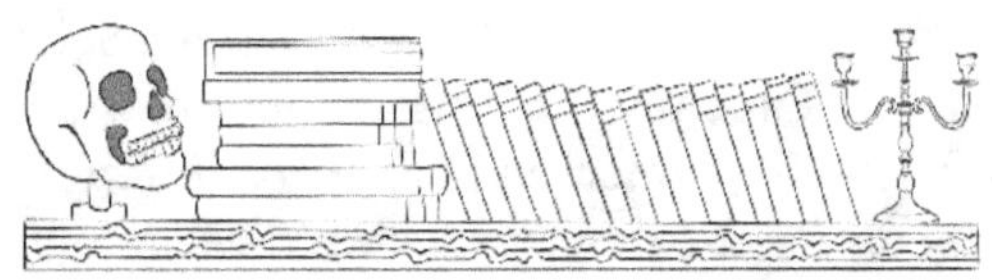

# Contributors

Writing from coffeehouses and bars where ever he finds himself, **Jon Black** is an award-winning author focusing on historical fiction with pulp, supernatural, or horror elements. He is best known for his *Bel Nemeton* series blending a quirky 6th century historical-fantasy reimagining of Arthurian mythology with brainy 21st century pulp, as well as his Jazz Age, music-driven supernatural mystery, *Gabriel's Trumpet*. Jon is an internationally published music journalist, bringing his passion for music and music history to much of his fiction. He is a regular guest on the convention circuit, where he speaks on the craft of writing, historical fiction, alt-history, and other topics. Jon's other writing activities include ghostwriting, speechwriting, and tabletop roleplaying games. To find his most recent work, check out Jon's novella, "The Dreamquest Beast," in the anthology *Shadows Over Avalon* vol. II, presenting an explicitly Mythos tale set in the world of *Bel Nemeton*.

**M.H. Norris**' mystery series, *All the Petty Myths*, combines forensics and mythology in a unique brew. The first volume featured the premiere novella "Midnight," which won #2 Best Mystery Novel in the 2018 Preditors and Editors Readers' Poll. Other stories in the collection took home #1 Science-Fiction/Fantasy Short Story and #1 Steampunk Short Story. The first full-length All the Petty Myths novel is forthcoming with Jazz Street, featuring the investigations of Dr. Rosella Tassoni.

*Badge City: Notches*, earned her the 2016 Pulp Ark New Pulp Award for Best Novella, and *The Whole Art of Detection*, took #4

Best Mystery in The 2016 Preditors and Editors Readers' Poll.

She wrote the December 2020 *Doctor Who* Subscriber Short Trip, "Crime at the Cinema," for Big Finish Productions.

Her short fiction has appeared in *Speakeasies and Spiritualists*, *The Black Beacon Book of Mystery*, and *Silver Screen Sleuths*.

**Kara Dennison** is an author, journalist, and presenter from Virginia. Past works with 18thWall include short stories in *Sockhops & Seances*, *Pizza Parties & Poltergeists*, and *Shadows Over Avalon*. She has also penned entries in the *Iris Wildthyme*, *City of the Saved*, and Black Archive series from Obverse Books, as well as their popular *Forgotten Lives* charity anthology series. Kara is half of Altrix Books with Paul Driscoll and the creative duo TopShelf2 with illustrator Ginger Hoesly.

Outside of fiction, Kara regularly contributes articles to Crunchyroll News and Otaku USA magazine. Updates, book reviews, and more can be found at karadennison.com.

**Heidi J. Hewett** writes mysteries, science fiction, and romantic comedies about nice, sometimes nerdy, straight-laced men who get their socks knocked off by luminous women. Currently, she reads and writes mostly queer romance. Heidi plays the violin, badly but with gusto, inspired by Sherlock Holmes. She also enjoys tinkering with recipes and inflicting strange food combinations on her unsuspecting family. Her other loves include screwball romantic comedies, Nordic police procedurals, and Hong Kong cop movies.

**Liam Hogan** is an award-winning short story writer, with stories in *Best of British Science Fiction* and in *Best of British Fantasy* (NewCon Press). He helps host live literary event Liars' League and volunteers at the creative writing charity Ministry of Stories. More details at http://happyendingnotguaranteed.blogspot.co.uk

**R.C. Mulhare** was born in Lowell, Massachusetts and grew up in a nearby town, in a hundred year old house near an old cemetery. Her interest in dark and mysterious things started when her mother read the Brothers' Grimm faery-tales to her, while her Irish storyteller father gave her a fondness for strange characters and quirky situations. She's also fond of hiking in New Hampshire's White Mountains, and browsing antiques shops. An Amazon best-selling author, contributor to the Hugo Award Winning Archive of Our Own, and member of the New England Horror Writers, her work previously appeared with Atlantean Publishing, FunDead Publications, Deadman's Tome, NEHW Press, Hellbound Books, Lovecraftiana Magazine, Tales of Wonder and Dread, and Weirdbook Magazine. She shares her home with her family, a young parakeet who loves vintage music, two thousand books and an unknown number of eldritch things rattling in the walls.

For many years now, strange ideas creep into **Michael O'Brien**'s head in unguarded moments and make him write them down, draw them, perform them, or make web sites about them. Recently, he did all that at once in the online serial podcast *Managlitch City Underground* at http://managlitch.com. In the past, he's written a fair amount of OC *Star Trek* and *Doctor Who* fanfic—sometimes in the same tale—and of expansion material for tabletop gaming settings. Currently he's hip-deep in the second volume of the podcast, a novel, a novella, several short stories, and an assortment of vignettes that will eventually belong to some larger tale.

In his professional life, Michael has administered networked macOS systems in the printing, educational, advertising, entertainment, telecommunications, and aerospace industries. He currently lives in North Carolina with a catgirl, a girl cat, a foxgirl, a bewildered dog, and an eclectic wardrobe of non-gender-compliant clothing for which he's gained minor notoriety at fan conventions. He's currently learning Japanese via Duolingo to increase his repertoire of terrible bilingual puns.

The winner of the 2017 Kindle Book Award for Horror and a Pushcart Prize nominated author, **Sean Michael O'Dea** has also played the roles of an officer in the US Navy, a local beat cop, a mindless corporate drone, an apprentice chef, and an overly enthusiastic personal trainer. And now, as a high school history teacher, he spends most days diving into world history, art, and philosophy. As a writer, he has always had an affinity for exotic locales, maniacal villains, and the flashy heroes of turn-of-the-century pulp fiction. As a reader, his shelf is brimming with science fiction, fantasy, and horror thrillers.

Currently, he is in Denver, CO hard at work writing and teaching while attempting to raise two crazy boys with his lovely wife (and biggest fan), Rachel.

**Karen Thrower** was born and raised in Oklahoma. She lives in Tulsa with her husband and their rambunctious ten-year old. She graduated from The University of Tulsa with a bachelor's degree in Deaf Education in 2005. She is also a member of Oklahoma Science Fiction Writers and has served in several capacities such as President, VP and is currently the Facebook 'Wizard' which she suspects has something to do with her young age. You can find the rest of her works on her Amazon Author page: amazon.com/author/karenthrower

**Fio Trethewey** is a writer and artist based in London known for their love of *Doctor Who*, Arthurian Legend and 80s cult classics. He has written a variety of audio dramas and short stories for Big Finish Productions for their *Doctor Who* box sets, most recently writing for the *Gallifrey War Room* series, both 'The Last Days of Phaidon" (2022), and "Transference" (2023). Fio has also contributed their work both as a writer and artist to charity anthologies and raised money on a charity drawing stream for FareShare UK back in October 2020 raising $4,762.

## DID YOU ENJOY WHAT YOU JUST READ?

**If you enjoyed this book,**
***please* review it on Amazon and GoodReads!**

**It's the best way to support the author.**

***For fantastic fiction, in-depth articles by your favorite authors, open submissions, and more, please…***

## VISIT OUR WEBSITE

*18thwall.com/*

## LIKE US ON FACEBOOK

*facebook.com/18thwall/*

## FOLLOW US ON TWITTER

*@18thWall*

**We'd love to hear from you! You help make these books possible.**